REVERB
by J. Cafesin

THIRD EDITION
Entropy Press, 2019

Library of Congress Cataloging-in-Publication Data is available.

ISBN-13: 978-0615756394 (Entropy Press)
ISBN-10: 0615756395

Romance—Fiction.   2. Romantic Suspense—Fiction.
3. Fantasy Romance—Fiction. 4. PTSD—Fiction.   5. Adult—Fiction.

Printed in the U.S.A

Cover design by TargetMediaDesign

-
-
-
-
-
-
-
-
-
-
-

For men,
and women who love them...

-
-
-
-
-
-
-
-
-

REVERB
PROLOGUE

\-

JAMES

"Get 'em, Ian!" I held the mud covered kitten and paced the water's edge trying not to cry.

"No. You get them." Ian stood on the grassy hillside several feet up from the pond. "It's your fault they're in there. I wouldn't have tripped if you hadn't been chasing me." He shrugged his gangly shoulders and held up the empty shoe box home I'd made for them.

"I can't swim. Get 'em Ian, please!"

Two kittens struggled to stay afloat, clawing at the washcloth moving towards the center of Miller's fishpond. Their whimpering sounded like children screaming in the distance.

"I'm not drowning in that scummy water over some feral cats." Ian just stood there, watching. "Get them if you want to, but I'm not. They're probably rabid." He held the shoe box away from him like it was diseased, then flung it into the pond.

I paced, filled with outrage. I was so excited to see my teenage half-brother, only the second time in all my seven years, but I hated Ian right then. I never should have shown off the Lynx kittens I'd found near the marsh behind Miller's farm. I looked at the barn on the hill. Mr. Miller was away at work all day. And it would take too long to go back to my house for help.

I clutched the muddy kitten I'd plucked from the bank to my chest, and held it against my mounting terror as I stepped into the murky water. My feet sank into the soft, slimy bottom. Cold water rushed through my socks and around my ankles, then seeped into my sneakers and weighted me.

"You'd better learn to swim fast because you'll never reach them from there." Ian's rosy, full face was suddenly angular and hard in shadow as clouds hid the morning sun.

I shivered and waded deeper, the water to my knees, then my waist, but I still couldn't reach them. Then one of the kittens disappeared below the surface and I lunged for it, then I was suddenly kicking water, searching for ground. Sharp pain pierced my shoulder from the kitten's needle claws, then my neck as it scrambled up me. I screamed but it was garbled as I gulped in mouthfuls of grimy water. I couldn't get air. My lungs felt as if they were bursting. I kicked and grabbed at the surface above. The excruciating pain in my chest became numbing, almost relieving, and my vision tunneled as I sank. I saw Ian standing at the edge of the pond watching me with the exact same blank expression he wore watching the kittens drown.

What I recall happening next seems impossible, even cliché, but the memory is vivid and visceral. I could see Ian from under the water, then something burst behind my eyes and everything went white. Then my view was from above my body, maybe six feet up, and I was looking down on myself sinking in the pond, watching Ian come in after me, the pain gone. I watched, but didn't feel my limp body being dragged to the shore. And though I saw Ian kneel beside me, I did not feel him pounding on my chest.

"Come on, you little shit." Ian yelled as he practically pounced on me. "You die on me and I'm screwed. Come on! Get up!" He put both his palms on my rib cage and pounded again.

Blinding pain shot through my chest and up my throat as the water was forced from my lungs. And suddenly I was back in my body on the ground, gritty water burning my throat and nostrils as it poured from my nose and mouth. When I finally stopped choking and sat up everything was quiet. The kittens were gone. The pond was still.

"You tell and you'll regret it." Ian stared down at me with a sinister grin plastered on his face. "I'll make it all your fault. It'll be easy too. I could almost tell the truth. And father will believe me, since

I'm his only *real* son."

Not anymore.

Fast forward twenty years, and now I'm the only one left.

Damn you, Ian.

I stare at the pine casket that lays perched at the edge of the hole in the ground. I picture Ian lying in there with that smirk fixed on his face. The priest is saying something but I don't hear and don't care. I want to be someplace else, anyplace else.

Damp, dead air. Then a hint of an icy breeze stings my cheeks. Brown leaves dance across the clipped lawns of the High Halden Church graveyard as I watch them lower my half-brother into the ground. "All the leaves are brown, and the sky is gray..." 'California Dreaming' with its ubiquitous chord progression, mirrors the scene before me. *"I'd be safe and warm if I was in L.A..."* I'd be surfing, working with The Zone, finishing the remix for Caravan, arguing with Julia, instead of freezing my ass off in this graveyard, trying to figure out why I agreed to come.

The casket is settled in the hole and I want to feel something, but I don't. Most memories around Ian are of him taunting me—stupid shit, like putting razor cuts in my guitar strings so they'd snap when I played, or threatening to slam the piano cover closed while I was practicing. First day I came to Castlewood, six years after the kitten incident back in the States, Ian walked into the music room blasted on something, came within inches and whispered, "Do you ever dream about dead cats?"

I tried to avoid him, but he sought me out at first, angry I was there, or maybe just bored. We came to a head when I trashed his stash after he put LSD in my iced tea at our father's appointment to the Shadow Minister. Dumped his box full of weed, speed and assorted pharms into the Thames the next morning. After that, Ian left me alone.

The priest hands me a shovel filled with dirt. I pour it onto the casket. The noise is surprisingly loud, and hollow. I wonder if Ian is really in there. Perhaps he's given up all those millions for the warm Sicilian sun. *"All the lonely people, where do they all come from..."* And a young Paul McCartney is in my head singing Eleanor Rigby. I hand the shovel back to the priest and step back, keeping my eyes downcast, consciously avoiding my father. Again the question of why I agreed to come strikes me, but I can't hear an answer above McCartney's rich tenor.

The priest crosses himself and wipes his hands as he walks from the grave. *"No one was saved."* McCartney's melodic voice unveils the story of the lost. That was Ian. The man had no center. Maybe he felt that and couldn't live with it. I stand with my hands in the pockets of my overcoat, hold it closed against a gust of biting wind, feeling the music resonate in my body and shroud me against the cold.

Everyone starts milling about, coming up to me and shaking my hand with the canonical sympathies. What am I supposed to say to these people? Am I sorry Ian is dead? Won't affect me much either way. It was expected really. There isn't a person here who could deny Ian was on self-destruct, except maybe dear dad, who spent a lifetime denying it, or just couldn't be bothered. Ian was screwed from the start. *"All the lonely people, where do they all belong..."*

Gray domes the sky and feels suffocating. I want out of here. Now. But how? Everyone's watching me, checking me out.

I hate that. No sanctuary with everyone always watching.

The limo that brought me is just across the lawn, not fifty yards away. The driver that picked me up at Heathrow is standing next to it, smoking a cigarette. I can just walk over there, get in, and go. But I don't. I've no interest in shaming my father in front of his constituents. Instead, I pull up the tune for the Zone's lead track I worked on the entire twelve hour flight here, and compose it in my head while I shake hands and nod.

Open with all power, hard and fast—like a freight train comin: G-C-F-A- then back off, G5, sustain 1-2-3-4, and pick it up, faster, and faster, hold the rhythm with the change to E—

"James Michael Whren." The priest extends his hand. Tall, thin, gray hair, trim beard, simple black suit with a thin white collar. His smile is warm, but affected. "How many years has it been? My word, look at you." He clasps my hand in both of his and shakes firmly. "Welcome home, son."

This is not my home, and I am not your son.

"Hello, Father." I reclaim my hand. Can't remember the priest's name to save my life.

"James, you may remember Father Tenant?" Edward Charles Whren XXI comes up behind me and I'm chilled straight through. "It has been quite some time, Albert."

"Of course, Edward." The priest turns back to me. "Father Albert Tenant. It has been a long time, hasn't it?" He sticks his hand out again and I shake it again. "I know your father is glad you found your way here today. I'm sure Ian would have felt the same."

Ian wouldn't have cared less. And my father required me for display.

Again, I wonder what the hell I'm doing here. *I want to get out of here.*

The priest and my father exchange glances. Then the priest looks at me. "How long will you be staying, son?"

"I'm leaving in the morning." Total lie. I hadn't booked a return flight yet. The funeral was a sidebar, an excuse to give myself a few days at Trident, lay down a demo of the Zone's track before going back to the L.A. mania.

Another quick exchange with my father, then the priest looks back at me. "So you'll be staying at Castlewood this evening then?"

An involuntary shiver at the notion of entering the cold stone walls of Edward's estate. "Actually...I'm going over to Trident, in London, lay down a demo. It'll be a late night, and my flight's early...and, well—"

"I'd like you to come to Castlewood this evening, James." Edward's phrasing masks the command as a request.

Fuck. "Like I said, I've got this gig going on in the city. And my flight is like at five in the morning,Well, my flight's at like six in the morning and—"

"Stefan will take you to the recording studio later this evening, as well as get you to the airport in ample time for your flight in the morning." Edward keeps his green eyes fixed on me.

"Yeah... Okay, I guess." What else can I say? My father just buried his only other child. The priest nods approvingly. I feel like flipping him off, but manage to refrain.

"Good." Edward nods just once. "I'll see you back at the house soon." He turns back to Father Tenant. "Albert. Join me."

"It's a pleasure to see you again, James. I'm sorry for the circumstances, and your loss." Priest sticks his hand out, and I shake it, again. Then Father Tenant and Edward walk across the misted lawn to the cobbled road and the waiting limousines.

"Master James." Curtis Weston, one of my brother's strung out cronies mocks me. "It's been a while, man. Too bad about Ian, huh." An anorexic model-type clings to his arm wearing a little black dress so short you can almost see the cheeks of her ass. "How ya doing?"

"Okay, Curtis. How you doing, man?" Curtis looks like crap. Emaciated, with vacant eyes peering through long, greasy hair.

"Gettin' by. You still making the L.A. music scene?"

"Yeah. What about you? You still with The Ravens?"

"Na. Don't play much anymore. Hang out mostly. You know…"

No. I don't. And I don't ever want to know a life without music. Take away music and I'd have no life at all. Probably end up like Curtis. What a waste. He used to be a damn good bassist.

"Weren't you in that remake of Wuthering Heights a couple years back?" the woman asks.

"No."

She smiles slyly. "You aren't that British actor that played Heathcliff?"

"Nope."

"Well, you sure look like him—same chiseled cheekbones; the tousled hair, the wild-child thing you've got going," Her eyes scan my body, shoulders, chest, maybe lower, though it's hard to tell. "You should consider acting, or modeling. Lots of money in it for your look."

Curtis laughs condescendingly. "James doesn't need money, love. You know who this *is*? May I present Ian's little brother—Sir James Michael Whren, the Fifteenth? Sixteenth? What's ya all up to now?"

"I don't know, Curtis." I look away, at Edward walking with the priest across the lawn. Gray mist twirls around their black, polished leather shoes, and up round the cuffs of their pressed slacks as they stroll.

"Still have that killer place in Zuma, man?"

"Yeah." I try and come up with something to say to send Curtis on his way.

"You should see his crib, Alexis—totally secluded, overlooking the Pacific, the latest and greatest studio set-up. This man is *famous* in the music biz, baby, the best of the best, a truly amazin' player. Master James and I performed together way back when." His accent is thick, East End. "Remember Red Rocks, man?"

"Yeah." I lie. Don't have a clue what he's talking about. I'd backed up Incubus to The Lumineers at Red Rocks but have no recall playing with the Raven's there. "Look, I've got to go, man. Take care." We shake hands. I flash a quick smile at the woman and turn away, move across the misted lawn towards the limos, following my father's path.

"My God, Curtis, he's brilliant. I mean, *perfect.* Do you have any idea how much a face like his is worth..." I hear her say as I walk away. A flash of anger, then surrender with a heavy sigh. I shake my head in bewilderment at the value so many place on physicality—an accident of birth, over achievement—an accomplishment of will.

Edward is talking to the priest by the waiting limousines. He glances at me across the lawn, then turns away with a sweep of his cloak and gets into the first limo lining the old road. I watch it drive away, pull my coat tighter around me.

Agreeing to go out to Castlewood was a bad idea. *Stupid.* The sonofabitch arranged this whole thing, set me up to meet with him by 'requesting' I attend the funeral. I'm an idiot. What the hell does he want? Clearly, more than a show of family solidarity. I never should have agreed to come.

I've nothing to say to Edward, especially after so much time. We never got on. I recall our first dialog, two days after my arrival: "Diligence is the only path to excellence. I expect *both* of you." *Yes, sir.* "Paul Michelson will be your piano tutor until you begin the

Royal Academy. You'll have the full three months to work with him before beginning school." *Yes sir,* though I had no interest in the piano, or attending the suffocating Royal Academy of Music in London through my teen years. My father didn't give a damn what I wanted. At first, I resisted, or outright ignored him. That first summer with Edward, I took off with a punk band to tour Europe. He had me arrested in Munich. I was thirteen, a minor, a runaway, without parental consent to travel.

The man is maniacally controlling. And I'm an idiot. Should have said I had a red-eye and had to get back to Heathrow.

I'm angry and freezing as I approach the limousine I came in. "Stefan, right?"

"Yes, sir." Maybe twenty, adorned in an ill-fitting black suit—a beanpole, with clear blue eyes and white/blond spiked hair peeking from under his black cap. He opens the door of the now first limousine in the long row. "I'm sorry for your loss, sir," he says again, as he did when he picked me up at the airport only hours earlier, though it feels as if I've been stuck here for days.

"Thank you." I get in. Apparently Stefan knows where to take me because he doesn't ask.

The door shuts and I am entombed. Feels like the oxygen is sucked out of the vehicle, along with the damp afternoon. *Breathe! Inhale. Slow. Keep going. Hold.* The limo gently glides forward along the cobbled drive. *I have to get out of here,* is loud and clear above the rhythm of the tires over the old stones. *Release. Exhale. Slowly. Control your breathing.*

I knock on the tinted partition blocking the view through the front windshield, and hiding the driver. "Can you keep this down, please?" I have a need to see where we're going.

The partition rolls down and sandwiches in-between the front and rear benches. "Glad to oblige. Just let me know if I can do anythin else for ya, sir. Some music, maybe? Your brother uploaded a great collection of tunes. Fancy some bootleg Segovia, then, sir?"

"James. Please. Just James. And thanks, but no music right now." Segovia will be one more distraction from my own composition. "How long is it from here?"

"Should be about ten minutes or so. I'll make the ride as smooth as possible, sir...James." He's looking at me in the rear view mirror every other second. "Maybe pour yourself a drink, Mr Whren? There's scotch, and gin back there. Even a twist of lemon in the—"

"I'm good. Thanks." I'm not looking for banter. And booze won't mix well with my body chemistry already crashing from too much speed. I flash on Julia calling me out about using, that last night in my studio. *I want to go home* now.

Try relaxing into the warmed leather seat. Rich wood burl lines both sides of the limo. A minibar with four small glasses and a two crystal decanters of hard liquor is inset on one side. A flat screen monitor on the other. I stare out the tinted window at the graveyard as we leave the church and enter the High Halden countryside.

Driving through the tree-lined, rolling plains of Kent, rows of ancient walnuts and aged oaks look like black sentries against the matte gray sky. Foliage was planted centuries back as boundary lines for the vast estate properties. *Breathe.* There'd been no mention of a wake for Ian, at Castlewood, or anywhere else, that I recall...I track back in my head to the church service, sitting a few rows behind my father, between Ian's mother's sister, Aunt Rose, she'd introduced herself, and her daughter...what was her name? Rose made sure to tell me her obviously fertile 30-something daughter was a single mom, which wasn't hard to figure out. She looked rather haggard, spending the entire service both in the church and at the grave site shushing her two kids, reminding me how glad I am to have none.

We turn off the main road, onto a small back road. Huge, almost flat fields are lined with foliage, as is the narrow, rough road Stefan is traveling on. Though the limo is long, it is not excessively stretched, like rentals for events that are meant to impress. This limousine is a custom Mulsanne Grand Bentley. The ride is smooth, but the curvy road is making me feel mildly nauseated. I stare out the window at the colonial farmhouses and grand estates, some practically castles, that dot the open landscape.

Right about now, I'm craving the simple elegance of Spanish Craftsman houses. A Spanish Craftsman, and palm trees.

I try pulling up the Zone track I'd been working on at the grave site, but it's impossible to hear music in my head, now crowded with pop-flashes of mental imagery from my years here, and aching for home, my studio, and Julia. Maybe I shouldn't stay, screw working at Trident and just go back to L.A. It'd nix the risk of my father insisting on any other discourse beyond this one. I owed Edward nothing. What the hell does he want, anyway? I really don't care, but that doesn't quell the panic building inside me. *I shouldn't have come.*

"Hey, Stefan," I say, louder than intended.

"Yes, sir?"

"Any chance you can take me to London, or back Heathrow?"

"None, Mr. Whren. My instructions were to bring you directly to Castlewood, sir."

I figured as much. No point in arguing. It would be unwise of the driver to cross my father if he wants to stay employed, anywhere in Britain, at least. Edward usually gets what he wants.

Stefan slows, then pulls the limo onto the estate's driveway, if one could call it that. It's almost a quarter mile long. He stops at the closed iron gates attached to a six foot stone wall that borders the entire 428 acres of Edward's legacy, handed down through generations of Whren's, dating back to the early 1500s.

The gates open silently, and my skin starts to prickle. Stefan accelerates past the foot thick wall and moves slowly up the perfectly straight gravel drive. Manicured emerald lawns fifty feet on either side of the road are lined with blue spruce, Italian pine, and interspersed with coiffed bushes clipped in elongated ovals. It's impossible to see the softly slopping grasslands, punctuated with forested parkland that stretch hundreds of acres, that I know is beyond the foliage.

And suddenly I'm on Razor, riding bareback, full throttle along Cutter's creek. It's pour icy rain. I'm soaked. And freezing. Shaking, holding onto his mane with both hands, locking my knees to his ribs, my ankles round his belly to stay on him. I knew it was stupid, riding along the ledge of the muddy creek, but I just didn't care. I absolutely had to get outta here, or fucking hang myself in my bedroom threshold with a guitar string.

As the road clears a small hill, the central front facade of Castlewood appears at the end of the long drive. It gets harder to breathe, like hands narrowing round my neck. The gravel pops and crunches under the tires and my heart pounds so hard it's reverberating in my throat. I'd walked away from here the day I turned eighteen, leaving behind my father, Ian, and the five years I'd been forced to live with them. That was over a decade ago. I'd most likely never have come back, had Ian's funeral not given me a convenient excuse to put Julia, the band, the entire team at Capitol on hold for just a bit. I'd justified this trip, thinking a few days conflict free, and a change of scenery, may give me the head space I've recently lacked to finish the Zone's first track. And, assuming Julia read my text, she'd think me magnanimous for attending today, being here for family I hardly know. Win. Win.

*Ah, Jules...*Flash on my last image of her, standing in the studio doorway in her lavender silk camisole and purple panties, mad as hell that I was still working. *Have I abandon you again?* I grimace, in mock shame. I'll make it up to her when I get back—take her on a date she swears we never go on.

Limo finally pulls up to the front of the massive Elizabethan brick mansion. Three main floors, and two more on that for servant's quarters. Forty french windows grace the front facade, the floors separated by thick, brick ledge, blackened with age, that surrounds the building. Almost an acre wide, the 72 room estate spreads out from the center tower into matching wings. At the end of each are imposing square towers, topped with actual turrets. An exasperated sigh escapes me. My skin prickles again, feels like the fine hairs covering my body are rising independently. I lean forward to see through the front windshield, but I can't see my old bedroom window, my prison in the North Tower, from my angle.

Stefan opens my door. Dread is so pervasive I just sit there, paralyzed. Nothing good can come from this encounter with my father. I shouldn't have come.

Stefan stands shivering by the door in the cold, wet air, and waits. I sit in the car feeling angry and trapped until I can't take the absurdity another minute. "What are you waiting for?"

"You to get out, sir."

"Well, what if I don't?"

"Well, then, I have to wait here, sir, until you do." Puffs of steam escape his thick, violet lips as he speaks.

I grab my bag, get out of the car, even manage, "Thank you, Stefan. That will be all for now," as I cross the gravel drive towards the mansion's principle entrance. Jesus, I can't wait to get back to L.A. where people are normal. I hear Stefan slam the door to the limousine, then the pops and crackles of the tires on the gravel as he drives to the Garage House, which used to be the Carriage House in 1558, a two-story stone building near the stables, where my father houses his collection of Jaguars, Bentley's, Benz.

I move under the domed marble-columned portico. *Breathe!* Take a deep breath, then release it slowly as I climb the five steps to the blackened cherrywood vaulted double doors. I was thirteen when I stepped through them the first time. It was Howard that escorted me inside Castlewood the day I'd arrived. He'd waited under the portico to help me "get situated" when I was deposited on my father's doorstep. I stood in the drenching rain wanting to jump back in the car, get back to Boston, to our house in Concord, to when my mom and step-dad were still alive. Edward was in Brazil. Shoot me if I don't remember why.

*Inhale...Exhale...*I turn from the doors and look out at the property. The front lawns beyond the gravel plaza, currently empty of any other cars, are immaculate—cut green grass for acres. Only the road we came in on disrupts the endless green, divides it in half. The driveway extends on either side of the gravel plaza. Take the north, or left road to the delivery bay on the backside of the estate near the kitchens, or drive down the road a bit to the Garage House, or the stables behind it. The right road leads to the Rose Gardens, the Hedge Maze, and the Garden House behind the estate.

I ran away the first time a week after I got here. I hid in the Garden House for days, in the attic, crowded with planting tools and potting containers. I was just thirteen. I had no money. No passport. No I.D. at all. And I had nowhere else to go. At their funeral, back in the States, none of my parent's friends, or my friend's parents, could give me "what my father could provide," several told me apologetically. My step-father was estranged from his mother, who raised him alone, though he was proud of making it on his own, with *music* nonetheless, at just thirteen. I don't know that I ever heard why I never met Mike's mom, or why she wasn't there to bury her son. No family on my mom's side either. Perhaps it was on this common ground that her and Mike first bonded beyond music. She was an only child, just eighteen when her mother died of breast cancer. Her dad passed of dementia a few years later, but my mom always said it was loneliness that killed him. Edward, my biological father, was all the family I had left.

And with Ian dead, I'm the only blood relative he has now.

A thick, misty drizzle starts falling. Even the greenery seems gray. It's always raining here. I hate it here. *Run*. The sudden urge to descend the stairs, get a car and get out of here almost puts me in motion. I don't have to go to Trident. I've got another twelve hours on the plane home to come up with something for the Zone. The Garage House is a hundred meters up the gravel road. I can find Stefan's room upstairs, demand keys to a car, take it and go to Heathrow, try and get an early flight—

A low rumble and I spin around as one of the heavy doors opens. Howard stands inside, looks at me critically for a second, though it's impossible to get any bounce what he's thinking.

"Your father would like to see you in his study at 6:00 p.m. Sharp," Howard says abruptly, then steps aside for me to enter. Dressed in his impeccably tailored, dark wool suit, he looks virtually the same, except maybe more gray around the temples, perhaps less hair there as well. His thin lips are set in a straight, unreadable line, his gray eyes impassive as ever.

I step onto the checkered marble floor of the Grand Gallery, and drop my travel bag on the floor against the wood-paneled wall. Across a large, open space, is a massive oak and iron-railed staircase, lined with red carpet that covers most of the dark wood steps, like the tongue in a giant mouth. It splits at the mid-level landing into two staircases, in opposite directions, onto the wings of the second floor. Enormous portraits of stone-faced dead relatives I don't know, nor ever care to learn about, hang on the landing wall, virtually looming over the Gallery entrance. Their gilded frames radiate a golden glow from the soft light coming through the domed leaded-glass ceiling above the staircase.

"You have one hour to rest, bathe, and dress before meeting with your father. You'll find the appropriate attire and toiletries in your room." He says nothing else, not even, "Good to see you after all these years, James." He turns away before I conjure a witty response. The muffled squeak of his leather shoes on the marble floor recede as he retreats through one of four arched thresholds under the right staircase, with that ivy-league stick up his ass.

"Nice seeing you, Harvard," I call after him as he disappears down the hallway. My father's personal secretary since their Harvard days, for the five years I lived on the estate, Howard was, if not attentive, at least more available than my father ever was. Perhaps I owed him for that alone. It's just, well, why did he have to be such a cold prig?

Light streams through the archways that line the hallway Howard disappeared into. I move across the spotless, black and white floor, past the sitting room to my left, and the parlor to my right. Both are empty, though there is a fire blazing in the wide fireplace in the parlor. The flames reflect in the black resin of the Bösendorfer grand piano tucked just inside the threshold of the expansive room. The two French windows that take up much of the front wall should light up the room, but thick red velvet drapes cover most of them.

There are two grands and one baby grand in this house, but I like the rich resonance of the Bösendorfer the best. I remember playing it at 3:00 in the morning when my father was home. I knew he could hear me, but he'd never stop me from practicing, regardless that I was likely waking most everyone else up running scales till dawn. By the end of my first summer here, after I was delivered to my father by the cops, I couldn't wait to go to the Royal Academy in London.

Check my cell for the tenth time since leaving the church. No connection. Lost it after Ashford and haven't gotten it back since. No way to call Julia, let her know I'll be home late tomorrow night. My text said I'd be gone a few days. But I was delusional thinking cold, soggy old England would inspire me. The weight of this place has always been suffocating. *I have to get out of here.*

Searching for a cell connection, I continue past the red-carpeted tongue of the lower staircase, and past the double arches on both sides of the Grand Gallery that lead to the north and south wings. Cross the arched hallway and enter the Grand Room. It's still breathtaking, the walls coated in gold leaf panels carved with complex Victorian floral patterns. The outer wall is lined with five, floor to almost the ceiling double french doors, topped with half round transoms. Two more sets of double doors cap the sides of the room. Half my Zuma house would fit in here. I open the center doors and walk out onto the slate terrace overlooking the curated formal gardens, the tennis courts, the glass pool house, the manicured lawns and the foliage beyond, but I can't get a cell connection outside either.

No land line phone in the Grand Room...or back in the Grand Gallery...or the adjoining parlors. Still searching, I climb the tongue, then the left staircase, and go up to my old room, but the phone that used to be on the antique writing table isn't there anymore. It's cold in the cavernous room, even though there's a fire blazing in the marble-mantled fireplace. My traveling bag is on the bed, though I'd left it by the front door. Several plush, violet bath towels lay next to it. *Damn.* I'm expected to stay the night.

Edward can't stop me from leaving, though I've no idea how to get out of here now. It's past five, and getting dark. Cold and wet outside. And two hundred and thirty acres to the next estate. At this point, my only way out's a taxi.

No phone connection. No taxi. I can take one of the horses to Hythe, find a ride from there. Fat droplets of rain now hit the French window above the front door threshold. Already tried, and failed, navigating a horse, through heavy rain and mud...I can try bribing Stefan to get me out of here. Probably cost a lot, if he'll do it at all, which he's already indicated he won't. Smart dude. No way out until morning. I compulsively shiver at the notion.

I glance around the opulent room I stayed in on holidays and breaks between sessions at RAM. It looks the same as it did the day I'd moved out. The framed newspaper ad from the Globe for the Boston Pops Fourth of July, my last year in the States, is still mounted on the wall by the door. My four poster bed is up against an interior wall, perpendicular to the fireplace, already ablaze. Maybe twelve feet from the bed to the Louis XV writing table. It sits in front of the huge French windows that provides a sweeping view of the front of the estate, but keeps the room perpetually damp and cold. Running the length of the outer wall is a padded bench three feet from the floor. Arched wood panels cover the base of the bench, the bold pattern repeating along all the walls in the room. I'm trapped in the sixteenth century, except for the small rehearsal space I'd bordered with music and guitar stands, instruments and amplifiers where the bench meets the interior wall. The two custom Hiwatt amps, the closed case with the Stradivarius my father gave me, the Fender electric, and an Ibanez bass I never liked the sound of, are still exactly where I left them the day I moved out, though they are dust free, polished clean.

Inhale deeply, exhale slowly to chill. An hour with my old man in ten years probably won't be near the deal I'm making it out to be. Crashing from all the Adderall and Didrex I've been doing lately is making me edgy. Julia's right. Been using too much for too long now. Gonna have to knock it off, even if it means working less.

Check my cell for a signal again. Nope. The display reads 5:25 p.m., and under it, London, over my blue-violet screen. I strip, pile my suit on the bed, grab the towels and go to take a tub, then shave. The bathroom, like all the others in the estate, was added in the last century, taking over the bedroom on the opposite wall of my old bed. It has been entirely redone many times over the years, though it has remained spare. A flush toilet, running water and electric lights were added with each new architectural advancement. The interior designers were careful to keep the minimalist Renaissance look and feel with the lion-claw tub, the long oak table with the thick marble top and washbasin, and the full-length standing mirror near the window.

I turn on the tub's tap and cold water falls from the iron faucet. It takes a while to get the water hot, so I wrap myself in a towel, cinch it round my waist, and go back to the bedroom. I pull my tablet from my bag and sit on the bed with it, turn it on and input the chord progression I'd created at the grave site. Check for an internet connection, email Julia instead, but I get a popup requiring a password to access, which I don't have.

Moments later I'm slipping into the tub, warm water already gathered an inch or more with the small drain unable to handle the faucet's flow. I put the rubber stopper sitting on the side of the tub on top of the drain, then lean back and let the hot water stream through my toes, over my feet, and fill the tub.

Holding the hard rhythm on E, then G, C, Am, and back to E. Sustain, 1, 2, 3, 4. Full stop, 1, 2, then Power G, C, Em...

...I'm towards the back of the stage with my electric as the lights come up. They're blinding against the blue twilight for a minute. My eyes adjust to the dim amphitheater before me, and the massive red rocks jutting up around it. The stadium seating sweeps up the rocky hillside. Almost ten thousand people stare at the stage, waiting for the boys in The Zone standing before me to start playing, but they don't. The silence is like a vacuum. I can't hear the audience clapping, or even my own voice when I yell, *"What the fuck!"* to Pete Devlin, on bass, standing six feet in front of me on stage. He turns to me, and I can see it's not Pete, but Curtis Weston. His eyelid are half-mast, and seem sunken. He looks totally blasted as he grins and aims the long neck of his bass at me. He laughs maniacally, then suddenly it's an assault rifle, and he shoots me.

I wake with a start, splashing water from the almost filled tub onto the checkered rose and white marble floor.

I get out of the tub and go back into the bedroom. Check my phone for a signal, again, but of course there is none. The display says it's 6:18 p.m. Seems I've already blown my 6:00 p.m. with dear dad. Regardless of whatever I may or may not owe Howard, there is no way I'm staying here tonight. I stow my black suit in my bag, then put on worn jeans and a hoodie. *Screw formality.* I put my tablet back in my bag, zip it and sling it over my shoulder, then slide on my boots and head back downstairs to my father's study.

I'll meet with my old man, express my condolences, then listen to what he brought me here to say. I script in my head as I move down a dim, narrow hallway, lined with more portraits of dead people, with the occasional Dutch or Italian masterpiece interspersed. He wants anything from me, I'll politely decline, clue him in to the demands on my time. I pass closed doors to more bedrooms, sitting rooms, even a chamber suite for dignitaries, then descend the back staircase. There are two huge bouquets of red and white roses at the base of the dark wood stairs. Galley, kitchens, dining hall are to the left I recall. I go right, down the Long Gallery, the arched hallway behind the entrance gallery staircase, then pass the Grand Room, to the south wing hallway, and my father's study at the end of the South Tower. I'll express my sympathies again, like everyone did for my parents, and Ian earlier today, I continue scripting. Then I'll tell Edward I got a text to lay down a few tracks with some old mates from RAM before leaving London in the morning, and request a car take me to the city. I'll be here a couple hours, tops.

I check my phone one more time for a signal, but of course there isn't any. It's 6:30 when I finally get to Edward's study. I drop my bag by the threshold of the arched doorway, breathe in and out slowly, then move towards the open door. The fireplace is ablaze and casts a rich golden glow to the enormous wood paneled room. Two of the four walls are lined with bookshelves packed with hardcovers that likely date back centuries. The scents of leather and wood polish sparks a flash memory of our first 'talk' in this room. I don't recall when I was told, but I'd known Edward was my biological father for as long as I can remember. I'll never forget his opening line that February afternoon a decade and a half ago, three days after I'd arrived at Castlewood. "I am profoundly sorry for your loss. I, too, am deeply saddened by your mother's passing. She was taken, from all of us, far too soon." That was it. No mention of losing my step-dad, the only dad I ever really had, along with my mother. He spoke as if she'd been taken from him, personally, as if *he* were her husband, not Mike.

My father sits at his massive Partners mahogany desk, focused on his laptop. Two huge French windows behind him creates an almost black backdrop to his imposing figure, with night having settled in. Only the small lights that line the straight road to the estate can be seen moving off to a singular point in the far distance. Edward looks up at me, passively. He's wearing glasses but takes them off and stands as I come in, though he does not extend his hand. He's still in the black suit he wore to the funeral. He looks exactly the same as a decade ago, hasn't lost one hair from the mass of thick peppered gray that sweeps across his forehead, still cropped short on the sides. Remarkably, he's retained his tall, stately stature, and even more remarkably, he is still trim and looks fit. Though he's almost eighty, he can easily be mistaken for early sixties. He hasn't changed one iota in ten years. Perhaps he sold his soul to the devil.

The coffered ceiling now sports halogen lights in every other square, highlighting the polished antique Renaissance furniture in surreal blue/white. Edward walks over to the bar, pulls a dark brown bottle from the fifty or more terraced along the smoked mirrored wall. "Would you care for a whiskey, James?" The puppeteer is still orchestrating the scene.

"No." *Back off. Keep it light.* "Thank you." I stand a few feet from his desk, caught in one of the many circles of recessed lights. About the last thing I need to add to my messed up chemistry is alcohol. I tuck my hands under my arms, shifting from one hip to the other, edgy in the extreme.

My father opens the beveled glass cabinet, selects a crystal tumbler, and pours himself a drink. Neither of us speak, and the silence between us becomes the rhino in the room. I cram my hands into my hoodie pocket, and wander over to the expansive bookshelves that line two of the interior wall, rise almost to the ceiling, and require the ladder to reach the topmost shelves. I randomly scan titles. *Pillars of the Earth. The Principles of Mechanics. The Prince.*

Okay. Breathe. Relax. *Loosen your shoulders. Say something. Say anything.* "I'm really sorry about Ian," is the best I come up with.

"It is your loss too, son. It would serve you to recognize that."

Here we go. "Yes sir. It is my loss, too. I'm sorry Ian's dead. It's really a tragic waste."

"Yes. It is." Edward speaks as if to himself. He leans against the bar and takes a sip of his whiskey. "A tragic death—a tragic waste of a life. Wouldn't you agree?"

"As you know, Ian and I weren't close. I'm not in any position to judge how he lived his life."

Edward takes another drink. "It's unfortunate that you and your brother were never able to cultivate a relationship. Perhaps by your example, Ian could have developed some focus, some self-discipline."

"I doubt I could have provided the influence that would have saved Ian, sir."

"Of course not." A sardonic laugh. "Ian's issue was not a lack of discipline, but a lack of self. Most assuredly, neither of which are your issues."

Like you have a clue what my issues might be. "What is it you want to talk with me about, sir?"

Edward swirls the whiskey in his glass and takes another sip of his drink. "It is time to discuss your upcoming role in our family's future."

Prickling rush sweeps through me, like the kind that follows just barely missing the Mack truck. "Let's not go down that road, Edward. I'm not interested. I never have been, and you know it. I've made my own life, which is very demanding of my time—"

"We're here to discuss obligation, responsibility, not choice, James."

"Not a choice for Ian, maybe, but it is for me. I'm just lucky, I guess, that I wasn't your first born, or legitimate." *Watch out.* I'm letting him get to me.

Edward's eyes narrow. "Your arrogance is only surpassed by your ignorance." He shakes his head slowly, then takes a gulp of his drink, moves from the bar and begins circling me. It's unnerving. "Your brother was a lazy, spoiled, contentious, undisciplined brat. I had no expectations of him managing the family estate since he could not manage his own behavior." Edward stops a few feet in front of me, close enough to smell his sour breath.

Every part of me tenses. It takes considerable effort to relax my balled fists. Flex my fingers discreetly. We're the same height. I'm almost fifty years younger, and in good shape. But I'm still afraid of him. "I'm very sorry for your loss, Edward. But I can't fill it."

"No. You can not," he said, and I detected the weight of his sadness, a crack in my father's stoic facade.

"Then what do you want from me, sir?" I add to soften my irritated tone.

"An easy transition." Edward takes another sip of whiskey, "Though that seems unlikely." He drains his glass in one final gulp. "James, did you honestly expect to walk away and sever all ties to your family? If you did, I'm afraid you were sadly mistaken, son."

"What ties?" He has to be kidding. "We have no ties. We haven't spoken in a decade. You know nothing about me. When you had the opportunity the five years I lived here, you chose your constituents, your agenda, other commitments."

"I had two sons." Edward almost shouts. "Now I have one." He goes back to the bar and pours himself another drink, then takes a long, slow draw and looks at me. "Am I to expect the same petty contempt from you as from your brother?"

My heart's coming through my chest again. All I want to do is get out of here, away from him. "What do you want me to say? What are you looking to hear from me, Edward?" It suddenly strikes me what Edward wants. I have to laugh. "I can't give you what you want. I won't. I'm about the last person to grant you absolution."

Edward laughs heartily. "Absolution?" He shakes his head with a twisted grin. "You are young, and naive, so you are forgiven." Then raises his glass to me, brings it to his lips and drains it, goes back to the bar and pours himself another.

"I don't need your forgiveness, Edward." *I need to get out of here.*

Edward stands at the bar studying me, then finishes his drink and places the glass down gently. I've never seen my father drink so much. Worries me. Never got on with drunks. This could turn into a very bad scene.

"Please, sit down, James." Edward indicates one of the two padded hardwood armchairs in front of his desk as he goes behind it and stands waiting.

I glance at the door then look back at my father.

"Please." Edward is casual, somehow making the command sound like a request, and again he motions to the antique chairs with a sweep of his hand.

I don't sit until he does.

He presses a few keys on his laptop and closes it, arranges some papers on his desk, then leans back in his wingback leather armchair, folds his huge hands casually in his lap, and looks at me.

"With Ian's passing, you will become the sole heir to the family estate upon my death. The estate is currently valued at over two billion in assets. Most of it is tied up in real estate holdings, though a good percentage is incorporated into a variety of business ventures, some of which—"

"I can't believe you are insisting on this conversation." I stand abruptly and my chair slides back silently over the polished wood floors. I back away from his desk, move behind the chair and grip the carved wooden back with both hands. "I told you, I'm not interested. I don't want any of this, or any of your money. If this is all you wanted to talk to me about, then we're done, Edward."

"This isn't about money, James."

"Well, excuse me for being vulgar, father, but whatever it's about I'm not interested in any part of your estate. This is absurd. You can't honestly expect me to walk away from everything I've established, worked for my entire life."

"I've not suggested you abandon anything. I am expecting you to absorb your additional obligations, and invest the time necessary to become effective at overseeing our collective assets—not overnight, of course, over time. You have lived a lifestyle known only to the privileged few. Do not minimize the role your heritage has played in your accomplishments."

You pompous, self-aggrandizing prick, almost falls out of my mouth, but I manage to swallow it back. "I have devoted my *entire life* to music. I work my ass off, round the clock, since well before *you* came along. I've made millions on my own, without your money or connections. And somehow, according to you, I owe all my success to this family? Well, that's bullshit, Edward."

"It's not my intention to minimize your achievements. Your dedication is beyond reproach. However, there is no denying that attending one of the world's most prestigious music academies, as well as private tutoring from some of the finest musicians of our time has undoubtedly assisted in the advancement of your career. I am hopeful your commitment to this family will be equally fulfilling when you invest some of the energy you've given so exclusively to your music, and redirect it into managing the Trust."

"I have no commitment to you or this family. And you sure as hell have no right to sit there and tell me that I am behaving like a spoiled child, following the path you not only paved, but shoved down my throat." I'm almost shouting. My heart's racing. It's hard to catch my breath. "I don't want to be part of your world, Edward, and I won't let you pull me away from the one thing I love."

"It is narcissism, at best, that the only thing you know of love is your own talent."

"That's not what I meant. You're taking what I said out of context."

"Am I?" Edward rises and spreads his long, spider-like fingers on his desk. "You have served yourself and no one else all of your adult life. You've cultivated relationships merely to satisfy your muse. Two years from thirty, you've not even the prospect for a wife, or children to inherit your name." He shakes his head and takes a few measured steps from his desk and looks at me. "Serving the family Trust will compel you to step outside of yourself, and the infinitesimally small world in which you exist. Like it or not, you are a part of this family, inexorably linked to its past, and destined to help carve its future, and the thousands of lives we affect. The only question is how you will play the hand you have been dealt." He moves to the front of his desk as he speaks and stops in front of me, not two feet away. His eyes are fixed on mine, boring a hole right through my head.

He's too close. Run. *Escape while I still can.*

"There is no such thing as destiny. I choose, father. Just like you. And I will not let you manipulate me into taking a position for which I have no passion, or interest. It's *my* life. Everything is transitory, Edward, even this family. I am not the answer to your need for immortality. I can't save you. This conversation is over. I'm leaving."

"Sit down, James."

"Fuck off, Edward," comes out of my mouth and I feel strangely vindicated, until he backhands me. My right cheek and eye explode in pain. Stumble back, out of his range, wipe my tearing eyes on my shirtsleeve, and cradle the side of my face in my hand, nestle it to counter the throbbing.

I'm shaking uncontrollably, but frozen, like a deer in the headlights, shocked. Until now, Edward's never raised a hand to me, or Ian, as far as I know. Can't recall my father *ever* being violent. He'd always been so contained, controlled. I stare at him, trying to gauge his state of mind. He doesn't look at me. He goes to the bar and pours himself another whiskey, and in one swift gulp drains the glass.

EDWARD

His inability to maintain even a modicum of decorum makes it clear to Edward that his son is on something. Edward expected this type of behavior from Ian, but not from James. The boy has been far too productive to be ravaged by drug addiction. Yet, his behavior is fundamentally disturbing.

James holds his cheek, stares at him as if he's Satan. Tears in his eyes, and Edward sees the grief stricken boy, a few days after he'd arrived at Castlewood. He'd been unable to talk to his son then. It is unfortunate they have yet to move off that mark.

"Please, sit down, James."

James stands his ground. He has Anna's striking beauty, with his thick, fine chestnut hair hanging over his brow and in his eyes— worn wild, just as his mother did, framing his square jawline, his full lips. His son's wide, glassy green eyes, *his eyes*, Anna had told him, are fixed on Edward's.

"I'm leaving, Edward. Tell Stefan to take me to Ashbury, or give me a phone, or I'm taking one of the horses and riding to Hythe or Folkestone to get a cell connection for a taxi." He folds his arms across his chest and tucks his elegant hands against his sides. He glares at Edward, waiting.

"You must have become a hell of a rider, son. Doubt I'd be able to make a ten mile journey in the dark, in the rain, without injury to the horse or myself." He pauses, but doesn't bring up what happened to Razor. "But, of course, the horses are yours, as is everything here. You don't need my permission to take one."

"Damn you!" James glares at him. "*I. Don't. Want. It.* Any of it.

What part of 'I'm not interested in your estate,' don't you get it, Edward?"

Edward's ire spikes. "Do not address me with that tone again," and he would have smacked James a second time if the boy had been in range. "I have neither the right nor the will to break five hundred years of tradition by passing on the Whren legacy to anyone other than a blood heir. Your pedigree is the last remaining bloodline of this family. Ownership of the Trust will transfer to you upon my death, a simple fact to do with what you will."

James runs his hand through his hair, clearly agitated. "You're just not getting this are you," his eyes narrow on Edward's, as if he's trying to gauge his father's demeanor, then he scoffs and turns away, and anxiously looks around the study.

"On the contrary. I understand that you have worked hard to achieve the admirable level of success you have garnered with your music, James. In addition, you have made yourself abundantly clear that you do not wish to be involved in our family's affairs." As he often does with his colleagues and constituents, Edward captures his son attention by agreeing with the disagreeable, and the command of his concentrated gaze. "While I acknowledge your position, I must again remind you of your heritage, and the shoulders on which you stand that paved and paid for your early path—"

"My mother and Mike paid and paved my "early path," Edward. You were 3,000 miles away, managing this little empire, instead of being a father to the children you sired. Ever wonder why my mom refused to marry you? Or Ian followed his mama, your ex-wife, over the edge?"

Edward struggles to keep his voice steady while flushing with the heat of anger. "You can construct whatever narrative you choose, but you will restrain yourself from speaking about that which you know nothing of." He considers another whiskey, then reconsiders. It is already hard enough to retain control faced with his son's impudence. He narrows his eyes on James, studies him closely. His son's disheveled appearance, the darkness around his eyes, are of grave concern. If he is using drugs, like Ian was, the outcome will likely be the same. An icy chill of panic rushes through his chest. The sweatshirt James wears covers his forearms, so Edward can not see if he has track marks, as Ian's did. "What are you on, James?"

"*What?*" James eyes his father suspiciously. "Nothing!" He turns away from his father, runs his hand through his hair again, pulling it out of his eyes for a moment, but when he turns to Edward, it falls back over his brows. "This is *bullshit*. I told I'm done. I want to leave. You can't keep me here, Edward. I'm not thirteen anymore." He shakes his head with obvious disdain. "I want a car, a ride, or a phone. And I want it *now*."

"You are not a prisoner here. This is your home, James. You agreed to this meeting tonight, which I assumed you were well aware of its content, having come to attend your brother's burial."

James laughs, rather manically. "You think I came here to claim my prize since Ian died? You're delusional, Edward. I fucking came here to get away from my girlfriend for a few days peace so I could work." He fixes his eyes on Edward's again. "I don't give a shit why you think I'm here, or what you *assumed* would come of this meeting. I just want to leave. OK? We're done."

"We've yet to resolve any business here tonight. I'd like to do that before you go."

"What makes you think I care what you want." His tone is low, angry, practically growling. "I'm leaving. Tell me where there's a goddamn phone to call a cab, or I'm going to rip this house apart to find one. *Do you understand?*" He's infuriated, sweating, his eyes wide and unblinking, confirming Edward's fear James is either on drugs or withdrawing from them.

Howard gently knocks on the study's arched threshold.

"Come." Edward says.

Howard enters, his thin lips pursed, he narrows his brow at James then looks at Edward. "May I be of assistance?"

"Thank you, Howard. Please notify Stefan he's to be available for my son throughout the evening, and to deliver James to Heathrow for his flight tomorrow morning."

Howard nods. Again he glares at James, scrutinizes him. "You are here to bury your brother, not malign your father. Enough, James." And he turns around and walks out of the room.

James spreads his hands in surrender, shakes his head and laughs at Howard condescendingly, then looks back at Edward. He studies his father, they stare at each other for a long, tense moment. "I'm sorry for you, father. You've lost one son by playing God, and you're about to lose the other."

"I've no illusions of omnipotence, son, hence our meeting tonight. I have been, and remain humbled by that which is greater than me. What humbles you, James?"

He shoots Edward an insolent grin. "Not you. Not anymore." His grin fades as his jaw line tightens, hollowing his cheeks, revealing his mother's high cheekbones. "Watch out, Edward. You're not in control." Deep forest green eyes stay fixed on Edward another moment, then he turns and walks out of the study.

Edward watches his son leave, but James' insolent grin remains in his mind's eye. He recalls that same grin on the boy's face when he was seventeen, on the hillside overlooking the Kinloch Hourn Estate. He'd disappeared from Castlewood after refusing to even discuss attending the acclaimed Social Sciences PhD program at King's College upon graduating from The Royal Academy. An unusually warm afternoon for the Highlands, and Edward remembers being winded when he made it to the top of the hill to talk to his son. He'd tried to impress upon James why it was important to prepare himself for his responsibilities ahead, in part, as the landowner of all they could see—the locks that fed the farms; the forests their timber companies harvested; the commodities they sold, the people they employed.

"Some friends from school got signed by Capitol Records, and they're paying me two hundred thousand dollars to co-write and produce the music for their first release. I'm leaving on the twenty-ninth, my eighteenth birthday, and moving to L.A." He looked at Edward passively. "And you can't stop me." Edward had wanted to slap that insolent grin off his face, but refrained. Perhaps that was a mistake...

His impudence at seventeen can be excused as teenage angst. But at twenty-eight, there was little justification for his disrespect—drug abuse the most obvious. He'd traveled this road with James only once, when instead of the agreed upon Blue Danube, he played something about American idiots with a lot of foul language at Edward's appointment as the Shadow Minister of State Foreign Affairs. It was obvious to everyone at the celebration that his son was on something. Howard took him back to Knightsbridge. Some interaction transpired between them, and since then, drugs had ceased to be an issue with James.

It has been ten years since he'd last seen his son on that hilltop in the Highlands of Kinloch Hourn. When James returned to Castlewood to collect his things, Edward was in Glasgow, negotiating with the STUC to delay a wage strike. When he returned home, and went to his son's room, little had changed. James took only the acoustic guitar he came with, which his step-father had given him as a child. Upon inspection, he'd emptied his armoire of his casual clothes, and taken the 12-string Takamine that Anna had given him, that he'd kept in its case on the window bench, but never played.

'What makes you think I care what you want,' and the memory of his son's wide-eyed, impudent glare spikes his ire again, and Edward's body flushes with heat, this time accompanied by nausea.

Images of Ian come to the fore, with the same insolent expression. He's slumped in Edward's wingback chair, stoned out of his mind and spinning it round and round. He sings television jingles to shut down what he calls Edward's diatribe on responsible behavior.

Edward pictures the chair twirling faster, and Ian's face becomes a grinning mask, and he starts to feel faint as Ian's face flashes by. Then the chair stops, but now it's James that Edward sees sitting there, Death standing behind him holding the chair still.

The study is suddenly stifling. Edward has to get out. He keeps his pace measured, and somehow makes it outside to the rose garden without faltering. He draws in the misted air with great gasps, then sits down on the marble bench near the Rodin and watches the condensation as it collects and drips from The Madonna's carved breasts.

He recalls his last exchange with Ian, four months earlier, entering the Knightsbridge house and finding Ian unconscious on the parquet floor of the entrance hall parlor. He revived his son, who promptly threw up on to the intricate wood inlay, which Edward then noticed was marked with bloodstains from careless injections and burn holes from once lit cigarettes. Thanks God Ian, or any one of his cronies hadn't burned the house down, along with the block of attached homes and apartments, yet. Stench throughout the house revealed Ian, and likely many others had been there quite some time. Detritus of paper waste from fast food bags to pizza boxes were left strewn about many rooms, and along the halls on most every floor. When he threw Ian out, along with the leeches and lost souls that day, it never occurred to Edward it would be the last time he would see his son alive.

First born dead from the talons of addiction, and his remaining child likely heading down the same path. If Edward lets James return to the States and the lifestyle he's adopted there, it could lead to his undoing. Could mean scandal, prison, or worse—end up where Ian took it, and my sad, fragile Kathryn, before him.

Edward shudders as if a ghost has passed through him, huddles into himself for warmth, but the cold does not pass. It clings to his bones and Death sits down with a groan beside him and refuses to leave. "I won't let you take my son," he whispers aloud to no one. Warm tears spill on his cheeks and to his disgrace he's crying—grief, sadness, frustration consuming him until he's able to delineate the voice of reason through his fear.

This time he isn't going to turn a blind eye and do nothing. Edward will not lose his only remaining child. A month or two in a private, discreet recovery program could teach James self-restraint, help him achieve some measure of balance by learning to moderate his obsessive behavior. He'd emerge drug-free, slave to nothing. The experience may even impress upon his son some of the privileges that come with positions of power. But Edward must act now, tonight, before James leaves Britain. He must use his resources to prevent his remaining son from harming himself, the family name, or God forbid, succumb to addiction, and sever Edward's only real connection to his beautiful Anna.

Creaks and pops of his bones echo in the quiet garden as he stands. Death does not accompany him as he walks back inside. It stays out in the damp night, filling the air with plumes of steamy laughter, and gives him a sly wink just before he enters the portrait-lined hall.

Edward returns to the study, sits down in front of the laptop and pulls up Home Secretary Rt. Hon. Douglas Perkins profile. Five hundred thousand dollars in donations to his Reform Referendum should be more than enough to call in one small favor.

-

-

-

BOOK ONE
Entropy
Chapter One

-

MARTIN

Martin Risner stares out the living room picture window and watches the towering redwoods sway against the deepening indigo sky. He counts seconds between the lightning flashes and the sound of the thunder. Storm's still off a ways. But it's coming, and a smile creeps across his face. Martin loves storms—the power, the drama, the rain. Had John shared his enthusiasm, they'd be enjoying the storm together right now.

Christ, we're so old and boring.

He looks through the telescope—John's housewarming gift to the both of them years ago—and spies lightning cells dancing along the southern ridge. He watches, astounded by the beauty, and saddened by another shared moment lost.

Front gate buzzer sounds.

Can't be anyone for John's clinic. Everyone in the area knows to use John Muir in Auburn if there's an emergency after five. Has to be some idiots looking for wine tasting who didn't bother to read the sign on the stone wall that says 'Private Residence.' Martin can't see who it is. Gate camera is still out. John promised to fix it about a hundred times already. *Promises. Promises.*

He ignores the first three rings, but by the fourth he goes down the hall and presses the button. "What is it?"

"Martin, is that you? It's James Whren. Could you open the gate?"

His heart practically skips a beat. *No. Couldn't be.* The voice, and

British accent sounds familiar, but strange, more East End than cultivated. Besides, James hadn't used his father's last name since he left England.

"Who is this?"

"Martin, it's James—Logan. Will you please open the gate?"

"James?" He can't believe it. "Is that really you?"

"Yes! Open the gate, Martin."

He presses the gate release. It has to be some sort of joke. James has never just shown up. But Martin isn't too concerned with letting whoever it is in. Cameras at the front of the house still work. He can see who it was without ever having to open the front door. Would be wild if it *was* James. *My beautiful James.* Last time Martin saw him was at Ian's funeral, over a year ago now. Was some weird rumor going around about him after that. What was it?

He turns on the floodlights and lights up the front of the house like daylight. He'd heard James was on a DreamWorks project at Apple in London. No. It was something else. Something stupid and he'd dismissed it. *Oh well.* He'll think of it later.

Martin stands in the foyer and watches a white SUV come on to the security monitor. Windows are up and reflective so he can't see who's inside. He waits for the car to stop when it comes to the center circle, but it doesn't. It keeps going, very slowly, and sideswipes the fountain. Martin stares at the screen in shock. Car finally jerks to a stop. Then the horn starts blaring.

He can't believe it. And right then it hits him he's not watching TV. Martin runs from the house and out to the car, hesitating only a second when the driver's door swings open.

A young woman sits behind the wheel. She has one hand on the horn but releases it upon seeing Martin. Her other hand cradles the head of a young man seemingly asleep in her lap. Upon closer examination Martin sees the man is James.

"Are you Martin Risner?" she says above the *beep, beep, beep* of the open car door.

"Yes."

"Your friend needs your help. I'm not sure he's breathing." She looks at Martin. Tears streak down her freckled cheeks. Flaming red hair tumbles over her shoulders and frames her wide, delicate face.

Martin reaches over and presses the ignition to shut off her car and stop the incessant beeping.

James suddenly opens his eyes, gasps for air and bolts upright. He sits in the passenger seat holding his right side, choking, struggling to breathe. He's very pale. His lips are purple, bordering on blue. He stares at Martin, a momentary delay before a flash of recognition, then looks back at the woman driving, glares at her actually.

"Fuck! Why are we here, Kate? You told me you'd drop me at a motel—" Then he takes a deep breath and starts coughing again.

"I never said that. Look, I'm just trying to help you—"

"You're not. You're making it complicated." His face contorts in pain as he starts to get out of the car, but he keeps moving with only a moment's hesitation. Moves his legs out and onto the gravel drive, and then just sits there.

Martin goes around the car to the passenger side, and sees John coming from the clinic toward them, his white lab coat whipping around his lanky frame.

"It's James Logan." Martin yells as John approaches. "Something happened to him."

James pulls himself out of the car, stands, almost falls. Martin moves to help, but James pushes him off. He leans against the car panting icy smoke, holding one hand out to keep distance, with the other he clutches his right side, all his attention focused on the simple act of breathing. Worn jeans hang loose on his hips. A dark blue flannel shirt ripples against him with the wind. He looks at Martin as if to speak, then his eyes roll back in his head and close as he slides against the car onto the ground.

Martin moves to catch him but misses. Kneels next to James slumped motionless against the SUV, and shudders in sudden terror that James is dead. Then John is kneeling in front of James, pushing Martin aside, almost pushing him over. Martin stands, moves out of John's way, where he so often finds himself these days.

"James," John says, but James is unresponsive.

The woman James called Kate comes around the car and stands beside Martin.

"Are you hurt?" John glances up at her.

She shakes her head as John turns back to James and feels his neck for a pulse.

"No! Fuck! Get away!" James wakes, panicked, punches John in the chest with the base of his palm then slugs him in the jaw with a closed fist as he scrambles to get up.

Martin gasps as John's head snapped back, but then John turns back on James, grabs his wrists and pins them against the car on either side of his head.

"*What the hell's wrong with you!* James! It's me. John. Look at me!"

James freezes under John's grip. Trembles violently. Eyes are black, wide, and vacant. "Get the fuck off me or I'll fucking kill you." He speaks in a harsh whisper but Martin hears him and is stunned. The James he knew abhorred violence, and rarely cursed.

"James, *look at me*! I'm John. *You know me.* Focus on me." John releases him, holds his hands up in surrender. "I'm trying to help you. Okay?"

James doesn't respond. He sits there shaking, his hands still clenched in a fist, against the car, black eyes fixed on John—but not on him, more like through him, locked in some terrible place. When he blinks, tears fall. Then his eyes roll back in his head again.

"Hey! Stay with me, James." John stays kneeling in front of him. "Hey. Hey! Focus on me."

James looks at him then. Connects. His dazed gaze travels to Martin, then Kate, then back to John. He brings his arms to his sides and spreads his long fingers wide on the gravel drive. "Shit. Man. I'm sorry...I...I thought...You okay?" He reaches up to John's face where he'd hit him, but in doing so it must have hurt because he sucks in his breath sharply, brings his hand to his side and holds it, still struggling to breathe.

John studies him. "I'm going to check out your ribs, okay?" He moves slowly, gently probing James torso. "Can you stand?"

James stares back at him blankly.

"Come on, man. Stay with me, James. Focus on me."

He does, squints at John then flashes his infamous wily, single dimple grin.

Martin smiles, can't help himself. Even totally ravaged, James is still magnificently adorable.

"You need to lie down before you puncture a lung, if you haven't already." John glances up at Martin. "Let's take him to the guestroom. He'll be more comfortable than in the clinic. Get his left side, I'll get his right." He looks back at James as Martin takes position. "I'm going to take your arm and put it around my neck. And Martin is going to do the same with your other arm. Ready?"

"Hey, Martin." James says casually as Martin kneels down beside him. His usually stunning green eyes are now black marbles. His hair is longer than Martin has ever seen it—hangs just past his shoulders in soft waves, framing his slightly stubbled cheeks and accentuating his square jaw.

"Okay. Here we go. Ready?" John takes James' hand and draws his arm around his shoulder and nods at Martin to do the same. "And this is going to hurt, so brace yourself," John adds as he slowly rises, and nods again at Martin to follow his lead.

James sucks in a gasping breath just this side of a scream as John and Martin help him stand.

John looks at Kate as he guides them forward. "What happened to him?" James takes a few drunken steps but for the most part, Martin and John carry him.

"We were in a car accident up near Tahoe." Kate follows them. "He wouldn't go to a hospital. He wanted me to just drop him off at a motel but I wouldn't, so he told me to take him here."

"Was he unconscious most of the time, or was he in and out?"

"In and out, but more out after a while."

"What was his longest period unconscious?"

"The half hour before we got here."

James' flannel work shirt ripples in the fierce wind, the blue and black plaid like a flag wrapping round him. He looks absolutely gaunt. He's easy to carry, surprisingly light, especially for almost dead weight. James is close to six feet, *was* an avid runner and surfer, a beautifully built athlete. *What happened?*

"It's going to be okay, James. You're going to be fine." It soothes Martin to repeat it endlessly as they round the car and head for the house. Cold wind whistles through the trees, and before they make it to the front doors, an icy rain starts to fall. Martin feels James shivering.

"Did he vomit at all? Spit up blood." John continues the third-degree.

"He didn't throw up, but he spit up something and it may have been blood. I couldn't see." Kate paces John, practically yelling her responses over the wind and rumbling thunder.

"We're almost there. You're going to be okay, James," Martin chants as they drag him through the doorway into the warm house. They make their way through the foyer, down the hallway to the guestroom. John tosses aside the quilted maroon comforter, and they gently release him onto the double bed. His eyes are still open but he looks dead, like he's been dead for quite a while. "You're okay, James. John's going to take care of you. You're going to be fine."

"I'm sorry, Martin. I shouldn't be here." James closes his eyes. "This was fucking stupid..."

-

-

Chapter Two

-

John sits on the bed next to James, now unconscious. "Would you get his boots off, Martin?"

More a command than request, as again was so often the dialog between them of late. James does not stir as Martin removes his boots, and John gently unbuttons his shirt. Martin feels that familiar twinge of desire watching John strip him. James was on the bed, unconscious before him, not frenetically working, enraptured with his muse. Martin's spent many hours fantasizing about having James in his bed...He looks away, at Kate, to suppress his misplaced, unrequited lust.

She stands in the doorjamb, as if unsure she's welcome, staring down at James. Young, mid-twenties; her red hair pulled over her slender shoulders is offset by an oversized black cashmere sweater. Irish ancestry most likely, by her fair skin tone and blushed cheeks. Then all the color suddenly drains from her freckled face. Martin looks back down at James as John peels back his flannel shirt.

Torso still defined, but red, purple and gray bruises spot his flat, tight stomach. A three inch gash across several ribs is oozing blood but has started to clot. White of bone presses under his skin below the gash along his right side. It's disgusting.

"Oh, my God. He's a mess." Kate whispers. She draws in a quick breath, her soft mouth quivers. She blinks and tears slide down her cheeks.

"He's got a fractured rib. Lying flat will keep the pressure off his lungs." John retrieves a penlight from his lab coat pocket, lifts James' eyelid and shines it in his eye. James doesn't stir, his black eye stares ahead blankly. "Could be a concussion, or drug overdose, or both with his pupils blown out like this." John lifts James' other eyelid. "Concussions are tricky. Bleeding in or around the brain can cause seizures, coma." John releases James' eyelid and it closes. "And it's even trickier if he's on something." Then he unbuttons James' shirtsleeve and pushes it up his forearm. "God damn sonofabitch," he whispers.

Martin's breath catches in his throat. He hears Kate gasp.

James' wrist is callused, bruised, the skin stripped to red in parts, like irritation from restraints. But even more disturbing is the long vertical cut on the inside of his forearm. The jagged red scar runs from the base of his wrist, six or more inches up the middle of his arm. John unbuttons James' other shirtsleeve and pushes it back. His left arm is equally disfigured.

"These wounds are fairly recent, maybe a few weeks old." John runs his fingers gently over the cuts. "And they're not defensive wounds." He glances at Kate. "You know anything about this?"

Kate stares back at him and shakes her head. "I met him like two hours ago, when he smashed into me."

Martin is sure he's going to be sick. "Why would James do something like that?"

"I don't know, Martin. But it looks like he was serious. I think your friend is in some major trouble."

It annoys Martin how John phrased that. *My friend*, like he hasn't known James for the last fifteen years, too.

"My uncle Calvin killed himself." Kate stands rooted to her spot in the doorway and speaks just above a whisper. "Sliced his wrists and bled out in the tub. I was the first one in the bathroom. I was six. I remember because it was right after my birthday party. I was going to show my mom what a big kid I was taking a bath all by myself."

Martin tastes the tofu curry at the back of his throat and swallows repeatedly to keep lunch down. John is engrossed in examining James and does not acknowledge she's spoken. Martin hates that. John does that to him all the friggin' time lately.

"I'm sorry," is all Martin can think of to say. And suddenly he remembers the rumor. It was a few days after Ian's funeral. Who was it that told him, James was busted for meth at Heathrow on his way home, and had to do mandatory rehab? Martin didn't give it a lot of thought at the time. It seemed absurd. He'd known James to indulge in various amphetamines that work cronies supplied him during sessions. Working twenty hour days, most everyone did something. Martin, and other friends of Bill W., lived on triple espressos. James was addicted to music, not drugs. Martin had never known James to use meth, or any hard drugs, and he'd never be so stupid to carry it overseas. Gossip abounds in the Industry. Martin had figured James was totally immersed in studio. It was easy to lose James. It happened often.

John pulls the comforter up to the middle of James' chest and tucks it around him, strokes the hair from his face gently. Martin caves. He loves the softer side of his husband.

"I need some things from the clinic. I'll be back in a few minutes." And John gets up from the bed, hesitates only a moment for Kate to step aside then exits the guestroom.

Martin turns to Kate now standing in the hallway. "Come in. Come in. Sit down. You must be exhausted. Are you sure you're not hurt?"

"I'm fine."

"Good. I'm Martin Risner." He extends his hand to her from where he stands near the bed so she'll have to come into the room to shake it.

She does, hesitates before crossing the threshold and planting herself next to the Deco dresser before shaking Martin's hand. "Kate McConnell." Her eyes fill again and she looks back down at James as her tears fall. "I'm real sorry about your friend."

"Thank you for helping him, bringing him here."

Her hand covers her mouth. She inhales sharply, her entire body trembles as she pulls her hair back then wipes her eyes and nose on her sleeve. "I did this. It's my fault. I didn't see his car. The accident was *my* fault." She takes a quivering breath. "I'm really so very sorry." She never takes her eyes off James.

"Hang on a minute, girl. Kate, right?"

She nods.

"Hey. That's why they call it an *accident*," Martin assures her. "And accidents happen all the time."

She finally looks at him with glassy green eyes.

"I was texting, Mr. Risner. I was looking at my phone and I ran a red light, right into him."

Rage, compassion and regret consume him almost simultaneously, and Martin can't think of what to say. The only sound in the room is James' labored breathing. Martin flashes back to the memory of the cyclist flying over the hood of his BMW on his way home from yet another drunken Halloween in the Castro, and shame encases him.

"It was an accident," he assures her again. "And, please, call me Martin. I may be old enough to be your father, but Mr. Risner is my dad, and the inference is rather...*disturbing*." He's trying to lighten things up but it isn't working. Kate stares down at James.

"He is extraordinary looking, isn't he?" Martin knows it's catty, especially given the circumstance, but he sees the way she looks at James, like everyone looks at James.

Kate glances at Martin. Her face flushes.

"He's going to be fine, Kate. John will take good care of him."

She nods.

"You didn't have to bring him here. You could have dropped him at a motel and driven away. But you didn't. You've done all you can to help him. Your conscience should be clear."

"Right." She shakes her head. "He'd be in Tiburon, safe and sound, with his very expensive sports car by now if it weren't for me."

"Maybe." Martin flashes the faintest smile. "But a mile down the road he may have hit a jackknifed truck and died."

Kate looks at him then, gives him a faint smile. "Are you always this philosophical, or are you just trying to make me feel better?"

"Bit of both." Martin studies her. "How do you know he was going to Tiburon?"

"He told me on the way here. He said he was coming from Boston on his way to Tiburon and that he didn't live anywhere. But I really doubt he's homeless."

"No, James isn't homeless. At least he didn't use to be. He has a gorgeous house in Zuma Beach, near L.A. At least, he did. What else did he say to you?"

"Not much. He was pretty out of it." She looks back at James. "His car was totaled. Instantly. Then it blew up. *God....*"

"Blew up? With him in it?"

"No. He'd gotten out by then."

"What kind of car was he driving?"

"A little sports car, a Porsche Spyder I think, like the kind James Dean got killed in. Why?"

Martin leans back against the dresser, three feet from where Kate stands. "James had a hybrid, or electric of some sort. He never owned a Porsche, not that I know of, anyway."

"He told me it wasn't his. He said it was a friend of his, and she'd got it from a divorce settlement so she wouldn't care that it got wrecked. But I care." She takes another quivering breath. Tears slide down her cheeks again.

Martin watches her but she doesn't look at him. She stares down at James.

John comes back right then and sets a small black case, some washcloths, a bottle of something clear, and the iPad under his arm on the Mission end table. He sits on the bed, opens the case and pulls out a filled syringe.

"John?" James blinks heavy-lidded at him. "Am I dreaming?"

"No. I'm here, James."

James looks confused, like a child upon waking from a nightmare. Martin moves closer to the bed. "Martin?" His eyes open wide. "What is this place? What's happening?"

"You're at Paradise, James, at our vineyard in Sonora, in our guestroom."

"Do you remember coming here with your friend tonight?" John glances at Kate. She gives James a quick smile as he looks at her.

"Kate? *Shit.* What are you doing here? You shouldn't be here." He tries to sit up, grabs his side and falls back against the pile of pillows.

"Relax." John holds his shoulder to the bed. "You need to be still, flat on your back. You've got a broken rib, which is why you're having trouble breathing, and what looks like a concussion, unless you're on something. Are you on drugs, James?"

His black eyes almost twinkle. He half-laughs, thick with irony. "Nope."

John nods once, to himself. "Okay. Then we've gotta get you over to Muir, get you stabilized. You're gonna be fine—"

"No. Can't go to a hospital." He stares at Kate. "Must be why I told you to take me here…"

"I can't do a CT here. There could be swelling—"

"I don't care. No hospitals. *Please.* You'll crucify me if you force me into a public position." He stays on John a minute then fixes his gaze on Martin. "And no one knows I'm here. You get it, Martin? No gossip. No bullshit."

"I get it, James. Relax. I won't tell anyone you're here."

James narrows his eyes on Kate. "You shouldn't be here. You have to leave." His gaze stays on her until John lifts the syringe and James catches sight of it. His eyes go wide and he scrambles up but John pins his shoulder against the pine headboard. "No! No meds. You're not putting me out." He glares at John, trembling, his huge hands on John's arm and chest trying to push him off.

"It's Fentanyl, James, for the pain." John releases him and sits back on the bed, needle still in hand. "It's only a low dos—"

"I don't want it." James slumps back, struggling to breathe again, hand clutching his ribs. "Unless you OD me." He flashes a sardonic grin, but Martin's sure he's not joking.

John stares at him, shakes his head, drops the syringe on the end table. He glances at Martin, brows furrowed, clearly concerned, which concerns Martin. Then he reaches for his black bag, takes out some bandages and lays them on the bed. He wets a cloth with rubbing alcohol and James recoils on contact as John cleans the bloody gash.

"Breathe, James." John commands.

James releases a wheezing breath and gasps for another.

"Want to tell us what's going on?" John inquires as he bandages the wound.

"No." James retorts, flinching with John's touch.

"Try and relax. This will just take a minute." He wraps James' ribs, guiding him gently forward as he brings the ace bandage around his back.

"Kill me or be done, John." Sweat trickles down James' face.

John's pause is barely perceptible before he clips the bandage closed and smooths it out against James' torso. James sinks back into the pillows piled up against the pine headboard. His hair is scattered in his eyes which are half-mast, red-rimmed and surrounded by dark. He looks like the lead in a punk band.

Martin recalls their last encounter, at Ian's funeral. They didn't really talk then, just that quick handshake in the chapel. At the grave site, James was across from him, rocking out to some tune in his head. The man was possessed. He was fine then, gorgeous as always. He'd been the silent center of attention. Martin wonders if anyone else caught him fingering.

"Well, that's about all I can do right now." John says as he checks James' eyes with the penlight again. Martin spies a thin ring of luminous emerald around James' enlarged pupils before John pockets the light, then pulls his tablet from the end table and begins filling in fields of a chart.

"You need to leave, Kate. Now." James lays slouched against the pillows watching her.

She stares back at him, her face flushes crimson.

"Ignore him." Martin senses Kate's embarrassment, and knows her guilt. "He's out of his mind, clearly. You're welcome to stay, Kate, as long as you like."

James scowls at Martin, blinking to keep his eyes open. "Couple hours sleep and I'm outta here, too."

John glances at James and shakes his head but doesn't say anything.

"This is too fucking hard. I want to be done." James whispers then closes his eyes. Then his body goes slack and he sleeps, his breathing even for the first time that evening.

Kate stands stone still at the end of the dresser by the doorway. "Is he going to be okay?" she asks in a small voice.

"I have no idea." John stands and faces her. "I don't know the extent of his injuries. We'll give it until morning, monitor his vitals. If he doesn't respond the way he should, then he goes to Muir. He's probably better off here right now. It'll take an hour or more to get to Auburn in this rain, and the winding roads wouldn't help him any. He needs to be still. Warm, dry, and still." He gathers his syringe off the table, caps and pockets it, then picks up his iPad, tucks it under his arm and looks at Martin. "I have to find the power pack for the heart monitor, and the portable defib, and research seizure meds. I may be a while. Call me if you notice anything weird."

"What do you mean, 'weird?'"

"If he stops breathing, Martin. Call me if he stops breathing."

Martin ignores his condescension, sort of. "What's the likelihood he'll stop breathing?"

"I don't know. I'm a doctor, not God. He just needs to be still, flat on his back and he'll probably be fine. Don't worry about it." John looks at Kate. "I'm more worried about his friend here. Kate, isn't it?"

"Yes."

"And you were not injured in the accident. Is that correct?"

"No. Yes. I mean...I'm not hurt."

"Good. Your car seems fine, too." He reaches in the pocket of his lab coat and pulls out her keys. "I moved it into a parking space by the clinic."

"Oh God, I'm so sorry for wrecking your fountain!" She'd completely forgotten about hitting it when James passed out in her lap. "I'll pay for whatever it costs to repair. I'm really sorry."

"No need. The damage to the fountain is minimal as well. Nothing a bit of concrete won't fix. Your follow-through in bringing James here is admirable. Thank you." He stays focused on her a moment. "Well then, Martin will look after you. He can fix you a strong cup of green tea." He glances at Martin then leaves the guestroom.

-

-

Chapter Three

-

Martin retrieves his favorite Goofy mug from the cupboard, puts it on the glazed concrete counter top next to the other mug. Kate is in the bathroom freshening up, and after, she's agreed to join him for coffee before leaving. He leans back against the counter by the enormous stainless sink and stares across the virtually sterile kitchen out the glass breakfast nook. It's completely dark out, rain pelting the French windows exaggerating the warmth within, and Martin revels in it for a moment.

Muffled voices and spontaneous bursts of laughter surround him while he watches the coffee drip into the carafe. The rich bitter/sweet aroma takes him back to that café in the Village, all those years ago. He sat on that splintered bench, banging on the piano. James was perched on that rickety stool strumming his acoustic so fast Martin could barely keep up. They worked together a lot back then. James was more of a fixture in their lives, back in the glory days. The days before age and illness.

He leans back against the hard counter and recalls John tease that Martin and James together reminded him of Donald Duck and Peanut's Schroeder. Those were the days John used to be jealous.

Dripping stops. Carafe is full, and Martin fills his cup and leans against the counter, cradling the warm mug next to his soft belly. Those were the days…

Martin hears screaming. Tortured screaming. James is screaming. He puts his mug down and runs down the hall and into the guestroom to find James locked in a nightmare.

"NO! *Fuck!* STOP!" are the only intelligible words through the screaming.

"James!" Martin sits on the bed and tries to wake him. "JAMES. Wake up!"

James slugs at him, throwing wild punches. "NO! Get off me! Get away!" He scrambles off the bed, falls onto the floor and clambers up against the wall. He sits hunched in the corner, shirt hanging open, his hands spread wide on the ground, trembling to the point of convulsing. His eyes are open, but it's clear he is still stuck in his dream.

Martin stands and slowly moves around the bed toward him on the floor by the bay window.

"Get away!" James practically growls. He's breathless, wide-eyed. "Why are you doing this? Why are you hurting me?!"

"James! It's Martin. I'm not hurting you. WAKE UP!" Martin kneels in front of him and James recoils to strike but freezes. So does Martin.

James' eyes are open hugely wide—black, glassy, riveted on Martin, and suddenly he connects. Martin feels a tangible pulse between them. He unclenches his fist and brings his hand to his side. "Sorry. Sorry. You okay? Sorry." He flashes a guilty smile, and a quick laugh, then runs his hand through his hair and looks around the room, shivering uncontrollably.

Martin kneels in front of him, lost for what to say.

James pushes himself up against the wall until he's standing. Martin stands, too, fixed on James who stares back at him.

"I know how this looks." He flashes a grin that borders madness. "But I'm not crazy." His eyes drift past Martin to John and Kate standing near the doorway. "I'm not. It was just a bad dream. I'm not crazy."

He looks crazy. He stands plastered against the wall, his eyes still open wide, black and hardly blinking. He stares at Kate. She stands just inside the guestroom doorway, her delicate nipples protruding through her sheer, deep red camisole which is minimally tucked into her jeans.

John moves past her into the room, takes the small black case from under his arm and puts it on the edge of the dresser. "You need to be lying down, James."

James stays glued to the wall, eyes now on John.

"You don't get it, do you?" John speaks gently, but precisely. "You have at least one broken rib. Dislodge it, and it could puncture your lung. You have a type-three concussion. Swelling around your brain, and you traumatize it again, even slightly—maybe move your head around too fast, you die instantly." John studies him. "Anything but rest can possibly kill you. Get the picture? Do you care?"

James and John are fixed on each other, the two of them exchanging some hidden dialog. Martin stands there trying to decipher what's going on exactly. He has this nagging suspicion it isn't good.

"You don't get it." James narrows his eyes to black slits. "Three weeks ago I left a maximum security mental hospital in Scotland— without permission. I'm wanted back there, and in the States now, too." He gives a quick, disdainful laugh. "But I'm never going back there. Not ever. No one can make me go back there. I'll meet them in hell before I ever let them take me back there. Get the picture?"

Rain drums the windows. Only sound in the room. Martin is speechless. What James has just told them is incomprehensible, and Martin blanks.

James laughs, low and hollow, filled with irony and anger. Then he runs his fingers through his hair and looks around the room. "I shouldn't be here. I have to get out of here."

"You've got nowhere to go tonight, James." John keeps his tone gentle but clinically commanding. "You need to rest."

James stays against the wall staring wide-eyed at John, and slowly shakes his head.

"Who knows where you are right now but us?"

He looks at Martin, then quickly at Kate, then back at John. "No one."

"And what are the odds of someone, anyone, figuring it out overnight?"

A conceding smile spreads across James' face. He looks down.

"You need to rest, James. You're safe here."

James glares at John with disdained amusement. "Safe. Right." He gives another quick laugh and speaks to himself. "I'm fucked. In a world this wired, how far is gone? They're going to find me. It doesn't matter where I go. They're going to find me. And then I'm fucked." James shivers, looks away and laughs again, and keeps laughing. It's out of control, maniacal. He starts coughing, then manages to stop. Gasping for breath, he slides to the floor, buries his face in his hands and seems to curl into a ball. He sits on the floor crying, rocking, his long fingers grip his hair and dig into his head.

Uncertain of what to say or do, Martin stands there watching. He's never seen James break down before. Never seen any man come apart like James was. He shoots John a quick glance, but John is fixed on James. Kate stares down at James, too.

Martin kneels in front of him and speaks softly. "It's okay, James…" He touches James' arm lightly, but James hits his hand away—hard. Martin falls back and lands on his butt. He sits there stunned and feeling stupid.

"Sorry. You okay?" Again, James' grin touches insanity. "I'm okay. Really. Don't worry about me." He laughs again. "Sorry. I'm not crazy. I'm not." His breathing comes in quick quivers. His face is tear-streaked and chalk white. Eyes dart to John and then to Kate, and stay on her for a moment, then he looks back down. "Please, go. Leave me alone." James sits on the floor, his back to the wall, knees to his chest.

Martin looks up at John and John nods, then he looks at Kate. She's still fixed on James.

James stares at the ground. *"Get out!"*

John touches her arm, grips it lightly and guides her towards the door. Martin gets up, looks down at James who stares at the floor. He waits a few awkward moments then finally leaves, follows John and Kate down the hall as he tries to control his breathing and slow his pounding heart.

"I'm calling Shelly Pasquel to see about getting James over to Sutter." John says it definitively as he pulls his cell from his lab coat pocket when he enters the kitchen. He has that directed efficiency about him, where he forgets to factor in feelings.

"John, wait a minute. We need to talk about this. I think it's a bad idea."

"You're not a doctor, Martin. You're not a psychiatrist, and neither am I, and James needs a psychiatrist now."

"Didn't you hear what he said? He just got out of being locked up. He's running. He's scared. Getting him locked up again my not be the best way to help him, John. James isn't a manic depressive teen. Not everyone is Phillip, you know."

Apparently, that was the wrong thing to say.

John glares at him. "What do you want me to do, Martin? Your friend is laying in there half dead, and I don't think he gives a damn whether he recovers or not. Do you understand that? He's still suicidal. I can see it. He should be in a hospital where they can get him on the right medications to balance him out."

"Or zombify him."

"Don't be so melodramatic."

"I'm not. Thorazine, Lithium, all that crap does is numb your brain."

"James is ill, Martin. He's distraught, maybe delusional. He just admitted to being hospitalized, probably for attempting suicide. Do you have any idea what the stats are for a long life with people who seriously attempt suicide? Of course you don't. You write show tunes for a living."

Martin looks at Kate standing near the butcher block island, flashes her a small, apologetic grin, then turns back to John. "He'll never agree to it."

"I don't care." John snaps back.

"You lock James up and you may be hurting him more than helping him. You ready to shoulder that, John?"

John glares at him. "*Damn you,* Martin. We let him walk out of here now and it's like letting a drunk get behind the wheel." He stays fixed on Martin another second then turns away in frustration.

"Let me talk to him, John. Find out what is going on before you do anything." Martin waits for John's response but gets none. "I'm going to talk to him," he says definitively as he passes John, and stops in front of Kate. "You okay, honey?"

She nods. She doesn't look okay. Her freckled face is ashen. She hugs herself with bare arms, the thin spaghetti straps of her camisole hang on her bare shoulders.

"Well, come in. Sit down," and he indicates the kitchen table tucked into the glass enclosed breakfast nook. "John will get you your promised cup of coffee. I'll be back in a jiff. Hopefully with a reality check." Martin flashes John a quick glance. John scowls back at him as Martin leaves him in the kitchen with Kate.

-

-

Chapter Four

-

Thunder rumbles close by as Martin walks down the hallway. He's blinded by lightning through the bay windows as he enters the guestroom. Thunder cracks almost simultaneously. Storm cell is passing overhead. Lightning strikes again and this time silhouettes James standing in front of the bay windows looking out. He glows for an instant, translucent, like a ghost.

"You okay?" Martin feels anxious seeing him standing after John repeatedly said he should not. He moves beside James, within catching distance should he collapse again.

"Yeah. Sorry about earlier." James holds his ribs and stands slightly hunched as he stares outside. "This is wild. The air is electric." His voice is soft, filled with wonder. "Feel that?"

Fine hairs on Martin's skin feel like they're standing up. "Yeah." Lightning strikes again, and thunder cracks and crackles so loud the windows vibrate. "*Cool*," Martin exclaims his wonder too as he flips on the Tiffany lamp set on the Mission table between them. "So, how do you feel?"

"Like shit." He whispers then shoots Martin a quick grin. "I'm okay." He stares out the windows, now reflecting his image with the lamplight. His shirt hangs open. He's practically bare to the waistband of his low slung jeans.

"Really. You look like hell, well, for *you*."

James laughs. "Thanks, Martin." He squints at the light then looks back outside.

"Want to tell me what's going on, James?"

"Not really."

He watches James stare out the windows and feels uncertain how to proceed, then decides on the direct approach. "Is it true you were busted for speed at Heathrow on your way home from Ian's funeral?"

Lightning crackles horizontally over the valley, spreads like a million tiny fingers.

"Wow! See that?" James whispers in amazement, just like a kid.

"Yeah." Thunder booms. "Is the rumor true, James?"

He half-laughs, shakes his head. "Is that what you heard? That's what everyone thinks?"

Window resonates with the wind as it howls through the split redwood frame.

"D-major. Hear it?" James grins at Martin, then it's gone and he looks back out. He seems a million miles away, and for a moment Martin sees the old James, lost in his head.

Martin stares at him. An ace bandage wraps his ribs to his waist, accentuating the muscles of his chest and arms. Stacked abs peek through and below the bandage. His hands are shoved deep in the pockets of his worn jeans, pulling the waistband down in front, exposing his bellybutton and the graceful line of his pelvic bones. And even though Martin knows it is completely inappropriate, he still wants James to want him.

Lightning crackles across the valley again. James startles from the clap of thunder that follows. He glances at Martin with a quick, demented laugh.

"I've become a bit jumpy." He flashes a twisted grin.

"I can see that." Martin meets his black-eyed stare. And the old James is gone. The James he knew was casual and confident—to the point of arrogant. The James who showed up this evening seems positively unhinged. He's the same exquisite work of art, but Martin does not know this man. "God, someone really messed with you, didn't they?"

James stares out at the storm. He nods slightly. "You think I'm crazy, Martin?" He whispers the question. The James he knew never would have asked it.

"You mean now, or have always been?"

James smiles. "Let's start with always."

"I'm not qualified to judge crazy, James. But I recognize obsession. I've lived it, with you at times. Actually, *anytime* with you."

James scoffs, then looks at Martin. "That wasn't obsession. It was love."

"That's not love, James. Music can't love you back."

His expression hardens and he looks back out. "Yeah… I got that, alone in hell…" He stands stone still, completely absorbed in his thoughts, but not like the old James—clearly rapt in the sounds he created. Now his face is expressionless, like a mask on top of many.

Thunder rumbles but it's distant. Storm cell is passing. Half-moon peeks out and lights the rolling hills of vineyards in dark grays and deep blues. Ambient light cast James in marble, like a Greek god. But then Martin notices him trembling. And the indestructible archetype is gone.

"Do you think you're crazy, James?"

He shoots Martin a quick look, then turns away, pulls the blanket off the bed and wraps it around his shoulders. He stares outside. "I know what crazy is. I lived it, with it for the past thirteen months." He gives a dismissive laugh and shakes his head slightly. "I'll admit to being obsessed, but I don't think I was crazy. I don't know if I am now. I may be." Another quick, derisive laugh. "They tried to make me crazy." He speaks as if to himself. "I know John thinks I'm crazy."

"John thinks you're still suicidal." Martin waits for a reaction but gets none. "And I must admit, I'm concerned, too, after seeing what you did to yourself. Care to fill me in on the accuracy of John's assessment?"

James looks at Martin and cocks his head. "What's the deal, Martin? What difference does it make to you? I mean, really? We haven't seen each other or worked together in years. If we never saw each other again, what impact would it have on your life? Honestly, why does it matter to you what I do with my life?"

"Jesus, James. What the hell kind of question is that? How long have we been friends?"

"Is this a test?" Soft, quick grin. "I don't know, Martin. But we've known each other a long time."

His comment cut. It was careless, and so *James*. "Fifteen years. You've been a part of my life for *fifteen* years. Whether by default or design, you've affected it. I've done some of my best work with you. You got me my first Broadway gig, and my first Tony nomination for Christ's sake."

"You're a talented composer, Martin. It was always a privilege working with you."

Martin softens. "And for me, with you, James."

Sad smile dances across his full lips. He stares out the bay windows at the blue valley. He looks like a monk, or one of those young fantasy novel heroes. "We made some good music together." James whispers, as if to himself again.

"And we'll make more down the road—"

He laughs, like Martin is absurd.

Martin finds it deeply disturbing. "Are you looking for permission to kill yourself?"

James shoots him a black-eyed stare.

"I'm not going to give it to you, James." Martin glares back at him. "You impact everyone you touch whether you acknowledge it or not. You've affected my life way beyond just music. I mean, John and I might not be together today if it weren't for you, and that time up in the Hampton's."

He stares at Martin blankly. Obviously, he doesn't recall one of the most important weekends of Martin's life. "Look, I've known you to be incredibly perceptive and brutally accurate when you're paying attention. The trick has always been *getting* your attention."

Rain begins again, and within moments sheets the windows, encasing the room. James stares out. "I pay attention, Martin. I just never cared to engage."

Again his sharp edge cuts. Martin is nothing more than a colleague, one of many to the man. He sighs, exasperated. "You know, I hope sooner rather than later you'll discover how magnificent your life can be when you let yourself be touched by the people in it."

James narrows his eyes on Martin. "Is this an inquisition?"

"Think of it more like an intervention." Martin smiles to lighten the tension. It doesn't.

"It's harsh, man. And not true." He runs his fingers through his hair and stares out. "I've just been better with music than people."

"Because you want to be, James."

He shoots Martin a sideways glance. "You sound like Julia."

Martin laughs. "I've often been accused of sounding like a woman."

James smiles, but it doesn't last. "Have you heard from her?"

"Only once. She was calling around, looking for you."

"When?"

"It was winter, around this time last year, I think. Maybe a few weeks after Ian's funeral."

"What did you tell her?"

"Just what I'd heard—either you were busted for speed at Heathrow, or you were doing a studio gig in London with Phil Sinclair."

James looks down, pulls the blanket around him tighter and huddles in it, like it's a cave. "Damn lies, stats and rumors." Again he seems to speak to himself.

"Wait a minute, James. We had no idea where you were in trouble, locked up in some mental institution somewhere."

"I used to wonder if anyone was looking."

"I don't know. I didn't. There was no reason to. Julia confirmed what I'd already heard—that the Zone guys got Zack Pearson to finish their release after a call from some lawyer in Britain on your behalf. I thought you offered the gig to Pearson to work with Phil Sinclair on Pandora's EDM single." Martin crinkles his brows, stares at James with his puppy-dog eyes of apology. James does not look at him. "Look, even at worst, and you *were* busted, you'd have been held up for a few months, gotten out and absorbed in working again. Honestly, I thought it was bullshit, James, and that you were in London, working with Sinclair."

He smiles. "Thanks for the vote of confidence, Martin."

"You know, just a heads up—Julia said she didn't believe the rumor either. She thought you were working, too. Gotta give her credit, cuz it was all over the net rags that you were at some rehab for the rich and famous after getting busted at Heathrow for dealing speed." Martin pauses, watches James for some sign of denial or admission, but he remains stone still. "When she didn't hear from you, she was sure you were holed up in some studio in London. You 'ran away to make it with your muse again,' I think she said, or something like that."

"She knew I went to Ian's funeral. I texted her from the airport."

James seems bewildered.

"Then it's a text she never got, because she was surprised when I told her I saw you at the burial. She didn't even know you had a brother." Again Martin waits for James to respond, but he doesn't. "She told me about the fight, right before the funeral. And that she still didn't believe the rumor, well, makes her a friggin saint, don't ya think?"

James shakes his head. "I wasn't addicted to speed, Martin. And there are multiple points of view in any argument, or relationship."

"What does that mean, exactly?" Martin pauses again. James stares out the window. "This isn't Rashomon, James. It's real life." Still no response. "Do you honestly believe Julia's misguided, and that you made a concentrated effort to keep that relationship vital?"

James practically whispers, "No. Probably not." He pulls the blanket tighter, huddling into himself. Martin knows he should stop interrogating James, but he just can't stop. His associate, his friend needs a reality check.

"Probably? Julia body slammed you at the Palisades studio, grabbed you by the hair and smashed your head into the wall to get your attention."

James laughs. "She was just screwing around, Martin."

"You still don't get it, do you? Our dear Julia carried out a fantasy many of us harbored towards you James. We all have to compete with your composer, your muse."

James scowls at him. "Well, since I no longer hear music in my head, you'll be pleased that I don't hang out there anymore. You have my attention, Martin, just above the screaming."

Martin stares at him. What is he supposed to say to that? "Screaming isn't good. The dreams probably won't go away either until you deal with whatever happened to you, find a way to live with it and move on. You won't get away with trying to bury it."

"Watch me. I bury it or it buries me. It's warped and distorted and I just want it to go away. Dissecting the past won't change it."

"It may help you come to terms with what happened, and why. Nothing happens in a vacuum, James."

"What's that supposed to mean?"

Martin hesitates. The path he's taking James down might not be the best one right now. James seems on the edge of contained, and Martin doesn't want to push him over.

James glares at him. "Straight up, Martin. What are you getting at?"

Still Martin hesitates, but with James staring at him, waiting, there seems to be no turning back. "Remember Ian's funeral? I do. You couldn't stand still. At the grave site you were actually rocking to some tune in your head. That's pretty far gone, even for you. It was your brother's funeral, James. You should have been paying attention."

His eyes narrow to thin slits. "So you're saying this is all my own fault?" James holds the blanket to his shoulders like a cloak, and paces a few steps, putting distance between them, then stops and glares at Martin again. "Well, screw you, Martin. Nothing I've done justifies what they did to me. They may have robbed me my ability to ever play music again." His anger is palpable, his East End accent thick. "*Damn you...!* You say 'move on.' *To what?* If I'm not a musician anymore, than *what the hell am I?*"

Rain pelts the window pane in a soft, even rhythm. James stares at him waiting for an answer, but Martin feels afraid to say anything now.

James stays on him, his black eyes piercing. Then he sighs, shakes his head slightly and turns back to the bay windows. "I'm sorry. I'm tired." He stares outside through the blurry silvery ribbons streaking down the three giant panes. "Relax, Martin. I won't lose it again."

Again the Greek statue comes to mind, especially with the blanket around him like a hooded cape. But then Martin sees the tears streaming down his face and the classic image is replaced with the lost man before him. "You can be whatever you want to be, James. Music doesn't have to be all there is. You just made it that way."

He wipes his tear-streaked face on his hand then looks back at Martin. "I've just spent three hundred and ninety-five days in hell repenting for my sin of omission. Does that satisfy you, Martin?"

"Only if you learned something, James."

James looks back outside, but Martin catches a hint of his smile. Hail begins hitting the windows. Little white balls strike the glass with pings, slide down the panes and gather on the weathered wood frames.

"I learned many things," James says softly. "Things I never knew, and never wanted to know, Martin." He pauses. "I was raped," he almost whispers. "Tortured, isolated for weeks at a time. I've been intimate with Lonely, and a blackness I never knew existed. And now I know fear. It is pervasive." He glances around the room, then looks at Martin. "The weird thing is, I still see things like before, only now I feel them too, more viscerally than ever before. I get you're afraid for me, even *of* me right now. I can feel your anxiety, like it's inside of me. I feel everything now, except the tips of my fingers." He holds his hand up in front of him and rubs the tips of his long, slender fingers together. "And I don't know how to live like this." His jaw line hardens and hollows his cheeks.

James stares at him. For a second Martin is certain he's pleading for salvation. Direction, maybe. Then the mask returns, he drops his hand, and looks back outside.

Martin is dumbstruck, nauseated, yet tantalized by James'

confession. Tortured? James restrained and *gently* sexually assaulted were some of Martin's bondage fantasies, though in his imaginings James was always a willing participant. Guilt for conjuring these twisted scenes suddenly consumes him. Again, Martin's lost for words.

"Details of my torture play into your fantasies, Martin?" James' tone is impassive, not accusatory. He doesn't look at Martin with the question.

Martin blushes, face and body flush and he breaks out in a sweat. James doesn't seem to notice. *Bless him.* "Do you hate me?" He blurts, unable to contain his guilt.

James still doesn't look at him. "No. Seems you're not alone, Martin." A quick shake of his head. "It doesn't matter to me what you think, only what you do."

Martin smiles. The old James stands before him—the brutally perceptive, fluid philosopher. He runs his hand through his hair and it tumbles back into his eyes and onto his shoulders. All these years Martin believed James was a narcissist: doing what he wanted, when he wanted, because he could. But it suddenly occurs to him that James was actually a solipsist. Unless you were of immediate concern, he didn't know you existed. "You know, that you don't have music to shelter you anymore may not be such a bad thing."

James shoots him an irate glare. "Go to hell, Martin."

"I'm trying to help you out of it." The tension grows between them but Martin feels a need to give him direction out of the tunnel he's seemingly stuck in. "Think about it, James. Just imagine the possibilities when you let people in."

His black eyes flash irritation, but Martin is certain he sees humor, perhaps enlightenment, as James looks back outside.

"Tell me what's going on, and between you, me, and John so we can figure out how to help you. Resolve your past, take what you learned and start with a clean slate—recreate yourself, become whoever you want to be."

"I want my fucking life back. I want it to be how it was."

"And what was that? Where did it get you?"

Quick laugh. Sad smile. He stares out, but Martin gets James heard him.

Ice balls gather in the corners of the five square panes that top the three long bay windows. Pinging grows louder, and harder, and combined with the resonance of the wind creates a soft but audible symphony.

"It's beautiful, isn't it?" James whispers in wonder.

"It is." Martin watches him. He's expressionless, inside his head again. "I'm sorry for whatever you've been through, James. And I don't mean to minimize it, or seem harsh, but you're here, now, and have to play it as it lays. You have a choice, right now. Keep running, or stop and deal—get a lawyer, a team of them, whatever it takes."

James shakes his head then fixes his black-eyed stare on Martin. "No." He brings his hand back to his ribs, his long fingers around his slender side. "I can't afford to lose. I told you, I'm never going back there, Martin." His jaw tightens with his resolve, and Martin is chilled by it.

"John will be all over me if he finds out you're out of bed," Martin says, feeling apprehensive about pushing James further. "You should lie back down. Get some rest."

No response. James stares out as moonlight breaks through the clouds, the vineyards suddenly awash in silver droplets against royal blues. Locks of fine hair spill over his brow and brush his long lashes. He blinks repeatedly, as if to keep his eyes open.

"You really ought to rest. We'll talk in the morning. You're gonna have to fill in a few blanks for us to help you out of the mess you're in. But for tonight, get some sleep, James."

He stares outside. "Thank you, Martin."

"No problem. Hope I helped."

James does not comment.

Hail begins blending with rain. Fat raindrops mix with the small white dots which become fewer and fewer until only water slides down the glass. Martin waits another second but James does not look at him. "Good night, James." He shakes his head in defeat as he leaves the guestroom, suddenly overwhelmed with exhaustion. Hallway to the kitchen looks long and feels daunting. And right about now Martin wants a drink. Correction. Many drinks.

-

-

Chapter Five

-

JOHN

John sits in his office in front of his laptop reviewing the over thirty thousand search returns on 'James Michael Whren.' 'James Michael Logan,' his mother's married name, yielded almost a million results, most highlighting his music career, producing and writing credits and the like. John is looking to find out what's happened to him recently. Can't possibly help the man without some understanding of what is going on.

He'd never have guessed James would attempt suicide. People driven by an internal obsession were usually unscathed by the external world. Whatever happened to him must have been powerful enough to rip him from the cocoon he'd built with music, which John wouldn't have believed possible. Not James.

A piano or a guitar is a fixture in every memory with James, from the first time John saw the boy pounding away on the piano on the empty stage at Covent Garden. 'That's the child prodigy,' Martin had told him. 'He's fourteen.' Martin was in his mid-twenties then, back in the days when he was hot, and healthy. The thought is so overwhelmingly depressing he pushes it aside and continues his reverie... And the prodigy became a man, and John recalls James on the beach that winter in the Hampton's, in those worn jeans and that gray sweater, running scales on the guitar at three in the morning. No denying the man's talent, or beauty. John used to tease Martin for his interest, but there had been times even he'd harbored fantasies.

James had always been Martin's friend. Really, they were more like colleagues, since James never integrated into their lives like so many of Martin's other work cronies. Mentally compromised, possibly suicidal and clearly ravaged, and Martin still wants him. John doesn't. He has no desire to be with someone so insular. John wants to *be* James. Or, at least, have the looks, possess his talent, and have his family money. Martin doesn't look at him the way he looks at James. No one ever looked at John the way most people look at James. John wants to try that on for a day. Wear it awhile. Bask in being the object of lust. Hard to remember feeling desired.

He relaxes back into the chair and rubs his eyes, then focuses on the page of links, seemingly different versions of the same story, all around the same time frame from over a year ago:

James Whren, Sole Heir to Whren Family Fortune Arrested in Drug Scandal.

John clicks on the link and brings up a year old article in the London Times Mirror. Picture of James in his late teens conducting the

London Symphony Orchestra at the Barbican. His eyes are closed, his arms up and extended, he's holding thin white batons in both hands. He looks like he's making it with God.

John stares at the picture. He doesn't really want to be James. There's a price with everything. With looks comes fickle lust. With money, especially inherited money, comes responsibility. Great talent is only achieved through focused practice, letting most everything else fall away, which is exactly what James had done. If John doesn't watch it, he's about to go there with Martin. He laughs, surprised to see himself reflect James, and even more surprised to feel shamed by it. And it suddenly dawns on him why James may not want to be James anymore.

-

"James Whren, son of Edward Whren, twenty first Earl of Carham, was arrested Tuesday on drug related charges.

Chief Constable Richard Brunstrom of New Scotland Yard made the arrest at Heathrow airport before Mr. Whren boarded a flight back to the United States with allegedly close to half an ounce of methamphetamine.

Sir Edward Whren, a Conservative heredity peer of the House of Lords and a Shadow Minister of State Foreign Affairs, withheld comment in regards to his son's arrest..."

-

The article goes on to enlighten readers of Sir Edward Whren's grave loss—his son Ian passing from an overdose of heroin just days before his only remaining son's arrest for drug trafficking. It ends, like any good cliff hanger, with James' case pending trial. Like all the other blurbs and full length stories John's read, there is no followup with the outcome of the trial, and does not shed any light on his existing knowledge. He knew of the rumor, of course. Martin had told him ages back, and like Martin, he'd dismissed it. After reviewing several more sites, he rubs his eyes, shuts the laptop, then collects what he needs and leaves his office.

Air is wet, windy and cold. Fine mist falls from the soaked trees but the rain has stopped. The moon shines brightly on the small wet stones of the gravel drive. John crunches across them, then wipes his feet on the welcome mat as he crosses the threshold into his warm house. He brushes the beads of water off his wool sweater as he walks down the hallway to the guestroom.

The bed is empty. He looks around the vacant room as he places his black bag and portable defib on the end of the dresser. James is gone, and for a moment John feels a surge of anxiety, but then notices the door to the bathroom is ajar. As he gets to the threshold he sees James on the marble floor, slouched up against the glass shower wall. His eyes are half-mast. His shirt hangs open, his ribs still wrapped. He holds his side with one hand. John kneels in from of him, but he stares ahead, focused on nothing. "James. Hey. What are you doing? You OK?" James' eyes finally travel to John's, but it's clear he's totally out of it. "What's going on? You with me? Hey!" Then John notices the amber prescription bottle next to the almost empty glass of water on the counter near the sink. "Oh God, what did you do?"

John rises, goes and grabs the empty bottle off the Carrara marble counter top. Valium, the prescription John had given Martin after he'd quit drinking to help him with the transition. There were twenty pills in that bottle, 10mg each, and Martin had taken only a few. Said it made him nauseous. James has just taken the rest.

"Goddamn you, James!" John throws the empty bottle at him in fury, but misses, and the plastic container rattles along the dark oak floor.

"Damn me to hell, John." James whispers, and grins.

"What's going on in here?" Martin stands in the bathroom doorway with his mouth gaping.

"James just ate a bottle of Valium."

"No worries, John," James practically groans. "It doesn't agree with me." He uses the tub ledge to pull himself up off the floor, then grabs his side as he moves unsteadily to the sink, leans over it and vomits starchy white fluid until it turns into dry heaves. He finally collapses back against the counter but manages to stay standing. He looks at Martin, then John, then laughs that maniacal, lunatic fringe laugh, then wipes his mouth clean on his shirt sleeve. Then he staggers from the bathroom, past John and Martin, back to the guestroom.

From the mirrored wall, John sees him practically fall onto the bed and then curl onto his side.

Martin still stands in the doorway. "What the hell is going on?" He looks from John to James on the bed, his eyes now closed. "We were just talking ten minutes ago."

John picks up the empty bottle on the floor and puts it on the counter. "Why didn't you call me after you spoke with him?"

"This isn't my fault, John."

"I'm not blaming you, Martin. James did this to himself." John stands over the sink and runs his index finger though the vomit.

"What are you doing?"

"I'm looking to see if all the pills dissolved. Gives me a window to how much got into his system." The starchy liquid mess has many small round white dots floating in it.

Martin comes closer to look in the sink. "Is he going to be okay?" He steps back as John faces him.

"He'll live, for now, but he's not okay, Martin. I tried to tell you before. James is not okay." John turns on the tap and washes the vomit down the sink.

Martin goes back to the bathroom doorway, leans back against it and looks at James, now lying on his back, apparently sleeping. "All that talent and beauty, and he wants to blow it all away."

"That's what used to boggle me about you, when you were drinking yourself to death." John looks at Martin's reflection in the mirrored wall in front of him. Martin doesn't respond. He stares at James. John sighs, shakes his head and goes back to the guestroom. "James! Wake up. Come on. Open your eyes." John sits on the bed next to him.

James opens his eyes and glares at John through narrow slits. "Give me a break. Would you leave me alone, please." He tries to curl up again but John pushes his shoulder back against the bed. He grips James' face in one hand, holding him to the pillow, pulls his penlight from his lab coat pocket with the other and shines it in James' eyes. James tries to push him off, but doesn't really manage it until John stops his examination. The moment he does, James shimmies to the head of the bed to get away from him. "Get off of me. Leave me the fuck alone."

John stares at him, now huddled against the headboard holding his ribs. "Why, James? You show up here, out of the blue, and kill yourself? This is our home. What the hell were you thinking?"

James closes his eyes, but John's on him.

"Wake up! Look at me! Pay attention, you selfish son of a bitch."

James opens his eyes to slits again and stares at him.

"You took three quarters of a bottle of Valium, James." John gets up off the bed, goes to the bathroom, gets the prescription bottle, comes back to the bedside and holds the amber bottle an inch from James' face. "What the hell were you trying to do?"

"Ease up, John," Martin says.

"Shut up, Martin."

"I didn't count 'em, John," James says thickly. "I just wanted to shut down. Turn off. Sleep without dreams. Pills were right there." He squints at Martin across the bed. "You got it right, Martin. I spent the last thirteen months in hell wanting to be what I was, which turns out to be nothing."

Martin's jaw literally drops. "I never said that James—"

He blinks at Martin several times then his eyes drift back to John. "Just need to sleep a bit…please..." His eyes roll back in his head a little then he fixes them back on John. "I'm fine. Really. I swear. Just sleep it off for an hour and I'm outta here." He blinks a few times then his eyes stay closed. His body goes slack and he slouches back against the pillows, unconscious.

-

-

Chapter Six

-

John stares down at him. He looks Christ-like, his slender, muscular body lay over the pillows, his arms slack at his sides. His huge hands are face down and spread loosely on top of the maroon quilt. He looks perfect. Undamaged— but John knows it's a lie. Anger wells in the pit of his gut. The man is going to walk out their door, and unless he gets help, in a week, a month, a year down the line, he'll likely be joining Martin at James' memorial.

"I'm calling Shelly Pasquel and getting him over to Sutter." John looks at Martin standing at the foot of the bed. "He needs to be in a hospital, Martin, where someone can watch him around the clock, get him on the right meds to quell his death wish." John strokes James hair away from his eyes gently, then feels his forehead but there's no fever. "I'm an internist, just a GP. I handle cuts and colds and broken bones. I've done what I can for him. I'm getting him over to Sutter." He stares down at James a second more then glances at Martin before leaving the room.

John takes his cell from his coat pocket as he moves down the hall. He searches for Shelly's contact numbers, finds her listing as he enters the kitchen and calls her. Kate is at the table in the nook, nursing a cup of coffee. She stands when he comes in.

"Is everything OK? With James?" Her face is pale, delicate, but pretty, even with the freckles. "I heard you yelling."

John had told her to wait for Martin in the kitchen when he went to his office for medication and the defib. He hadn't planned on getting distracted playing detective like he had. "This is Shelly. What can I do for you, John?" Dr. Pasquel is on the phone.

"Sorry about the hour, Shel, but I have a patient. White male, late twenties, physically and mentally unstable. He's already attempted suicide at least twice." John paces the kitchen with the phone to his ear. "I need to get him in on a 51/50 asap."

"Since when did you start taking on adults?"

"Well, he's not actually my patient. He's more like a friend."

"Sounds like your friend's in trouble. Were the attempts serious?"

"Yes."

"Were both attempts recent? Possibly a response to critical life changes?"

"Yes. I believe so. The thing is, I'm afraid he's going to try again. He's experienced some major trauma, and I don't know exactly how to help him."

"Bring him in, John. Will he come?"

"No. I don't think so."

"Well, we can get an ambulance over to you. EMTs can handle him once they're there."

'Or zombify him.' John hears Martin in his head. He turns around to continues pacing sees Martin standing in the kitchen doorway.

"He wasn't trying to kill himself, John," Martin says flatly.

"James just overdosed in our guest bathroom on three quarters of a bottle of Valium," John seethes.

Kate gasps.

"And you're standing here telling me he didn't mean it?"

"Yes. I don't think he was intentionally trying to kill himself." Martin responds to John but looks at Kate.

John glances at her, her hand to her mouth, her eyes wide in horror. *James is right. She shouldn't be here.*

"John? Is there a problem?" Shelly's tone is so damn clinical.

John stands in the center of the kitchen glaring at Martin. "James crossed the line, Martin. I can't just let him walk out of here now."

"Don't get him locked up, John." Martin stands near the doorway staring at his partner of twenty years with his puppy face on. "At least wait until we find out why he took those pills. I spent half an hour talking to him earlier. He's lucid, John. I'm telling you, James is not crazy."

"John?" Shelly's voice sounds shrill. "Should I send someone?"

Martin stares at him. "Phillip was locked up, and it didn't do him any good."

Martin's words cut to the core of John's certainty. "At the very least, James is reckless, Martin."

"John." Shelly is speaking to him again. "I can get someone over there in half an hour if you feel it's warranted. You understand that once he's in our system you won't be able to see him for at least forty-eight hours, and only then by professional courtesy."

John pictures on James institutionalized, imagines him sedated, blank. If James isn't suicidal, John may be sentencing him because of his own fears. And once James was 'in the system'... "Thanks, Shelly. I'll call you back. Thanks a lot." John disconnects and holds up the phone for Martin to see. It takes considerable restraint not to throw it at him. It feels as if he's surrendering a weapon as he put his cellphone on the butcher block island between them.

"You're doing the right thing. Thank you for trusting me."

"I don't. I just don't trust myself." John looks at Kate still standing in the nook by the table, then back at Martin. "James is not your entertainment du jour, Martin. This isn't a Broadway score you two are constructing. You're playing with his life."

"I'm not playing, John. I'm well aware of the gravity here." Martin sighs, shakes his head and shoves his hands in the pockets of his baggy parachute pants. "You know, locking him up may postpone his death, but it won't save his life. James has got to want to do that."

"*God,* I'm so sick of AA platitudes. But you're right, Martin. James has got to want to live. The problem is, I don't think he does."

"And you can't stop him if he's hell bent on killing himself." Martin delivers his cutting words softly.

"Excuse me." Both men look at Kate. "I don't know if I'm allowed an opinion here—"

"No." John glares at her.

"Yes." Martin glares at John.

"Well, I can't tell you what the right thing to do for your friend is. But I get the feeling if you force him to do something he doesn't want, well, he'll run the first chance he gets—one way or another." She looks at John. "I just mean, well, you could push him into a position where his only way out is to do the very thing you're afraid of."

John glares at her, stays fixed on her a moment, then turns to Martin. "I'll watch James tonight. If at any time I feel it warranted, I'll do what I think is right, with or without your consent." John shakes his head then walks out of the kitchen.

-

-

Chapter Seven

-

KATE

Kate watches Martin watch John leave. Martin looks down when John is gone, his pudgy frame seems to slouch, and Kate witnesses sadness consume him. She recognizes black. "I'm sorry. I didn't mean to aggravate anything between you."

"You stop right there, girl. This isn't about you. John and I have been together a long time. Relationships go through stages, and we're not at a particularly great one right now." He gives her an apologetic grin and shrugs. "When he's actually present, he seems to think his way is the only way of late."

"Well, he could be right. Maybe being hospitalized would be the best thing for your friend right now, especially if he just tried to OD."

"He didn't."

"How do you know that? Taking three quarters of a bottle of Valium isn't rational behavior, Mr. Risner. Maybe James needs more help right now than you can give him."

"So now you're taking John's side?" Martin stands near the massive Sub-Zero PRO stainless fridge and glares at her across the large modern kitchen.

"I'm not taking anyone's side. Look, your friend's in trouble, much more than I caused him. I just want to help."

"Why? Why is that?" Martin moves toward her slowly. "Is this a guilt thing? A fantasy thing? Disney mess with your mind, Cinderella?" He stops three feet from her. "He may look the part, but James is not the Prince Charming type. Trust me."

Kate can hardly breathe, though it probably wouldn't feel so choking if he wasn't right about her. Maybe that's why she wants to stay, why it's so important to make sure James is OK. Perhaps if she rescues this knight, he'll fall for her in turn. Or maybe losing her uncle is driving her desire to save him. Or maybe she's still there because she has to be sure he'll be fine, since she caused their car accident, and will burn in Hell for eternity if he dies. She shivers at the notion and would have crossed herself right then, except for Martin Risner. She looks away.

"I'm sorry. I'm feeling very anxious. And when I get anxious I get snippy." Martin sits in one of the six maple Windsor chairs around the elegant River table. The epoxy 'river,' set between two thick burl slabs, reflects deep turquoise with moonlight now coming through the glass enclosed nook. "I've been snippy a lot lately. Gonna have to cut that shit out," he muses.

She smiles but doesn't look at him. She stares down at the perfectly fitted strips of oak and marvels at how spotless the floor is—no dings, gouges or stains. The pink and white checkered linoleum tiles in her apartment are a mess.

"John's not usually this...edgy, either." Martin says softly. "Guess it threw him, seeing James like this. He's a good doctor, but suicide kind of freaks him out. A year ago his sister's teenage son killed himself. Jumped off the Golden Gate bridge." He seems lost to the memory and Kate isn't sure he's actually talking to her. "Did you know there are like, forty suicides a year off that bridge?"

She feels a sudden surge of compassion for John. He knows what it feels like to lose someone through suicide. Kate sits in the chair next to Martin's, but still doesn't look at him. "After my uncle killed himself, my mom kind of melted down. It was her baby brother, and I think she felt responsible. She couldn't forgive herself, so she turned to God. She became a fervent Christian— 'Praise the Lord' was every other sentence. She even pulled me out of public school and stuck me in private Catholic school, with the nuns, the whole nine yards." She feels Martin watching her and finally looks at him. "Sometimes the worst part when someone kills themselves is the ripple effect. You never know how it's going to touch you."

"I'm sorry about your uncle. But the outcome may have been the same no matter what was done for him. We all have to deal with what life throws at us. James does too, just like the rest of us. Whatever happened to him, he's going to have to find a way to live with it. Or not. But ultimately it's his choice."

Kate flushes with anger. "There are no choices when you're dead, Mr. Risner."

"Martin, *please.*"

She pictures her uncle huddled on the gold shag carpet, leaning up against her mother's bed, tears streaking down his stubbled cheeks. Her mom was giving him the 'grow up' lecture. It was the morning of Kate's sixth birthday. Uncle Calvin had his knees up, his arms over his head like he was trying to hold in his brain. "I think John is right, Martin. Suicide is insane. And insanity doesn't make rational choices. I think what my uncle did, and James did, *is* crazy. Life is a gift. It is selfish and careless to throw it away. That's why it's a sin." She pauses, looks down. "Killing yourself is never a *reasonable* choice. And sometimes people need help making better choices."

Martin sighs and shakes his head. "God, you sound like John. That's probably why I like you." He smiles at her.

She smiles back, grateful to be accepted, even welcome, especially after what she'd done. She likes him, too. It starts to feel safe, almost familiar sitting next to Martin. As an interior designer for Kendall Wilkinson, Kate is used to gay men. Even prefers their company. Usually bright, creative, often intuitive and nurturing, like women, but with a directed, efficient male perspective. And hanging out with her colleagues, there's no worries of getting hit on.

"What is the defining line of crazy?" Martin asks, posing the philosophical question. "And how often do any one of us cross that line?" He raises one eyebrow at her. "Scratch the surface and we are all fatally flawed. We just run around pretending were not."

Kate studies him, wondering what Martin's fatal flaws are. Clearly successful, living in his gorgeous estate vineyard, aptly named 'Paradise,' happily ensconced with his doctor/partner that he's obviously in love with. What could Martin Risner know about living an ordinary life. "I suck at pretending. It's probably why I'm still single." It just slips out. She blushes.

Martin cocks his head, seemingly mystified. "Honey, any man who is fool enough not to recognize your beauty and compassion, should not be graced with your time and attention."

Tell that to Kyle, she thinks of her latest ex, but her smile broadens with Martin's kindness. She looks outside to hide her blush. Beyond the floor to ceiling French glass, clouds shadow the earlier moonlight. The deep blue and ultraviolet landscape dims to blackness. The windows reflect the huge, virtually pro kitchen now. She marvels at the Decor range, the Viking double oven. White marble throughout. Really tastefully done, and Kate wonders if either Martin or John designed it. Rain begins again, sheets the windows, the noise striking like a melody. She's sure she can hear bass...and piano, as if the drops are keystrokes of music notes.

"James..." Martin says.

She looks at him. He has this broad smile on his face, like a kid discovering candy. He holds up his index finger, as if to stop any questions, inviting Kate to listen too. It takes her a moment to discern the now heavy rain from the eerie piano melody coming from somewhere in the house.

"He's in the music room."

They both sit listening for a moment, the music moving up and down the scales virtually in time with the drops striking the panes. Tune is haunting, cascading flats and majors, like a storm on a churning sea, and masterfully played.

Music stops. Martin gets up. "Come on."

Kate follows him through the large family room off the kitchen. Windows extend floor to ceiling between thick squared beams of redwood every yard or so along the exterior wall. A center glass door slider opens to the back of the house, but it's impossible to see what's back there in the dark. A huge TV hangs on a stone wall perpendicular to an enormous fireplace. Westminster sectional sofa in slate gray leather is set in a u-shape and dominates the Mission and Deco pieces in the room.

Music starts again, sounds crisper, louder—the same haunting melody.

They pass through a cozy study with a large bay window. A wide bench extends the length of the exterior wall, two feet off the ground at the base of the window, supported by cabinetry. A great place to huddle for reading. Bookshelves line the three interior walls. Books are tightly packed, and many others are stuffed haphazardly on top of the compact rows.

Music stops again.

"Shit," she distinctly hears James say.

Music starts again as they enter a stylish Grecian bathroom. A huge sunken tub takes up most of the exterior wall. Two of the walk-in shower walls are made entirely of glass bricks. Kate practically runs into Martin when he stops abruptly at the bathroom threshold that adjoins to the music room beyond.

-

-

Chapter Eight

-

She sees James over Martin's shoulder. He sits on the bench at a huge, black grand piano with his eyes closed. His shirt still hangs open but the sleeves are buttoned now. His fingers move fluidly, like spiders dancing on the keys, note for note, then he mixes in descending chords holding a perfect tempo. He stops abruptly, opens his eyes, shakes his head and starts massaging one hand with the other. Then he notices Martin and Kate in the bathroom doorway.

James stands, knocking the piano bench back, and the sound of it moving over the wood floor is all that breaks the tense silence. He moves to the side of the piano, running his hand along the black resin surface, glaring wide-eyed at Kate. *What the fuck*. What are you still doing here, Kate? I thought you left."

She flushes, and looks away so they won't see her blush.

"I invited her to stay at Paradise as long as she likes, James." Martin says with resolve as he comes into the music room. "Chill on Kate, will ya," he adds, then looks back at her and winks.

Kate sticks close to Martin, following him into the room. It looks like a recording studio with the grand piano, two electronic keyboards on heavy stands, multiple guitars, amps, and speakers lying about.

"She needs to leave, Martin. Like an hour ago...or has it been longer. I passed out a while." And James seems to space a minute, like he's lost in time.

Kate stands on to the massive, intricately patterned, light blue and white Persian area rug that covers all but a few inches of the dark oak floor. She stares boldly at James a few yards from her. "I'm still here because I'm trying to do the right thing. I screwed up, and I'm sorry. Deeply and forever sorry. But now I have a debt to pay, and I need to make sure you're okay, or at least taken care of," she pledges, and it actually feels empowering.

"And so you have." James sighs, leans against the piano, puts one hand flat on the black top, his long fingers spread like a spider's legs on a black mirror. "Look, I'm sorry to offend." With his free hand, he runs his long fingers through his hair again, clearly a habitual response to irritation. "It's just...I'm really not the best person to be around. I probably never was, but right now is particularly bad." His hair falls in soft waves around his sculpted face and hangs in his eyes, his dark lashes creating a tiger-like frame around a thin ring of vibrant green irises.

She stares back at him, but feels naked under his scrutiny, suddenly exposed in her thin camisole. Her sweater is in the bathroom where she left it when she'd heard James screaming from his nightmare.

"We're square, Kate. You're off the hook. Get back to your life," James says softly. "And once you get your car fixed, and get back to your routine, this will all become distant, an ethereal dream. Like it never happened."

She folds in shame. "Maybe for you, but not me." Kate looks down at the complex geometric pattern boarding the large rug. "And we're not square. I wrecked your very expensive sports car, even if your divorced friend didn't want it anymore. You're standing there holding your smashed ribs because of *me*." Say goodbye and she'll be back to no life, going home to no one missing her. She'd been texting her dog's kennel when she crashed into James. "I'll take to you Tiburon. I owe you that much. I live in San Francisco, the Marina District, just me and my pound hound, Ed, and—"

"Thanks, but don't worry about me. I'm gonna be fine. Really." James flashes her a soft smile.

"Nothing catastrophic happened in the accident to either of us. A few scrapes and bruises, and I'd say we both got lucky. You've done all you can for me, bringing me here. But there's really no need for you to stay." He watches her, no, *studies* her, then flashes a quick, knowing grin, seemingly to himself. "There are no white knights here, Kate. You don't need one. Go home, and rescue yourself from the ideology that you need saving."

"*Whoa.* Back off, buddy," Martin snaps. He looks at Kate. "James gets a bit too close to the bone when he bothers to grace us with his insights."

Kate blushes, shamed again, then looks back at James. "Seems like you're more the one who needs saving. Your friend, Dr. John, doesn't think you're fine, which isn't a stretch with what you did to yourself." She flushes with anger—at his razor sharp perception, at herself for opening her mouth, now unable to shut it with his eyes narrowed on her. "He called a psychiatrist to get you into some kind of hospital, but Martin stopped him." As the words leave her mouth, she knows she should not have spoken them.

"John wants to get me locked up?" James glares at Martin.

"I wouldn't put it that way, James," Martin begins. He scowls at Kate, then looks back at James. "He's scared for you. We all are."

"*Damn* him." James whispers to himself then fixes his gaze back on Martin. "Did he tell anyone about me? Or that I'm here?"

Martin shakes his head. "No. He called a colleague to discuss your case. That's it. Never mentioned your name."

Kate attempts to repair her breach. "I'm absolutely sure John just wants to help you—"

James looks at her, his face drained of color. He takes his hand from the piano, sucks in a sharp breath and holds his ribs, never taking his eyes from hers. "I'd like to reconsider your offer. A ride to Tiburon would be great. If the offer still stands, I'd like to go now." He slowly begins buttoning his shirt.

"Don't be an asshole, James," Martin snipes. "You leave now and it could kill you, puncture your lung with a fractured rib, or give yourself a brain hemorrhage if you move your head too fast."

"Don't be so melodramatic, Martin," James says as he continues attempting to button his shirt. "I'll be fine, nothing that a bit of time and rest won't heal." He's having trouble lining up the buttons on one side with the holes on the other. Kate moves in front of him, hesitates only a second before reaching up and buttoning his shirt.

"You can not leave here now, James," Martin is practically pleading. "John will fucking kill me if I let you go. At lease wait for him to check you out. I'll just run down the hall and get him," and Martin heads towards the music room doorway.

Kate finishes buttoning James shirt. He gives her a grateful smile. "Thank you."

"You think it's a good idea for you to leave now? Are you sure you're OK to travel?" Kate asks, checking his response for even a flicker of doubt.

"You bet. Like I said, scrapes and bruises." James grins. "You ready to go?"

'Yes' is on her lips.

"No!" Martin practically yells as he comes back in the music room. John is behind him, hovering breathless in the doorway, holding her black sweater. "I told you. He's leaving!" Martin is getting pissy, but he feels scared and can't help it. "You said you were going to stay on him. Where the hell were you?"

John ignores him, glares at James instead. "I woke up. You weren't in bed…and I thought…"

"That I slit my wrists in your bathtub or something." James offers teasingly. "Don't worry, John. I wouldn't mess up your stone floors."

"Just our marble sink."

"*John*," Martin shakes his head, ashamed.

James gives Kate a quick, uneasy glance, then John a wary smile. "Sorry about that. Thought I was immune to the stuff after what they fed me. Gross miscalculation."

"Is that all it was, James?"

The two men stay fixed on each other. "A momentary lapse of reason," James practically whispers.

John stops a few feet from Kate and hands her her sweater. He's stands between James and the doorway, leaving a few yards between them. She feels the men mentally circling, and their tension scares her.

"Thank you," she says gently to John, then slips her sweater on and pulls her hair out from under it. She looks at Martin. His brown, puppy dog eyes are wide and fixed on John and James.

"I'm leaving, John." James speaks softly.

"I don't advise it. You need to rest, be flat on your back—"

"I'm leaving. Kate has generously offered me a ride." James glances at her.

She looks at John. He does not acknowledge her.

"You don't need his permission." James glowers, then looks back at John. "You don't understand the risks. Obstruction of justice, aiding and abetting—they carry time if someone wanted to push it."

"You are my patient, James. No matter what you've done, I am under oath to administer care. Martin is a theater queen with HIV. No one wants him in prison." John glances at Martin. Martin purses his lips in an air kiss at John. Not exactly a 'fuck you, honey,' more humor, like a shared joke, but Kate can tell there's an edge to his gesture.

John glances at Kate, then looks back at James. "At least let me check you over before you go."

James still clutches his ribs, and is standing somewhat hunched. "Not gonna happen. But thanks, man. You've helped me all you can. And I appreciate it. Really." He flashes John a quick, adorable, single-dimpled smile, then looks at Martin. "Hey Martin, good to see you're good. Sorry 'bout this." James half-laughs. "And thanks for the assist."

"Maybe you ought to let us assist a bit longer? You really look like hell, James." Martin says. It doesn't sound like he's joking but James laughs anyway.

"Tell me I'm not making a mistake letting you walk out of here." John moves in front of James as he speaks, blocking his path. They're two feet apart, eye to eye.

James raises an eyebrow. "Try and stop me and I'll kick your ass, John." His smile broadens to a Cheshire grin, but like with Martin and John's exchange, Kate catches a very sharp edge. "You've got it wrong about earlier. The pills. Just flat out stupidity. I wasn't aiming to off myself here. If I was, I'd never have attempted it with half a bottle of 10 milligram Valiums. I'm not crazy."

John narrows his eyes on James forearm, now covered by his dark flannel shirtsleeves."I don't know if you are now, but you clearly were, and not too long ago." He narrows his eyes on James. "You have one life, James. One. Whatever it is, *this is it*. Deal with it. Make it what you want. Don't throw it away."

James shakes his head with a soft smile. "You guys rehearse this stuff? Just had the same 'Come to Jesus' speech from Martin. You two are a tour de force." His smile fades. "Slicing my wrists was the sanest thing I did in my entire incarceration. I was justified, not crazy." He stays with John another moment then he looks at Kate. "Ready?"

She hesitates before nodding. She looks at John, then Martin. "I really want to thank you for your kindness. Your home is beautiful. It's been a pleasure meeting you both—"

"Come here, you." Martin takes her by the hand and pulls her in. "Thank you for looking out for our friend." Their bodies connect. She feels Martin's appreciation with his hug, and returns it. He keeps his eyes on hers when they separate. "You are every bit as beautiful as," he points to James, "he is. You've just got to believe it, girl."

"Thank you." Kate wants to kiss him right then, but she doesn't.

James and John stare at each other silently. After a moment, John moves aside to let them pass. "I'm letting you go because I think it'll do you more harm than good to force you to stay. But watch yourself, James. Insanity feeds on justifications."

James smiles and nods slowly, then extends his hand to John. John hesitates, then grasps James' hand, shakes it once and releases him. James looks at Martin. "Catch ya on the flip side, Martin," and he flashes his single dimpled smile.

"Right back at ya, James." Martin smiles, and they have a visceral exchange to which Kate is not privy, but wishes she was. She's so tired of being on the outside looking in. They seem to share a palpable affection as Martin takes James' extended hand in both of his, and they shake hands heartily, till James grimaces in pain and pulls back.

"Take good care of each other." James says to Martin, then glances at John, then Kate. "Let's go," and he grips her arm lightly and leads her to the doorway. He stops before leaving, turns and looks at John. "If you're looking for a test of my sanity, well, I can see what's going on between you and Martin. And I'm lucid enough to know if you let what you two have established slip away it would be madness." He gives John a quasi-grin, smiles at Martin, then turns away, takes Kate's hand and leads her out of the music room.

"If you need me, I'm at Paradise Pediatrics in Placer County. My service can reach me twenty-four seven." John calls after them.

Martin follows them down the hallway. "Any chance you'll fill me in on where you're off to, so I can track you down if need be."

"Nope. You suck at lying, Martin. I don't want to put you in a position of having to." James stops in the guestroom, retrieves his suede boots and pulls them on.

"Then what am I supposed to tell anyone who comes looking?" Martin asks.

"The truth. I showed up injured from a car accident. John patched me up and I left. Keep Kate out of it. You can do that, Martin. Omission isn't a flat out lie."

"Well, now, that depends on the circumstances, doesn't it. But your anonymity is safe with me and John, dear Kate. Not to worry," Martin says, as they make their way past the floor to ceiling etched glass wall of Mucha's Four Seasons women, separating the living room from the foyer. "Keep in touch, James. If we don't hear from you in six months should I gather a posse and come looking?"

They cross into the foyer and James lets go of her hand and turns back to face Martin in what looks like awe. "If you don't hear from me in six months there'll be no reason to come looking." He stares, fixed on Martin. "Appreciate the offer though. You are forever humbling, Martin." And he bows slightly, in the Asian fashion, his hand to his ribs.

"About time you noticed, James." Martin flashes a whimsical grin but it fades quickly. "Just wish John did."

"He does," James assures him.

Kate sees John standing by the etched wall. James sees him, too, but Martin doesn't.

"Pay attention, Martin. He's right behind you, where he's always been." James looks at John.

Martin swings around and looks at John. Kate feels them connect, just a hint of a smile from both men simultaneously, and she's suddenly consumed with envy of their obvious bond.

"Take it easy, James," John says cautiously.

James nods, then laces his fingers in Kate's again, clasping her hand. He leads her out the front door, leaving Martin standing in the threshold.

-

-

Chapter Nine

-

Cold strikes her in the face and chills her nose and ears. Air is dense, thick with wet foliage and moist soil. The silhouetted pine trees that line the front courtyard, and the rolling hills covered in grapevines beyond are saturated in blue-violets from the bright, three-quarter moon.

James pulls her gently by the hand and starts down the steps. Kate sees her car parked beyond the fountain, in one of the five parking spaces meant for the clinic across from the house. They crunch across the glittering, rain glazed gravel and stop next to her car. James lets go of her hand to examine the damage. The left fender is crumpled from the accident, but doesn't touch the wheel. Left headlight is fractured too, but that's about all that happened to her SUV from the collision that destroyed his Porsche.

"Well, it looks driveable." James straightens, winces, looks at her. "I'd like to drive. I feel safer driving." He gives her a teasing grin.

She blushes. She can't exactly fault him for not trusting her driving. "Sure, I guess." A gust of wind whips her hair across her face, as Kate pulls her keys from her jeans pocket. "Electronic starter. I'll keep my keys." She pulls her hair back. "I did get you here, though," Kate feels a need to add.

"So you did. Thank you." James takes the keys. "It'll just be easier if I drive. I know where I need to go from here." He grasps her hand again and leads her around the car to the passenger side, possibly to accelerate her pace. He opens the door and ushers her in, like they're on a date or something, then shuts her door and goes around the back of the Blazer to the driver's side and gets behind the wheel.

His body seems to melt into the seat. James rests his head back and closes his eyes. His body seems relaxed, but his breathing is too quick, too shallow, like he's gasping for air.

"You okay?"

"Yeah." He takes a heavy breath, like he's trying to slow his breathing. "Give me a minute."

Kate hesitates, suddenly realizing the gravity of giving James a convenient way to leave Paradise. "You sure you can drive?"

"Yeah." He takes another couple of breaths, his breathing slowing each time, then opens his eyes, and straighten behind the wheel. He seems OK, but then he reaches out for the open car door and sucks in a muffled gasp. His jaw tightens as he pulls the door shuts, then he glances at Kate for just a second before turning his attention to driving. James presses the ignition button, starts the engine, backs up into the rotary driveway, and then pulls the SUV around the fountain. He doesn't see, or acknowledge Martin and John in the doorway of their house as he passes them and continues down the sloping gravel drive, but Kate waves, for both of them. James' long lashes mingling with locks of his hair. He blinks several times in a row as if to clear his vision, or keep his eyes open.

"Maybe it's not the best idea to leave your friends right now."

Road crunches under the tires as they move down the hill. The valley shimmers in pinpoints of silver—rain droplets clinging to endless rows of grapevines reflect the moonlight. James turns left off the gravel drive to Paradise, and on to Gold Hill Road.

"I'm trying to keep everyone safe, and free, including me." James combs his hair back with his elegant fingers. "Regardless of the accident, Martin is a known colleague of mine. If anyone's looking for me, they'll look here eventually. Maybe the CHP will connect the dots, and place me at the scene with the Porsche, but they won't do it in a day, if at all. As far as we know, no one knows you were involved in the accident. And you're nobody to me."

Boy, he's right about that. She's nobody to James. Worse, she's nobody to anybody. Almost a year together, and Kyle breaks up with her last November, calling her out for wanting too much from him, for *being* too much for him. It was only a week after her mom passed.

James stops at the crossroad of Hwy 49. She feels him look at her, can see him watching her in her peripheral vision. She stares out the windshield at trucks whizzing by.

"I'll take off as soon as we get to Sacramento. Old Town is only about forty minutes from here. I'll find my way from there."

"I told you I'd take you to Tiburon. I want to." Her voice sounds childlike to her.

He shakes his head. "It'll be safer if we separate."

"Why? I'm no one to you, right? And no one is looking for me." Kate wonders if she sounds as small as she feels, throwing his words back at him.

"I didn't mean safer for you." James glances at her again, then turns right onto the slick blacktop heading west. "I'm obliged to take care of you when you're with me. You're a liability, which is why we need to separate."

Ouch. Feels like he's slapped her. She stares ahead to hide her shame. She does not speak, but the silence looms large between them, for her at least. She searches for something to say to fill the void but can think of nothing before James pushes the audio player button on her dashboard monitor. Four Bose speakers fill the car with the fast picking of steel string guitar, and quickly becomes the sound track for the scene. She'd gotten the Premium package on her SUV for the sound system alone. They move through the blackness on the practically empty, narrow highway, every few minutes momentarily blinded by blazing bright headlights on the other side of the road.

She looks at James. His cheeks are flushed, his skin tone ashen in the dim light; his full lips deep red. Trace stubble hardens his baby face. He looks unscathed, normal—drop dead gorgeous kind of normal. His left palm is on the top of the wheel, his long fingers extending past it, and they're moving with the music. Kate is certain he's not consciously aware he's subtly, but clearly, picking air guitar in perfect time to the complex guitar piece. Of course, it's obvious he's a player, but she'd only made the connection when she saw him at the piano at Paradise. She lets the piece end before speaking.

"That was a beautiful piece you played on the piano earlier."

"Ravel's, *Gaspard de la Nuit.* But I massacred it."

"I wouldn't know. So, you play piano, and the guitar, too." It's more statement than question since she knows the answer. His fingers are still contorted in the closing pick.

James glances at her, his eyes narrow, like he's suspicious of her question. "I used to." He drops his hand from the top of the wheel and grips the bottom. "Don't know that I can anymore." A quick, angry laugh with a shake of his head. "You've seen my wrists. The restraints they had on me cut the circulation to my hands. I may have lost the dexterity. I don't know." He shrugs. His expression is somber. His eyes are glassy as he squints at oncoming headlights, and only then does Kate notice his long lashes sticking together from tears. He blinks and they stream down his face. James flashes her a quick glance, half-laughs, but not like it's funny, and wipes his eyes on his shirtsleeve. "I suppose it doesn't matter. Even if I could get back to where I was, I'm not so sure I ever want to go back there."

"Why? Music is very powerful. It touches a lot of people."

"Maybe my music did, but I'm finally getting that I probably didn't." His jaw hardens. He stares straight ahead.

"Are you famous? I mean, should I know you, know your music?"

"You may have heard things I've written. But I'm in the background, in the studio mostly."

"What other instruments do you play?"

He flashes a smile. "Most all of them."

"That's impressive." Kate is awed by people with passion, as she's yet to find her own.

"Not really. Most anyone can get good at anything with practice. And I've been playing all my life. My stepfather taught me to play the guitar when I was five." He speaks as if telling a tale. "He was a violinist with the Boston Pops. My mom was a piano teacher at Berklee School of Music. She could pick the harmony out of a vacuum." He seems to drift, like he's hearing her sing. "She had the most amazing ear, and perfect pitch. I mean *perfect*."

"Are your parents still in Boston?"

"No. They're dead." And he's back in the car with Kate.

She's astounded by his admission, and for the first time feels a real connection to James. "Mine, too." She practically whispers. "My dad died of a heart attack about a year ago. My mom, of cancer in late November, almost three months now." She shuts her mouth, holds her breath and swallows back the lump in her throat.

"I lost my parents when I was thirteen, in a plane crash on their way home from a benefit concert in Haiti. So much for Karma." He stares out the windshield. "Everyone said it would hurt less with time. But the longing is often still intolerable."

Kate crumbles. He's right, of course. She still thinks of calling her mom almost every day, the impulse always followed by that horribly empty realization no one's there to answer the phone. Tears spill down her face, and she can't stop them. She stares out the windshield.

James stops at the crossroad of Hwy 50 and looks at her. "No shame in grief, Kate." He reaches out to her and wipes her tears away with his huge thumb, strokes her cheeks gently, first one, then the other, his glassy eyes filled with compassion focused on her. "The real price of love is losing it. I get it. Longing is a bitch of a mistress."

She wants him to pull her face to his and kiss her. Tenderly. Passionately. Save her from longing and loneliness.

Truck whizzes by, startling him. Mist and droplets sparkle in the headlights as he brings his hand back to the wheel, focuses forward, guns the engine and enters the crowded, fast-moving highway.

"I'm sorry for your loss, Kate," he says gently, his accent momentarily refined.

"I'm sorry for yours, too, James."

He slowly nods. "Fucking sucks, being orphaned."

Kate manages a smile through her tears. Again, she's surprised by his acute perceptions.

They listen to several tunes of smooth acoustic rhythms. James keeps his fingers still. The tune changes to a wailing electric guitar, fronting a fast, pounding beat of electronic drums, the unnatural vibration adding to her angst that grows with each passing mile. Kate feels herself falling into the rabbit hole, blackness looming. Beyond Sacramento is San Francisco—home—alone. Again. Still. Back to the seemingly endless search for her prince.

"We should be in the city in fifteen minutes. It's where I take off, and you get back to your life." He doesn't look at her.

She imagines asking him to stay with her until he's well. She'd care for him. They'd bond, and like in the movies, he'd leave to reconcile his past then come back to her. She considers offering to take him to Tiburon again, give her the opportunity to network with more of his friends, keep track of him, but doesn't. "Okay," comes out of her mouth. "So, you're off to Tiburon, then?"

He nods.

Kate looks outside. Housing developments line the highway on both sides now. The tall glass buildings of Sacramento sparkle with moonlight against the black backdrop of night. Brandon Boyd sings the old tune, *Drive,* against the wet road din. "What's in Tiburon?"

James stays focused on driving, as if she's not spoken. Kate thinks he won't answer, but then he says, "Money. Enough to get me set up some place safe. If I've got any left."

"And if you don't have any left?" *I can save you...*

"Then I'll be living a whole other kind of lifestyle than I hoped. Probably be a lot colder, at least in the beginning." He flashes a quick grin. "Don't worry about me, Kate. I'll be fine. Money or not, I can be very resourceful."

"I don't doubt that. For the asking, you could probably get most anything you want."

"Clearly not. Or I'd have my life back."

She stares at him. "You mean the one you tried to throw away?"

James glances at her with a furrowed brow.

Kate's broken the glass wall and steps through. "Why did you try to kill yourself?" She has to know. She just can't leave it.

"I don't want to talk about it."

"Did you really want to die?"

"Yes." He stares at the road.

"Do you still?"

"I don't know. Sometimes." He glances at her again then looks forward. "It doesn't matter. I told you, I don't want to discuss it."

"Why? I've thought about it in dark moments. I'm sure lots of people have. Suicide isn't exclusive to artists and intellects, ya know."

"My decision to slit my wrists wasn't motivated from melancholy. I was trapped in hell and it was the only way I could think of to get out."

"Pretty radical solution."

"A permanent one, to be sure, but at the time it seemed warranted."

"Don't you care that it's a mortal sin to take your own life?"

He smiles. "No."

"Well, then don't you care that you'd be hurting people that love you?"

James stares out at the highway. His jaw tightens, his expression darkens, then veils, but Kate feels the weight of his sadness. She watches him for a second then has to look away. She's all too familiar with that level of alone. Just hard to believe someone like James knows it, too.

Tall glass buildings of downtown twinkle and loom in the distance. James stays in the left lane and keeps pace with traffic. They pass a blue Acura on the right, and Kate looks at the white, middle-aged male driver on his cell phone. He never glances her way. The world is so insular now. How was she to find a partner with all of us so immersed in our tight little worlds.

She looks at James. His long lashes look even longer with wetness.

He'll be gone in five minutes—the Prince Charming that never was. His beauty belies his manic behavior earlier, his battered body under his dark fleece shirt. "Promise me you're not going to kill yourself. Ever." She stares at him, searching, wondering if her voice sounds as ambivalent as she feels. "If you kill yourself, I could burn in hell for handing you the opportunity."

He laughs, but grimaces, like it hurt. "You're concern is touching, really." His smile fades quickly. He does not address her request. He looks straight ahead and Kate is sure James is consciously avoiding looking at her.

"God, your friend John was *right*. You're still suicidal." Anger, disgust, guilt jockey for lead emotion. Suddenly the car feels stifling. She can't catch her breath. "I'm such a sucker for letting you talk me into this."

"You're not." He glances at her quickly then back at the highway. "You can't save me, Kate. And I can't save you. We're going to have to do that for ourselves." He glances at her again, sighs, like he gets his words cut. "Look, a lot of people I meet along the way get caught up in my façade. But there's nothing behind it. Not anymore. There probably never was, I just didn't notice. Too busy jacking off with my muse."

"I don't think achieving excellence is nothing. And I'm pretty sure tuning out is a typical guy thing."

James laughs. "It may be. But I've been told that's a lousy excuse."

"What was her name?" Kate asks, even though most of her doesn't want to know.

He doesn't answer, and again she's wondering if he will. "Julia. But it never really was, and now it never will be. And I don't want to talk about this."

"Well, what about Julia?"

James shoots her a piercing glare. "What about her?"

"Don't you care you'd be hurting her if you killed yourself?"

"Either way, I'm hurting her. So I'm alive. We can't be together. I'm wanted for drug trafficking, escaping lawful custody. Murder." He does not look at her. "To her, I'm dead either way."

Kate watches at him. He said 'murder,' that he's wanted for *murder*. And for the first time she feels afraid of him. James could be crazy—one of those guys who's calm most of the time, then goes psychopath every now and again. "You told John you left a mental institution in Scotland 'without permission.' Were you there for killing someone?"

He jaw tightens again. "I won't discuss this. I'm sorry I mentioned it." Quick, nervous laugh. "I wasn't putting you off when I told you I wasn't the best person to be around right now." He glances at her again and sort of shrugs, wipes his nose with his shirtsleeve and runs his fingers through his hair again, but it falls back in his eyes.

All fear of him dissolves. Kate can not fathom him as evil, or even crazy. He'd just admitted to 'trafficking.' A drug dealer seems plausible, though not probable as a career musician. She imagined drug dealers to be hardened people. Underneath his manic behavior, James seems fundamentally a gentle man. Kate feels it to her core. "I'm not scared of you." She blushes. Aloud it sounds taunting, defensive.

James laughs, and winces. "I'm not scared of you either, which is a first for me with a stranger in quite a while."

"I didn't just tell you I murdered someone."

"I didn't say I murdered anyone. I said I was wanted for murder." He glances at her for an instant before he catches sight of a road sign. James changes lanes abruptly and turns off Hwy. 50 on to Hwy. 5 heading north. He takes the first exit, then drives back under the freeway, then takes the next right into Old Town Sacramento.

It's like stepping back two hundred years as they cross the train tracks into the old western town. Streets are lined with wide wood boardwalks, covered by decorative balconies supported by slender wood columns every few feet.

"Damn if I remember where the hell it is..." James pushes the stereo off hastily.

"What is?"

He doesn't answer. She's not sure he heard her, his attention focused on navigating the narrow streets.

-

-

Chapter Ten

-

Buildings are all gold rush era, with lavish Victorian facades, crammed right up against each other, each with their own intricate designs. All the shops are closed for the night, the tourist town virtually deserted. Though the roads are paved it feels as if they're not. James slows the Blazer almost to a crawl to get around several horse drawn carriages meant for tourists along the side of the street.

He turns off the main drag, back under the freeway into modern downtown Sacramento, then into the large parking lot of an Amtrak train station. He parks near the entrance and turns off the headlights but leaves the car running, then looks at Kate.

"You okay?"

"You're asking *me?*

"You okay to drive?"

"Yes." No. "Don't go." She hears herself whisper. "I'll take you to Tiberon—"

He shakes his head, looks around at the almost empty lot, then back at her. Sighs. "Thank, you, Kate."

"Right. I wrecked your car, likely broke your ribs, cracked your skull, and that's just what John could *see*. And you're *thanking* me?"

He smiles. "Thanks for helping me out tonight, *after* the accident. For taking me to Martin and John's. Giving me a lift here. We're square. You did all you can. Thank you." James stays fixed on her. "You take good care, Katie McConnell." He takes her hand and kisses her palm, his warm, thick lips tingling, spreading warmth up her arm, through her chest, belly, right down to her crotch. He looks at her a moment longer, gives her a soft smile, then looks back out at the lot. He does not meet her eyes again as he gets out of the SUV, nor glance at her as he moves to the front of the Blazer holding his side, then stops and puts both hands on the hood for support.

Kate gets out and joins him at front of her car. "I'm an idiot for listening to you. You're *not* okay."

"I'm just a bit off balance. Give me a minute." A moment passes and he straightens, then runs his hand through his hair as he surveys the parking lot again.

"James, get back in the car. We can go back to your Martin and John's. You can come home with me, just until you're well..." She sees the cop car as it crosses the intersection bordering the lot.

James sees it too. He slides his arm around her shoulder and pulls her into him, hugs her, holds her tightly, and for a second she feels him with her. She buries her head in his chest, breathes in his musty, masculine scent.

He speaks softly into her ear, "Godspeed, Kate." Then he gathers her face in his huge hands then kisses her, on the forehead. He lets his hands slide from her face, holds her captive with his eyes another second, then glances at the cop approaching the parking lot and walks away, towards the train station, and a moment later disappears inside the building.

And James is gone.

Cop enters the lot and cruises slowly toward the front of the station. Buzz cut, stern expression, he eyes Kate suspiciously as he approaches. She's done nothing wrong, but he still intimidates her. She glances at the station, then goes around her car, gets behind the wheel and waits for the cop to leave the lot before she drives away, onto I-80, toward home.

"Kiss him goodbye, Katie." She speaks aloud to no one. Then loneliness sucks her in. Longing for her mom, her dad, even Kyle, or Drew before him, feels physically painful, almost *intolerable*, as James said. Tears stream down her cheeks. She hastily wipes them with her sweater sleeve. She's become so isolated, with her friends from college and high school getting married, moving on. She rarely hangs out with her newly wed assistant, Zina, anymore. They used to go bar hopping after work with their boss, Ed, (who renamed himself Fred, ah la Freddy Mercury) in the Castro. Great for eye candy, but not much else. It's easier to stay home in her warm apartment, read a novel at night, and get swept up into more exciting lives than living her own. It's easy to fall for the hero, always the archetype of a knight with a bit of bad boy thrown in, saving the heroine from longing, and loneliness.

The rain starts again. Fat drops hit her windshield. She turns on the wipers. Their smooth rhythm, continually clearing the dots of water obscuring her vision, feels rather hypnotic. She flashes on James as she's passing Davis, just west of Sacramento. *'There are no white knights, Kate. You don't need one.'* She smiles with his memory. He's right, of course. No one, nothing can save her—but her.

'Go home, and rescue yourself from the ideology that you need

saving.' Again, Kate sees James in her head, his irritated pout, and can't help the chuckle of humility that escapes her. Two for two, James. For a felon, and a suicidal, likely drug addicted musician, he was surprisingly cognizant. She'll miss him, and forever forward compare other men to him. So much for forgetting about their encounter. *OK. Strike one, James,* Kate ruminates. The impact we have on others, by our deaths, but also our lives—our reverb effect extends well beyond our random, or even our most casual exchanges sometimes.

It's time to rescue herself from her self-imposed isolation. Instead of just going online, she'll get out and about from here on out. No more wasting weekends binge-watching garbage, or *reading* about romance. She'll get back into building furniture, hang out at the machine shop in the Mission, try and sell her own designs this time. She'll go to meetups, make some new friends with common interests, expand her circle. Have *fun*, and start living days to remember, like this night has been, only not by accident, but with purpose. She'll work at overcoming her pervasive fear of loving, that comes with being recently orphaned and dumped, since she now knows this is just a tired excuse to isolate. She must create the life she wants to live, as Martin said about James. This time around, she'll actively participate in creating her own version of 'happily ever after,' instead of living vicariously in antiquated fiction that she, or any woman requires a knight for a joyful, fulfilling life.

-

-

Chapter Eleven

-

STEPHEN

The doorbell rings. Steve opens his eyes, momentarily blinded by the sun rising over the East Bay hills through his bedroom's massive picture window. Angel Island comes into focus, then the sparking

San Francisco bay, and the city beyond as he gets up and pulls on his sweats from the floor where he'd left them last night. The doorbell rings again. He glances back at his sleeping beauty, and is grateful the bell has not disturbed her. It's disturbing him though. Who the hell is at his door at this hour? It's likely not a burglar since they're knocking. Probably the old lady from next door looking for her damn dog again. He plucks his t-shirt from the headboard where it landed last night after she pulled it off him and tossed it during sex.

Steve smiles with the memory, can practically taste her smell as he slips on his shirt and descends the carpeted stairs. The hardwood is painfully cold under his bare feet, but it's only a few steps to the throw rug that dominates most of the foyer floor to the front door. Even through the distorted peephole view, Steve recognizes him. It's hard to mistake him for someone else, looking like he does. *Great.* James is just about the last person he wants to see. But Steve always knew the man would come back to haunt him. He decodes the alarm behind the potted palm and opens the door.

"Hey Stephen."

"How are you doing, James?"

"Been better. Sorry about the hour."

He stands aside for James to come in. Stephen knows what he's come for. And the hour might just work to his advantage. It's possible James could be in and out before she wakes up, *and we were up late last night…*

"You know why I'm here?"

"I'm assuming it's not for the killer waves at Maverick's."

He smiles. He looks exhausted. His face is thinner, the wild-child look even more pronounced with his hair longer and hanging in his eyes. She'll see him. She'll want him, and want to save him. And

Steve will be screwed.

Send him away. Arrange it for later. Hide him in the office. "There's something you should know." *Damn me.*

James' eyes scan the entry, then up the stairs and connect at the top. Steve follows his line of sight to Julia, holding the balcony rail with both hands, wearing only his Stanford tee shirt over her lacy panties. She's ghost white.

Just great.

"*No*... This isn't happening." James whispers as he stares up at her, then looks at Steve.

"I was about to tell you she was here, James…"

James looks back at Julia. They're fixed on each other. Steve feels something tangible pass between them. His stomach tightens, like he's been sucker punched.

"I know what you came for." Julia says softly. "Get it and go, James, if that's what you need to do." She looks down at Steve. "It seems my holiday surprise was more than intended."

"Wait a minute, Julia. I had no idea James was coming here this morning."

"He didn't, Jules."

She looks back at James. "Whatever. Please don't let me break up your little tryst. I'm sure Steve will be very accommodating."

"Damn it, Julia. Don't get mad at Stephen. Be mad at me."

She glares down at him. "You lost the right to give me direction the day you left." She comes down the stairs, her hand barely touching the handrail as she descends. "You disappeared, for over a year. Got so wrapped up with your muse in London, or New York, or wherever the fuck you were, you didn't bother to acknowledge that you left me. Not one word, in thirteen months, James. How can you just show up like this?"

James watches her. "I'm sorry, Julia. I didn't know you'd be here."

"Why not? Did you expect me to wait forever? Besides, Stephen is one of the good guys. Isn't that what you use to tell me? And what are you sorry about? Leaving me? Losing me? That I'm here? With Steve?" She's trying to hurt him. Steve doesn't know if she is, but it cuts him that she still feels the need.

She stops directly in front of James, not two feet away and examines him. "You look like shit, if that's at all possible."

He looks down, shakes his head. "Julia, about the last thing I want to do is hurt you again. But I can't deal with the fallout between us right now. I need to talk with Stephen for a bit, then I'm gone. Okay? Like I was never here. If you can't handle that, then I'll go now." James fixes his eyes on hers and they are together.

Steve feels the wall go up around them and can only watch from the outside. And he hates himself right then for just standing there instead of trying to sever their bond.

"Don't go," Julia whispers. She turns and walks toward the kitchen, then turns back to face him. "Your timing just sucks, honey. I'm here maybe once a month. Most any other time and we would have never crossed paths. And you could have just stayed gone. And I could have kept pretending that you were dead." She glares at him, then at Steve, then leans against the swinging door opening it. "I'm going to make coffee." And she disappears into the kitchen.

"This is bad." James looks around the room as if he's trapped, runs his fingers through his hair. "Damn it!" He practically shouts it, then looks at Steve. "I'm sorry if I'm messing you up, Stephen. Say the word and I'll go. We can do this another time."

Steve believes he would leave, even though it's clear he's in dire straits and needs what he's come for. "I figured you'd be back eventually, James. Assuming you weren't dead." He manages a grin. "Julia and I got together a few months ago. You were gone, she was wrecked, and I was here."

He nods, acknowledging the words, but doesn't say anything.

"I've always been here, from the day you introduced us five years ago."

"I know."

"I was hoping when you did show up you'd no longer be between us. But obviously that's not the case."

"I'm sorry."

"Don't be. Fix it. I've been up against your ghost for the last year plus. Now that you're here, and she is too, maybe you can take a few minutes to fill her in on why you left, so she can move on."

He shakes his head. "Actually, I'd like to minimize her involvement as much as possible." James looks at the kitchen door. "This *sucks*," he whispers to himself, then looks back at Steve. "Look Stephen, I'm in trouble. A lot of it. And I don't want Julia involved. I'm sorry for bringing you into it. But I need money. Do I have it? Is that doable?"

"You've got it. And it's doable, James."

"How long will it take?"

"Depends on what you need. We can go downstairs to my office, talk about what to pull and put it in motion."

"Yeah. Okay. Can we do that now?"

Steve stares at him, bewildered. "*No*. You're going to have to deal with her, James. She'll be on me if you avoid her."

James smiles, glances at the kitchen door again. "This is a mistake, Stephen. She'll want the truth. And all that'll do is hurt her more."

"I don't think it's possible you could hurt her any more than you already have." Steve means to cut, but feels bad when he sees how deeply his words hurt. James looks like he's about to cry—his eyes fill and he looks away. "Come on. Let's get some coffee and maybe some closure." Steve moves toward the kitchen. James reluctantly follows.

Julia's on him the moment they come through the swinging door. "Are you going to tell me what is going on and where the hell you've been?"

James stands at the end of the butcher block island, wraps his spider-like fingers around the two inches of aged oak and holds it as if to keep standing. Either he doesn't hear her or he's ignoring her because he doesn't respond to her question.

"*Damn you* son of a bitch." Her eyes cloud. She goes back to filling the grinder with coffee beans. She blinks, and tears spill down her soft cheeks.

Steve feels his shoulders tighten, his ire rise. James could be such a heartless son of a bitch. "James has just informed me he's in some kind of trouble, major trouble, and needs money. *His* money." Steve ignores James' piercing glare. "He needs my help, Julia. It's my job. It's that simple."

"Don't patronize me, Stephen." She turns away, gets three mugs from the cupboard and sets them on the counter top. "You know I really hate it when you do that. I deserve better than that." She stands with her finger on the switch of the grinder glaring at him, and with a heavy sigh flips the switch. No one speaks over the noise.

Steve leans against the cold granite counter top near Julia and folds his arms across his chest. She stands next to him, not two feet away, but he feels the void between them. She's fixed on James. She crosses her bare legs, her slender, curvaceous body rigid beneath her casual display. Her short dark hair is tousled from sleep, framing her striking oval face.

She's shamed, and Steve doesn't blame her. Choosing to remain silent, James is damning her to her self-effacing ego. When he disappeared, she'd come to Steve, true to form. And they've just begun closing the distance, tearing down her walls and replacing them with foundation. He'd been enamored, even smitten from the day he'd met her. Brilliant, beautiful, passionate and accomplished, but until a few months ago, Julia had insisted on only friendship. That fantastic night on the deck of Liquid Asset finally set them on course together. And Steve was sure he had her this time, until now.

"You have fourteen million dollars." Steve speaks the moment the grinder stops. He knows it's the only way to break their connection. James looks at him. "Give or take a few hundred thousand. At least, you did the last time I checked, which was about a month ago."

A barely perceptible smile creeps across James' thick lips. "Can we cash it out right now?" James looks at Julia, as if asking for permission.

Again the intimacy of their exchange bothers Steve. "How do you want the money? Can't really transport a suitcase of cash anymore. You setting up accounts? How many? Where?"

"I'm going to have to be moving around quite a bit. At least at first." He grimaces, grips his ribs with his huge hand as he paces a few steps.

"What's wrong with you?" Julia sounds concerned for the first time. "Are you hurt?"

James fixes on her. "Yeah." He glances at Steve then stares at the floor. "No. I'm okay. I'm just tired. It's been rather hellish lately."

He looks at Steve. "Can you set me up an account in Rome with a few hundred grand? And a couple mill in a Swiss account. And back that up with the rest in the Caymans or something? I speak French, and passable Spanish and Italian. I should blend okay if I stay out of the mainstream."

Who's he kidding? James isn't exactly the blend-in type. "Whatever you want to do, James. It's your money." Steve glances at Julia. She and James are fixed on each other again. Looking at the two of them together reminds him how slim the odds that she'll choose him for the long run. They are the beautiful people. And Steve—isn't. Then Julia turns his way but she doesn't look at him, not even a glance. She loads the coffee maker with the fresh ground. Was she consciously avoiding him? Did she want him gone? James was right. This meeting is a mistake.

"The quicker we can set this up, the quicker I'm out of here." James looks at Steve, then slides onto the bar stool as if to avoid falling. "I need you to put everything under a new pseudonym." He rests his elbows on the butcher block, then his forehead in his hands and stares down at the oak island. "If you get together the signature papers, I'll back them with I.D."

"What is the matter with you?" Julia studies him. "Are you on something?"

"Give me a break, Jules. I'm not on anything. It's not the same as before. Clearly." He glances at Steve then back at her, and they're connected again.

And Steve wants to bash James' head into the hard oak. He swallows back his humiliation and releases a deep breath. Somehow James always manages to make him feel inept. "Your I.D. better be solid. We start moving a lot of cash around, and I guarantee someone's going to notice."

Julia fills the mugs with coffee and passes them around.

"The I.D. is good. I've been using it for a few weeks now." With effort, he shoves his hand in his back jeans pocket and takes out a thin black billfold, then takes out a driver's license and social security card and put them on the butcher block.

Julia gets the sugar tin and slams it down in front of James.

He looks up at her. "Thanks." Then he turns back to Steve. "This is all I've got for right now." He pours close to a half cup of sugar directly from the tin into his coffee. "My birth certificate and tax I.D. papers kind of got…well…burnt up. I've contacted my source to get duplicates, but it's going to take quite a bit of cash to get them." He holds the mug to his lips, blows the steam off, then takes a sip and closes his eyes as he drinks the hot liquid. For a minute Steve thinks he might pass out. Julia still watches him. It feels to Steve like she's forgotten he's in the room.

"I can overnight the signature cards with copies of what you have here as long as you can produce the hard copy they require the first time you access the accounts. But the money won't be available for at least three days."

"Three days?" James puts his mug down and winced as he stands abruptly. "You can't be serious. This is the electronic age for Christ's sake. I don't have days. I thought we were talking about a few *hours* here, Stephen." He holds his ribs as he moves from the island. "What the hell happened to the internet?"

"James, I can sell all the stock you want in real time at a key stroke. But standard practice is T plus 3-trade day, plus three business days to settlement of cash. I can't open the accounts without the cash, and it will take a minimum of three days to get it. This is going to take the better part of a week. That's just the way it is."

He stops pacing. "This is a bad idea." He speaks to himself. "I should have watched the house a while. I just assumed you'd be alone. This is a mistake. I should leave." Then he looks at Julia. "I had no idea you'd be here. *Why the hell did you have to be here, Julia?*" He practically yells.

Every muscle in Steve's body tenses. "Wait a minute, James—"

"*How dare you*—" Her voice is deep, filled with outrage.

"I'm sorry." He runs his hand through his hair and stares at the floor. "That was completely out of line. I apologize."

"Don't you dare act like you give a shit, you son of a bitch."

"That's not fair, Julia. It's not right."

"You walk away thirteen months ago, just disappear, and then come back for *money*. What's not right, James?"

"I didn't walk away."

"What the hell does that mean?" A few more tears escape from her soft brown eyes. "Tell me what is going on and where you've been." She screams at him. "I absolutely *need* to know. You owe me an explanation!" She's quite literally begging him, and Steve feels ashamed for her…of her.

James shakes his head then looks away. "You know what happened, Jules." His voice is low, almost a whisper. "It seems there was a rumor…"

Her mouth literally falls open, her eyes widen and stay on him. "Oh my God. *No.* I was sure it wasn't true. I know you'd never deal, and I couldn't fathom you bringing speed on the plane, through all that security, and customs. I didn't believe it. Michael Flint told me you were arrested for *trafficking*, but I didn't believe him, or the press, not even when you didn't come back. I thought you were in London on the Pandora project, and that we were over."

Steve knew the rumor, of course. And like Julia, he too thought it unlikely. He'd never known James to be more than a casual user. Carrying drugs overseas was reckless and stupid, and Steve knew James to be neither. Beside, he didn't need money. The backup accounts Steve managed for him alone made him if not rich, at least wealthy, as did his Zuma beach home. James disappearing, getting swallowed up in his music was far more likely. And leaving Julia behind was typical.

James glances at Steve, shakes his head slightly, then looks back at Julie. He shrugs and spread his hands in surrender. "Julia, I need to deal with this now. And right now I need money. I'm getting money, and I'm going." He stays fixed on her. "I'm sorry Jules. I don't know what else to do. Blink and I'm gone—like I was never here, and we all just move on."

Julia is fixed on him but her expression has softened. "That's it? The best you've got? Forget the last five years of my life and 'move on.'" She sighs, but keeps her eyes on his. "I didn't know you were in trouble, James. *I didn't.* I thought we were through—"

"We are," James whispers, looks at Steve then down again.

Weighted silence. Julia stays fixed on James. Her expression, her countenance is suddenly calm, professional. Steve can feel the wheels in her head turning as she assesses him.

"Please just tell me what is going on?"

"There's no point. It won't make any difference. You can't help me, Julia."

She glares at him, then shakes her head. "You really are a self-serving prick."

James sighs and turns away, looks at Steve for salvation.

Damn him to hell. He deserves it. He's sucked Julia in, but Steve doesn't want to know the details. There are laws against wealth managers assisting criminal clients. "Clearly, you two have things to work out. I wish to hell you didn't. I wish we were on the same page, Julia." He picks up his mug then he swipes the driver's license and social security card off the butcher block and heads for the kitchen door as he speaks to James. "I'm going down to my office and put what you need in motion. You're going to have to sign some paperwork. Come down when you're ready." He looks at Julia. "You okay with that?"

"Does it really matter? You can see he needs more than money. But you're going to help him run, aren't you?"

"I'm going to do my job, Julia. I'm not choosing sides."

"That's not how it feels."

"I'm sorry. It's up to James what he wants to do. Not me. Not you." Steve stares at her, and for the first time that morning they connect. She's looking for James to validate her, and that cuts.

How can Steve draw her in? Why isn't his respect, his desire, his love enough? He doesn't try to mask his disappointment as he leans into the swinging door and leaves the kitchen. He's confident that James will leave as soon as he gets what he needs. Steve's counting on the fact that he loves Julia enough to go alone.

-

-

Chapter Twelve

-

JULIA

The shroud that veils Steve's dark blue eyes etches in her brain as she feels him withdraw, and the weight of his demeanor remains even after his exit. It's not lost on her what he must be going through with James here. She's humbled by his civility, his moral fiber. Stephen really is a good man. And Julia's suddenly struck by how much it hurts—hurting him. She has the urge to go after him, comfort him, reassure him of her love, but burning curiosity keeps her where she is. And she hates James all the more, for bringing her to her knees again.

He stands at the French doors staring out at the bay. Morning sun pours in through the rippled glass and drenches him in light. His dark, long sleeve fleece or flannel shirt practically glows around the edges. It's haphazardly tucked into his jeans which hang loose on his hips. Gold highlights in his hair are lit up with the sunrise and halos him. He looks like he's in a Vermeer painting. Stunning. How many times had she rationalized away his culpability because of his beauty? Untouchable, like fine art, that's what he was, and always had been, except in spectacular moments.

He hasn't come for her. She has to face that. Chance brought them together this morning. *Entropy*, James would have said, a lifetime ago. She leans against the counter top to help her bear the weight of her shame. But as she stands there watching him, she experiences that familiar rush of pleasure. Her magnificent work of art is twelve feet from her, blissfully unaware of what he'd done to her, and the mess he'd left when he went away. And she isn't going to let him get away with that.

"The first few weeks you were gone gave me time to miss you." She tries to control the quiver in her voice. He turns to face her and she draws a sharp breath before continuing. "The next month I started to feel anxious and angry. By the beginning of the third month, when it started to dawn on me you may not be coming back, I started coming apart. For the next six months after that I came unglued virtually every day, putting friends, my family, my residency at UCLA—my career, in jeopardy."

He stares back at her. She waits for his response but none comes.

"Stephen's constant support and Saint-like patience saved me from caving in on myself completely." And she isn't going to let him see her cry. She turns away and fills her cup, then leans back against the counter top and looks at him again.

Part of her is glad he found her with Steve, and she hopes it's hurt him. She'd played his return countless times, rehearsed speeches in place, but suddenly feels afraid to speak. She absolutely refuses to come apart. But as the tension grows with the silence between them, she finally can't take it anymore. "If the rumor is true, then why on earth would you carry drugs overseas?"

"I didn't."

"Then why were you arrested?"

He laughs, cynically, angrily, and looks away. "My father set me up."

She only knew his father through his descriptions, which were few. Julia had an impression of a tall, imposing general type, with German origins. In all the time she'd known him, James had not seen, nor spoken to his father. "Why would your father do something like that, James?"

"I don't know. I used to think it was because he was insanely controlling, but I'm not so sure anymore. I'm not so sure of anything anymore." He stares at her through the brass pots and pans that hang above the butcher block. His hair hangs in his eyes and looks dark against the whiteness of his skin. His shirt is loose on his shoulders. He looks gaunt. Strung out.

"Have you been using since you left?"

"No. I haven't touched anything—that wasn't forced on me for the last thirteen months."

"What does that mean?"

"Forget it."

"No."

"Why?" He glares at her. "What difference does it make now? You're with Stephen. Be with Stephen. Go have a life." He turns away and looks out the French doors again. "As soon as I get set up here I'm gone. I'm dangerous to be around and I don't want anyone else getting hurt, especially you."

"You've reserved that right for yourself." She regrets saying it as the words leave her mouth.

He shakes his head but doesn't say anything.

"James, I can see you're in trouble and I want to help you. Whatever it is, we can deal with it. But I can't help you unless you tell me exactly *what is going on." Don't get mad. You'll lose him. Stay even. Be very specific. Take him step by step.* "What happened after I left you in the studio that morning at your house the last time I saw you?"

He turns around and faces her, fixes his eyes on hers with an intensity that connects them. "You can't leave it?"

"No."

He sighs. "Okay, Julia. You want a recap of our conversation before you left, or just the highlights that followed?"

"You actually remember one of our arguments?"

"I've replayed it a thousand times in the last thirteen months."

"Why don't you just tell me your version?"

"Okay..." He cocks an eyebrow. "I'm assuming you remember our... *discussion* in the studio that last time we were together?" He pauses. She nods. "Then you'll recall you came down that night and we got into it, and you walked out, to the kitchen, I think, to draw me out of the studio thinking I'd follow you."

She blushes, exposed by his insight at her transparent attempt at manipulating him.

"Well, I was gonna come after you, but my father's solicitor called right then, before I even got up from the board. My half-brother, Ian, had died of an overdose, and my father *requested* I attend the funeral. He'd chartered a jet to collect me, but I didn't want to be beholden to his terms, so I told him I'd get there on my own, which meant leaving in the morning to make it to the UK for the service." He moves to the butcher block and spread his huge hands on the oak top. "And then you came back into the studio, remember? All bent out of shape I was back to working. But I wasn't. I was booking a flight. I was going to talk to you about it, but you stormed out of the house."

For a minute it's hard to breathe as memories of that night flood her head. She flashes on him sitting in front of the multiple monitors in his studio, totally absorbed in the wave forms streaming by on the screens, never noticing she had come in the room. Julia forces herself back to the present. James straightens under her scrutiny, tucks his hands in his jeans pockets. "Why didn't you call me, or text me to tell me what was going on? Why did I have to find out about Ian a month after the fact from Martin—"

"I *did* text you. From LAX. And again from Heathrow, after I landed. I don't know why you never got them." He shakes his head, then shrugs. "I knew if I told you about Ian's funeral before I left Zuma you'd want to come, but it was pointless to get you involved with my family. My father and I were estranged. Ian and I were never close. I hadn't seen, or spoken to either in ten years. Then Howard, my old man's personal secretary, guilts me out that Edward is under media scrutiny, and I'd be publicly shaming him if I didn't attend my own brother's burial. I had no ambitions of hurting my father, at the time, anyway. And, well, you were coming down my throat, and I couldn't exactly deny your reality. So I figured the funeral would give me some distance from using, and give us a break for a few days."

"What *us*? We were done. It was over. You released me and left."

"*Released* you?" He shakes his head. "Julia, we're having this conversation because it's what you think you need. But the truth isn't going to set you free, my dear. You're going to have to do that yourself."

She glares at him. He's doing it again—pulling the focus from him by putting it on her. She isn't going to let him. "So you're father set you up and you've been in jail in England for the past *year* plus for using speed?" It sounds ludicrous. First arrests in the States for possession got a slap on the wrist and *maybe* court ordered outpatient rehab.

"I wasn't in jail. I was remanded to rehab, but I wasn't there for most of that time. And I was arrested for *trafficking*, not just using."

"You just told me you weren't using. Were you or weren't you?"

"I wasn't, Jules. I swear it. I trashed all the pharms I had before I left home 'cuz I couldn't get you out of my head. But they found an eighth-ounce of *crystal meth* in my jacket on x-ray at Heathrow. And when I tested positive for amphetamines from the Didrex you railed on me for abusing, well, it made their case. My father couldn't have timed a drug set-up better had he premeditated it."

"Do you know how bizarre this sounds?" She studies him, trying to assess his cognitive level. He looks exhausted, totally spent, but he doesn't seem delusional. "If you weren't in rehab all this time, where have you been?"

He folds his arms across his chest, tucks his elegant hands against his sides and looks away. "I got sentenced to a one month 'recovery' program in Priory Manor, enforced rehab at a private clinic outside London. Third night there, before I even got phone privileges, I heard screaming, and went to help a woman I thought was being assaulted. Found four guys, all privileged class and strung out on heroin, holding her down." He pauses, virtually expressionless. "Ended up killing one of the sonsabitches." He takes a deep breath and shudders as he releases it. "Just so happens the little prick turned out to be some judge's son. And that judge had me locked me up in

Langside Priory Hospital for the criminally insane, outside Glasgow, for killing his kid." He stares at her, almost blankly. "That's where I've been, until about a month ago."

She has no idea what to say. She tries to associate what he's just told her with related college studies, or recall a PTSD patient having gone through something similar for some context. But she hasn't work with soldiers, or trauma victims. She handles mostly accidents, domestic and gang violence, and ODs in Emergency. James may be delusional, of course. Developing paranoid schizophrenia was a real and increasing possibility in white males from their mid to late twenties.

Perhaps he had some conflict with his father after the funeral. Assuming he isn't crazy, it's *possible* with Edward's money and resources he could have set up his son. But why? And what James said about killing a man doesn't resonate. He felt bad when he killed a spider. Even with sports, like surfing or racquetball, the competition was always secondary to mastering the game. "Let me get this straight. You've been in a mental institution in Scotland for the last year for killing a judge's son?" Hearing herself say it makes it all sound even more surreal.

He laughs, this deep angry chortle. "Up until a month ago." He gives another quick laugh. "Right out there, isn't it? If it didn't just happen to me, I wouldn't fucking believe it."

Julia isn't quite sure she does believe it. At least all of it yet. "Where have you been for the past month?" *Why didn't you come to me?*

"I was in London for about a week. I made it to the States after that, went up to Boston and stayed there about two weeks, at the Devlin's place in Cambridge."

"Harry and Michelle Devlin?"

He nods.

"Aren't they divorced?"

"Yeah, they are."

"So you stayed with Harry, or *Michelle* for two weeks?"

"Michelle."

"How did you end up with her?" *And why didn't you come to me?* Michelle was Harry's trophy wife, a Victoria Secret's model. "I didn't know you really knew her."

"She knew me. She used to hang out when I was producing Harry's album. About a month ago I ran right into her in Harvard Square. I was pretty messed up, even more than I am now, if you can believe that." He grins. "She really helped me out, helped me come up with a plan and put it in motion. She got me together with her lawyer who put me in contact with a guy who set me up with a new identity. She gave me Harry's old Porsche to drive here to Stephen's, to cash out, go someplace safe, hide for a while, get my head together."

"Why didn't you come to me?" *Stupid Julia.*

"I couldn't, Julia."

"Don't give me that, James. You managed to get here. You could have come to me."

"No. You're wrong. Any contact puts you at risk. Stephen too, but…" He pauses, and shrugs. "I need money. I need to be able to move around, and that takes money."

"Clearly, money isn't all you need."

"You're right, I'm sure, but right this minute it is." He takes his mug from the butcher block, comes around it and pours himself another cup of coffee. "So as soon as Stephen gives me some numbers, I'm gone. It'll be best for everyone that way."

They stand two feet apart. Julia fights the urge to slap him. "Is that right? Is that your professional opinion, or just what works best for you?"

No response. He takes a sip of his coffee.

She glares at him. "Why do we always come back to what works for *you*?"

"It's different this time." He speaks without looking up.

"Not for me, James."

"Tell me what you want to hear, Julia." He looks at her, sets the mug on the butcher block and wrapped his fingers round the edge of the island behind him. "You want to know that every fucking moment in hell, the thought of you was my lifeline; that day after day I searched for something to save my sanity. And it was never music. It always turned out to be you." He glares at her. "Does that help you, Jules?"

In a way it does, then shame consumes her. Despite his suffering, she needs to know he had feelings for her. She wants to hold him, have him hold her. Surrender into him. Protect him. Forgive him. And she isn't going to let him see her cry.

"Julia, you need to listen to me now. Look at me."

She does. He leans against the butcher block slouched on one hip. He stares at her, but it feels like into her. "Stop crying." He leans forward and brushes the tears from her cheek with the side of his thumb.

With his touch comes that sudden rush of pleasure, and she grabs his hand before he pulls away. She holds her breath. He grips her hand and pulls her to him and hugs her against him, their bodies pressed into each other. She can feel him breathe, his heart beating. "You are intoxicating," he whispers. "Every time I got wrapped up in you—

with you—it was all consuming. So I pulled back. I never let myself really be with you. Not all the way. Not like I should have. And I am profoundly sorry."

She leans into him, surrenders to his words, to the feel of him, his arms around her, and cries.

"I have to play this as it lays now, Julia. I'm in way over my head and there is no way in hell I'm going to let you drown with me."

"Then let me help you."

"You can't. Ya gotta just let it go. Don't blow away what you have with Stephen. Don't measure what you've got with what you imagine we had."

The rush hits her and it feels as if she's sucking in water in search of air. She pushes him off and backs away from him until she's up against the counter behind her. "*Imagine*? Don't make me crazy, James." She glares at him. "Don't stand there and tell me I imagined the most profound connection I've ever felt to anyone in my life."

He leans back against the butcher block, crosses his legs and buries his hands in his pockets. "Makes no difference now, Julia."

"*It does to me.* God, how can you be so *blank*? The times you crawled outside of your head and into mine, your perceptions were virtually flawless. For *four years* I counted on you for direction, guidance. I went to medical school because of *you*. I am a psychiatrist because of *you*! I felt closer to you than any man, or woman I have ever known."

"Why is any of this important now?"

"Let's just say I need a reality check. I need to know that I didn't spend all those years lying to myself about what we shared."

He inhales as if to speak, pauses, then his eyes narrow but he keeps them on hers. "Okay, Jules. Here's some reality I gleaned over the last thirteen months of dead time. I was making it with music *way* before my parents died. A year into living with Edward, and it became my Savior. I was just abandoned, left rotting in hell because I never developed anything with anyone real, not even with you. We could have spent the rest of our lives together and you never would have gotten what you needed from me. *And you knew that*, which is why you tried to lay it on the line that last night we were together." He pauses, studying her. "Why do you do this to yourself? Why do you remember only the best of what we had instead of what actually was?"

She looks away, shamed. "Because the times you plugged into me, with that same focus you gave to your music, those moments were...electric." She looks back into his eyes, searching. "I know they were for you too. *I know it*. I kept thinking that if I just gave it enough time, you'd learn to trust me. You'd figure out that love wasn't going to consume you, but complete you."

He stares at her, then shrugs and spreads his hands in surrender. "It's the past, Julia, and we have no future. I'm a wanted felon. For murder, drug trafficking, escaping from lawful custody. Any contact between us only compromises your professional position, and your safety. I have nothing to offer you now. Nothing. Do you understand me?" He stares at her then looks away toward the kitchen door.

-

-

Chapter Thirteen

-

She feels him separate, pull away from her, wall up. And though there is tenderness in his eyes, the Grand Canyon is between them. A part of her brain is screaming, like an addict going through withdrawal, and she wants to grab one of the pans hanging above the butcher block and hit him in the head with it.

"What are you going to do, James? Where are you going from here?"

"I'm not sure. I've been in the States too long though, longer than I'd anticipated. For a while at least, I think I'm going to have to keep moving around."

"How manageable is that? I mean, look at you. Are you really that far gone? It must be obvious, even to you at this point your current course is not sustainable."

"But I'm about to change it, with a lot of money." He flashes a cocky grin, his tiger eyes shrouded by his thick lashes. "Julia, I'm sorry for what I put you through, for the years we were together, and the last thirteen months that we were not." He stays fixed on her. "You've started something good with Stephen. Stick with it. Make it what you want. He'll go there with you—for the long run. I'm sorry it isn't me—that it wasn't me, and won't ever be."

Tears spill down her face again and she can't stop them. She looks away. The son of a bitch has already separated. He's closed the lid of the box to which she belongs and shelved it, even though she's standing right in front of him.

"I'm going to talk with Stephen for a bit, and then I'm leaving. And now you know why. I hope it helps you, Jules."

She watches her tears fall onto the clay tile floor. She feels him watching her. She refuses to look at him. The lump in her throat is so choking she cannot speak.

"Blink, Julia." He partially whispers. "Shut your eyes, and when you open them, don't look back." He stays fixed on her another second then picks up his mug from the butcher block, crosses in front of her, and leaves the kitchen without looking back.

She can barely breathe as she sinks back against the counter. Tears blur her vision. Sunlight strikes the hanging brass pots and bounce golden rays around the room. She squints to dim the brightness, and focuses on the blue of the bay out the kitchen windows. The Art Deco towers of the Golden Gate are lit blazing red from the rising sun.

Blink of an eye and he'll be gone. She feels ambivalent about trying to stop him. She's afraid for him. Whatever happened has clearly traumatized him, but she knows she can't convince him to get help. He won't listen to her. Back to the cat and mouse game with James. It's exhausting, and demeaning.

He's right about her and Steve. They are good together, in a quiet way. Stephen makes her feel valued, safe. She and James should have been as short-lived as her singing career. She knew who he was, *how* he was, from the beginning. In five years, she probably should have figured out she couldn't change him. They really were through a year ago, the night she laid it on the line. And again Julia flashes on James focused on the monitors of streaming music at his home studio in Zuma that last time they were together…

--

It was well after midnight when Julia got to the beach house. She'd come all the way from Westwood to be with him, instead of going back to her condo in Brentwood only a few miles from work. Her tension spiked when he didn't acknowledge her as she opened the door to his recording studio.

James sat in front of his computer, making notations on wave forms of music streaming by on the monitors. His right ear was covered by a headphone, which was beating out the percussion, while he listened with his exposed ear to the melody, if you could call it that, which filled the studio.

She moved beyond the threshold and he finally noticed her and gave her a quick smile. His attention never really left the multiple screens, nor did he take his hands off the electronic piano or computer keyboards. She went and stood behind him and rubbed his shoulders. He relaxed with her touch, turned his head back towards her slightly and she saw him smile, then she lost him again to the computer. The music was loud, hard, electric, with a lot of digital starkness. It was clean though, and she liked it. Julia liked mostly everything James crafted.

"Who's this for?"

"The Zone. Lead track for their debut album. What do you think?"

From punk to popular, Bach and beyond, James was a master musician. "Your brilliance never ceases to amaze me, my love."

He laughed. "And I thought you were only with me because I'm beautiful."

"True dat, honey," Julie teased. "You do make a good arm piece." She bent down and kissed his neck, then leaned her chin on his shoulder as she slid her arms down his chest. "You're very impressive at all the fancy parties, that is if we actually went to any parties, or really anywhere for that matter." She slid her hands a little further down. "Why don't you knock this off for the night and come upstairs?"

"Give me another twenty minutes and I'll meet you up there." He took both her hands in his, kissed them, squeezed them and released them, then focused his attention back on the computer. She straightened, sighed loudly enough for him to hear her, and looked back only once as she left the studio. He was lost inside the wave forms, totally absorbed, and did not look at her.

Julia went upstairs and took a shower. She'd just come off evening rotation, dealing with all the homeless psychotics and crashing junkies the cops dropped on the hospital doorstep. She was tired. The second year of residency seemed even harder than the first. The hours were just as brutal, but dealing with the anger and violence of the patients was becoming exhausting.

She lay down in bed after showering and fell asleep, woke at

4:20a.m., according to the bright red numbers on the digital clock on the mission-style night table, and James was not in bed. She knew he'd still be in the studio, and she fought the urge to go downstairs and confront him. But the longer she lay there trying to fall back asleep, the more agitated she got. He'd been using amphetamines to sustain working endless hours, letting music consume him. Again.

He'd gone through periods like this on and off since she'd met him, where he'd use for a couple of months to get through some project and then not touch anything, not even wine, for months at a time. Julia never considered him having a "drug problem," since it never seemed to negatively impact his life, and he walked away from it for extended periods without repercussions or change in behavior.

She didn't know why it was bugging her so much that particular night. Maybe, while she lay there counting the number of months he'd been using, the final figure was too high. Maybe, when she counted the number of times they'd actually made love in the past few months, the number was too low. A half-hour into lying there, she couldn't contain her anxiety any longer and went down to the studio to talk to him.

Of course, he was still awake, still at his computer staring at the wave forms streaming by on the monitors.

"Hi." He gave her a guilty grin, and she realized that he'd never come up that evening to find her sleeping.

She took a cleansing breath to keep her anger in check. "Hi. I think we need to talk." She sat down on the old leather couch.

"Uh oh." He pressed some keys on the computer. The music froze on the screens, and silence created a vacuum in the room as he swung in his chair around to face her. Black of enlarged pupils took up most of his green eyes, which were open too wide, and red rimmed. His full lips were chapped and scarlet. He sat slouched, his lean muscular body relaxed, hands clasped against his flat stomach. He stared at her waiting for her to continue.

"I think it's time you stopped using Didrex or Adderall, or whatever the hell you're using."

He laughed. "Jules, aren't you working the Dependency unit right now?"

"Don't patronize me, James. You're taking it too far out there. You're doing it almost every day now. You hardly eat. You need Ambien to sleep. You're hurting yourself. Do you get that? Do you care?"

He cocked his head and flashed a condescending grin. "Come on. You know this is temporary, and I can pull it back anytime. What's this really about Julia?"

"Let's go to Maui for a week or two over spring break. Or we can take a drive to Yellowstone, or fly to Italy. Get you out of the loop you're in, away from the Industry for a while."

"Music is not the issue."

"It never is for you, James. You've been using consistently since mid-summer last year. It's almost the end of January."

"Epic wants the Zone's release by the summer. That makes it really tight. We're right on the edge here, Jules."

"You've been over the edge since way before the Zone. What is going on with you, James? Before you started working with Max Harding and his band, it was the remix for Caravan. Before them it was…God, I don't even remember, but something that was consuming all of your time. You've been involved in one project or another for most of last year, working eighteen, twenty hour days with no breaks in between, except for that week in Bali for Christmas over a year ago. We used to have *some* time together, a life outside our careers. What happened to that?"

"You got involved, and so did I. And that's okay. It's not a bad thing. You've given yourself some substantial goals in pursuing your doctorate, and it's going to take sacrifice to get there. I admire your tenacity. Really. I've a lot of respect for what you're doing."

"You're doing it again."

"What?"

"You're making the conversation about me and taking it off of you."

He spread his hands in surrender and laughed. "Okay, Jules. You're afraid I'm abusing speed. And that's fair. I probably am *right now*. But the real issue here isn't about me using, or abusing, whatever you want to call it. What you're looking for is an emotional commitment from me that you don't feel I'm investing. Isn't that right?"

"Yes, James. That's right. But that's not what I'm talking about *right now*. You're using too much so you can work too much. You need to take a break from your muse for a while."

"Ah. We're back to that." His expression softened. "I'm sorry I'm hurting you, Julia. Not my intention. It's true we used to have more time together. But things change, and we both have to deal with other commitments, which doesn't mean I love you any less, I'm just less available."

She sighed. "You know, James, love, like intention, is meaningless unless put into action."

He just stared at her.

"I admit I want more of your time and energy. And I'll even confess to being jealous of your passion for and commitment to music. It will always be the mistress between us. But this conversation is not about *us*. Using speed allows you to cross the event horizon and get sucked inside. And you can't be with me when you're making it with yourself."

He bent his head to one side, mulling over what she'd said. Then he looked back at her, half-smiled apologetically, and ran his fingers through his hair. "Touché." He sat up straight in his chair. "I'm sorry I can't give you all you need. I understand that you want more from me, but I just don't know how to give you more right now. You deserve to be with someone who can give you what you want, and I think you should pursue it, if that's what you need to do, Jules."

She wanted to roll into a ball and right off the face of the earth. "God, all I'm asking is that you stop using. Why can't you just make that commitment to me?"

"Because that's not all you're asking and you know it. Think about it." He stared at her for a moment, studying her, and she felt raped.

She blushed, shamed, then got up and walked out of the studio. She didn't want him to see her cry. She went into the kitchen and started making coffee but got lost in the view of the sun rising over the L.A. basin. The Santa Anna's were up, the strong, hot winds out of the east churned up the coastline, the sun lighting up the foam of the whitecaps all the way out to the horizon. Julia kept waiting for him to come into the kitchen after her. She kept waiting…then hoping. By the time the sun had arced over the Huntington Hills, she went looking for him.

He was still in his studio, still on the computer playing with the wave forms on the monitors. That son of a bitch had compartmentalized their discussion already. Julia was waiting to continue their conversation, and James was back to fucking working.

She left. She slammed the front door on her way out and went home.

He was gone before noon that day. She had not seen him, nor heard from him until he walked into Stephen's door this morning. And though she thought about going to London, imagined showing up at the studio where he was likely working a thousand times, she never would have followed through. Julia was too busy mentally tormenting herself with what she did to chase him away.

-

-

Chapter Fourteen

-

"Have some numbers for me?" James comes into Steve's office, sits on the tan, crushed leather couch and puts his coffee on the steel and glass table in front of him.

"Yeah. Almost." Steve sits at his glass top drafting desk. Through the glass wall in front of him, and in the reflection of the enormous O'Keefe print on the wall behind his desk, orange sunlight arcs over the Bay Bridge and spreads across the tall buildings of San Francisco, lighting up Alcatraz, and the Golden Gate beyond. Only Tiburon afforded this view, which was why he had to live here. "I set up a temporary email account— surfinmavericks@hotmail.com." He grins at James. I'll stick the accounts and corresponding numbers in there so you can access them anytime, from anywhere. Thirty days without logging on and the email account disappears."

"Good. Great. Thanks." James picks up his mug, cradles it with both hands, and takes a drink of his coffee. "I appreciate this, Stephen. You have what's left of my assets. Turns out you weren't so whacked setting me up under a pseudonym to cover my ass, though at this point I'd preferred to have been sued." He scoffs, shakes his head. "They seized everything in my name. And they took the Zuma house—the studio, the equipment, most everything."

"Who?"

"The DEA. Once Due Process is complete, and the States uphold my UK conviction, they're going to auction it off. And the Justice Department walks away with an easy seven million. Poof. No more house." He gets up, walks over and stands in front of the glass wall.

"I'm sorry, man." It feels awkward getting personal. Their only connection outside of business, other than surfing, was Julia. And though Steve is curious for the details of the bizarre situation he's been drafted into, he wants to keep it about business, especially now. "Well, the good news is you have close to fifteen million. As a matter of fact, at this very moment, the computer says your portfolio is worth $14,609,265.05. Close to three million is tied up in long term ETFs and Muni's, but the rest is in various securities and liquid for trading."

Steve isn't sure James is listening, but keeps talking anyway. "We can set you up with six or seven million in the offshore account, back that up with another four or five in a Swiss account, and you can personally open as many accounts in Europe as you need them. The interest should be enough to live on so you don't have to touch the principal. What do you want me to do with the rest of your assets?"

He doesn't answer. He stares out the window.

"I can leave your remaining bonds exactly where they are, under Stephen Kennedy LLC in Trust for Michael James Thomas, or transfer it over to your new I.D." Steve picks up his driver's license that says the man he knows to be James Michael Logan is now James Matthew Pierce.

He stands perfectly still, watching the sunrise through the glass wall. "I'm sorry I lost it up there." He speaks softly. "It's just... I'm not feeling well. I'm really very tired..."

"I get that. Look man, I'm really sorry for whatever is up with you right now. I hope money will help you out. It can fix a lot, but not everything."

James looks at him. "It'll give me a chance to breathe." Darkness surrounds his eyes, making the green of his irises radiate. His unruly hair shadows his brow and hangs in his eyes. He looks like a runaway teen. "Feels like I've been suffocating forever," he whispers.

"Relax, James, we'll get you set up." Steve looks back at his monitor. As with all his clients, he'd spread James' holdings across a fairly wide range to keep him diverse. "I've killed most of your popular tech stocks, Apple, Cisco, Oracle, Samsung, Google and the like. That gives you close to nine million. We can raise the rest of the cash with your SPDR's. Want me to hold on to your bonds, or cash out now and you take the hit?"

"Keep them. Their yours. Payment for services beyond the call. It's the only way I've got to repay you."

"You don't owe me anything. It's your money, James, much of which has helped me make mine. You have every right to claim it." Steve retrieves a tablet and stylus from his desk, gets up and hands them to James then points where to sign. "Full signature on pages two, four and five, and initial pages six through ten, then sign and date at the end. And remember to sign Michael James Thomas. You'll have over two million left. What should I do with it?"

James scrawls his signature on the screen repeatedly. "Do whatever you want with it." He puts the tablet and stylus back on the desk. "Donate it to a worthy charity before the Feds find it and take it. I don't care. If twelve million can't salvage me, a couple more on top of that sure as hell won't."

There's something in the finality of his phrasing Steve doesn't care for.

"I just need the accounts set up as soon as possible. And I need some cash, Stephen. I have like ten bucks left on me."

"I'll give you the cash I have here, but it's not much. Likely less than a grand." He goes to the wall safe behind the Monet print, spins the dial four times and opens the safe. "I'll hold on to the rest of your money, James, invest it, hopefully multiply it, do my job." He pulls out a small stack of cash and counts it, then hands it to James.

"There's only eight hundred and forty bucks here. If you need more, I can go the bank. It's down the hill in town. I can be back here in half an hour." Steve lifts the license and social security card off his desk and hands them to James.

"This'll do. Thank you." James retrieves his wallet from his back pocket, inserts the cash and I.D., then slides the billfold back in his pocket.

"I'm thinking it may be wise to liquidate all of your assets in the near future, then reestablish your portfolio in a living trust under James Matthew Pierce. Only you and I will have access to your account. When, and if you need money again, it'll be here for you." He pauses, swallows back his trepidation. "But Julia won't be. I'm going to ask her to marry me, when the time is right. If you've got a problem with that, James, we ought to work it out now."

James stares at him, it feels like probes him, then he manages a quick smile. "You really are one of the good guys, Stephen." He bows slightly then straightens, winces. "Are we done?" He holds his side, and Steve thinks his breath because he doesn't see James breathing.

"You okay?" Steve has to ask. The man looks like he's about to pass out.

He nods. Steve sees him swallow, his jaw line tighten. "Fuck," he whispers. His skin tone goes ashen. Sweat trickles down his face and neck. He runs both hands through his hair then clasps them on top of his head. His sleeves pull back a bit with his motion, and Steve notices chaff marks and bruises on his wrists, like scarring from restraints. Jagged red scars at the base of his wrists continue up his forearms under his shirtsleeves. James catches him looking, folds his arms across his chest, tucks his hands under his arms, turns away, and freezes.

Julia stands on the stairs, a step from the bottom, three feet from him.

"What did you do?" She glares at him, her brown eyes wide, her brow narrow. "Come here." It sounds like she's commanding a dog.

James stares at her wide-eyed, frozen like a deer in the headlights. Julia moves on him, comes off the stairs, grabs his hand and pulls his shirtsleeve back exposing his forearm.

Steve literally gasps. An ugly red scar runs along the full length of James' forearm.

James pulls his hand away, moves back, but she stays on him, grabs his other wrist but he pulls his arm away before she can pull up his shirtsleeve. *"What did you do!? Why!?"*

He just stands there staring at her, shaking his head.

She begins slapping him about the arms and face. He moves back, but doesn't try to stop her, as if he deserves to be hit, like he's a child being scolded by a parent. He backs away from her until she has him up against the glass wall.

"*Stop*, Julia." Steve moves to pull her off him, grabbing her around the waist but she resists him.

"You lied!" she yells at James, and continues hitting him.

"I didn't lie, Julia!" James yells back, finally grabbing her wrists and holding them.

"You weren't institutionalized for murder." She yanks her arms down, freeing herself from James' grip. James winces, grabs his side again. "They locked you up for trying to kill *yourself*, didn't they?" She pushes Steve back, then glares at James a foot from her. He stares back at her but remains mute. *"Talk to me,"* she screams. "And I want the truth this time!"

"What is going on!?" Steve interjects, but they ignore him.

"I swear, everything I told you is the truth—"

"Omission is a *lie*, James. You didn't tell me everything." Julia's crying now. Tears streak down her face while she glares at James, outraged, undermined, clearly afraid for him.

"I tried to kill myself in *Langside,* Julia. I was in hell and it was intolerable." He speaks only to her, as if Steve isn't there. "They messed with my head. They screwed with my body, and I couldn't get out of there, couldn't get away from them—it was my only way out." Tears streak down his gaunt cheeks. He holds his ribs, his eyes fixed on her. He's begging her for absolution.

"I didn't know," Julia whispers. "I thought we were through." She turns to face him, all the blush gone from her tear-streaked cheeks. "I'm sorry, James."

"Don't go there, Jules." James shakes his head, glances at Steve.

Julia finally looks at Steve, and her eyes fill with tenderness, he's sure of it. "He's sick, Stephen. You can see that. He needs more than money. He needs professional help," she says softly. "Now. Today." She turns back to James and he recoils, bangs his head into the glass wall behind him.

"Don't talk about me like I'm one of your fucking psychotics, Julia." He glares at her as he moves past her to the center of the room, holding both sleeve cuffs in his fists, hiding his scars. "And I sure as hell don't need some academic prescribing me meds to reorient my perspective. I've had enough of those already. Money, and lots of it, is the only solution for my immediate issues."

"Ultimately not, James. Unless you deal with what happened that allowed you to justify taking your life, you will forever stand on the precipice of that exit," Julia says rather clinically.

James stares at her and shakes his head, then looks at Steve. "My humblest apologies for all this, Stephen. And profound gratitude."

He wipes the tears from his eyes and cheeks with his shirtsleeve. "surfinmavericks@hotmail, right?"

Steve nods, suddenly exhausted, drained of all anger, resentment, jealously of James, watching the broken man before him. "I'll set up the accounts with your liquidated securities as we discussed. You can expect them to top out by the end of the week." He looks at Julia. She glances at him, her expression more defeat than anger, then she turns away, goes to the glass wall and stares out. James watches her, but Steve talks to him anyway. "My suggestion would be that you invest a good portion of it in real estate, bonds, stocks, whatever—be good cover to have a strong portfolio under your new I.D."

"Yeah. Good idea. Thanks again, for everything." He looks at Julia. She turns around to face him, and Steve feels them connect with an intensity he knows he'll never share with her. "Did you know that even though she professes to be an atheist, she prays." James keeps his eyes fixed on hers as he speaks. "You're a lucky man, Stephen." He finally looks at Steve, gives him a pensive smile and extends his hand.

"Good luck, James." He grips James' hand firmly and shakes it.

James releases him then fixes his eyes back on Julia. "In a different life, my dear..." He whispers. "Have the time of your life in this one." He doesn't acknowledge Steve. He stays on Julia, and she on him. A moment passes between them, as if they are the only two people on the face of the Earth, then James turns away and disappears up the stairs.

Julia stares at the staircase a moment, as if hoping he'll come back, but then she looks down, seemingly, consciously, avoiding Steve. "I'm sorry I've hurt you, Stephen. I'm sorry I made this hard. You deserve better, better than me."

"I want *you*, Jules. Unless you can't get him out from under your skin. I want a lifetime with you, without James between us."

Steve hears James padding across the wood floor of the living room above his office. He watches Julia as he hears the front door shut.

"James is gone, Stephen. He's not coming back. He's no longer between us. The truth is, he was never really here at all."

She looks at him then, her eyes still wet with tears, shakes her head slowly and looks down again. After a moment Steve moves to her, lifts her head with his forefinger, cups her cheek in his hand as she looks up at him. His eyes connect with hers, and he feels her sadness, confusion, doubt, fear. He extends his love, his longing, his desire for her as he moves his other hand to her face, lets his eyes travel to her lips, hesitates for her response then catches the hint of her smile. He pulls her to him, meets her body halfway, and kisses her.

-

-

Chapter Fifteen

-

JAMES

I'm in a mammoth aqua curl. Wave arcs over me and I glide on my board through the tunnel of water. Reach out and touch the curling wave, water streaming off my hand like liquid mercury. Rushing wave sounds like a symphony—highest treble to lowest bass of a tempestuous orchestral sonnet. I fly towards the light beyond the breaking wave, but it doesn't get any closer, and I look back just as the wave engulfs me.

I'm on the sand, the sun lifting the wetness from my skin and baking me warm. Can't remember how I got here. Just glad I survived the wipe out. Tickle of sand sprays my torso, and I open my eyes as Julia, wearing her black one-piece straddles me with her long, slender legs and sits on my stomach. She has a beer in both hands, and takes a swig of hers as she puts the other icy bottle on my bare chest. I gasp with the shock of the cold and she laughs, more mean-spirited than funny, and it kind of creeps me out. The laugh is familiar, but I've never heard it from Julia before.

Then her lips are on mine, her tongue in my mouth, she's sucking me in. My body responds before my brain and I feel pulsing in my groin, my cock hardening. She slides her hand down my body, under my swim shorts and wraps her fingers around my shaft. And while it should feel good, it doesn't. Her touch is aggressive, overly rough as she moves her hand up and down my length. She laughs again, that cold laugh, and I look up at her, but she's now kissing her way down my torso. I see the top of her head, her long, thick brown hair cascading across my stomach, but instead of soft, it feels stringy, damp, like an old-style mop.

But Julia wears her hair cut short.

She's running her tongue along the line of my pelvic bone, then stops at the base of my penis, and Parker looks up at me.

I'm naked. Exposed. No longer at the beach.

Her black eyes are wild. She's blazing on smack, or some derivative thereof, per usual. She smiles, laughs coldly, holding my dick with her laced, goth-gloved hand. I try to get her off me but can't move my arms—they're spread and pinned at the wrists by leather straps fixed to the armrests extending from metal frame of the examining table I'm on. Desperately try kicking her off me, but I can't move my legs either. They're spread wide, pinned to the sides of the table's frame by leather straps around my knees and ankles.

I go berserk, writhing, fighting against the restraints. Feel her hand on my ass and every part of my body tightens as she slides her fingers between my balls to my anus. Squirm to get away from her, but the restraints cut into me, holding my legs back and forcing my body to arch upwards at the hips fully exposing all of me. I can't move. I'm beyond prostrate, and helpless, and scared out of my mind.

"No! Stop!" I try and yell, but something's in my mouth, a hard leather rod, holding my tongue down and my mouth open so my words are garbled, my voice slight. Tears of frustration, rage, shame, well, then stream down the sides of my face into my hair.

She runs her finger round the rim of my anus then sticks it up my ass. I groan with the painful pressure, and continue to grunt with the cramping in my stomach and groin as she rotates her finger, finally release a panting gasp when she finally pulls it out. I struggle to lift my head but the gag around the back of my neck is so tight I can only lift it an inch or so. Parker looks at me, smiles as she releases my cock, draws her fingernails across my stomach as she turns away from the bed. I hear high pitched clanking of metal instruments. My terror mounts.

I'm trembling uncontrollably, drenched in sweat, and succumb to tears for a moment. Peeling plaster reveals ancient stone brick walls. Bare light bulbs hang on wires from the ceiling, which is also coated with peeling plaster exposing the arched Cathedral vaulting. There are no windows.

Parker returns, and looms over me. She holds a six inch metal wand by its black plastic handle between my spread legs, but keeps it from touching me. Then she flips a switch on the wand's handle. It glows bright blue at the tip, like a dentists tool for hardening fillings, and emits a low, electronic hum. Parker grins at me broadly, her face awash in blue light. Her yellowed teeth look bright against her black lipstick and blue skin, the scene right out of *Clockwork Orange,* but it's happening to *me.*

"We gonna put on a good show today, baby?" Parker slurs her cockney delivery. Her breath is sour, stinks of liquor.

Then searing pain shoots through my balls, my groin, right to my brain as she touches the wand to my testicles. Scream—loud, long, then I'm choking for breath, the restraints cut into my wrists and knees like knives as I recoil from the white hot shocks.

"Ooh. Very good, puppet." She laughs again, touches the wand to my thighs, my pelvis, my stomach, my cock.

Light worms squirm across my eyes, obscure my vision, the pain so agonizing it's commanding all my attention, overriding even my fear. My body jerks convulsively with each shock, my hips coming off the mattress only a fraction with each electric pulse, my limbs ripping as I pull against the restraints.

Parker is all smiles as she bends over me, grasps my flaccid dick and starts sucking me, touching the wand to my ass, scrotum, inner thighs again and again, putting me into a convulsive rhythm. She holds my cock so the head stays between her lips and goes in and out of her mouth as I contort against the pain.

I'm screaming at her to stop, to let me go, begging her to stop hurting me, the sounds coming out of my gagged mouth more animal than human.

My screaming wakes me. I'm on a train, sunlight coming in through the picture window momentarily blinding me from the view beyond, but then I catch a glimpse of the flat, chaparral landscape and somehow know it's the Sacramento Valley. The compartment is old-Europe though, with two bench seats for three, facing each other, like in Harry Potter. Kate sits across from me, her enigmatic smile on her freckled face, her long red hair tumbling over and blending into her thin, burgundy camisole.

We enter a tunnel. The lights blink, then go out, then come back on, and Kate is gone.

I stand, bang my head on something above me and wake with a start. I've smashed my head into the elaborately carved wooden headboard of the huge king size bed I'm in. Lay back into the pile of down pillows rubbing the side of my forehead to counter the throbbing, then throw the heavy white quilt aside. Sea breeze coming in from the open balcony door sweeps over my sweaty skin and cools.

Daylight shimmers through the sheer white drapes over two thirds of the glass wall. Beyond is the sparkling Ionian. I lay in bed staring at the textured ceiling, recalling the dream about Julia, integrated into the memory of Langside. I shudder picturing Parker again, shocking the shit out of me with her electric wand. I'm writhing in agony, screaming with each stinging pulse, *No! Don't! Stop!* I try and scream as my dick grows under her grasp, her warm wet mouth...

Tears of rage and shame well in my eyes and I get out of bed to stop mentally cycling. I go out onto the patio overlooking a sweeping view of the rocky shoreline of Govino Bay, and over the rolling chaparral covered hills of the island of Corfu. The turquoise Ionian Sea glitters with the early morning sun. Greece lies beyond the horizon.

I stand at the short, marble railing bordering the balcony of my private villa, surveying the scene of what money buys. Below the bedroom and sitting room is the living room and kitchen, which open out to a patio complete with dining area and jacuzzi the size of a lap pool. A small path leads down to a private dock which sports a small speed boat for my amusement. No beach to speak of, mostly rocky and shrouded with low trees and ground foliage that hides the villa next door.

Haven't left this bungalow in weeks. Haven't seen nor heard any neighbors, and haven't spoken to anyone in as long. Been subsisting on the nuts and candy set in bowls around the villa they keep refilling when they come in to clean. Doesn't bother me. Not really hungry. More like exhausted all the time. Don't sleep much though. Too scared of dreaming.

Gonna have to stop hiding in this bedroom if I want any semblance of a life. I get that. Just don't know how to convince fear to let me walk out of here.

-

-

BOOK TWO
Recovery
Chapter One

-

ELISABETH

Elisabeth wakes to Cameron crying and brings him out on the roof garden to suckle her breasts. She strokes his silky fine golden hair and cradles his face, seeing Jack there, feeling every fiber of her being extending to her son with love. And she cries, as she always does lately, sitting on the lounge chair, perusing Google Maps on her tablet for where to go from here, with tears streaming down her cheeks. Cameron doesn't seem to notice, which sometimes gets to her, though she's probably expecting way too much of an eleven month old.

Her mother says to come home. Insists it would be best, for whom, Elisabeth isn't quite sure. Without a doubt, it won't be for her. Her parent's house is not good grieving ground. The endless judgments of her parenting, the constant little digs she'd have to endure for 'following' Jack to Israel, then having a child here, and *staying*. A gust of wind comes off the Mediterranean and whips the U.S. and Israeli flags fluttering half-staff on separate poles in front of the Hilton Hotel several block from her flat. Four soldiers, and eight civilians were killed in a suicide bombing yesterday. Just another day in Tel Aviv.

Going home might be better for Cameron. Having grandma and grandpa fuss over him could compensate, even minimally, for not having his father anymore. But grandma is sure to make her life hellish, however unwittingly, and that won't be good for mommy. If she's sad now, she can't imagine how miserable she'd be within a few short days of being *there*. And ultimately that wouldn't be good for Cameron. No. Going back to L.A., running back to her family is not an option.

She'd given thirty days notice to Helen and Clive over three weeks ago. She and Cameron have to be out next week because Helen arranged for Clive's cousin to move in at the end of the month. They were all very sympathetic when Jack was killed, but seemed hardened to such events. *How is that possible?* Her mother is right. It is simply unfathomable how losing loved ones through terrorism could ever become part of the norm.

Every day for the past six weeks, Elisabeth goes up to the sundeck to breastfeed Cameron. She comes back up after putting him down for his afternoon nap, stares out across Tel Aviv, her home for the last five years, affirming it's time to leave. She scours maps, drilling down to street level and virtually driving cities and suburbs in the States and Europe, searching for some place that *feels* right. Safe. Money's not an issue. Between the two of them, they'd put away a couple million, and that doesn't even include Jack's life insurance through the AP. *The world is my oyster*, though there is no joy in this cliché. She wants to crawl inside and close the shell. What difference does it make where she goes? Every place is like every other place without Jack.

Almost dark by the time she puts on her khaki's and the gray cashmere sweater that Cameron likes the feel of. She puts him in the baby carrier, and buries his head between her breasts for safety. She ties her hair back and tries to become transparent as she walks down Ben Yehuda to get a falafel, trying to ignore that they're about a million calories and she still needs to drop twenty pounds. She avoids eye contact, but notices everyone in Muslim garb.

Elisabeth hates herself like this.

She absolutely has to get out of here. Jack haunts every street in the city. And she feels scared a lot now. Israel has always been a dangerous place, only now, since Jack was killed, she sees murderers everywhere, on the face of every Palestinian, in the eyes of every Muslim child. She really has to leave as soon as possible.

Four doors down from the sandwich shop she notices the travel agency and goes in.

"What is the first flight out of Israel in the morning?"

The agent sits in front of her flat screen monitor. She's dark-skinned, plump, mid-fifties. "To what destination do you wish to travel?" Arab or Israeli—it's impossible to tell, but she's definitely native born. Her accent is thick, and of the area.

"Anywhere. I just want to get out of here."

She seems unfazed by my desperate need to escape this place. "How many will be flying?"

"Just me and my one year old son. Do I need a separate seat for him, or can he sit in my lap?" The thought of putting Cameron in the car seat carrier next to her leaves her cold. Elisabeth *needs* to be holding him.

"You may hold your son." The woman looks at her with the most sympathetic expression she's gotten since Jack was killed. The agent focuses on her monitor and taps on her keyboard. "The first flight that has available seating is to Athens, Greece. It departs Ben Gurion airport at 8:45a.m. and arrives in Athens at 9:40a.m. Will that do?"

Elisabeth has been to Greece only once before. She attended an art history extension program at an international college the summer of her junior year. "That'll do."

She boxes her portfolios and various personal treasures back at the flat that evening, then gives them to Clive to mail to her parents. She leaves everything else she can't send or carry to Clive's incoming cousin. When all is packed, and Cameron is down for the night, Elisabeth goes to the roof deck, stares out at the city lights, recalling her years with Jack here, silently saying goodbye to both, then sits in the lounge chair for the last time, and cries.

Next morning she and Cameron are on their way to Athens. Cameron clings to her, wraps his little arms tight around her neck from the moment the engines start, through lift off. Elisabeth strokes his head, rubs his back slowly, assures him they're safe. She points out the window at the puffy clouds, the blue sea below, picking out islands and ships with excitement until Cameron releases her, puts his tiny hands on the window, presses his face to the small glass and stares out. All the way across the Mediterranean he's captivated, mesmerized, and again she sees Jack in their son's wide brown eyes. She has to peel him away from the window to strap him in her lap for landing. He throws an embarrassing fit as they descend through the thick brown sky, quelled only as they land in the ancient, smoggy city.

Being off-season, she'd been able to book a room from Israel the night before. Two weeks at the Best Western in Kolonaki, an upscale neighborhood at the base of the Acropolis she'd stayed in during her summer here. She ventures out daily, toting Cameron around Athens in the carrier. If not exactly fun, with just the two of them, at least it's distracting visiting the tourist traps and local eateries. Jack isn't in every cafe and on every street like in Israel, or so many other cities they'd traveled. Though they'd been together forever, he'd been doing an internship at the New York Times and did not join her in Greece that summer all those years back. Elisabeth tours her old college, the cafes she'd frequented. She turns Cameron on to her favorite pizza place, miraculously still there, and shows her son the four story walk-up on Zenocratis Street she'd rented, what now feels like a lifetime ago.

Athens is more crowded, noisy and hectic than Elisabeth remembers. The people seem angrier too, probably since Austerity took effect. Riots in the streets every few months now. And while it's still only bottle tossing and a lot of bravado, it keeps her on edge when she's out and about with Cam. Her only real peace since arriving is in the mornings, at the bakery across from the Best Western. Cameron munches on his moon cookie, and Elisabeth sips espresso and stares at the poster of the island of Corfu, taped to the cracked plaster wall. It shows a pristine white sandy beach with turquoise blending to ultra-violet water lapping a lazy, *deserted* shore. That's where she needs to be.

Two days later she takes Cameron on a ferry from Igoumenitsa to

Kerkira, Corfu, then checks them into the Hotel Omiros in Gouvia for the next two weeks. They spend the first day exploring Corfu City. Then, every morning for the next week, Elisabeth and Cameron get on a bus and discover tiny old towns to resort villages nestled in the hills and along the mostly rocky beaches of the small island.

Corfu is everything the poster displayed. Stunning, full of tree-covered hills rushing down to meet the crystal Ionian and Mediterranean seas. Everywhere they venture is fairly deserted. Tourists haven't arrived yet. Even Corfu City is mostly locals who only speak Greek, of which Elisabeth doesn't know a word. But it feels safe here, even familiar, though she's not been to this island before. Everyone she encounters is gracious, polite, seemingly relaxed, like the Greece she remembers from her college days.

Beginning of their second week on paradise, Elisabeth discovers a real estate office that caters to Brits and Americans. Somehow, she lets the pleasant, golden skinned, mild-mannered English broker talk her into a three-month lease on a two bedroom *villa*. Photos he presents on his laptop show a charming, adobe 'saltbox,' with a Spanish tile roof, situated at the base of a hill bordering a sandy beach north of Agios Gordios, a small resort town on the west side of the island. Summer, he'll get five times the seven hundred and fifty Euros he's willing to offer her per month, which is why the lease goes only to the end of May. Still, it's better than the five hundred and twenty-six Euros a *week* she's paying the hotel. Three months of down time should be enough space to figure out what direction to take the next phase of her life, the one with a child, and the one without Jack.

The two-bedroom could easily pass for a one-bedroom by knocking down the dividing wall between the two small rooms. But the house is clean, wood floors throughout, the living room the largest in the house with a fireplace and a big picture window framing the exquisite ocean view, the pebbled beach only a couple hundred feet down the small hill. The kitchen has a vintage GE fridge and an O'Keefe & Merritt porcelain stove and oven, and enough space to put a small table and Cameron's high chair. Formica counter tops complete the 1950's look. Best part—the house is nestled in a small grove of pines, a mile or so from town. There are only a few other houses behind her rental, up the hill. A few more to the south dot *her* stretch of beach, though most are empty until summer. She can finally be with her son, and her memories, without feeling afraid.

She wishes Jack could have seen this place. He'd have loved it. He loved the ocean, any ocean, and they'd explored many together. He kept promising her they'd escape to Avila Beach or Pacific Grove when they were ready to settle down. And she wanted to believe him, so she stayed with him in Israel, gave birth to their son while he was reporting in Beirut, and spent the last year arguing about going home to the safety of the States, and the sweet, salty air of California.

She should have laid it on the line, left without him. He would never have gone for pizza that night if not for her. Jack didn't even like pizza. Funny how things work out. *Not ha ha funny.*

-

-

Chapter Two

-

She sits on the patio lounge chair feeding Cameron, staring out at the sea when she first sees him. It's mid-day, the west winds blowing in the first hint of spring. The beach is deserted as usual, so it surprises her to see him walking along the water's edge. He's too far away to see in detail, the sea meeting the sand well over three hundred feet from the house, but she can tell he's fairly tall and slender, and by his cadence, which is smooth and graceful, she's pretty sure he isn't an old man.

She leaves Cam on the patio with his Thomas trains and gets her Nikon from the kitchen counter, mounts the 500mm lens, and comes back out to the deck. She focuses on the beachcomber, turning the lens, sharpening his profile to clarity when he turns towards her.

He's beautiful. Young, early twenties, maybe. Stunning, like he just walked off the cover of a Burberry catalog.

She drops the camera to her side and moves behind the extending branches of a pine rooted just off the patio. She doubts he sees her. He doesn't keep looking her way. He continues up the beach, and within a few minutes he's out of sight, around the cliff that meets the sea several hundred yards to the north.

She smiles to herself as his picture replays in her head. Soft, sculpted features framed by dark, tousled hair. His image fades and Jack comes to mind. And guilt. Then comes the void and with it the tears. She sits on the pine bench that runs along part of the back of the house and cries. Cameron doesn't notice, lost in his toys, lining them up contentedly. As it should be. He's safe, the patio surrounded by a three foot high pine plank fence, and a locking metal gate at the step off the deck. Elisabeth sighs heavily, takes a quavering breath to stop crying. She leaves Cam to his bliss and goes inside to make them lunch.

They spend the rest of the afternoon on the pebbled sand, digging for sand crabs, searching for shells, getting soaked by the waves. The entire time, Elisabeth keeps looking for the model guy to reappear. He doesn't, but she can't let go of the overwhelming sense that she and Cameron are being watched.

In the weeks that follow, she sees him every day, running at dawn down the beach while she sits on the back patio feeding her son. She assumes he knows she's there, watching him, but he never so much as glances her way. He comes out of the north, running south along the water's edge, fast, fluid, full force. He's back two hours later, right after she puts Cameron down for his morning nap, and like clockwork, she sees him through the living room picture window, his pace more casual, his intensity spent. She usually wanders out to the porch in time to watch him climb the path up the cliff and disappear into the stone house up the hill behind hers.

At first, she imagines he's some rock star on holiday from his wild and crazy life. But as the weeks turned into the next month and he's still out there every day at dawn, she conjures many scenarios. She likes making up stories of who he is, and what he's doing living alone in one of the few old stone houses on the hill. He may be a recluse hiding from the wicked world, like her. Elisabeth has no desire to find out the truth. The guessing game is entertaining. She isn't interested in talking to anyone beyond Cameron, and the vendors at the Friday street market. She just isn't ready

-

-

Chapter Three

-

A spring storm rages. Elisabeth thinks it's the thunder that wakes Cameron when she hears him crying late one night in early April. She goes to check on him. He's burning up. Panic replaces every other feeling. She's in the middle of nowhere with no vehicle. No cell service this far from town. Phone's out, a frequent occurrence she's come to expect with storms. She gives him some infant Tylenol to bring the fever down, and holds him to her in front of the fireplace for almost an hour but the fever remains high.

Jack. I need you. I'm scared. Jack!

Horrific thoughts of losing her son run through her head as she sits there rocking him. Closest hospital she knows of is in Corfu City, and there's no way for her to get there.

Think!

She'd seen the runner driving a Jeep around town on occasion. Maybe he can help her get to the hospital, or at least to town so she can call an ambulance. She wraps Cameron in a woolen blanket, stuffs him into Jack's zipped North Face jacket, and climbs up the muddy, winding trail virtually in the dark, except for brief moments of moonlight peeking through the fast moving clouds. She slips and slides, praying all the way that the runner speaks English, until she finally arrives at his door ten minutes later, though in the day, and good weather, it'd take her under five.

It's three in the morning, and Elisabeth's surprised to find him awake. She sees him through the large picture window, sitting cross-legged in jeans and an open shirt, in front of his fireplace, reading, the firelight casting him in a Vermeer painting. She knocks and he startles, stares at her through the window. Then he gets up, comes and opens the door.

"I'm sorry to disturb you at this hour, but my son is sick. He has a high fever, and I have to get him to the hospital. You're the only one I've seen around here with a car, and I really need your help. I live just down the hill—"

"I know who you are. Come in. The car's in front. You can go through the house." His accent is British. "Let me get my keys. I'll meet you out there."

No furniture in the living room, only a sleeping bag on the floor by the fireplace. There are books everywhere though, piles of them against the walls, some strewn about the room, others stacked along the hallway. She holds Cameron to her, feeling his hot little body, her attention focused on his labored breathing. She goes through the front door and gets into the Jeep.

Keys jingle, and moments later he comes out to the carport, pulling on a worn black leather jacket. He's even more stunning close up— tall, trim, his tight build obvious even under his dark flannel shirt and worn jeans. He gives her a quick, warm smile. His sculpted features and hint of stubble belie his baby face. He runs his hand through his soft dark hair. It falls to his shoulders and back in his striking green eyes. He glances at her, then Cameron as he gets behind the wheel, starts the engine, and they're on their way.

"The closest twenty-four hour medical facility I know is in South Corfu. It'll be quicker than trying to get to the city, and from what I've heard the staff there is good. How long has your son had a fever?"

"A few hours, I think. I tried to bring it down with Tylenol, but it didn't go down as much as I'd like. He's still very hot. I took his temperature before coming to you and it was 103." Panic washes over her again, and she can't hold back tears.

"Hey. Your son's going to be just fine. I don't think 103 is all that high for little kids. When did you give him the Tylenol?"

"About fifteen minutes before coming to you."

"Give the Tylenol a bit to take effect and he'll cool down." His accent is refined, his tone soft, reassuring. He holds the wheel with one huge hand at the top; his fingers wrap around it and back over his palm. His slender form is molded into the driver's seat as if car and driver are one. He navigates the narrow, winding road quickly and with ease. Pine trees are whipping around in the strong winds. Branches are flying everywhere, but he manages to miss hitting anything.

She unwraps Cameron's head and kisses his forehead, and he actually feels a little cooler. "I think the Tylenol is working. Feels like his fever is coming down." She clings to her child, pushing back her panic. "I don't know how to thank you."

"No problem."

"What's your name?"

"James."

"I'm Elisabeth. This is my son, Cameron."

"How old is he?"

"Thirteen months." She stares ahead, suddenly shamed to look at him. "I know it probably seems irresponsible of me bringing an infant out here to the middle of nowhere, alone. I did check the medical facilities on the island before renting my place. I figured if anything came up I could always get an ambulance from town if I really needed to. I didn't know I couldn't get a cell signal, or that the land line went out with every storm." She sighs heavily. Crisis averted. "I'm really grateful for your help. When I felt how hot he was, and the Tylenol wasn't working, and I couldn't call anyone for help..."

"Really, it's not a problem. I'm sure your son is going to be just fine."

They pull into the driveway of a pink, two-story building. Pink cloth banner attached to the upstairs railing announces Kérkyra Nótia MediGuard. All the lights are on when they go inside. A middle-aged, compact woman with short, white hair and piercing blue eyes wearing teal scrubs rises from behind a linoleum counter and immediately attends to them.

James speaks to her in Greek. The only word Elisabeth gets is Tylenol.

"What are you telling her?"

"Just what's going on."

The nurse speaks to James in Greek, then she picks up the phone and calls someone, says something quickly then hangs up. "Eláte me aftón ton trópo." She speaks to both of them.

James indicates for her to follow the nurse then he falls in step behind them.

The examination room is small but clean. It has two examining tables in it, and the nurse points to one while she gathers several forms from the plastic bins on the wall and puts them on a clipboard.

Elisabeth sits Cameron on the vinyl cushioned table. She holds him to her as he looks around the room, then fixes his sleepy gaze on James. Cameron suddenly flashes his adorably welcoming grin at him.

A wide smile forms on James' exquisite face as he stares back at her son. Cameron reaches his tiny hand out to James lingering in the doorway, but James stays where he is. Elisabeth releases a deep, shaky breath as she holds her son on the examining table. She strokes his forehead, which seems much cooler, and suddenly she feels silly that perhaps she's overreacted and doesn't really need to be here.

The nurse attends to Cameron, takes his temperature with a digital ear thermometer, unzips his sky blue onesie and listens to his small chest with a stethoscope, then checks his ears with one of those magnifying flashlights. She leaves the instrument with Cam as she steps away, fills in forms on the clipboard, has a quick exchange in Greek with James, hands him the clipboard and points where to write, then hands him a pen.

He looks at Elisabeth, pen in his left hand poised to write. "Cameron what? C,a,m,e,r,o,n, right?"

"Yes. Whitestone, spelled as it sounds." Cameron gets up on his pudgy legs and tries to stick the ear magnifier in Elisabeth's ear, but nearly puts it in her eye. "Stop that." She picks him up, takes the instrument from his tiny fingers, which apparently isn't the right thing to do because he starts fussing and whining and leaning, trying to get it back.

"Oh. Shh. Shh. Eivai Wpaia," the nurse says, startling Cameron into silence as she takes the instrument from Elisabeth.

She rocks her son gently and he actually snuggles into her, rests his head on her breasts and sticks his thumb in his mouth. Elisabeth watches James write. His fingers are very odd, unnaturally long, and very slender. He stops writing and looks down the hallway, watching someone approach.

"Hi. I'm Dr. Nikolaos Avgoustis." A tall, athletic, Mediterranean man in his late forties maybe, stands in the doorway, extending his hand to James.

"Hi." James shakes the doctor's hand. "Good to meet you."

"You must be the concerned father?" He glances in the room at Elisabeth and Cameron. He's olive skinned, clearly Greek, yet speaks perfect English with only the slightest swarthy middle-eastern accent.

"No. Just a friend." James doesn't offer his name.

"You must be the worried mother." The doctor addresses Elisabeth as he comes in. He gives her a wide, white smile and extends his hand. She shakes it, feeling the weight of worry dissipate.

"Elisabeth Whitestone. This is my son, Cameron. He's thirteen months. He had a fever of 103 earlier this evening. I gave him Tylenol, and I think it's coming down now." Cameron is snuggled in, the top of his head under her chin feels much cooler than it did earlier.

"Okay, then. Let's take a look, shall we?" He turns to his nurse and they exchanged some words in Greek, then he turns back to Elisabeth. "Put him on the table here, and I'll just take a quick look at him, okay?"

She peels him off her and puts her son back on the examination table, but he's not happy about it and his small, round face contorts into a frown as his eyes well. The doctor shows Cameron his stethoscope, diverting his fear into wonder. He holds the device to his own heart and let's Cam listen before reversing the roles. He examines her son, showing the child the instruments before using them, explaining what he's doing the entire time in simple, exaggerated language. She resists the urge to kiss that doctor right then.

"Okay. Looks like your son has influenza, or the flu as you Yanks call it." He flashes a teasing, white smile. "The inflammation in his throat is moderate, and his lungs are only slightly congested. I don't see any signs of an ear infection, but it often follows the flu so I'm going to give you some Amoxicillin, just in case. It's good to have around anyway." Doctor Nikolaos retrieves the clipboard from James and starts writing.

"What should I do if the fever returns?" Elisabeth picks up her son.

"Tylenol. And lots of it. Cradling him will comfort him. Half the cure is in the contact." Doctor smiles that charming grin again. "You have any more questions for me?"

"No. Thank you. You've been really great." She feels stupid now. "This is the first time Cameron's ever been sick, and we're so far from anywhere if he needed real care, and...well..."

"I'm assuming Cameron is your first child?" The doctor gives her a gentle, tired smile.

She nods, looks at James watching her.

"Ms Whitestone, Elisabeth, your son is just fine. He appears to be a healthy child who at the moment has the flu. Take him home, keep him as hydrated as possible—water or juice are fine, and all of you get some rest." Doctor Nikolaos glances at James. "I'm sure a good night's sleep will do you all some good."

The doctor retrieves a bottle of Amoxicillin from a white cabinet, hands it and several sample boxes of Children's Tylenol to Elisabeth. She pockets them with thanks. They follow the doctor back down the hall to the waiting area where he joins the nurse behind the front desk. Elisabeth and James thank them again and leave the clinic. No payment for service required. Health care in Greece is socially funded for all residents, permanent or not.

-

-

Chapter Four

-

Elisabeth swaddles Cameron in the woolen blanket, then secures him back in Jack's jacket, zipping it up to his chest. She buckles them both in for the ride back. Exhaustion sweeps over her with the gentle swaying of the Jeep. She can hardly keep her eyes open. James is focused on driving. He looks tired, darkness around his eyes she'd not noticed or wasn't there earlier. It's close to dawn. She's kept him up all night, and is feeling kind of bad about that. "I'm sorry for dragging you out of your house in the middle of the night. You must think I am just another over-reactive *mother*." She doesn't mean the last word with disdain. It just kind of comes out that way. She can't stand being solely characterized by her role as a mom with twenty plus years in the trenches.

"You're trying to do right by your son. No fault in that."

"Thank you, for all your help. Even if I'd gotten to the clinic, I would never have been able to talk to that nurse. I'm surprised you speak Greek. It's not exactly a common language."

"I've been studying it since I got to the island, about three months now. I have a pretty good ear for this sort of thing, though I'm still not very fluent. I missed half of what the nurse said and I'm not so sure what I said to her was accurate. I'm glad she got the message."

"Me, too. What brings you to Corfu?"

He doesn't answer. Elisabeth starts to think he isn't going to, but then he says, "Space. And I find I enjoy the pace. What about you?"

"Same thing, I guess. My husband, Jack, Cameron's father, was killed in a terrorist bombing in Israel a few months ago, and this seems a good place to preserve what's left of my sanity."

"I'm sorry." His square jaw tightens hollowing his cheeks. "And for your son's loss as well."

"Thank you." She holds Cameron tighter to her. "Are you a permanent resident of the island?"

"I'm not sure. Maybe. I like it here." The Jeep is drafty. Fine strands of his hair blow about. He runs his hand through it to tame it. "It's quiet, secluded and beautiful."

She stares at him. He really is magnificent. Classic profile, straight nose, full lips, ultra long lashes surrounding big, almond shaped eyes. *Wow.* Elisabeth looks back out the front windshield hoping he doesn't see her blush. "It is beautiful here, right out of a postcard. Can't stop taking pictures. I'm hoping to sell some to a stock house, but most of them will probably end up on Instagram with the rest of the travel blogs."

"I didn't realize that you were a fine photographer."

"I'm not. I'm a photojournalist." The way he phrased his statement irked her, and she remembers feeling the same when he'd originally answered his door this evening. "When I came to your house tonight you said that you knew who I was. How is that? I don't recall having ever met."

"I bought the house on the hill. It came with forty acres, which includes your house on the waterfront. The broker that manages the property ran your application by me."

"You own the house I'm renting?"

"Yeah."

"What did you find out about me?"

"Pretty much what you've already told me. Look, don't worry about it. Like you, I'm kind of hiding from the real world, too. Corfu is a good place for that, don't you think?" He smiles at her, this wide grin. She smiles back. He focuses back on the road. His smile fades but he seems relaxed, weaving the Jeep along the winding road. The rain has stopped and the wind calmed with the dawn. Sky is just beginning to get light.

"You must be very tired. I'm sorry I kept you up all night."

"You didn't. I don't sleep much anyway."

She's not quite sure what to say to that, but she gets the distinct impression she should not ask why. We'll be back at my place in a minute. I'd take you to yours, but I'd have to drop you off in the parking area, which is a longer hike to the bungalow than it is from my place." James pulls into his carport. "Sorry about this." He turns off the engine and looks at her.

"Don't be sorry. I'm so grateful you were here, *are* here. I can't thank you enough for your help tonight." Cameron starts to fuss. The top of his tiny head feels too warm again, and with his fever comes her fear.

"What's up?" James is fixed on her, like he's trying to read her.

"He's getting warm again." She kisses her son's head. "Think it's too soon to give him more Tylenol?"

"That's what the doctor recommended if his fever should return." James gets out of the jeep as Elisabeth loosens the blanket around her son, setting his small arms free. "Why don't you come inside and give him some Tylenol before you go," James gently suggests. "By the time you get home, his fever should be way down."

Elisabeth follows him into the house, Cam to her chest, still cradled in Jack's jacket. James leads her down the dusty hardwood hallway, past the unfurnished kitchen and into the furniture-free living room. A fire smolders in the fireplace, sparks of gold and red suck up the chimney. She retrieves a sample bottle of Tylenol from her jacket pocket.

"Me! Me!" Cameron yells, reaching out to grasp the bottle she's trying to uncap while holding it out of his reach.

"Little help?" James takes the Tylenol from her.

"NO! MINE!" Cameron wails, kicking and screaming for the bottle. James takes the plastic serving cup off and presses down on the childproof cap with his palm. A surprising grimace, as if responding to a sharp pain, and he retracts his hand quickly. He looks at Elisabeth meekly, like checking if she's noticed.

Elisabeth extends her hand towards James, visually requesting the Tylenol bottle back. Takes him a minute to respond, and again, Elisabeth wonders if he will, but then he puts the serving cup back on the bottle and hands it to her. Cameron launches for it. She holds him fast to her so he doesn't fall, and palms the bottle, but Cam keeps trying to get at it. "I can't open the childproof cap with him going at the bottle. Will you take him a minute, please?" She lifts Cameron from Jack's jacket, and out of the loosened papoose she'd made with the woolen blanket.

James hesitates only an instant before gingerly taking her son. Cameron is surprised, but not startled, his attention now focused on James instead of what his mama is doing. James brings Cam to his chest, his arm a bench for her son, one huge hand wrapped around Cameron's torso supporting his back.

It takes her son about two seconds to realize the ploy, and feel frustrated by the diversion. Cameron starts fussing for the dropper that Elisabeth is now filling with red liquid.

"Check this out, little buddy," James says to Cameron as he takes an iron poker leaning against the stone facade of the fireplace and stirs the embers alive. Cam is instantly captivated by the sparks rising in the flue. James sets the poker back against the stone and sits loosely cross-legged on the sleeping bag in front of the fireplace, letting Cameron stand safely inside his crossed legs. He holds her son at the waist with both hands, his long fingers practically meeting in front of Cam, keeping him from moving towards the rain of sparks. The sparks die down. Cameron settles, sits on James' leg and smooshes his face into James' soft shirt, sticks his thumb in his mouth, and sucks.

Crackle of charring wood is all that breaks the silence that follows Cameron's near tantrum. She stares at them. James looks at her and smiles as he gently rocks her son. She smiles back. Then she squeezes three drops of Tylenol into Cameron's mouth just to the side of his thumb, which he sucks incessantly. By the time she seals the cap back on the bottle, Cameron's asleep in James' arms. And at that moment she can't tell who is more beautiful, the man or the child.

"Thank you," she whispers.

He smiles but doesn't say anything. Elisabeth scans the titles of the books lying around. The range is extensive—from Dostoyevsky, to Machiavelli, to Michael Crichton. He has a lot of non-fiction too, from learning conversational Greek, to coping with loss, and dealing with anger. He seems so even-tempered. It's hard to believe he needs an education in anger management.

"What are you doing out here in the middle of nowhere? Do you just sit around and read all day?"

He smiles. "Pretty much. Right now anyway. I blow a lot of afternoons playing Tavli— Backgammon, with the old men who hang out at the cafés, but I haven't really integrated beyond that yet."

"Why are you here?"

"To get away from out there."

"What did you do 'out there' that you're trying to get away from?"

"It's not important."

"I see you running every morning. I've imagined all these crazy things about you. You know, make up stories about who you are, what you do. My best guess, I'd say a musician."

His eyes narrow. She feels him tense. "How do you know that?"

"Relax. It isn't rocket science, James, not with hands like yours."

"Well, I'm not a musician anymore." He looks down at Cameron. "Anyway, I can walk you down the hill now if you'd like."

That's her cue the conversation is over and it's time for her to leave. "That's okay. I'm sure you're tired. You've been very kind. I can manage from here. Thanks."

He gets on his knees, and gently hands her back her sleeping child, then strokes the hair out of Cameron's eyes. "He feels much cooler now. Perhaps the fever has broken." He looks at her, stares actually. A gentle smile spreads across his face. "He's going to be just fine, 'Lisabeth."

And she believes him. A warm wave of tired sweeps through her. She gently wraps her son in the woollen blanket, then zips him in Jack's jacket against her. She thanks James again. He bows ever so slightly, in the Asian fashion, but doesn't say anything. There is an awkward moment of silence, then Elisabeth turns away, and leaves.

-

-

Chapter Five

-

Heavy, labored breathing wakes her. She'd fallen asleep on the patio after putting Cameron down when they got back. Elisabeth opens her eyes to see James turning away from the three foot gate at the patio step.

She sits up, smiles. "Hi," she says, happily surprised.

James turns back to the gate. "Hi. Sorry I woke you. Just stopped by to see how Cameron's doing." He rests his hands on top of the gate, his long fingers fold over the wooden fencing, like spiders perched on the rim.

"I was hoping to see you this morning." Elisabeth gets up and goes to the gate. "Cam's much better, thanks. Sleeping. Has been since we got back. Thank you again, for everything. Would love to make you breakfast, show my appreciation."

"Not necessary. I'm glad to hear Cameron's doing better." He drops his hand from the gate. His long sleeve white shirt is unbuttoned all the way and hangs open, but clings to his sweat soaked chest, shoulders and arms. His face, neck, and slender, swimmer's torso glisten. Sweat even blackens the waistband of his dark gray sweatpants. What an odd choice of apparel to run in. *Hot.*

"Hang on. I'll be right back." Elisabeth goes inside to the kitchen, grabs a bottled water from the fridge and comes back out and extends it to him.

He smiles. "Thank you." He takes the water, drinks nearly all of it and sighs when he finishes. She smiles. He laughs. "It's good. Really good. Thanks."

"You're welcome." She studies him. "Can I ask you something?"

"I guess." But he doesn't seem he likes the idea.

"Why are you running in sweats and a long sleeve shirt in eighty degree heat?"

169

He grins. "I like to sweat." Then he gulps the last of the water, caps it and hands it back to her. "Thank you. I should be off."

She takes the plastic bottle. He seems to hold on a beat too long, and in that instant she feels his intensity, like a static shock, and gasps. He smiles, lets go. And it's gone. Then he bows ever so slightly and turns away, disappears into a grove of pines that canopies the trail at the base of the hill.

She pictures his soft chestnut hair falling into his striking green eyes and framing his stunning face; his flat belly, the gentle curve of his abs; his sweatpants hanging on his hips just right—

A sudden, choking wave of overwhelming guilt.

Jack. Damn you. I need you Jack. I miss you. I hate you for leaving me alone.

Elisabeth sits back down on the bench, stares out at the small waves crashing on the shore. The beach is empty as far as she can see.

"Damn you, Jack." She says aloud to no one, no one at all, and the tears come again.

-

-

Chapter Six

-

Cameron sleeps a good portion of the day, and there is no fever when she puts him in his crib for the evening. He wakes her several times throughout the night crying to be fed, and suckles her greedily. Though he wakes late, he seems back to normal the next morning, even eats half a bowl of Cheerios after breastfeeding. Elisabeth brings him out to the porch to play while she reads *The New York*

Times and savors her one cup of coffee for the day.

She sees James coming back from his run along the shoreline. She envies him his discipline. He slows to a walk and looks over at her then crosses the sand towards the house. Dark gray sweatpants hang on his hips, and are soaked around the waistband from the sweat dripping down his torso. His white shirt is unbuttoned and hangs open but clings to his wet shoulders. It's hard not to stare in awe.

"Hi." He's still breathless.

"Hi."

"Want to see something very cool?" Wide smile spreads across his face.

"Sure."

"Come on."

She picks up Cameron and follows him up the hill towards his house. About a quarter of the way up the cliff she notices them. Monarch butterflies. They're everywhere. They swirl through the knurled pines and swarm together in the leaves of the Eucalyptus.

"Oh wow…" Elisabeth is awestruck. Cameron bounds after them, and she feels his sense of wonder. "This is amazing."

"Isn't it? I saw them on my way to go running this morning. They're incredible, aren't they?" James stares at them wide-eyed, smiling. His expression is the same as Cameron's as he watches the ebb and flow of butterflies. His sculpted face sharpens against the background of fluttering color, and for a second she's lost in him, in his amazement.

"Oh God, I don't have my camera." She thinks of running home to get it, then Cameron goes chasing after the swarm as they take off down the hill. She races after him, James follows, and they all gather where the path meets the sand, and monarchs surround them.

Cameron grabs at them, though they're impossibly out of his reach.

James laughs. "This is wild." His smile is as infectious as her son's.

Butterflies rise from the trees and brush, flutter above them—orange and zebra black pulse against the clear blue sky. Then Cameron releases his high pitch shriek of frustration and suddenly they scatter, fly every which way then seem to disappear. The three of them stand breathlessly looking around, but only a few remain fluttering about.

Cam follows a lone butterfly towards the house, forgets about it as it flies behind the pines, instead he climbs up the one patio step, toddles to retrieves his toy on the deck, then scrambles back down the step to meet Elisabeth and James approaching on the sand. "Muki." He holds up his stuffed monkey for James to see and admire.

"Good to meet you, sir." James greets the monkey, bows slightly, shakes the monkey's paw.

"Come. Come. Come." Cameron repeats endlessly, takes James by the hand and tries to lead him to the patio.

James hesitated and looks at her.

"Just gonna make some breakfast. Please join us."

Cameron still pulls his hand. "Come. Come. Come…"

He looks around, then back at her and smiles. "Yeah. Okay. Thanks." James lets Cameron lead him onto the patio after patiently waiting for her son to navigate the patio step.

Elisabeth locks the back gate as Cameron leads James to his play area and plops down on the deck. James kneels beside him. Cam introduces his dump truck, cars and airplanes one by one. James examines and admired each.

"He can do this all morning, ya know." She feels a need to warn him.

"That's okay." He picks up a miniature Red Baron type biplane in the long row of toys Cameron has laid out, and sits on the lounge chair behind him. The plane looked big when Cameron held it. But in James' hand it seems tiny. "Look at this thing." He holds it out so it sits in his huge open hand. "It's a work of art. Solid metal. Movable parts." He lifts it and spins the wheels with a flick of his long, elegant finger. "And a damn accurate model of the real thing. It's beautiful. Isn't it? I'm a big fan of craftsmanship."

"Mine!" Cameron grabs the plane out of James' hand. James startles, a quick jerk back, barely perceptible, then he holds his hands up in surrender and smiles. She doesn't.

"Cameron, don't grab. *Ask*." She practically yells, then feels stupid, blushes, and avoids eye contact with James. Her son ignores her, in favor of putting his plane back in his line of collected objects. "You know, I was ready for the sleepless nights, the care and feeding, the continual concern with parenting. But the real shocker is the endless list of rules we live by, and the need to constantly impart them."

"I've never been big into rules." He shrugs, and flashes her a casual smile.

"A part of growing up you never mastered?" Elisabeth teases.

His smile broadens. "Something like that." He stays fixed on her until Cameron shoves a Hotwheels Formula racer in his hand. James startles, though, again, it's barely perceptible. "What's ya got here, little dude..." He affects a casual demeanor but seems edgy as he holds the racer in his palm and examines the car carefully.

Cameron stands at his knees, gazing up at it. Both their faces sharpen and the background blurs and Elisabeth has the urge to get her camera then thinks better of it. She snaps the image in her head and holds it to memory, watches them for a minute more then heads inside.

"I'm going to start breakfast. Are scrambled eggs okay?"

"Sounds good." James sits on the end of the canvas lounge chair and waits for Cameron to show off another toy.

Elisabeth goes inside and makes enough eggs for all of them, grills some bacon, and toasts two thick slices of sourdough. She keeps expecting James to get bored with Cameron's antics and come in, but when he doesn't, she finally looks out the kitchen window over the sink as Cameron crawls onto the lounge and lays next to James seemingly asleep on it. By the time she finishes the eggs and bacon, and comes out to announce breakfast is ready, she's not surprised to find Cameron curled against James, and both are sound asleep.

James lay on his side, his head resting on one arm, his other arm lay casually over Cameron, his huge hand covering her son's entire torso. Again, it strikes her how beautiful they both are. She can't help herself. She goes inside, gets her Nikon, comes back out and starts shooting.

They're like a work of art. *Click.* Father and child, there's nothing to tell they're not—the fine, thick, wavy hair, sculpted baby faces. Cameron looks angelic, like a cherub. James is spectacular in sleep, his square jaw relaxed, taking the sharp hallow from his cheeks, the full lips slightly parted. *Click.*

She burns through the first roll of film and is on her second, focusing on James' enormous hand over Cameron, made to look even larger with his shirtsleeve scrunched back, when she notices. Elisabeth kneels next to the lounge chair and examines his exposed wrist. James stirs and she freezes, holds her breath. He shifts slightly but stays sleeping. A jagged cut extending up his forearm is in the process of healing. She shudders, moves back quietly, lifts the camera from around her neck, and focuses on the scar. *Click.* What happened that would make him want to take his own life? He's so *young*, beautiful, probably well educated, obviously wealthy. *Click.* Why would someone with all he has want to die? She burns another roll and is on her third when he wakes to her lens in his face.

"What are you doing?" He slowly gauges what's happening, sits up gently and settles Cameron on the lounge as he moves off of it and stands. "Give me the camera."

"Why? You two were perfect. Like an Annie Lebowitz portrait. It was beautiful. I couldn't help myself. Please forgive me."

He walks over to her, takes the camera out of her hand casually and examines it, then opens it and pulls out the film.

She can't believe it. "Why did you do that? You have no right."

"Did you shoot any other rolls of me?"

"Why? What difference does it make? I'm not going to publish them. The pictures are for my personal collection, chronicling Cameron, that's all. You have no right to destroy them."

"And you have no right to take my picture without my permission."

"Well, actually, I have every right to take your picture without your permission, especially if you *are* famous. Do you really need the first amendment speech?" Her heart is pumping hard and fast.

"Where is the rest of the film you shot?"

"You just wrecked it. God, what is the big deal, James? I just took a few shots. No one besides me, and maybe my mother would have seen them. May I have my camera back now please?"

He stares at her, then runs his fingers through his hair and sighs. "You're right. I'm overreacting. Sorry." He hands her back her camera and the exposed roll of film and turns away, walks to the railing and looks out at the sea.

"What is going on? Who are you? What are you so afraid of?"

"Everything." He whispers it, but she's sure she heard him. "Nothing."

"Right." She studies him. "There are only two types of people I've encountered that are afraid of me shooting them. The superstitious, who believe that capturing their image on film is somehow damning them to death, and those who don't want to be seen, people who are hiding from someone or something they think can harm them. And you don't strike me as the superstitious type." For the first time since they'd met she feels afraid of him. "Why are you hiding here on this island?" Visions of him being a terrorist, or a mercenary flash through her mind, and she's suddenly very afraid for her son.

James turns back to her, leans against the railing and stares at her, then shakes his head. "Look, I'm just really tired, and you surprised me."

She glares at him. "Who are you?"

"James Matthew Pierce. And I'm nobody."

"I'm finding that a little hard to believe."

"Have I given you cause to fear me?"

Yes. "No." *No?* "Yes."

He laughs.

"Well, not really, I guess. Except for the camera thing. What's up with that?"

"Nothing." He laughs again, shakes his head. "You startled me. And I'm wound a bit tight these days. Sorry."

She stares at him imagining all kinds of horrors he could be, but with that tousled hair, those bedroom eyes, that baby face, she has to remind herself to feel afraid of him. And she really can't fault him for his reaction. Somewhere in the recesses of her early learning, before *'just get the shot,'* she knows it's not exactly on the moral side of *right* to take his picture without asking first.

Cameron stirs on the lounge chair, and Elisabeth goes and picks him up. He snuggles his face into her neck and she melts into his warmth. James watches them. She looks over at him and he looks away.

"I'm gonna take off, go home, take siesta." He gives her a quick smile and pushes away from the wood railing.

"I made breakfast—scrambled eggs and bacon. You're still welcome to join us. I'm really sorry about the pictures—"

"It's not that. Really. And I owe you an apology for wrecking your film. I was out of line. I'm just more tired than hungry right now. Sorry." He stares at her, studies her. "Enjoy the rest of the day." He glances at Cam, her son's face snuggled between her breasts then he turns away, leaves the deck, and crosses the graveled sand to the tree shrouded path.

"Bye. And thanks for the butterflies." She watches him wave without looking back and then disappear in the grove at the base of the hill. She holds Cameron to her, his warm body pressing into hers, and is mystified by the suffocating loneliness filling her chest and closing her throat.

You've left me alone Jack, to raise your child on my own. *Alone! And I hate alone. And I hate you. Do you hear me? I hate you, Jack! You always left me alone.*

She goes inside and takes the exposed rolls of film she'd shot out of her jacket pocket and drops them in her underwear drawer. Served James right after he wrecked the roll in the camera. Ironically, she knows in the future she'll be teaching Cameron to take the moral high ground. A pang of guilt. She probably should have modeled this behavior and given James these other rolls of film when he asked.

-

-

Chapter Seven

-

It's close to midnight when she closes the photo album. Elisabeth gets a cold beer, goes out to the patio and stares out at the calm black sea. It glimmers as it reflects the blanket of stars. And something else. Small waves breaking on the shore are *glowing*. Phosphorescent green. She's seen this once before, on a night crossing to Catalina with her father. Phosphorescent Sea he'd called it. Certain plankton emit light when disturbed in the water. Like a million microscopic fireflies, they light up with motion.

She has to get a closer look. Might be able to get some interesting shots. Digital won't pick anything up. Not enough light. Must have an old roll of 300 Kodachrome floating around the bottom of her camera bag. Still need a tripod though. She goes back inside, finds the film and gets the equipment she needs, then checks on Cameron asleep in his crib, and goes down to the shoreline. If he starts to cry she'll be able to hear him from quite a distance in the warm, still night.

The sea is even more amazing close up. She can see fish dart about, fully illuminated in the night water from the phosphorescent plankton lighting up around them. Long thin waves make a pattern of glowing lines along the shore. Elisabeth sets the tripod in the sand and mounts the Nikon. It'll be hard to capture the scene. Phosphorous light is bright aquamarine, but shines only briefly and never in the same place. She focuses on an radiant wave crest, then waits for it to strike the water and light it up.

Wait…Wait...

Click.

No way. Film speed is too slow, and the light too low to get anything but blur, even with the moon rising. She looks back up at the house and listens for Cameron's cry, but hears only the chirp of crickets. Small waves lapping the shore sound like footsteps in the sand. She looks around, up the dark, deserted beach then scans the hillside up to James' house. A light is on. She pictures him sitting cross-legged on his sleeping bag in front of the fireplace, reading, his slender form arched over his book. Then she recalls him with the butterflies—his expression of childlike wonder, so similar to her son's. Elisabeth smiles. She flashes on him through the lens that first time she saw him on the beach. *Click.* Too bad she'd missed it.

She wades in the shallows. Phosphorous illuminates her ankles and her feet as she moves through the water, trailing liquid green light. Jack would have loved this. Natural beauty turned him on. Some of their best times together were spent storm chasing. Their second or third date they spent photographing lightning over L.A. up top Blue Jay Way till 3:00 a.m. They spent their fifth anniversary covering Tornado Alley, barely escaping with their lives, but two others in their crew of eight did not. Elisabeth flashes on Jack's hazel eyes, his rust-colored hair blowing wildly around his stubbled face. He's yelling something at her, and laughing, then turns away, holds up his cellphone and starts filming a spinning black mass looming in the distance.

She moves through the shallow shoreline remembering, kicking, splashing and lighting up the sea. Droplets of phosphorus glitter around her. She laughs. *God, Jack, you would have loved this!* Elisabeth kicks harder, splashes harder, then harder—kicking, then slapping, then slugging at the water. *Jack! Damn it. Damn you, God!*

"I hate you, God! Do you hear me? I hate you for taking him away from us!" Then she looks up and sees him through her tears.

"Hi." James stands on the beach watching her.

"Hi." She feels awkward as she comes out of the water, her jeans and tee-shirt soaking wet and clinging. She stops within a few feet, facing him.

He looks away, surveys the scene. He has on a dark, long sleeve shirt haphazardly tucked into blue jeans that hang loosely on his hips. "Beautiful night. Spectacular sea."

She looks back at the water. "It is."

"How's Cameron?"

"Good. All better I think."

"Good." He moves beside her and looks out at the waves. "How are you?"

She gives him a quick smile, then sticks her tongue out, then quickly closes her mouth and swallows back the tears. "Have you ever lost anyone you've loved, James?"

"Yes." He takes his hands from his pockets, balls them into fists and tucks them under his arms. The change in his demeanor is palpable.

"Well, since Jack was killed, I've been having this war with The Almighty, or myself, I'm not really sure which. I need to believe now more than ever, but I find myself hating God."

"I've got a similar issue with anger towards entropy."

"What?"

"Forget it. Look, what I mean is, sometimes events in life won't always have a reason. Sometimes shit just happens." He looks at her, gives her a gentle smile. "Maybe you're trying to make sense of the senseless. Perhaps that's your real war."

"Maybe, but I just want to know why *now*, right after Cameron is born, and Jack had finally agreed to move back to the States. He was only thirty-two. I mean, what is the master plan here? Because I have a bone to pick with the Master."

"Sorry. I can't help you. Don't believe in a Master, or a master plan." He practically whispers as if not to disrupt the night.

"Do you really believe that everything is just random chance, that there is no higher order, no rhyme nor reason to anything?"

"Yeah. Pretty much. It's all just chaos. Random occurrences colliding with varying results, with respect to the laws of physics, which we've only minimally identified—like cause and effect, of course..."

She laughs, even though she knows he doesn't mean to be funny. "I think I get your general drift." Elisabeth looks back out at the glimmering sea, considering his perspective. She's known so few true atheists. Most everyone was affiliated with *some* religion, or at least a belief in *some* higher power. She glances at him, staring at the phosphorous sea. He stands with his hands in his jeans pockets. His dark, maybe flannel long sleeve shirt covers his arms and bunches at the pockets around the base of his palms, covering his wrists, the pockets hiding his hands. Elisabeth flashes on his cut up arms. "Some would say your perspective is rather...reckless. Without God, or a higher order, what gives your life meaning, or any purpose, any reason to stay living, especially in dark times?"

"I do—or don't, as the case may be." He states it as if it's obvious, without rancour or anger.

She looks back out towards the sea, lost for a reasoned comeback, or a wise, or emphatic response to his attempted suicide, especially since she isn't suppose to know.

"Does your belief provide you solace?" James inquires softly.

"It does...sometimes anyway. I struggle with believing in God, but I do believe there is a higher order. When I look out there, at this magnificent scene, I see design, and I'm humbled by the designer."

He nods, then looks back at the sea. The intimacy of their discussion strikes her as odd. Religion, even spirituality are generally taboo, often even with close friends and family. Jack wouldn't talk about it. He'd adopted his parent's vague sense of Christianity, and had no interest in discussing it further. She could never have had this conversation with Jack.

"Sometimes—at times like this, anyway, I wish I didn't believe. I wouldn't be wasting all this energy searching for a reason."

He laughs. "Yeah. Atheism is efficient that way. But I envy your faith. You're never alone, or without purpose."

Funny. She sure feels alone most days, these days, and most nights, when she wakes up at 3:30 in the morning aching for Jack to be laying next to her. They're quiet for some time, but it isn't awkward. Crickets fill the night with songs, and the repeating rush of water lapping on the shore sets an even rhythm.

James points to the camera mounted on the tripod. "Get anything?"

"No. Not enough light."

"Too bad. It really is extraordinary out here tonight. Did you develop the rolls from this morning of Cameron and me?"

Son of a bitch. She flushes. *He knows about the other rolls of film.* "I haven't set up a darkroom yet, so I'm not developing anything right now." She smiles at him.

He stays fixed on the sea. Doesn't, or won't look at her.

Now the silence between them *is* awkward. Should she apologize and offer the other rolls she shot? Elisabeth feels anxious, small, and then overwhelmingly tired. "Well, it's late. I think I'll head in for the night." She goes to the tripod and takes the camera off, then lifts the unit out of the sand and collapses it.

James watches her. "Need a hand?"

"No thanks. I've got it." She fixes her eyes on his for a moment until her guilt forces her to turn away. "Well, goodnight then."

"Goodnight."

Elisabeth walks back up to the house. She does not look back.

-

-

Chapter Eight

-

Several days pass in a blur. Elisabeth and Cameron keep to their routine—play on the beach, shop, cook, take a bus from town to various island attractions, laze in the warm afternoons, nap, read. She does not see James running in the mornings. She obsesses over why. She doesn't see him at the Friday morning street market in town either. *Was he avoiding her?* He knows she lied to him about the film. If she were him—she wouldn't trust her. She should just give him the stupid film. Go up to his house, hand it to him, and leave.

Around two, after lunch of spiral pasta salad, she and Cameron hike up the hill. Takes them twenty long minutes, but her big kid makes it all the way to James' house without having to be picked up once. Not bad for fourteen months. He's strong, just like his daddy. She picks him up before she knocks.

James doesn't answer so she looks through the window. She sees him, or someone, snuggled in the sleeping bag. She knocks again.

Cameron knocks too, but hurts his hand and his lower lip comes out. Elisabeth grabs his hand and kisses it, then sucks his knuckles. He laughs. So does she.

James opens the door, catching their exchange and smiles. "Hey. What's up? Come in." He leaves the door open, turns around unsteadily, goes back over to his sleeping bag and crawls back inside it.

She follows him inside and sets Cameron down, then moves to James.

Cameron giggles and toddles after his mama. He must think James is playing hide-and-seek, because he yanks back the sleeping bag and laughs.

James stays curled in the fetal position, doesn't startle, or react at all. Elisabeth kneels next to him. He's soaking wet. His dark, long-sleeve shirt, the one he was wearing several days ago, clings to him. His hair is matted to his face, and to the wet sleeping bag underneath him. His forehead is hot to the touch.

He blinks at her, and then at Cameron who stands bent over him, three inches from his face, still playing. James smiles back up at him, this wonderfully amused grin.

"So, what's going on?" His smile fades as he sits up and pulls the sleeping bag around his shoulders. Except for his rosy cheeks, most of the color drains from his face and it looks like he may pass out. His eyes narrow and focus hard on her. "What are you doing here?"

"I'm not exactly sure, now." She reaches in her jacket pocket and hands him the two rolls of film. "I came here to give you these."

He stares down at her hand, smiles, but doesn't reach for the small canisters. "Why don't you hang on to them, for your chronicle. Isn't that what you said you wanted them for?"

Cameron grabs the rubber film canister, plops down and examines it.

"Don't grab, Cameron. *Ask*."

He ignores her.

James laughs, gets up slowly and stands with his hands on his hips looking down.

"Are you okay?"

"Yeah. I'm really thirsty." He goes to the kitchen.

Elisabeth follows him in. "Have you been sick this whole time?"

He opens the fridge and takes out the only thing in it—a half full plastic container of bottled water, and drinks nearly all of it. "I guess. Whatever's going around got to me, too."

"You probably got sick from Cameron. I'm really sorry—"

"Could have picked it up from anywhere. I'm OK. It's just the flu. I'll get over it." He doesn't look okay. His eyes scare her the most. They're surrounded by black, like day old eyeliner. He leans against the tile counter top, holds the remaining bottled water to his forehead and closes his eyes. His face has regained color and is now almost crimson.

Cameron toddles in and starts opening cabinets, searching for hidden treasures. There's no food, no pots or pans. Every cabinet is empty. "Have you eaten anything in the past few days?"

"I haven't been very hungry." He runs his fingers through his hair, pulling it back off his face. Only a few wet strands fall back down, the rest stay matted in place.

"You haven't eaten *anything*? Are you crazy? You trying to starve to death?" Again she flashes on his cut up forearms.

"I just didn't think about it." He shoots her furrowed brows, like he gets her inference. "I don't have any food here and I didn't feel up to going into town and getting any." He slides down to the floor, sits with his knees to his chest, his back against the cabinet. Cameron comes over to him to investigate the bottled water in his hand. "How ya doing, sir?" He finishes it with one last gulp, then hands the empty, cap-less plastic bottle to Cameron. "You escort your mama home, my man. And take good care of her, okay? We don't want her getting sick, too."

"I'm pretty sure mom's have a natural immunity to this sort of thing. Do you have a fever?"

"I don't know. Maybe."

"Do you have any aspirin or any medication in the house?"

"No, but I'll be fine. I just need to sleep."

"You need more than that. Come down the hill to my house. I'll make you some soup, maybe some toast. You can have some tea, a glass of juice, and aspirin. And you can sleep on my couch, which is a hell of a lot warmer than this floor, and more comfortable, too."

He stares at her. "As much as I'd like to take you up on your generous offer, the thing is, I'm probably not the best person to be hanging out with right now."

"If you stay up here another few days like this, the point will be moot."

He shoots her a defiant grin.

"James, what's going on? What kind of trouble are you in?" Snapshots of car bombings flash in her head. She kneels and opens her arms to Cameron. He rushes into her and she sits back with his force, holds him in her lap and kisses the top of his head. James watches them, but when she looks over at him, he looks away.

"I had some trouble in the UK a while back."

"What kind of trouble?"

He studies her again. "I was set up for dealing drugs. I wasn't dealing. I wasn't even using. I was set up. I swear to you 'Lisbeth, I'm telling the truth. I don't use drugs now. Don't even drink alcohol, not anymore anyway."

She holds Cameron, and stays fixed on James. His arms rest on his knees, his long, elegant fingers are loosely laced in front of him. His hair is tousled around his now rather gaunt, stubbled face, and scattered in his eyes. A drug dealer? *No.* He said he wasn't. He doesn't look like a drug dealer. He isn't like those guys she'd met when she covered the Miami gang riots. James doesn't have that blunt edge. His confession is somewhat relieving, though. Even if he was/is a dealer, they generally aren't religious fanatics, or psychotics. The odds are against him being dangerous.

She strokes Cameron's fine hair. He lays his head on her leg and snuggles in. James drops his arms to his sides, spreads his hands on the floor. He looks like a kid carrying a macabre secret. "What are you so afraid of? What are you hiding here from?"

He just stares at her and she thinks he may not answer. "Myself. But I'm doing a damn poor job of it."

She smiles. "I know what you mean. But you know what I meant. Are there people pursuing you? Who, exactly, are you hiding from?"

"I'm not sure at this point." He shrugs, flashes a bewildered grin. "A few months ago I left Scotland rather abruptly, and not exactly legally. I disappeared off the face of the Earth so I'd never have to go back there. I changed my name, bought property, established a residence here because it's secluded, out of the mainstream. Safe."

"As if there were such a thing…"

He laughs. "Touche. I thought when I got here I'd be okay—I wouldn't feel so on edge all the time." His expression hardens with the clinching of his jaw and hallowing of his cheeks. "But it hasn't exactly turned out that way." Tiny pools of liquid emerald peer at her through long, wet lashes, accentuated by his black-rimmed eyes.

"You really are afraid, aren't you?"

"Yes." He looks away.

"Of what?"

"Getting hurt again."

"I would say that goes for just about all of us, James."

He stares at her, chuckles, then leans his head back against the cabinet and closes his eyes. "Not a whole hell of a lot of people know I'm here," James begins, but does not continue. They both listen to Cameron pressing his small hands into the bottle to illicit the crackling noise of bending plastic. James straightens his head, and opens his eyes on Elisabeth. "Those who do know I'm here, the people I interact with on this island, don't care who I am or where I come from, and I'm looking to keep it this way. I need to hear from you that you are prepared to protect my anonymity. If you feel a need to notify authorities, or pick up a news story, at least give me a head start."

"Believe it or not, I'm more concerned about your future than your past right now, James. Drug dealer or not—"

"I'm not."

"Well, either way, I don't think you're dangerous. To anyone but yourself." She catches the flicker of humor in his eyes. "Come down to our house, have some food and a good night's sleep. No one will know. I've got no one to tell." She tries to convey a relaxed demeanor with her promise, even though she feels rather panicked about getting him off the ground and down the hill. He just stares at her, like he's measuring the truth of her words. She needs something more powerful to motivate him to move. "There are easier ways to kill yourself then starving to death, James." She flashes a sardonic grin, then looks down at her son lying in her lap as she gently rubs his back. A silent prayer to anyone or anything listening loops repeatedly in her head.

Please, please, please, don't ever let my son want to end his life.

-

-

Chapter Nine

-

JAMES

She knows. No. She'd say it straight out. Or maybe not. She couldn't know. I've been careful not to let anyone see my arms.

Cameron is mesmerized by her constant stroking. Looks like it feels nice. I stare at mother and child, and am suddenly struck by a deep longing for intimate touch.

I had to tell her the truth. She'd looked at me as if I'm quite possibly a monster before I told her. So I had to tell her. Not sure she believes me, but I'm damn lucky she feels more sorry for me than afraid of me.

Fucking flu. I'm so tired. My body hurts, the floor *is* cold, and hard. Hot food and a soft couch sounds great. But I hesitate. "I've been on this island three months. No one's come after me yet, and it's somewhat unlikely they will with the name I'm using. That being said, I cannot guarantee your safety when you're with me. Do you understand?"

"You must be kidding me. My husband was blown to bits getting a goddamn pizza. There are no guarantees in life, James." She stares at me like I'm an idiot. "You need to eat something. *Now*. And aspirin, and then sleep." She stands, bringing Cameron with her to her hip. "Come on. Get up. Let's go."

They both stare down at me expectantly. They look remarkably alike, the same round face, the same pouty lips, the same huge hazel eyes. Their only difference is their hair. Cameron's is straight, strawberry-blond and ultra-fine. Elisabeth's thick auburn waves cascade over her shoulders and extend almost to the small of her back.

I don't have the energy to argue with her. She's given me a command, as if talking to her son, and I'm obliged to obey. Truth is, I want to. Maybe it's the haze of the fever, but I don't feel afraid of her anymore. Quite the opposite. I'm scared of her leaving, of dying alone in this kitchen. If she leaves, I'm pretty sure I will let myself starve to death. I could. It would be so easy.

You ready for nothing*, forever?*

Elisabeth watches me intently, as if she's trying to get inside my head, until Cameron yanks her hair, already impatient with my delay.

I sit on the floor trying to figure out how to get up. Standing on my own is out of the question. Then her hand is in front of me, and I take it. Somehow she manages to help me up off the floor while holding Cameron on her hip. I have to lean against the counter to stay standing.

"Can you make it?"

"Yeah." *Maybe.* "Let's go." I follow them down the hill. The sun is setting, a perfect orange ball sinking into indigo. Long shadows create giants of the dwarf pines. Time stretches and slows. Feels like I'm on acid, flashing back on my surreal experience with Ian's little joke at our father's inaugural bash all those years ago. Hillside is red—blood soaked earth. It's hot, or I am, or both. My stomach churns and stinging bile rises in my throat, hot and fast. I swallow it back.

I make it down the cliff without throwing up, passing out or falling. But five steps into their living room and I have to sit down. Sink onto the couch in front of the fireplace, lean my head back and close my eyes...

"James."

I hear her, but can't see her. *What's happening? Where am I?* I can't move, paralyzed with fear.

"James. Wake up."

Open my eyes, blink Elisabeth into focus. She's standing in front of me, and handing me a thermometer.

"Put this under your tongue until it beeps." She stares at me with a furrowed brow, a concerned look on her face.

"You okay?"

I smile at her to break the tension while trying to control my trembling. "Yeah." I stick the thermometer in my mouth.

"Yeah!" mimics Cameron. He stands at my knees staring at the thermometer. His expression is filled with the purest of amusement—curiosity. Can't help smiling at him. He puts his pudgy hands on my knee and the couch and tries to crawl up to me, but Elisabeth grabs him.

"Oh no, little munchkin. You've already infected him once." She cradles him in her arms. "And I don't want you sick again, either." Then she smooshes her face into his torso and blows on his belly. They laugh. And her laughter fills the room with lightness.

The thermometer beeps. I take it out of my mouth and she takes it out of my hand before I have a chance to look at it.

"104.2," she says, shaking her head. "Shit. You need to bring that down. Like *now*. Come in the kitchen, have something to eat. Line your stomach before taking meds. It will work better, last longer, and won't eat a hole in your stomach lining." She holds Cameron on her hip, his tiny arm wrapped around her neck. They stare down at me.

"Yeah. Okay." I stand. The scene recedes with what feels like the blood draining from my head. My vision tunnels. To avoid passing out, I stare at my feet, and will them to follow her into the kitchen. She puts Cameron in his highchair and points to one of the two chairs for me to sit. I collapse onto the chair as she sets a bowl of steaming chowder in front of me. Cameron's tray is full of small bits of things that vaguely look like food. He's using something, a carrot, maybe, as a crayon. Elisabeth prepares a bowl for herself and sits between Cameron and me at the small linoleum table.

By her grace, during the meal she does not question me. The soup is rich, and almost sweet, a perfect blend of salty clams and milk sugars. I take small sips and have to focus on swallowing to get it to happen. Elisabeth shares tales of her husband, Jack, of their friendship since childhood, of their adventures as journalists traveling the world together, with the occasional interruption to attend to her son. After dinner, she leads me back in the living room, and requests that I light a fire to warm the space while she settles Cameron with a quick bedtime story, and gets me some medicine.

I construct a pyramid of newspaper balls and split pine logs, then retrieve a blue-tipped match from a box on the bookshelf and strike it against the stone flue. I ignite the *New York Times*, all the while listening through the thin wall to her reading *One Fish, Two Fish* to her son. Finally sit on the couch, virtually spent. Hear her bid him good night, and the door to his room creak shut. She pads down the hall to the bathroom. I hear the click of the metal cabinet open, then the spilling of pills, then shut.

Elisabeth returns to the living room, and hands me two pills and a glass of water. "Take these," she says.

I flash on the cup of pills that first day at Priory Manor they expected me to take. And I did, knowing resistance was futile, all the while thinking I'd spend a week there relaxing on their meds, maybe even get some writing done, until I got phone privileges, and had a chance to call for help. I resist the urge to bat the pills out of her hand, say "Thanks," instead as I take them and the glass, and down the medication, which I assume is aspirin.

Elisabeth sits on the other end of the couch and stares at the fire. She's quite beautiful in the firelight, the orange glow haloing her graceful profile, bringing forward the rich brown in her hazel eyes. Light dances across her soft features, illuminating her long neck, the curve of her swollen breasts.

"I told you that I'd known Jack since childhood," she begins softly. "Though it was actually since infancy. Our mothers were neighbors and best friends years before Jack and I were born." She continues her reminiscing from dinner earlier. Her voice is soft, sultry, lots of resonance. I enjoy listening to her ramble. "Since we grew up together, played together in the crib forward, our friendship bonded without preconceived notions, like adult relationships always have to contend with. We've been, well...we *were* best friends, for as long as I can remember—from the playpen to Cameron."

"Sounds nice, having someone to share your life with."

"Well, it was, and it wasn't. It was always Jack and Beth, like one word or something. Everyone assumed we'd end up married, it was expected really, so we did, as a matter of course." She pauses. "And though I truly loved him for all those years we were together, there was something missing for me. For the longest time I assumed it was my failing, never considering what I was searching to bring out in Jack—he never actually possessed." She pauses again, still stares at the fire.

I feel her tension as she waits for my response, but I can think of none.

"Would you like to know what Jack was missing?"

"Okay." But now I'm thinking I don't want to go down the path she's surely leading me.

"Balls."

"What?"

"Not literally." She gives me a shy smile then looks back at the fire. "What I mean is, Jack was afraid to *feel* anything. So he shut it all down. His feelings. Mine. He objectified everything. The quintessential reporter. He didn't let anyone really touch him. Even me." Tears are streaming silently down her cheeks. "And though it's true I miss him every single second of every day, I kind of did when we were together, too."

I have to look away. Every part of me hurts. Somewhere in there I hear Julia.

"The thing is, living is all about feeling, James. Feeling pleasure." She pauses. "Feeling pain." She pauses again. "Angry, sad, hurt, scared, compassion, passion, love—letting yourself feel these things because in them lies the spectacular richness of being alive." She looks at me, her hazel eyes certain. "So the tragedy is not only in Jack's death, but that he never really let himself fully experience living."

Why is she telling me this? I know she has an angle. What is it? I feel afraid of her words. Stare at the fire.

"Do you think you're like Jack?"

"I'm sorry?" *Here we go. Look at her.*

"Well, it seems to me you'd have to be pretty far removed from feeling to slice up your wrists like you did."

Fuck.

I stand, cross my arms over my chest and bury my hands against my sides. Draw in a breath to speak, but I'm lost for words. *When did she see?* Maybe when she was shooting me and Cameron while we slept, or up at my place this afternoon. I should leave, but exhaustion holds me captive. *Then say something.* "I strive daily to feel as little as possible, actually. Death would be a nominal change." I raise an eyebrow, crack a grin, but she finds no humor in my comment. I have no idea what else to say to her. Comb my hand through my hair to get it out of my eyes. Scalp tingles and I shiver, then turn to the heat of the fire again.

"I'm sorry. Please forgive me. I apologize for my directness. Jack often accused me of being too forward. Really, I'm sorry if I was offensive." She gets up, goes to the storage bench below the window, pulls a sleeping bag out and spreads it on the couch. "I'm sure you're exhausted. Why don't you get some sleep. And again, I apologize if I was offensive." She puts on a soft smile, but I sense no remorse as she holds my gaze then turns away. "Good night, James." She leaves the room without looking back.

I stand in front of the fire watching the flames dance, listen to their crackle, try to pick up a bass line. My eyes burn.

Focus on the rhythm in the crackle.

But I hear none. It's just fire—random ignitions before it all turns to ash. No rhythm, no rhymes, no music. I picture her clear eyes, like still, mossy pools. *'The spectacular richness in being alive is* feeling.

I feel scared.

And MAD. *Mad as a hatter.*

I laugh, then flush with heat from fever, break out in sweat. The scars on my forearms itch, and I unbutton my sleeves and roll them back, then hold my arms in front of me and force myself to look at the jagged red lines. They're still so prominent. No wonder everyone who sees them has a reaction.

Warm tears stream down my face. I taste their salt. Stare at the fire and try to ignore them, but feel it coming, the wave forming, the drag as it draws back before cresting. My body reverberates with the pounding of my heart, fear suddenly gripping my throat and suffocating.

She's a *journalist*, for Christ sake. And now she knows about me. Quick search and she could easily find out who I really am, turn me into tomorrow's news. And I'd be screwed.

Run, James.

Right. Wouldn't make it ten feet up the hill.

My vision fills with floaters—sparkling light worms corrupt my sight. Knees buckle. I move to the couch before I fall, and drop onto it. Try to focus on the fire, on the crackle, listen for the rhythm. Still can't hear one.

Relax. Lay my head back against the large couch pillow. *Just listen...*

I hear someone screaming...in agony. Then I realize *I'm* screaming, my muscles so taut it feels like they're ripping. Back in the ancient infirmary, I'm restrained to the padded examining table in the ancient dilapidated room, arms splayed wide held pinned by straps on my wrists, my legs spread open, bound at the knees, arching my body, complete exposing all of me.

The pain subsides, and for a second I think they're done with me for now. Then white hot electric shocks slice through my inner thighs right into my groin and I involuntarily convulse with the stinging heat, hear myself scream again. See my trembling hands bound at the wrists, my fingers outstretched, contorting with resistance.

I struggle wildly, tearing my skin to a bloody pulp, my hands numb now—only feel wetness around my wrists and oozing into my palms between the blinding, agonizing shocks. Limbs ache, loin burns, my balls and cock feel like they're going to burst. Wires on the electrodes attached to the inside of my convulsing thighs tap against my ass even after the shocks stop.

"Get it off of me! Let me go, you fucks!" But either I'm yelling at no one or they're out of my range of vision, strapped to the table. Hot tears of frustration and outrage stream down my face. Struggle to lift my head, and see two metal bands with thin black wires coming off them around my cock. Panic replacing every other feeling except the searing, shocking pain, like a hot knife ripping through my groin. White hot prickles to the base of my cock arch my hips and force my head back onto the worn and torn vinyl pad, and somehow stimulate my dick. I feel it getting hard. *NO!* screams in my head. *No, god, STOP. Don't!* But I can't stop my growing erection. My hips arch upward again and again with each penetrating, intolerable lesion. Left groaning, panting, crying when the shocks subside for another minute, I manage to lift my head again, look past my knees through my spread legs and see a small, flashing red light. Several flashes reveal the light is on a video camera mounted on a tripod. They're filming my torture.

Recall snuff films and wonder if this is what's happening here, to me, and almost welcome the idea to end the pain. I'll be the latest in internet porn until the final scene with the ice pick in my ches—"

White hot stinging waves of agony through my thighs into my loins, my balls, my cock again, and another tortured scream escapes me as I feel ejaculate rising in my penis. Convulsively recoil against the restraints, but there are none, my arms and legs suddenly free. I bolt upright, and wake.

I'm at Elisabeth's. I came of my own volition. I'm sick, with the flu...well, a lot more than that, but...

I flash on my dream that wasn't a dream, but a memory. Similar scenes from my thirteen months at Langside wakes me with almost every sleep. *Get out of my head. It's done. There's nothing to do but forget it. It's over!* "Stop it." My voice surprises me. I look around and listen carefully. House is still.

Can't stop shaking. I pull the sleeping bag around me but can't stop shivering. No more sleep. Not here. *I shouldn't be here.* Look around the room. It's sparsely furnished, just the fabric couch, the storage bench, and the pine bookshelves on either side of the fireplace that the house came with. It's dark out the picture window. Can't see beyond the pines lit in deep forest green with the ambient light from the house. Gusts of wind rattle the windows. Blasts of cold air come in under the back door. I'm going to have to fix that...

Every cell in my body hurts. Again. Still. Maybe this will never end, and I'll never really sleep again—start hallucinating from sleep deprivation and get institutionalized for real this time. I'm so fucking tired...I can shut this all down. *Tonight.* Just go for a swim with the storm coming in, get as far out as I can into the white-capped Ionian...except there's no way in hell I can get off this couch.

Watch the dancing flames and recall her sitting next to me earlier, her long, oval face, those full lips, the curve of her neck, and swell of her breasts haloed by firelight. She really is strikingly beautiful. Close my eyes to study her picture in my head, and consider why I hadn't noticed when she was sitting next to me...

-

-

Chapter Ten

-

I wake but can't move, like I'm stuck in REM sleep paralysis. Leather restraints hold me spread eagle on the padded floor of the 'rubber' room, an 8 x 10 foot completely padded chamber. Shift and pull against the restraints, just checking, but I'm helpless, and cold. Fucking freezing, prostrate and naked on this floor.

Lay shivering, then hear the sound of sweeping suction as the door opens and closes behind someone coming in. Crane my neck to see behind me, my heart pounding so hard it's reverberating in my throat. Long, thin legs of a woman in dark, tight slacks, and I watch her move to my side and look down at me. Gaunt face, black hair, cut short, like the woman in *Pulp Fiction*. She wears bright red lipstick, a black pant suit and a white lab coat, and starts pulling gadgets from her big pockets.

I'm fucked. Literally. Figuratively. And every other way. "Please. Don't." My voice sounds strange, hoarse, no power.

She kneels beside me and smiles sweetly as she arranges metal fittings and plastic instruments on the padded floor next to me.

"Don't." I beg. Struggle, but she ignores me. *"Why are you doing this to me?!"*

"Oh, not just you, luv," she says in a thick Cockney accent. "How sooo like a man, to think everythins 'bout 'im all the time." She gathers my flaccid cock in her hand and I think she's going to try and jack me off, but then she ties a red cloth, like a tourniquet around the base of my shaft and my balls.

"NO! Stop! *God, don't!"* Cloth bites, like someone pressing fingernails into me. I writhe on the padded floor from the biting pain in my loins combines with the sharp stinging of the restraints around my wrists and ankles rubbing my skin raw. I want to black out but the pain keeps me conscious. "Please, it hurts. Take it off me. *Please...*" I beg her. But she's indifferent to my suffering.

"You should try and relax, Sir James. Ain't that the proper way to speak to you royals? You prefer James, or Sir James? Well, either way, you're really just makin things harder, on you anyways, fightin yerself from given it up." She retrieves a clear, hard plastic cylinder, maybe three inches wide by ten long, capped on one side. Attached to the side of the capped end is a circle gauge, like a blood pressure dial. Thin black tubing, a foot or so long, extends from the cap and has a squeeze ball on the end.

I can't catch my breath. "Let me go. *Please*, let me go!" Heart slams in my chest. Loins, balls and cock burn, pulse as the tourniquet constricts blood flow. Can barely feel her take hold of my cock again. *"NO! NO! Stop! Don't. Please. Please don't do this!"* I beg, but she flashes a sweet smile, like I'm talking about the weather.

"Just doing my job, Sir James. Pardon the intrusion." She stuffs my dick into the clear plastic cylinder and holds it up against me, and with her free hand lifts the ball at the end of the long black tubing and squeezes. Sharp pressure, then pain, deep in my groin, and I groan as my body lifts off the padding following the pull of my cock up into the cylinder.

"*Oh God. No,*" I moan, my body dripping and itching with sweat as I fall back on the padded floor, gasping, and struggling against the restraints. "Please...*No. Don't do this.* Don't make me do this."

She smiles at me sweetly again, then focuses on the gauge, and I see her fingers squeeze the pump. Searing, tearing pressure of my penis being ripped from my body, my hips lift off the floor convulsively and a scream escapes my lips.

"You fucking *bitch*," I manage, before I see her pump the ball again and succumb to the now dizzying pain and convulsing of my body, forcing my hips into a rhythm as the instrument virtually sucks me off, pulling blood into my balls and penis, stimulating an erection beyond my control. Struggle, cry, beg, pinned to the quilted vinyl floor, unable to stop her. "Why?! *Why are you doing this to me? Please...No...*"

She stares at the gauge that tops the cylinder. "Oh good. We're almost there. Just a bit more."

"*NO!*," screams in my head, but I have no voice, no strength left to speak. *God, it hurts,* my stomachs rock hard, every muscle taut, cramping, the restraints spreading my limbs wide, my legs and arms feel like they're tearing off with my resistance. Groin is hot, burning, engorging with blood as my cock hardens, commanding my attention. Bitch is gonna fucking take me. And I can't stop her. "No," I manage to groan.

She's fixed on the gauge, squeezes the ball more slowly now. I try and still my body, my mind, stop fighting, go numb to lose my hard-on. But each burst of suction convulses me, my dick now rock hard and filling the plastic tube, and ultra-sensitive to even the slightest change in pressure. I'm on the verge of orgasm, my mind fighting my body to resist, my brain imploding with cognitive dissonance.

I can't get air, my throat closing with what feels like every muscle in my body going rigid. I scream but there is no sound.

-

-

Chapter Eleven

-

"James!"

Get me out of here! Make it stop!

"James! James, wake up!"

Her voice is distant, and familiar, and not from the bitch torturing me. Not in the room at all— she's in my head.

"It's OK. You're OK, James. No one's hurting you. You're safe."

And it suddenly doesn't hurt anymore, so I believe her. Then it strikes me voice-overs only happens with insanity, in movies, and dreams. Open my eyes and Elisabeth is standing over me, holding my shoulders to the couch. "It's okay, it's just a dream. You're okay, you were just dreaming." Then she disappears. The room is lit in red and orange and glows yellow near the fireplace. Outside it's still night.

I shake uncontrollably, pull my hair out of my face, rub the sleep from my eyes, surprised to feel tears. I'm boiling hot and freezing cold at the same time. Shadows dance around the room with the firelight. Nearly have a heart attack when I notice her standing before me.

"Here." She holds medication in one hand and a glass of water in the other.

I stare at the three pills in her hand.

"They're aspirin. And you need all of them. Your fever is spiking. Take them."

I take the pills with a gulp of water. She takes the glass from me and disappears again. I stare at the fire, shivering. Wind blows fierce outside, resonating the doorjamb, like the sound track of a scary movie.

"Come with me." She holds her hand to me. "My room is much warmer, and I have a down comforter on my bed."

Take her hand and stand, but resist her pull. "I...I don't wanna sleep. I don't feel like sleeping."

"It's okay, James." She talks to me like she's soothing her son. "No worries. We can just talk—"

"I don't want to talk."

"Okay...Then I'll talk—help you stay awake. But it's less drafty and much warmer in my room." She fixes her eyes on mine like she's looking into me, to get inside my head. "You're safe here, James. Come."

I let her lead me into her bedroom. Double bed is centered in the room, and covered with a deep green quilted comforter. Two pillows are up against the back wall. She guides me to the right side of the bed, near the bay window. Then she drops her hand from mine, pulls back the comforter, and waits for me to get into her bed. I do. She releases the quilt onto me, and I snuggle under the down, still shivering intractably, but less violently. She goes back out, comes back a moment later with the sleeping bag, unzips it and lays it over me.

"Better?" She comes into bed beside me.

"Yeah. Thanks." A flash of terror with her suddenly next to me, then my rational brain convinces me *anyone* within her proximity will likely bother me for some time to come. Warmth is spreading throughout my body, easing my anxiety. I relax my shoulders back into the soft pillow, once Jack's, I assume.

She sits cross-legged in bed, leaning up against the wall, the quilt covering her legs to her waist. "It's going to take a little while for the aspirin to cool you down." She pauses, like assessing what to say next. "I don't know what's going on for you, other than what you've said, which I get is a small part of the full picture. But that sounded like a really bad nightmare. Want to tell me about it?"

"No. Sorry I woke you though."

"No worries. I'm not trying to pry. Sometimes it helps me if I talk about my nightmares, you know, put it out there so when I fall back asleep I won't go right back into the same dream. Sometimes just staying awake awhile helps with that too."

Painful prickles shoot through my muscles, into my hands, through my fingers. "You don't need to stay awake for me. Go back to sleep. I'll be fine."

"That's okay. Ever since I gave birth to Cameron I have this compulsion to mother."

"I'm okay. Really. There's nothing you can do anyway."

"I apologize for earlier." Her voice is soft, her tone tender. "I didn't mean to get on your case."

"It's okay." It's so damn *hot*. Throw the blankets back and lay panting. "You don't need to apologize. A lot of what you said is right."

She smiles at me. "I know it is. But I've never been any good with timing, and my delivery just sucks."

I laugh at her turn of phrase, acutely aware I've spent most of my life there. I'm freezing all of a sudden and pull the blankets back over me, curl up and snuggle down under them. I watch her, and this time notice her auburn hair cascading around the elegant lines of her long neck. One of the thin straps of her black camisole is falling off her smooth, tan shoulder.

"You never did give me an answer."

"What was the question?"

She sighs, shakes her head but with a hint of a smile, then her expression turns dark again. She looks down at her hands in her lap. "Ya know, I've seen and photographed atrocities from China to the Middle East, torture and cruelty beyond any semblance of sanity. And to the bitter end, most victims fight for life. How is it that you got so far from feeling, from caring, that you'd attempt suicide?"

I stare at the ceiling. *Good question.* Take a deep breath, feel the weight of it in my chest and release it slowly. "My decision to take my life was based on extreme, extenuating circumstances. What that experience has left with me is an acute awareness of the ugliness in all of us. And I'm not quite sure how to live with that."

"Welcome to the human race. We're all ugly sometimes, James."
Tenderness is gone. She turns off the bedside lamp and lies next to
me. Time passes in silence. Think perhaps she's fallen asleep, but
then I hear her draw a breath. "I try and picture Cameron grown, you
know, what kind of man he'll be. I want so much for my child to
love life, and really *live* it. I need him to know he's loved, so he can
love freely, be willing to risk caring deeply to embrace true
intimacy. I don't ever want him to be in a place where he would
consider taking his own life. It crushes the very heart of me to even
think about it."

I stare at the textured ceiling. "My parents died a long time ago.
Well, my mom and step-father anyway. I doubt my real father even
knows what I did. I am absolutely sure he wouldn't care." I close my
eyes, rest them a moment, my body heavy with warmth.

"I'm sorry," is the last thing I hear her say...

Someone's crying. A child. There are no children here. Where?
Where am I?

I'm afraid to open my eyes. Again. Still.

Open your goddamn eyes.

I'm in a bed. Alone. Under a deep green comforter. Outside the bay
window it's just getting light. Don't know where I am or how I got
here, but I'm fully clothed, untethered, able to get up and leave if I
choose to.

The crying stops.

I breathe.

"Mama's here, baby. Good morning, sweetie pea." I hear Elisabeth
through the wall.

Elisabeth. She's talking to her son, Cameron. I'm at her house, in her bedroom.

Listen to her footsteps as she leaves Cameron's room. Feel scared again. Scared she'll come in. See me scared. Hear the back screen door slam, and relax. Exhaustion sweeps through me and I have to rest my eyes for a moment...

-

-

Chapter Twelve

-

Someone is bouncing on the bed. Open my eyes. Cameron is in my face with this unfettered expression of joy. I smile back at him. He laughs.

"Ooo, you little devil." Elisabeth comes in and grabs him off the bed. "I told you to leave him alone." She looks at me. "Sorry."

"No problem."

"As long as you're up, come in the kitchen. I'm making lunch."

"What time is it?" I look out the bay window at the gray day.

"Close to 1:00. Come on."

Dark clouds come out of the west at a surreal pace across the Ionian sea towards the island. The house creeks with the heavy wind, the windows vibrate in their wood frames. I'll have to seal them. Move my feet to the floor, but have to sit a minute for the dizziness to subside before standing.

"You okay?" She watches me from the bedroom threshold.

"Yeah." Sit here shivering, trying to come up with a plan for standing.

"You may still have a fever. I'll get you some more Aspirin, but you should eat something first. Come on." She leaves the room with Cameron on her hip.

I stand. Ground feels like it's falling away. I look at my feet.

Walk... Good.

"I'm making omelets. What do you want in yours?" She stands at the stove holding a metal bowl whipping eggs with a fork. Cameron's in his high chair. Cheerios and blueberries fill his tray. He smashes the blueberries with one hand and with the other he stuffs Cheerios in his mouth.

Sit in the same chair as before, across the table from Cameron and watch him. He squishes a blueberry between his small fingers, licks the juice that streams down his hand. It's disgusting, but somehow the mess he's making seems...satisfying.

"I can keep it simple, just scramble them if you'd like." She puts an iron skillet on the stove, lights it, gets butter from the fridge and holds the stick to the pan.

"Scrambled is good. Thanks."

She moves the stick of butter slowly across the skillet surface. It sizzles. She looks at me, smiles. "How do you feel?"

"Better." *Like shit. Weak. Stupid. Pathetic.*

"Good. You look better. You're eyes aren't as black." Eggs sizzle as they hit the pan. "You want toast with these?"

"No." I don't want those, but I'm not up for an argument, and I know I should eat. She finishes scrambling the eggs, puts them on a plate and places it in front of me. I stare down at the steaming, fluffy yellow pile.

"Eat." She hands me a fork.

"EAT!" Cameron mimics perfectly.

She laughs, goes to him, holds his head to her stomach. "I love this head." She bends and kisses the top of it. Fine wisps of his hair cling to her lips as she pulls away. He lifts his tiny, pudgy hands to her— his purple, wet, sticky fingers reaching for her, and she recoils. "Keep those little things away from me. Arms up." Cameron lifts his arms and she lifts him from the highchair and holds him away from her as she takes him to the sink.

I watch their antics, and eat. The eggs are salty, and rich. It hurts to swallow. Chew them to mush and then sort of let them slide down my throat.

Cameron's on the counter top. Elisabeth has hold of his hands and is rubbing them together under the tap. He shakes his hands about, splashing water everywhere. Pure joy on his round face, his mouth open wide with fits of laughter. She turns off the water minutes later and Cameron protests with a long, low groan. She dries his hands with a dishtowel and sets him down. "Muki! Muki! Mama."

"Mr. Monkey is in your room. You can go get him."

"Get Muki. Bye-bye Mama."

"Bye baby."

We both watch his awkward gait as he toddles from the kitchen and disappears down the hall. She throws the dishtowel on the counter top, then leans back against it, and looks at me. "He'll be gone awhile. On the way to get his monkey, or once he's gotten Mr. Monkey, something will catch his attention and he'll forget about coming back."

"How great to be so easily captivated."

"I guess. Jack was just like that and it bothered the hell out of me."

I laugh. But her eyes narrow and her brow furrows, and I get that it pisses her off. "I just meant I envy Cameron's sense of wonder. Reminds me what it used to be like."

"Are you kidding? You were just as amazed as Cameron with the butterflies. I saw it on your face. It was beautiful." She gives me a soft, shy smile. "What I meant was, Jack was captivated by whatever struck his fancy at the moment, which rarely turned out to be me." Her gentle smile turns sad, and in her expression I see Julia.

Look down at my eggs, feel them coming back up. Try to hold them down by swallowing repeatedly, put the fork down in the scattered remains and push the plate away.

"You okay?"

No. "Yeah."

"You should go back to bed. I'll get the aspirin and bring it in."

I stand. Shiver. "Thanks for breakfast." I should walk out the door, go back up to my place, get away from them. I look out, at the rain now sheeting the kitchen's back window. Still doubtful I'd make it up the hill, especially in this weather. And, of course, I'd have to argue with her about leaving. The thought is exhausting. Her bed is soft, and warm. And I didn't dream, after the nightmares when I dozed. Best sleep I've had since I got to the island—

She takes my hand. At first I resist, but she looks at me, into me. "Don't be afraid to sleep. I'll wake you if you have a bad dream." She pulls me gently forward.

I let her lead me down the hall again. We pass Cameron in his room, sitting on a large couch pillow on the floor, flipping through the pages of a huge picture book. She pauses at the doorway, lets go of my hand and I almost run into her.

"PU! Could you be any stinkier?" She exclaims to her son. She turns back to me. "Go to bed. I'll be there in a minute."

I can't smell a thing, my nose and lungs still heavily congested. I continue down the hall, get to her room, crawl into bed and curl under the blanket.

I shouldn't be here...

-

-

Chapter Thirteen

-

Walls are beige. Ceiling's beige. The floor is fucking beige. And everything is covered with squares of quilted cloth. I'm in the rubber room. I'm not strapped down, though I'm naked, except for the straight jacket. Huddled up against a corner of the small room, trying in vain to get my arms out of the contraption that holds them pinned to my sides.

This is madness. I'm not crazy. *I shouldn't be here.*

I stand, move to the door and look out the four by six inch window but see only the row of rusting metal doors with tiny windows like mine across the dim, dilapidated hallway.

Let me out, I want to scream, but don't, afraid of the outcome. Instead, I slam my shoulder into the padded door to open it. There's the slightest of give and I try again, and again, wondering if the door is giving way or it's just me wishing. Move to the back wall and try slamming into it at a run, then try that again and again, slamming myself around the room like a madman.

Thick sound of suction as two huge orderlies come in. I'm against the back wall and charge at them full force, which isn't much momentum with just eight feet of launch. "NO!" I scream, knowing what they're going to do to me.

"It's okay, James. You're okay."

Can hear her but can't see her.

An orderly slams my face into the pillowed wall suffocating me. I'm pinned, choking for breath. Helpless.

"James! Wake up! No one is hurting you. Everything is fine. You're fine." Elisabeth strokes my hair. It feels nice. Tingles.

Orderly holding me shows me the syringe, and I struggle wildly to prevent him from poking me, then feel the needle in the side of my ass. Stings as the drug goes in and I know I'm going out, like it or not, fight it or not, and I'm scared out of my mind what I'll wake to.

"You're safe, James. Shhh...Just relax." Elisabeth's voice is soft but firm. "You're safe here with me."

I'm suddenly aware I lay in her bed. She gently runs her fingers through my hair. Don't open my eyes, though, afraid she'll see my fear.

"You're fine. Go back to sleep now." Elisabeth says.

Feel the drug knocking me out, heaviness encases me, the orderly release me, and I fall to the padded floor and stare up at him. Other guy grabs my legs and drags me to the center of the room, then spreads my ankles wide and restrains them with padded leather belts. But not even my terror will keep me conscious with whatever drug he's given me...

Elisabeth is beside me in bed, leaning up on her elbow looking down at me. I'm disoriented and tense, afraid, then feel awkward, exposed. I sit up and so does she. She sits cross-legged facing me. I lean up against the wall behind me, pull my hair out of my eyes. It's morning. Sunrise. Through her bedroom's narrow side window, and low, knotty pines, bright sun rays shoot over the hills behind the house.

"Hi." A warm, casual smile spreads across her face, eclipsing the sun that floods the room. She radiates lightness. Bells of her wind chime resonate with the morning breeze, the lazy Ionian lapping out a soft, even rhythm.

"Hi."

"How are you feeling?"

"Better, thanks."

"Good. You look totally different." She gives me a shy smile. "Normal, I mean. The color of your skin, your eyes, even your pupils look about right."

"I think the fever broke last night."

She reaches towards me to put her hand on my forehead and I pull back, tense, clench my fists but manage to refrain from striking her. She hesitates only a second then leans forward to rest her hand just above my eyebrows, and a tidal wave hits me.

Desire. Agony. Lust. Frustration, anger, panic overwhelm me instantly.

Run, James.

She pulls back and stares at me. "Are you okay? What's going on?"

I look away, pull my hair out of my eyes again. I do not look at her. "I'm sorry. It's just…" Stop to catch my breath. Feel like a foolish schoolboy.

"Hey. What is it?"

"I just felt dizzy, that's all." I try to give her a reassuring grin but know I don't quite get there. Her concerned expression remains.

"You feel okay now?"

"Yeah." *No.* "I'm feeling pretty good, in fact." *I have to get out of here.* "I think I'll try going for short run." *If I actually did, I'd likely pass out.*

"You really think running right now is a good idea?"

No. "Yeah. Quickest way to build strength. I'll take it easy, though." I get off the bed and stand, turn around and look down at her. "Thank you for the expert mothering." I crack a smile. She gives me a tentative smile back, but her confusion is not lost on me.

"You sure you won't stay for breakfast, at least ."

"No thanks. Not a good idea to eat before running. I'll fix something after."

"What? You have no food in your place. Come back down later. I'll make you something."

"I'm fine now. Stop worrying about me. I can take care of myself."

"Could have fooled me."

I grin. "I'll talk to you later." Then I turn away and leave without looking back.

It's cool, crisp and quiet outside. Listen to myself struggling to breathe all the way up the hill. Legs hurt. *Don't stop. Keep moving.* Lungs hurt. *Don't care. Don't stop.*

I hurt her back there. *Not good.* Should never have been there in the first place. She's not part of the plan. That was wild when she touched me. Electric, like static shock. Hurt. But felt good. Connected. *Talk about cognitive dissonance.*

My house is cold. The floor is hard when I collapse onto the sleeping bag, crawl inside and huddle into myself to get warm. Close my eyes, and again see Elisabeth's oval face, the curve of her neck, and swell of her breasts in firelight. Can't recall what we'd talked about, but her image lingers as I fall asleep.

-

-

Chapter Fourteen

-

ELISABETH

He sits on the floor of his kitchen, cross-legged in front of the refrigerator, door open wide, his head resting on top of the crisper drawers that line the bottom of the fridge.

"What are you doing? Are you okay?" Elisabeth holds Cameron on her hip while he squiggles and whines to get down.

James bashes his head into the glass shelf as he moves to get out of the fridge. A bottle of water falls into his lap as he moves back to stand. "I'm fine. Thanks. Just looking for water." He gives her this disarming grin, stands, opens the bottled water and takes a long drink. "What's going on?"

"I knocked."

"*I* knocked!" Cameron corrects.

"Yes. *You* did," and she kisses his knuckles several times. "Good job, buddy!" He giggles, rapt by their intimate exchange.

She looks back at James. "The back door was open." She suddenly feels stupid for coming up there. "I didn't see you running. You didn't come back down for supper...and I got nervous." He'd already proven himself to be suicidal, and had yet to deny he may still be.

"Sorry. Fell asleep." He takes another drink of water. He still wears what looks like the same jeans and dark flannel shirt he's been in for days. Shirtsleeves cover his hands, almost to the base of his long fingers.

"Down, mama. Down." Cameron manages to annoy her sufficiently to get her to release him. He toddles to the cabinet and began investigating.

"Have you been sleeping all day?"

"Mostly. Read a little. Thought I heard you two laughing on the beach this afternoon."

She smiles. "You did."

They both watch Cameron opening the cabinet doors, and then slam them with a bang! James flinches with every slam. Cameron's bored and it's guaranteed he'll get destructive if she doesn't get him out of here.

"Cameron, knock it off. Come here, baby."

James gives her a grateful smile. Again she feels awkward, silly for coming. "Have you eaten anything today?"

"No, not yet."

"Come down. I'll make you something."

"That's okay. I don't want to keep crashing in on you."

"I have to make dinner for Cameron and me anyway. Come down. Join us." The thought of him up here, alone, cold and starving bothers her. "James, unless you went down into town today, you still have no food in this house. I guess you can starve yourself to death, if you're still aiming to get there. But if that's your plan, could you leave me your jeep—just write up a short will bequeathing it to me before Cam and I take off back down the hill."

His eyes narrow—forest green peeks through dark lashes as his face breaks into an ear-to-ear grin. "What are you making for dinner?"

"Beggars can't be choosers." She grins back. "Come on. Let's go." She picks up Cameron who latches onto her hip and they proceed to the back door. James follows them out, down the narrow dirt path to their house.

She makes a vegetable stir-fry. Cameron goes to the living room and plays with his books and trains. James stands with her at the kitchen counter cutting up veggies, while Elisabeth wok fries onions and ginger. He cuts each precisely—the string beans perfectly even in length, the red peppers cut in equal width strips.

"You don't have to get Carthaginian with the vegetables. I kind of need them now."

He laughs. "A friend of mine used to use the exact same expression. That's wild." Her image must have come to mind because his expression softens and Elisabeth senses his distance.

"That is wild. Didn't know the story of Carthage was that common."

"She wasn't common." He pushes cut up vegetables off the cutting board with a knife into the wok. They sizzle when they hit it. He smiles, puts the cutting board back on the counter top and begins slicing the zucchini.

Elisabeth watches him as she stirs. He seems lost in his head. "Who was she?"

He smiles to himself. "She was brilliant, and beautiful, and driven. We were both driven, except I took it right over the edge." He pushes the rest of the vegetables from the cutting board into the wok, puts the board down, leans back against the counter, folds his arms across his chest and watches her cook. By his posture she knows not to probe further. The kitchen smells of onions and ginger. She spoon-feeds him a sample of the concoction she's created.

"Mmm. Good. Nice job." Then he snatches a slice of pepper from the wok.

"Cameron! Get in here sweetie pea. Dinner!"

James covers his ear with her shout. "Does that really work?"

She blushes. "Never, but I continue to be hopeful." She goes and gets her son.

Back in the kitchen, James stirs the contents in the wok. She sticks Cameron in his high chair and gets his small plastic Elmo plate from the drying rack. She takes the wooden spoon from James, piles a small bit of the stir-fry on Cameron's plate, and sets it on the tray in front of him. He munches contently while she prepares two more plates, and sets them on the table.

"Sit." She instructs James and hands him a fork. "Eat. Please. Don't wait for me. You want water, juice, or wine?"

"Water. Thanks."

She pulls off the top of a sippy cup and fills it with water from a bottle in the fridge and serves it to him. He smiles at the big red Clifford dog printed on the plastic cup. "I have a total of four plates, two bowls, one mug and three sippy cups, and a small collection of utensils. My wok, my iron skillet and my steamer are the only kitchenware I brought from Israel. And I haven't missed one of those things I so desperately seemed to need back in Tel Aviv." She sits down to join them.

James waits for her to eat, then takes a bite of his food. "It's good. Thank you."

"My pleasure." Elisabeth takes another bite. It is good. Onions are caramelized and coat the vegetables and shrimp with a touch of sweetness.

They munch contentedly. She feels relaxed, almost...*good.* For the first time since Jack died she recognizes what she had assumed left her with her husband—a grounded sense of calm. It's nice with James here, cooking with someone, having someone to cook for. His presence fills the hollowness constantly looming. "It's been nice living minimally, here on Corfu. I think I used to use *things* to fill me up. Crammed our place with furniture, artwork, photos of friends and family. A crowded house felt less lonely, since even when Jack was home, he wasn't really there so much of the time."

James flashes a guilty grin then takes on that distant expression again, like he's back with his *uncommon* love. Elisabeth keeps talking to keep him in the room with her.

"Don't find a need for things here. Cameron fills me up for the most part. Things just don't seem to do it for me anymore."

"Know what you mean. You've seen my place, how I live. There is a kind of freedom to having nothing."

The way he phrases it chills her. "When you have nothing, you've got nothing to lose. Is that it?"

He cocks his head, stares at her. "Something like that."

She frowns. "Committing to nothing is a harsh way to live. Lonely."

"Safe." He looks at his plate. "It can be lonely out here, in the middle of nowhere sometimes. The silence gets to me." James gives her a quick smile. "I've never been all that enamored with silence. And Lonely is a recent, and seriously unwelcome discovery."

"I don't understand." She watches him take another bite. "Do you mean to tell me you've never felt lonely?"

He looks at her. "Not never, but rarely. And never to the degree I feel it now. I used music to fill me up." She feels sadness encase him. "But not anymore." He looks back down at his plate. "I came here for solace, but sometimes the quiet out here lets my mind wander to all kinds of bad places."

"Well, Cameron and I sure blow the hell out of quiet."

"Thank you." He smiles. "It's been nice listening to you guys play on the beach. I find myself actually looking forward to hearing you out there."

Elisabeth can't wipe the smile off her face. "Well, we're much more entertaining up close and personal. You're welcome to join us anytime."

He smiles again. Nods. "Perhaps I will. Thanks."

Cameron has turned his red pepper into a writing implement and is rubbing it in broad strokes across his tray. James watches him, scrunches his face up in disgust then looks at the remains in his own plate.

She laughs. "Finished?"

He nods, gets up and puts his plate in the sink. Elisabeth gets up, takes her plate and Cameron's to the sink. James helps her clear the remaining dishes from the table, puts them in the sink and begins washing them. They work in silence, her drying what he puts in the rack, both listening to Cameron's contented cooing as he rolls peas around on his tray.

"Thank you again for dinner," James says when the dishes are done. "I should take off."

"Stay awhile. Give me a few minutes to put Cameron to bed, and have some tea with me."

He doesn't answer. He leans against the counter and watches Cameron, but she gets the impression he's somewhere else in his head.

"You with me, James?" She dries her hands on the dishtowel, sets it on the counter.

He looks at her, his piercing green eyes searching. "Yeah. It's just…well, it's been a long time since I've been in the real world. I haven't had more than a brief exchange with anyone in months. The other night, on the beach...the thing is, I'm not exactly sure how to be with people anymore. I don't know what to say, what not to. I'm not sure I ever did, but now..." He lets the statement dangle, and shrugs. "I'm sorry."

"Don't be. You're doing fine. It's nice to have the company."

A smile whispers across his gorgeous face before he startles.

"Down, down, down." Cameron bangs on his tray.

"Hold on sweetie pea." She takes Cameron from the highchair. "Give me ten minutes to get him to bed and we can have some tea. Put some on, would you please?"

She gives Cameron a quick rinse in the bathroom sink, then puts him in his airplane onesie. While reading *One Fish, Two Fish*, she hears the kettle whistle blow, then silence. Moment later, she hears James rattling around in the living room. By the third page Cam is asleep. Elisabeth gently deposits her son in his crib, kisses him goodnight and goes to join James.

"Thought I'd get a fire going. Bit chilly in here." He strikes a stick match along the stone face of the fireplace, and lights the newspaper he's places at the bottom of a small pyramid of wood. "Water in the kettle is hot. I don't know where you keep your tea."

She goes back into the kitchen and makes two cups of Tetley's. She takes a sippy cup, and gives James the mug when she comes back in. He holds it close to him, cradling the mug against his flat stomach.

"Thank you. It's good." He takes another sip. "And dinner was excellent."

"Suppose anything is when you're starving." She stands by the fireplace watching him. He shoots her an insolent glare, then shakes his head and gets sucked inside. She literally feels him separate.

He's focused on the fire but clearly seeing some other image. And Elisabeth wants to scream, shove him, slap him—anything to get him in the room with her. "Where are you?"

"Sorry?"

"You checked out. You did it before. You just did it now. Like you're not here. Like I'm not here. Where do you go?"

He laughs. "I'm sorry. I'm here. With you."

"You weren't a second ago. Where were you?"

He stares at her. "I'm not so sure if you get inside my head you'll like what you find there. You ought to check that one at the door before you go looking."

"Are you afraid of what I'll find, or what I'll show you?"

A smile spreads across his face. "Both."

She sips her tea. His eyes stay fixed on hers. Even though he stands still he seems breathless—anxious. He takes another drink from his mug and looks back at the fire.

"I have another question."

"Okay..." James turns to her.

"Do you get violent nightmares every night?"

"Pretty much. If I sleep for any length of time."

"How long has this been going on?"

"Quite a while." He looks at her, cocks his head to the side. "You're still at it. Look, it's violent, and ugly, and...the past."

"If I ask you to tell me what happened, will you?"

"Probably not. Not right now, anyway. I'm not exactly solid right now. The past seventeen months really messed with my head. I've only been free of it a few months now, and I need to keep it this way." He looks back at the fire. "Which is why I live with nothing, and talk to virtually no one. I leave tomorrow and no one misses me, or remembers I was ever here."

"Is this what you want? The life you want?"

"I don't know. It's different than the way I use to live, to be sure. A lot more isolated." Then he laughs. "Sort of—in the physical sense anyway."

She watches him stare at the fire, waits for him to continue, but when he doesn't she feels compelled to fill the silence. "I came to Corfu to get away from the world, a *'Stop! I want to get off,'* kind of thing. Thought the isolation was what I needed, but as it turns out, alone just sucks."

He looks at her, and laughs.

"Are you mocking me?"

"No. I agree with you, though up until a year ago, I wouldn't have known what the hell you're talking about. Alone is a lot more foreboding than it used to be." His tousled hair clings to his lashes and hangs in his eyes. He's the poster child for the lost. He's fixed on her, studying her, and his expression softens. "I'm sorry for what you must be going through, 'Lisbeth. I've never shared the kind of commitment you had with your husband. I cannot conceive the loss. And I can't fill it, either."

Ouch. She looks away, sits on the couch. "No. You can't. And don't. But you're a welcome distraction, James." She blushes with the confession.

"As you and Cameron are for me." He smiles a shy, single-dimpled grin.

He's adorable, and she can't help smiling back.

His smile fades. "I'd sure hate to screw you up with the backlash from my fucked up past, though." He stays fixed on her a moment, then sits on the couch beside her. "I escaped Langside Priory Hospital for the criminally insane almost five months ago now. But I'm not crazy. I wasn't when they locked me up, anyway, though I can't attest to now." He studies her. Somehow Elisabeth can feel him silently pleading with her not to recoil, so she does not. She listens like he's a lead telling his story to Jack, and she's there for the pictures. "I swear to you, 'Lisabeth, I'll never intentionally hurt you or Cameron. You don't have to worry that I'm a psychopath or anything."

"I'm not worried. I'm not afraid of you, James." In her head, and heart, she knows she's spoken the truth.

A faint hint of a smile that quickly fades. He looks back at the fire. "Thing is, there's likely law enforcement still looking for me, at least in Britain. The consequences of my leaving Langside illegally could *unintentionally* harm both you and Cameron if we're together when they come for me. I can assure you, I won't let them take me back there." His jaw tightens, the hollow in his cheeks exaggerating his high cheekbones. Then he's lost again, checked out, sucked back inside his head.

Her ire quickly spikes. She's back here again, on the outside looking in at a man lost in *himself.* "Oh God, you're just a more screwed up version of Jack," Elisabeth snaps.

James laughs. "You don't know the half of it."

She isn't so sure she wants to, but she can't help smiling at his comeback.

God, he'd be so easy to fall for. Smart. Gorgeous. Watch out, Liz. This guy is dangerous. And not just to himself.

-

-

Chapter Fifteen

-

JAMES

I have the oddest urge to kiss her—lean forward, pull her to me and kiss her. I don't. Look back at the fire but I can feel her staring at me. *I have to get out of here.* "It's getting late. I should take off."

"Okay." She practically whispers. She stays fixed on me then looks away.

I stand, put the mug on top of the bookshelf and look down at her. "I'll see you later, then."

"Hope so." She looks up. Her eyes hold me captive until she looks away. "Goodnight." She looks at the fire again.

"Goodnight." I turn away, go out the back door and close the screen gently behind me.

Dark, cool and crisp outside. Stand near the edge of the deck and suck in a deep breath. My eyes adjust to the saturated blue of the moonlit night as I cross the sand to the shadowed path. I look back at the warm yellow glow radiating from her house before entering the darkness up the hill.

Alone does suck. I smile at her vernacular. Elisabeth is quietly extreme. And she's right. Again. Three for three. See her standing in front of me, sipping her tea. Her hazel eyes were full of green tonight, confident. Is adult companionship all she wants. Or is she trying to save me, or maybe herself?... Does it matter?

Her infusion into my life has added an unexpected dimension. Without her, I could have died on my kitchen floor and no one would have noticed, for months maybe. But now that she's a part of the scene, entertaining getting dead feels reckless. It could hurt her, and Cameron. And I don't want to do that.

Do I still want to die? I hear Kate in my head.

Not when I'm with them.

I stop by after my run the next morning and she makes us pancakes and sausage. Heart still beats hard as I sit in my usual chair. We're alone. Cameron is napping.

"Juice or milk?" She sets a stack and some links in front of me.

"Juice, thanks." Sweet aroma wafts from the plate and suddenly I'm starving. I consume bite after bite, tasting each as if it were the first. Fluffy, buttery, sugary maple melts in my mouth. Salty, fatty pork sticks between my teeth and the greasy chunks fill me up, satisfying more than my hunger.

"I can make some more if you'd like." She has *one* pancake on her plate, sits down and starts eating it.

"That's all you're having?"

"This is all I want. I'm not that big a fan of pancakes."

"You made these just for me?"

"You and Cameron. He had his before you got here. He likes them almost as much as you do." Her broad smile makes me smile.

"They're fantastic. Thank you. I haven't eaten this well in a long time."

"I gather you don't cook much." She takes the last bite and brings her plate to the sink.

"Was never really into it. Cooking for one is a pain in the ass. Had a few specialties though."

"Yeah?" She playfully raises one eyebrow. "Like what?"

"My chocolate pudding was a favorite." Julia used to love my chocolate pudding. And I see her in my kitchen. Rain sheets the west windows of the glass nook, but I can see the storm racing across the Santa Monica Bay through the kitchen windows behind her. I'm feeding her out of the pudding-coated steel pot. She licks the spoon with long, slow swipes of her tongue then waggles it at me. I sucks on it, draw her into my mouth. She tastes chocolaty sweet, delicious.

The last bite of pancake sits on my plate and I finish it, then get up and put the plate in the sink. Elisabeth has stopped washing the dishes and is glaring at me. "You just did it again."

"What?"

"Checked out."

I laugh. She doesn't. She shakes her head and goes back to the dishes. "Where did you just go?"

"It's not important." I lean against the counter top and stare at the photograph of a war torn Palestinian settlement on the cover of the *New York Times* lying on the kitchen table. She finishes the dishes, wipes her hands on the dishtowel and looks at me.

"Is it really that good?"

"I'm sorry?"

"Your chocolate pudding."

"It got pretty good reviews. I'll make it for you and Cameron sometime. You can decide."

The photo is exquisite. A hole in the wall of the bombed out building reveals a mother, clinging to her dead child amidst the smoky ruins beyond. She is screaming.

"What do you feel when you look at that picture?" Elisabeth brings me back into the kitchen with her.

"The horrors of war. Isn't that what you feel?"

"How very abstracted. How male. Come on, James. What do you *feel*?"

Helpless. Hopeless. "Angry."

"Ah." Again the cock of her eyebrow, but more with acknowledgment than humor. "At what?"

"The stupidity of hate that's in all of us. What do you feel?"

No one's ever turned the question around, and she isn't sure how she feels exactly, so she hesitates to answer, until his eyes leave the paper and find hers. "Well, angry for sure. And so very sad, even though after all this time I probably shouldn't."

"Why?"

"I'd be a better photojournalist if I didn't. The key is to keep it impersonal to sell to the wire, if we want to get picked up for global distribution."

"What the viewer sees, or reads, depends on the perspective of the photographer, or the writer."

"Touché." She smiles at me. "In there lies the fundamental problem with objective reporting. You see the horrors of war because that's what the photographer wants you to see. He could have shown you Victory, focused on the Israeli holding up an Uzi out the Humvee passenger window as he's driven through the dusty streets of Jerusalem, lined with well-wishers." She picks up the paper and studies the picture. "Hey. Kurt Davies. We used to be rivals. Friendly rivals."

"Do you miss it?"

"Not at all."

"Wow. That's definitive. It was your career for how many years?"

"A decade plus. Jack was the writer between us, and my impetus to become a photojournalist. His suggestion, so we could get paid exploring the world together. And we did. And while I loved my husband, I never really loved photojournalism. It's harsh and ugly most of the time because conflict and adversity sell. And I have a hard time separating my feelings from the scene." She drops the paper back on the table and looks at me. "At this point, I've spent way too many years immersed in Photoshop, crying in front of the monitor while framing a picture or video *just so* for maximum impact. Jack used to tease me about being a bleeding-heart liberal, but I could not, and never *desired* to get to where he lived: above everyone he encountered."

I get she's ragingly angry at her husband for dying. It's typical to blame a loved one for leaving us, so I've been told. But I see no point in further focusing on her loss, so I don't touch her last line. Go for something more innocuous instead. "So what would you prefer to be doing then, besides parenting Cameron?"

"I have an MFA from Cal Arts in Film and Video. Studied a lot of art history, and photography in school. Fell in love with Brassaï's 1920's Paris street scenes. Mapplethorpe's flowers. Frans Lanting's landscapes for *National Geographic.* I've always wanted to be a fine photographer, you know, capture and share an intimate view of the *beauty* all around us, like Adams, or Leibovitz. But there's no money in fine art except for the lucky few."

"Do you need money?"

She hesitates, as if my question is threatening. "Well, no, I guess. Not so much anymore."

"Then why do you think you can't be one of the lucky few?"

"Because I'm a realist."

"Maybe it's time you become more of an artist, and produce some fine photography."

She laughs. "Maybe I will..."

-

-

Chapter Sixteen

-

Stopped by after my run the next day, and the one after, and the next after that. Month down the line and I'm still doing it. After breakfast, I usually go back to my place to bathe and change, then go into town and play Tavli with the locals most mornings. Around noon, I join Elisabeth and Cameron on their walk home from the street market for Siesta. Three of us lunch, then laze on the beach, talk, read, engage with Cameron, or nap until mid-afternoon.

Elisabeth makes elaborate meals with fresh ingredients she shops for almost daily. I help her prepare them, and during the last few months she turns me into a competent chef. I teach her how to make chocolate pudding. The days pass quickly. The hours pass slowly. The moments linger. And most are sweet.

The crispness of spring gives way to the heat of summer, and the days repeat and blur. We're in her kitchen this morning. It's just past noon and I'm cutting up peppers for the omelets she's preparing. She abruptly stops whipping the bowl of eggs she's holding to the linoleum counter. I look at her. She's staring at me, then cocks her head to one side.

"My God, you're gorgeous." Wide, seemingly triumphant grin spreads across her face.

I laugh. She says it as a statement of fact, like she's talking about a sunrise or something, and without sexual innuendo. "Thank you. You are too."

"No I'm not. Don't say stuff like that because we both know it's not true."

I look at her, stare really, trying to glean what she's feeling. I've upset her. *Why?* What did I say that was wrong? She's wearing her usual khaki's and black tee-shirt, but they don't hide her feminine form, nor diminish her natural beauty. "Elisabeth, I wasn't making a flip comment. I think you *are* beautiful."

"Right. Whatever."

"No. Wrong. Not '*whatever.*' Come with me." I put the knife in the sink, out of Cameron's reach, who's currently in the living room watching Clifford on Elisabeth's laptop. Then I take the bowl of eggs she's in the process of whipping and place it far back on the counter near the sink. Cameron is so absorbed with his show, he doesn't notice me practically drag his mama down the hall and into the bedroom, and stand her in front of the full-length mirror mounted on the back of the door. "Now, look. What do you see?"

"Botticelli's *Venus*, with bigger breasts. And behind me Mic's *David*." She gives my reflection a mocking grin and tries to turn away but I hold her shoulders, forcing her to stay facing the mirror.

"Now, I'll tell you what *I* see. Before me stands a voluptuous woman, with curves in all the right places. She has strong, defined features, with deep hazel eyes that reflect her mood, and passionately expresses her convictions. Her lips are full, red and inviting, and her smile radiates lightness. Look at yourself. Why is it you don't see this?"

"Standing next to you, honey, Audrey Hepburn would look average."

"You're a hard case, my lady."

"So are you. Let's reverse this, shall we?" Then she ducks from my hands on her shoulders and moves behind me so I'm in front of the mirror. "What do *you* see?"

Stare at my reflection. I know I'm considered attractive by social standards, from years, a lifetime really, of people fawning. But I've never bothered to examine my self-perception. "I don't know 'Lisabeth. Never taken much notice of how people look, unless they're extreme. Physicality is too transitory. No substance. It's given, not achieved."

"What do you *see*, James?" She grins mischievously.

I shrug. "What do I see...A man, close to six feet, a little too thin, not as muscular as I'd like, with green eyes and brown hair that's too long, and always a mess."

"Now I'll tell you what most everyone sees. Classic beauty. Strength. Virile perfection." On her face in the mirror is now a soft, sultry smile, as her eyes scan my reflection. "Wide eyes of a child, penetrating green with long, dark lashes creating a natural eyeliner most women would kill for. Soft full lips contrast the sculpted cheekbones and square jaw that sharpens the boy to man." Quick grin and she brings her hands to my shoulders and runs them lightly over my biceps.

Her touch is electric. Just beyond pleasure is pain. Every muscle tightens. Every nerve tingles with contact, right down to my groin. My heart beats hard and fast. Can she hear it, feel it vibrating my body?

"Tall, slender, *tight*—but not daunting, the solid build of an athlete." She slides her hands over my shirt sleeves and down my arms. "With huge, elegant hands," she laces her fingers in mine, "of a practiced musician."

Suddenly it isn't fun anymore. Can she see how scared I am? *Kiss her. Distract her. She won't know if you take control.*

She cocks her head to the side, stares at me in the mirror. She already knows, her smile gone.

I pull my hands away and turn to face her. Can't breathe. Everything spins, like vertigo. "I told you, I'm not a musician anymore. A musician is someone who plays or creates music. I do neither, and I don't want to talk about this." I leave the bedroom, head back to the kitchen, but when I get to the living room the back door beckons and I walk out of the house.

The sun is high. It's hot. I head towards the water. I see the startled, confused look on her face in the mirror over my shoulder. Feel her behind me, moments ago, her hands sliding over my arms. Feel someone grab my left shoulder and turn back to look, then feel a sharp jab in the right side of my neck. *"What the fuck—"* I whip round and push the fucker off me. He stumbles back, laughing, careening into one of the three other guys in the room also laughing, taunting me.

"You got him, Billy!" a hefty, preppy looking young 20-something mocks.

"Oh! You nailed the wanker!" one of the other similar looking kids says.

"Welcome to the party, mate. Better *with* us than busted for using in 'ere, egh?" Billy's holding up an empty syringe. Ostensibly, whatever was in it went into my neck.

"Are you fucking crazy?!" I demand. *"*What'd you...*fuck*...*"* The rush comes on like a wave dragging me backwards, slowing time, overwhelming me with dizziness and I suddenly feel queasy.

"Ooh, get ready for it. Best bloody buzz you'll ever 'ave, mate." Billy looks like the lead actor in *A Clockwork Orange*, early 20s punk, wearing black eyeliner, the whole bit.

I'm trying to gauge the scene, holding the stinking hole in my neck with one hand, the other in front of me to keep this guy away, but he's already turning his back to me standing near the doorway.

"Came in to play the hero, Lancelot? But there ain't no damsel in distress 'ere. Bitch's been *beggin* for it." He goes to the single bed in the sparse private room at Priory Manor. The other guys seem to part to let Billy have clear access, and that's when I see her—a white woman with long, tousled blond hair, likely in her mid-30s, sitting up on the bed, naked. "Join the party, sport."

"I want it *now*," the women is yelling at Billy and the others standing around the bed looking down at her like she's prey. "You promised I'd get some. We made a *deal*, and you give it to *him*?" She points at me. Striking blue eyes narrow on me like she'd like daggers to be launching from them.

I flash on hearing her voice while I'm dosing in my room the third night I'm at rehab. The drugs they kept me on made me drowsy all the time, so I wasn't sure if I dreamt her screaming, but I get up to check anyway. I remember thinking I'd get her a nurse who'd give her something for her withdrawals, and I could get back to sleep.

"You'll get yours, bitch. We got enough to go round," Billy is saying, and the others hardily agree as he crawls up on the bed. "But we all get first dibs." He grabs her knees and spreads her legs wide. She yelps, and tries to push him off, but two of the others standing on either side of the bed now grab her by the wrists and pull them back to the bed forcing her to lay down.

I lunge for the guy closest to me to stop him, but someone tackles me and we're thrashing at each other on the floor. I'm trying to pin him down, choke him out, but I'm coming on hard to what I assume is heroin because the heady rush is unlike anything I've ever felt. Everything slows, like slamming on the brakes at high speed. The woman on the bed continues screaming while the preppie and I scuffle, but Time keeps shifting from present to past. I can't hear specifically what she's yelling, but she's clearly in distress as I move down the immaculate white hallway of the expensive South London rehab facility dear dad had me locked in. It's literally sparkling clean as I near the threshold to the private room with the shinny wood floor I'm scuffling on now.

There's a lot of shouting, and shoving, and hands everywhere. Colors intensify, and light trails in long streaks with every movement of my head. I manage to get up off the floor, in what feels like super slow motion. The preppie and I circle in the small space, then a sharp pain in the side of my head, and I'm on the floor again, and all I can see is an animated Wiley Coyote vibrating from head to toe after the Roadrunner hits him with a metal mallet, because it feels as if my body is doing the same.

Then the naked blond woman is on the floor, leaning down next to me as I drag myself into a sitting position against the closest wall with one hand while holding my pounding head with the other.

"Come on, honey," she says as she pulls my hand off my head to help me stand. I look at her, but it's hard to see her eyes beyond the elaborately feathered mask she wears, like she's just come from a masquerade ball. Yellow and cream colored feathers fall in her eyes and cascade around her face.

"I'll do him gratis," she says as I let her help me off the ground and lead me to the bed. "But *only* him." She looks around the room at the others. "I get a hit for every one of you," and she turns back to me and pushes me on the bed, playfully. Then she's straddling my hips, grips my t-shirt at the collar, and forcefully rips it apart. It feels as if she's ripping open my chest. I gasp, searching for air and feel her grasp the waistband of my sweats. I push her back, but then they all move onto the bed like wolves pouncing prey.

I go ballistic, pushing and punching to get them off me, but their hands turn into reptilian heads, their arms to snakes slithering up my legs, across my torso, along my arms. Their scales are rough and grate but I cannot get them off me or stop them from biting into my flesh with my resistance. Faces are in front of mine, laughing, taunting, grins so wide it looks like bad CGI, and I'm trying to decipher the surreal from what's real...

My entire body tightens as I gag, stop walking and swallow back puking. I'm bent over, frozen in the hot sand, hunched like an old man and gasping for air.

-

-

Chapter Seventeen

-

Run. Stop thinking. *Move. Run.*

I start walking again, towards the sea, away from Elisabeth's house.

Breathe. In...Out. In...Out...

Quicken my pace as I regain control of my breathing, then take off in a casual run along the shoreline. Keep a steady, even gait for a bit, then hall ass along the water's edge, focus on my breathing, making sure I'm landing each step efficiently, and my stride is fluid.

I'm sweating in fifty paces. Must already be close to 90°. Beach is deserted. I take off my shirt and drop it as I run. I'll be back for it. Scars on my forearms are red and ugly. *Run faster. Look forward. Pump harder.* Loosely ball my hands and set my limbs into a fast rhythm.

I'm a machine. Breathe. Don't think. *Just breathe.*

I run out of beach a mile down where the cliff meets the sea, and instead of following the path up and over the hill, I suddenly feel sick again. Drenched in sweat, I swallow back this mornings samplings, but it's no use trying to keep it down. I double over and chunks of pepper and cheese are in my throat then my mouth. Can't stop puking until all that's left is burning stomach acid ripping my throat up. Swallowing it back repeatedly finally keeps it down. I sink to the hot sand, stare at the aquamarine Ionian, trying to shut down the screaming in my head, but it comes out of my mouth anyway. "I fucking HATE YOU, Edward!" my voice echoes off the cliffs and comes back at me.

Stop it! Bring it back in...Hold it together...Take a deep breath...In...Out...

I cover my vomit with sand, then look back out at the sparkling sea. How far would I have to swim out before killing my option of making it back in? Sink into oblivion and shut all this down for good...

Check out, leave, run, and he *wins.* Stop running, man. *Get mad! And find a way to take him down.*

No. Don't. What's the point? Play it as it lays. Bury it in the past where it belongs.

That's not right. The past is *never past.* It's fucking with me *now.* I see Elisabeth's enigmatic smile over my shoulder earlier this morning. I wanted to *be with her* right then... feel her, touch her, taste her. She was giving me every opening to at least ask her permission to kiss. But I couldn't. I can't. Not sure I can bear being touched anymore. "You *fucking destroyed my life, Edward*," I yell. "And I HATE YOU!" I'm not strictly sure if I'm screaming the last line at my father or myself.

Knock it off, James.

I stare out at the flat sea. Looks like the Santa Monica Bay did from my living room window sometimes—that electric blue/green the Pacific gets when a storm was breaking up or coming in. Or on really smoggy days, getting those spectacular red sunsets, the glowing orange ball sinking into horizon over the ocean...Or when the westerlies were up, the waves cresting at twenty feet...surfing all morning at Leo Carrillo, then lazing on the deck, knocking back the heat with an ice cold beer...

Julia's there. She's naked, coming through the sliding glass door. Shield my eyes from the blinding sun watching her approach. She's laughing at something I'd said, her long, tawny brown hair blowing wildly around her soft face. Then she mounts me, skin on skin all afternoon under the hot sun, and again that night beneath the stars. It's weird with moments like those. I'd missed their significant until

I was locked up in Langside, searching my memory for something to save me.

I dig my hands into the warm sand and let it run through my fingers. The scaring around my wrists from the restraints are almost gone, but the jagged red lines on my forearms will likely be visible for the rest of my life. Wish I had my shirt. I stand up, look around, scan the beach for people. Not a living soul in sight.

A sudden shudder, like a ghost passing through me, and I'm left suspended, without ground, alone. And scared out of my fucking mind. I'm breathless again. Abruptly consumed by what I've come to know as 'loneliness.' A profound longing to be seen, touched, known, to hold and be held, is tempered by an unmitigated terror that I'm now, or more likely always have been, incapable of intimacy.

I stand, and stare at the horizon—about twenty-six visible miles at sea level. How many could I make before going over the edge?

"Living is all about feeling, James." I hear Elisabeth, picture her softly sculpted profile, her elegant neck, the curve of her full breasts in firelight. *"Pleasure. Pain. Angry, sad, hurt, scared, compassion, passion, love—"* I see her clear, hazel eyes, so certain of the truth she's saying.

She has no idea how painful pain can be. I shudder, start walking back, looking for my shirt along the way.

"—letting yourself feel these things because in them lies the spectacular richness of being alive." I notice I'm smiling as I recall Elisabeth saying this to me that first night. And it's not lost on me I'm no longer free-falling, and fear has left me, for this moment, at least.

I pick up the pace to a casual run, heading back to Elisabeth's. I'm lost for what to say to her when I get there, especially for just taking off like I did. I flash on her bewildered expression when I pulled away from her this morning in front of the mirror. I recall times I left Julia at airports, train stations, standing in studio doorways with the same confused, wounded look on her face. I'd failed to acknowledge her feelings time and again, essentially ignoring her pain, so rapt in my own agenda.

I've lived an autonomous life. Self-serving. I hadn't noticed. And it didn't matter—until now, without music to absorb me, shield me, absolve me. *"Don't surround yourself with yourself. Move on back two squares..."* I hear Rick Wakeman of *Yes* in my head, and I have to stop running and laugh at the irony.

I stand on the beach laughing, strong and loud, but even I can hear it's filled with anger, almost maniacal. I spent thirteen months in hell and no one came looking for me. I was hating on everyone I could think of locked up in Langside. But I get it now. My entire life, my allegiance has been to an abstraction. I've never committed to anyone *real*.

The idea strikes me in an explosion of awareness: Music was never my savior. I may have lost myself in it, but it didn't really fill me up, which is why I played it obsessively, like an addict—asymptotically closing in on a buzz that never happens.

Instant headache, *intense*, with flashes of light, like a video filter of sparks overlap the serene Mediterranean scene. I'm not laughing anymore. Tears stream down my face. Close my eyes. Squeeze them shut tightly, then rub them with the base of my palms before brushing my cheeks clear of tears with the palms of my hands. Open my eyes and the flashing sparks are gone. Just the lazy sea lapping the shoreline where I stand, in small, soft puffs of foam is before me.

Run, James.

But I don't. I scan the beach along the baseline of the hills and spy a bit of Elisabeth's brick chimney 50 yards away, the small house mostly hiding by a thick grove of trees. I walk towards her place, along the water's edge. What the hell I'm going to say to her when I get there? If I go to her now, she'll drill me for details on my mood swing, especially since I'm the one that started the mirror thing. Turn about should have been fair play, she'll say. But I got pissed and split. She'll want to drill down on why, what's going on for me. And I'll have to get into it, because I can't keep mute every time I go dark, or she wakes me screaming from a nightmare during Siesta. And maybe once she finds out what happened, what I've done, she'll see who I've been, and likely still am. And she won't want to know me anymore.

I find my shirt in the sand where I left it, slide it on, cover my arms and hide the scars, from myself. I'm three minutes from Elisabeth place, then two, then one, but can't go back there just yet. I know I need to talk to her, apologize for taking off like I did. A year and a half ago, I never would have recognized I hurt her.

She's right about me personifying the worst in her dead husband. And about the last thing Elisabeth needs is a repeat of Jack. A year and a half ago, I wouldn't have noticed what she needed, and on the off-chance I did, I'd have figured I was her cross to bear in befriending me. Still, I cannot find the will to face her right now, without a clue of what to say that won't chase her away.

Probably close to 100° when I get back up to my house. Bathe and change into clean clothes, then walk into town. Maybe a few games of Tavli with the old men might give me the distance to formulate the right words to communicate my fulcrum, and satisfy, or at least pacify her justifiable concerns. Elisabeth is the daylight at the end of the curl; Cameron the sun— my lifeline. I may hide from the world forever without them, devolve to solitude, succumb to madness, become the crazy old man on the hill.

All the way down into town I work on the right words, phrasing and tenor for the apology I plan on delivering to Elisabeth, as soon as I come up with something worthy.

-

-

Chapter Eighteen

-

ELISBETH

She finds him late that afternoon in town, over a Tavli table at the Pelekas Café. He's playing an old man, a very old man with deeply wrinkled olive skin, crooked, yellowed teeth, and amazing brown eyes that shine with the vibrancy of youth. The old local gives her a pleasant little smile as she approaches, but James just stares at her.

"'Ames pay Tavi!" Cameron is on her shoulders but squiggles down the instant they stop at the side of the table. "Me like mommy!" He crawls into James' lap and messes up their board, stacking backgammon pieces and rolling others around. And Elisabeth lets him, too.

"Ohi! Ohi!" the old man yells, and stands to shoo Cameron away.

Her son startles from the hostile response and clings to James, who cradles Cam to him as he rises abruptly, and speaks rather aggressively to the old man. "Irémise. Ennooúse kamía zimiá. Távli eínai gia to pérasma tou chrónou tis iméras, étsi den eínai?"

The old man nods, then smiles tolerantly. James strokes Cameron's hair unconsciously while he stares at Elisabeth silently. She glares back at him, and they're both stuck in this void until the old man speaks to James.

"Oi gynaíkes eínai san tis skni'pes. Dio'htes makriá kai tha érthoun píso na se dankósoun."

"What did he say?"

"He told me to take you for a walk." James swings Cameron to his shoulders and takes her hand. "Let's go." He leads her through the maze of tables and onto the hot sand, now between her toes and the straps of her sandals. His fingers are laced in hers, extending over the back of her hand almost to her wrist. It feels oddly familiar. She's purposefully silent as they make their way towards the sea, hoping he'll begin.

"Look," he starts, and stops to look at her at waterline. "I'm sorry for just leaving like that. Guess I'm still not ready to get into my past with you quite yet. Even barring the last two years, I've been uncovering a long list of what's wrong with me lately." He gives her an awkward grin. "I tried to warn you—I'm really not the best person to be with right now. I probably never was."

Her heart caves. He must have felt it because he stops, lets go of her hand and looks at her.

"Hi mommy." Cameron smiles down at her. "Don't be mad."

"Hi Cam." She smiles up at him. "Kk. I'll try not to be mad at James anymore."

James watches her practically beaming up at her son, awestruck by the acute perception of her almost 20 month old child.

"I'm sorry, 'Lisbeth," James says. "About the last thing I want to do is hurt you."

She looks at him. He still looks rather gaunt, even with all these months of good meals together. But strikingly beautiful, nonetheless. She fixes her gaze on his green eyes—like ponds, they reflect his long, dark lashes. "James, you can run. From me. From you. Whatever. You can spend the rest of your life running, if you choose to. But you know truth here: you'll never outrun yourself."

He gives her a vague, passing smile, then his eyes veil to some internal thought.

"No running!" Cameron repeats her canonical refrain whenever he has food in his mouth. "Fy 'Ames. Fy! Fy!" Her son directs James to play their now familiar game.

James wide, infectious grin returns as he holds Cameron over his head and twirls him around and around. Cam sticks his arms out, like he's flying, and laughs hysterically. James stops spinning after half dozen or so full turns.

"'Gain! More! More!"

"In a minute, little buddy, or I'm gonna barf." James faces her, breathless, sticks out his tongue feigning nausea. He sets Cam on the sand in front of them. They meander along the water's edge, watching Cameron explore the shoreline. Her son is fully engaged in finding a treasure of interest, but when she glances at James beside her, it's clear he's not taking in the scene, but somewhere else in his head. She's lost him. Again.

"*Talk to me,*" Elisabeth says softly, but with force.

He shakes his head ever so slightly, almost involuntarily.

How do I reach this man, she wonders. Liz stops. James turns back after a few paces and looks at her. She fixes her eyes on his again. "Ya know, if you trust no one, James, and you can surely trust that you'll be lonely."

His pond moss green irises seems to darken, deepen to emerald, as if shadowed by passing clouds, though the sky is a cloudless, radiant blue.

"Either you are psychotic," she says to lighten the dark mood. He grins, half-laughs, then he turns away and starts walking again, slowly pacing Cameron. She falls in step beside him. "Or you remembered something this morning, in the mirror. I saw your expression change—go angry, dark—before you left."

He doesn't deny it, but he remains silent. She feels her ire rise. "So, before you mentally check out again, or leave before breakfast without a word, will you please share with me *what is going on*?"

"I don't know what's going on, 'Lisbeth," he says flatly. "It's like a tidal wave hits me. A flood of feelings comes to the fore and I'm drowning. I've always shut down anything that's stopped me from functioning. Relationships. Intoxicants. Feelings." He sighs heavily. "'Cept I'm not sure how to anymore."

She responds after a few measured steps. "You don't have to anymore. Talk to me. I'm right here." She waits what feels like a full minute, but manages to keep her mouth shut to give him the opening to speak.

"I'm free-falling, Liz. Music gave me ground, a foundation with walls, a controllable space of my own creation. The more focus, and hours I invested, the more I could accomplish." He pauses. She waits. "Now, I'm virtually non-functional. And I vacillate between anger, regret, and fear mostly. Except when I'm with you. You and Cameron." James glances at her quickly, then looks forward, seemingly at her son trying to outrun the thin foam line of the incoming tide.

Elisabeth smiles, hoping he does not see her blushing, momentarily lost for a response.

"Look! Look! Wow!" Cameron digs after a tiny crab that's scurried down into the soft, wet sand. "Ahh..." His pouty lower lip comes out when he can't find it.

James kneels next to him. With a scoop of his huge hand into the sand, he finds the crab and shows it to Cameron. They both watch it crawl across James' palm, then scuttle off his hand and drop back onto the wet sand. A small wave comes in, covering their toes. The water recedes, and the tiny crab has disappeared. Already on to the next thing, Cam toddles out of the water, trying to outpace the rising tide again. James stares after him a moment before rising, and they resume their slow pace.

"You're great with him. Very natural. How do you come by that?" Elisabeth asks, trying to return to the intimate exchange they had going before Cam interrupted them.

"Cameron is easy to please. Nothing complicated. No hidden agendas." He raises an eyebrow at her. "I have no living siblings that I helped raise. And no, I don't have any kids. None that I know of anyway."

"*Living* siblings?'" Liz asks, hoping he'll continue to be forthcoming.

He doesn't answer. She looks at him. He strolls beside her, but seems totally absorbed in his own thoughts, or whatever the hell is going on in his head. His expression is virtually blank, like he's sleepwalking.

Don't scream.

He's totally consumed, a million miles away.

Don't be mad. Don't get mad at him. You always got mad at Jack and it never did any good. Back off, Liz. Maybe if she gives him distance he'll eventually come to her.

James takes off like a shot, runs full force towards Cameron as he toddles into the sea while chasing a group of gulls. Just as a small wave sends her son tumbling into the water, James scoops his little body out. Soaking wet and screaming, Cameron clings to him. Elisabeth has to pry him loose, then he clings to her, body to body, his arms and legs wrapped around her, and she holds on for dear, sweet life.

"It's okay, baby." She smooshes her face into his neck. "You're fine, Cam. Calm down. You're okay." She rubs his back, rocks him gently. Cameron stops crying and loosens his grip around her neck. She looks at James and tries to hide her shame with a smile. "Thank you."

"No problem."

She holds Cameron tight. "I'm afraid of losing him. I think about it all the time. He was twelve feet away and I know he wasn't in mortal danger. But my heart is still stuck in my throat." She rubs her cheek to her son's, and he giggles and snuggles into her. He's soft and warm and wet, smells of sea salt and sweetness. "I've never felt anything like I do for him. The feeling is more powerful, intimate, connected, than anything I've ever experienced. And now that I know this kind of love, this magnificent *feeling* I had no clue existed before him, I can't ever live without it again." It comes out more dramatic than she'd intended. She looks away. Cameron's wriggling, so she sets him down. "He's already off on a new adventure, and my heart hasn't established an even rhythm yet." Elisabeth looks at James. He smiles and keeps his eyes on hers until Cameron takes off up the beach again.

They watch Cam explore what feels like every shell, lingering near him. The silence between them isn't awkward, but she feels his distance. He's watching her son, but not really, like he's lost inside his head again. Her mind races to find the words, and the right tenor to deliver them, that will engage James with *her*, instead of just himself.

"I don't know exactly how to help you with fear. I'm scared of everything, all the time, especially now, since Jack," she confesses softly, hoping to draw him in, but she's not sure he's listening. "And I don't know what to do with regret either. I live with a ton of it, like most everyone else, I guess."

"You're not kidding," he says quietly, like to himself, and still doesn't look at her. "Regret can be one hell of a motivator though."

"Touché to that," she smiles at him, but he stays fixed on Cameron. "What I *do* know, for me at least," Elisabeth continues when James does not. "Recognizing when I screw up helps me temper my anger. Acknowledging my culpability usually quells my outrage over being *wronged*."

She sees his brows furrow, his eyes narrow. She feels him tense.

"I was wronged" James says definitively. "And I have every right to be outraged." He takes a deep breath. "Look, Liz, even if I admit to some infinitesimal measure of culpability in setting up the train wreak that's derailed my life, I'm still disgusted—just at myself, too."

"But that's manageable. Learn from who you *were*, and there'll be no reason to be angry with the man you are."

He stops and looks at her. Then he smiles, almost to himself.

"Wow! Wut dat?"Cameron takes off up the beach.

They join him in front of a complex sandcastle collapsing with the incoming tide. Walled courtyard, four turrets with carved narrow windows and fluted tops, surround the interior castle.

"It's a *sandcastle*, baby. Like the ones we build sometimes. Only ours aren't as good."

James laughs. "Ours aren't close. This is pro. It's exquisite." A small wave from the incoming tide takes a piece of the sand wall away, and his lingering smile turns into a classic pout. Elisabeth almost laughs.

"Aww!" Cameron's lower lip comes out and his expression takes on the exact same pout. Cam pushes the wet sand of the castle wall back in place, only to watch it slide down again, taking more of the wall with it. "No! Fix, Mama!"

"I can't, Cam," she says gently. "The waves are just going to keep knocking it down. We can't fix it, baby."

Cameron looks at James. "Fix 'Ames. *Peeezzze!*"

"Your mama's right, little man. We can't fix this one. But we can build another one, a stronger one." James winks at her. "Come on, Cam, help me out. Let's create a masterpiece." He kneels and opens his arms to her son. Cameron runs to him. James picks him up, swings Cameron onto his shoulders and goes several yards from the water's edge. He plops down onto his knees, bows as if praying, and Cameron slides over his head and onto the warm, dry sand, still smiling.

They spend the afternoon building sandcastles, playing in the surf and on the sand, hunting for shells, making sand sculptures, burying their bodies. Their focus gravitates to keeping Cameron engaged. They head back to Elisabeth's house, sandy and sun-drenched around sunset. The masterpiece they created is the memory of the day.

-

-

Chapter Nineteen

-

Cameron shoves a fist of spaghetti into his mouth from the plateful on his highchair tray when Elisabeth doesn't supply him his next bite instantly. Olive oil smears his face, his hands, up his little arms.

"Ah, Cam. Can you please just wait a minute?" Liz is exasperated for the twelfth time today. Babies are *innocents*? Ha! Babies are solipsist, and it was turning out to be the job of her life teaching her son how to recognize other's needs beyond his own.

James retrieves the dishtowel and wipes him clean, then sits back down in his usual place to finish his shrimp and pasta. Elisabeth sits on the other side of Cam per usual. She takes one last bite of the fattening meal with a pang of guilt. She has to remember to leave more on her plate if she's going to lose weight. It all just tastes so great though. She sighs, picks up the mini-fork on her son's tray,

©2019 J. Cafesin   248

loads it with cut up spaghetti and feeds him the bite. "Acting civilized is part of what moved us past warring tribes of monkeys."

"You're mama's right, as always." James raises his fork to show Cameron, then puts it in the pile of pasta on his plate and scoops, demonstrating to Cam how to gather it.

Cam grabs the fork from his mama. "Me!"

"Don't grab! That's *not* OK," Elisabeth starts, and is about to explain, again, why grabbing isn't OK, except her son is trying to copy James. Cam is trying to fill his own fork with spaghetti, and she doesn't want to disrupt this teachable moment. Unsuccessful after multiple tries, he starts stabbing at his pasta, clearly frustrated, and Elisabeth feels her ire rise. "Maybe he's not ready—"

"He's ready. He just needs to be shown how." James covers her son's tiny hand in his enormous palm, grips the top of the bright yellow rubber fork handle and guides.

After multiple tries, with James assistance, Cam manages to get a few strands on his fork, and even several bites into his mouth. He and James high five with each success and after fifteen minutes of concentrated effort, her year and a half old son is feeding himself.

"Proud mama here." She beams at Cameron. "Thanks." She grins at James. "Learn something new every day."

"Only if you want to," James retorts gently, and turns back to Cam who pops a forkful in his mouth and then raises his hand to high-five James. "Good job. Keep practicing, little dude. Only way to get good at anything is to *practice*."

"Practice!" Cam repeats, and begins mushing spaghetti strands with his mini-fork, which is clearly more fascinating than eating it.

"Okay, okay," Liz say, exasperated, again, though Cameron is laughing, because James is. "I think we're done with dinner. It's shower time." She cleans up her son with the dishtowel again before lifting him out of the high chair. "We're going to get cleaned up and ready for bed."

"Sounds good." James finishes the last bites on his plate, gets up, collects the dishes and puts them in the sink for washing.

"Book, 'Ames." Cameron says over his mama's shoulder as she carries him out. "One fis. Two fis. *Peezze!*"

Elisabeth tries to ignore the sting of her son's new preference. "He wants you to read him a book before bed tonight." First time Cam has asked James for a bedtime read.

"I'd be honored, sir." He bows to Cam, then glances at her with a tentative smile. "Let me know when he's ready."

James is just finishing the dishes when she comes back into the kitchen holding a clean Cameron, dressed in his bright red nightie with the blue airplanes. "It's easier to read in his room, on the pillows on the floor, so he can go straight into his crib without distractions."

"Great. Let's go." He throws the dishtowel on the counter top and follows them into Cameron's bedroom, Elisabeth realizing only then he's never been all the way in her son's room before.

His eyes scan the room quickly and she wonders if he'll notice it straight away, which of course, he does. He looks at the guitar case leaning against the wall next to the crib, and then glances at her. Cameron squiggles out of her arms, flops onto the pillows, and waits expectantly.

"Okay. What are we reading tonight?" James asks casually.

She hands him *One Fish, Two Fish*. "It's his night time favorite."

He sits on one of the big pillows and wraps his arm around

Cameron, who snuggles into his chest as he begins to read. "*'From there to here, from here to there, funny things are everywhere,'*" He glances again at the guitar, then at her for only an instant, then continues reading to Cameron. Elisabeth goes back into the kitchen to finish putting away the dishes.

Was he mad? Glad? Did it matter at all? Clearly, it did. At least a little. His expression changed when he saw it. Hardened. What was that? Anger? No. Fear…

Why would the guitar scare him? He'd told her he wasn't a musician anymore, whatever *that* meant. It isn't likely he'd forgotten how to play. So he's choosing not to. Why? Or maybe he can't anymore. Maybe he cut some connection to his hands when he slit his wrists. *God, what a horrible price.* It's no wonder the man is lost.

"Your child has been tucked securely into his crib. I imagine you would like to go say goodnight?"

"Yes. Thank you. Be right back." She goes into his room, stands at his crib and takes in the picture worthy scene of her beautiful child sleeping. She kisses her fingertips, then touches Cameron's cheek. Elisabeth quietly bids him sweet dreams, then leaves, closing the door softly behind her.

"Whose guitar is that?" is the first thing he says as she comes back into the kitchen.

"It was Jack's. It's one of the few non-essentials I took with us. Other than his laptop, that guitar was probably Jack's most treasured possession. He played it pretty well for an amateur, and Cameron likes to fiddle with it every so often. Why do you ask?"

He shakes his head, shrugs, spreads his hands in surrender.

"Would you like to play it?"

"No." Then, "Yes." Then he laughs, but it isn't with humor. "Thing is, don't know if I can play anymore."

"Well, give it a try and see."

He gives her a quasi-grin. "Risky. If I can't, I'm not quite sure I can bear the loss."

"Maybe you won't have to." She goes back into Cameron's room before James can protest and meets him in the living room with the guitar. Elisabeth sets the case on the floor, flips open the locks, and lifts the lid. An unexpected wave of profound sadness, then guilt as she stares down at Jack's guitar. And suddenly she sees her husband sitting crossed-legged in front of her with the guitar in his lap. It's three in the morning, in the basement of their Tel Aviv flat. Building foundation vibrates with the passing jet fighters, but at least they can't hear the city sirens from down there. Cameron is just two months. He's fussing in the bassinet. Jack tries to soothe him to sleep with music. Elisabeth is too exhausted to move, or she'd have gotten off the floor and kissed him right then.

She looks up at James standing behind her. His arms are folded over his chest, hands tucked against his sides. He stares down at the guitar, his expression steely, unreadable. He finally glances at her, shakes his head slowly.

"I can't do this now. I'm sorry." He turns away, goes over to the window and looks out.

Elisabeth strokes the strings softly, just once, then closes the case and puts it back in Cameron's room, fully expecting when she comes out that James will be gone. But he isn't. He's still standing by the window, staring out. She doesn't know what to say to him, consumed by her own sadness. She sits on the couch, grabs the pillow, hugs it to her as she buries her face in it and succumbs to her grief.

"I'm sorry, 'Lisbeth. I know how much it hurts losing people you love." He leans back against the wall, one bare foot up against it. His soft linen shirt is tucked loosely into his jeans. Thick waves of silky hair frame his sculpted face and are scattered in his striking eyes, which are fixed on her. And as magnificent as he is, right now, she wishes he was Jack.

"God, I miss him. I miss him so much it physically hurts." She hugs the pillow tighter, and with every blink tears fall down her cheeks and she can't stop them. "I'm sorry. I get you've got your own shit going on. I'm sure you don't need mine right now." She sniffles, and wipes the wetness from cheeks with the back of her hand, then gives him a quazi-grin.

"Don't apologize for grieving, Liz. I buried my parents when I was thirteen, and then myself, in music. Lost my muse a year and a half ago." He looks down. "Been nothing since. Believe me, I understand loss."

She's floored by his words. Grief funnels into anger, and she's suddenly incredulous. "Being a musician was what you *did*, James, not all of who you were, or are, or could be. Don't you get it? Jack's loss as a reporter will be marginal. A thousand others precede him. His loss will be felt much more profoundly by the son who will never know his father; by me, who won't grow old with the man I committed to spending my life; by his parents who now have to face every day without the child they raised to outlive them."

"I've no family. No partner, nor children. I've cultivated none of these things. My loss will be marginal." He shoots her a cheeky grin.

"It wouldn't be to me, and Cameron." She sighs, shakes her head and sadness consumes her again.

"I'm sorry, 'Lisbeth. I was being flip. It was careless."

"But honest. You're still there, aren't you. You're still on the cliff staring into the chasm."

He half-laughs, shrugs then looks down again.

"Harboring the notion you're nothing to anyone just makes it easier to check out, James."

"Maybe. Probably." He looks at her then, searching. "But if I can't play, it feels like that just may push me right over the edge."

"Only if you let it. *You choose*." She stays fixed on him. "It's as important as you make it." She thinks she catches a quick smile as he looks down again. She sighs. "James, you want to find some ground? Maybe it's time to figure out what you have to give besides music, don't you think?"

He looks at her. "You don't get it. I don't want to think."

Jerk. "God, I'm right back where I left off with Jack," she practically growls at him. "No. Worse. You're *consciously* avoiding yourself." She buries her face in the pillow and screams.

He laughs. She glares at him. "Okay, Liz, what is it you want to hear? Wasn't it you who told me on the beach this afternoon that you're scared of everything all the time? Well, I'm with you. You should be."

Blank on a witty retort. She's surprised he heard her earlier. Pleasantly surprised. "I might feel afraid a lot, but I refuse to live that way." She stares at him. "Look, you said music gave you a foundation once. Maybe it can again. Take the guitar. Go play it, James. Prove to yourself you can, and that it's not the end all. No matter how brilliant a player you are, it won't ever really fulfill you."

He studies her. "'Lisbeth, I'm not your second chance at fixing Jack."

"Jack is dead. And I can't possibly fix you, honey. You're going to have to do that."

His eyes narrow, but there's humor in them. "Woman, you really are a hard case." His expression hardens. "You're mad at Jack. I get it.

But I'm not Jack. You can share your anger with me, but I'd prefer not at me. I may deserve it for past crimes, but not with you. Not yet, anyway."

"Not counting when you walked out this morning." She instantly regrets saying it. It's crass and shames her.

He sighs and shakes his head then pushes away from the wall. "It's getting late. We're both tired. We'll talk tomorrow. Goodnight."

She doesn't say anything to stop him. He walks out and shuts the screen quietly, and she's glad he's left. She sits on the couch and cries. She cries for what she and Jack shared, and what they didn't. She cries for Cameron, and the father he will never know. She cries for James, and the losses he's suffered, of his parents, of his music, of his sense of self. She's consumed with emptiness, aching for contact, with Jack, with James...

Never again with Jack. And though the notion hurts—an ache in her stomach and chest—it surprises her how distant the past now feels. *Never again with Jack,* is less weighted. She's finally done with trying to fix him, and getting nowhere—but contentious.

I'm sorry, Jack.

She sits on the couch and swears at herself, then to herself she'll never try to fix anyone but herself again. James believes his worth is his music because it's all he knows. And though music may ground him, it will never complete him. But he's going to have to come to that on his own.

It's close to four in the morning when Elisabeth goes into Cameron's room and gets the guitar. She covers her son, tucks the blanket around him firmly and strokes his small head, then closes the door to his room and leaves the house. She makes sure all the doors are locked, something she hasn't bothered with since moving in, though she'll only be gone a few minutes.

She climbs the hill as quickly and quietly as she can. She doesn't want him to hear her, doesn't want to see him right now. All the lights are off when she gets up to his house. Elisabeth leaves the guitar on his back porch with a note. She hopes when he finds it in the morning, he'll accept it in the spirit it's been given.

-

-

Chapter Twenty

-

JAMES

I read the note.

Since it's meant to be played, I thought you could be of greater service to this instrument than Cameron or I. Perhaps this guitar can help you find what you feel you've lost.

I'm sorry for last night. I was out of line. I apologize.

E.

I bring the guitar in the house and set it on the floor, kneel in front of it, flip open the case and stare down at it. Jack's guitar. Cameron's father's guitar. A dead man's guitar. *No use to him now.* It's a beautiful instrument, a Martin D45, LE, I think. Only 50 or so made as I recall, rosewood with pearl bordering, fourteen fret fingerboard. I vaguely wonder how well Jack played it. I'm scared out of my mind to find out if I still can.

If I can master the guitar again, I can surely re-master most other instruments. And I'll have my life back. Except not really. I'll only have music back. And that hadn't turned out to be enough. *'I'm afraid of losing him.'* I see Elisabeth smoosh her face into

Cameron's neck and hold on tight after I lifted him out of the water yesterday. The image lingers, their exchange of love was palpable. And I know right then, with a clarity often sought but rarely attained, that even if I can make it with music again, it will never be enough.

I stare at the guitar.

And suddenly I'm five, sitting on the gray woolen couch in the playroom watching TV. Mike comes in carrying two guitar cases covered with snow, sets them down carefully in the foyer and brushes them dry with his scarf. One of the cases is Mike's, with the stickers, dings and tears. The other I've never seen before. Mike brings both into the playroom and turns off the TV.

I protest loudly, but Mike silently flips open both cases, takes out his guitar, and hands me the other. He sits down on the couch and starts playing—very slowly, and instructs me to copy him. And I do. I sit on the floor at Mike's feet and copy his fingering, getting it wrong more often than right at first, but Mike doesn't seem to mind.

"Again. Again. Again." Mike repeats it softly, for an hour or so until mom calls us for dinner.

By then, I'm playing Frere Jacques right along with Mike. Mom joins us with her flute. Mike sets a fast rhythm, strums double time behind my slow picking. The flute quivers like snowflakes, dancing around our melody. Sound resonates off the walls and moves through me, and we are one. Mom. Mike. Me. Connected. And I am complete. I had to have more...

I'd missed the significance of that moment all those years ago with my parents. I mistakenly assumed it was the music that filled me up, but I realize now that deep resonance I'd felt had been the love we shared. We were simply creating the soundtrack for the scene. The music intertwined, blended with feelings of security, contentment, profound joy, that were subsequently rekindled every time I played.

Jack's guitar mocks me, and I glare at it. *'Take the guitar. Go play it, James. Prove to yourself you can, and that it's not the end all.'* I hear Elisabeth, recall the certainty in her clear hazel eyes, even wet with tears of grief. A sweeping wave of sadness rushes through me for her loss, which reminds me of mine.

I miss you, mom. I need to feel *you hug me, hold me, make everything OK. I miss you Mike, and the music we made together.* The ache is palpable. I feel my eyes fill with tears, and I don't even try to stop them from falling. And I see my parents again, that night in our kitchen, mom's short, dark hair is in her striking green eyes as she blows on the flute. She kisses Mike on the lips after we stop playing and he turns to me with his broad bearded smile. I smile with the memory, but it hurts inside—the gnawing, unrequited longing for them.

I sit on the sleeping bag and lift the guitar slowly from the case, position it in my lap and strum it. It's horribly flat, so I start tuning it, but as soon as I put pressure on my fingers sharp pain goes shooting through my hands.

Put it down. Put the fucking guitar back in the case.

No. Don't.

"Let the music suck you in and block out the pain." Mike's talking about the fatigue in my fingertips that day I was learning to play. "It'll get easier, I promise. Don't stop. Focus on the music and keep playing, James." Mike coaxes me on. 'Don't quit. Keep playing and the pain will go away.'

I tune the guitar, repeating Mike's words in my head like a mantra. 'Don't quit. Keep playing.' *It hurts.* Block out everything but the music. *Listen...a little higher. There it is. Perfect G. Hear it. Feel it resonate in you, through you.* It still hurts, but the intensity ebbs.

I'm doing it, Mike. Exactly what you told me to do. I'm blocking out the pain. I've been doing it my whole life now.

Laugh at the thought. "Internal, external, I've been shutting it all out with music..."

Except I can't anymore.

My hands are killing me, ribbons of pain shoot through my fingers as I pluck the strings. E, A, D, G, B, E. *Perfect. Good. Okay.* I shake my hands out, ball them and shake them again, trying to relieve the aching. The piano at Martin's had been a lot easier. I played like crap, but at least it didn't hurt as much. Strumming sends cramps through my palm straight into my head. I stifle a scream and stop playing. My hands are shaking. Fingers are rigid, contorted. *Christ, it hurts.*

I grit my teeth against the pain as I strum a simple Am7-Bm7b5-E7-Am progression. Tears still streak down my face, sadness now joined by the pain in my hands. I stop playing, wipe them away on my shirtsleeve. Stretch my hands out again, resume playing, go back to picking—arpeggio first. *Smooth it out.* Move to tremelo. *Keep it smooth.* Okay. And alternate. Okay. Watch my fingers move, find the groove, sync the riff. *I'm doing it.* The pain numbs, subsiding, but tears come again as images of my parents, Julia, then Elisabeth snuggling with Cam flash like a slide show in my head. Sudden suffocating heaviness in my chest for missing that it's the *people* in my life that really matter, and to date, I'd failed to give them their due. I stop playing. My hand closes around the neck of the guitar and I squeeze, letting the stings dig into my palm.

I put the guitar back in its case, close and snap it shut. Ball and stretch my fingers again, then pick up the case and put it in the bedroom I never use, among the stacks of books and clutter of clothes scattered about. I take off my jeans, pull a pair of sweats off the floor and slip them on before leaving the room, then go for my morning run.

I stop by Elisabeth's, as usual, on my way back. She's in the kitchen, wearing a gauzy white summer dress I've not seen before, making scrambled eggs and bacon. She looks stunning, her auburn hair, tied back with a scrunchy, is cascading down her back. Fine strands have escaped the hair tie all around her face, softening her defined features. Cameron's in his highchair rolling blueberries around his tray, and then taking delight in smashing one, and finger painting with the juice. He offers me the smashed berry as I sit at the table.

"No thanks, little man. You go ahead."

Cameron pops the blueberry in his mouth. "Mmmm. Yum, yum." He smiles this delightful grin and I'm pulled into his lightness, smile back at him.

"Thank you for the guitar." I watch her cook the eggs, flip the bacon. "I know it meant a lot to you. I'm really touched. It's very kind."

She flashes a shy smile. "Did you play it?" She tucks a fine, loose wisp of hair behind her ear.

"A little. Hurt like hell. Been awhile. My fingers aren't ready."

"Your fingers, or your heart?"

"Both, probably." She goes straight for the truth. No holds barred. It's unnerving. And humbling because she nails me so much of the time. She puts a plate of eggs and bacon in front of Cameron and me, then joins us at the table with a plate of her own. We eat in silence for a while, but I feel her tension mounting.

"I know I apologized about last night in the note, but I want to let you know face-to-face that you were absolutely right. I was taking my anger at Jack out on you. It was uncalled for, you didn't deserve it, and I'm sorry."

"And a lot of what you said is right. Again."

She gives me a temperate smile. "Either you missed your calling as a diplomat, or you're mocking me, James."

"I'm not, 'Lisbeth. Love is costly. The pain of loss is almost intolerable, so I've deftly avoided emotional commitments by burying myself in an abstraction. And you called me on it last night." Stay fixed on her with my confession. "I don't want to ever go there again."

She watches me for a minute. She turns to feed Cameron, then changes her mind and hands him his fork. She grasps his tiny hand and helps him scoop the eggs, then guides him, lifting the fork to his mouth without losing them. Her unwavering patience and tenacity as Cam misses or plays with bite after bite belies their incredible bond, the unconditional love she feels for him. 'You're safe here,' she'd said a while back, and right now, I believe her. I'm sated, grounded, glad to be a part of the scene.

A mischievous smile appears on her face.

"Why are you smiling?"

"Because you are." She stares at me. "What are you thinking about?"

"That foundation can be found in many things."

Her smile softens. "You're coming along."

I laugh, take another bite of eggs. Warm, rich and salty. Every mouthful tasted better than the last. I want more. *Need* more. I'm starving.

She rubs her nose against Cameron's. They exchange Eskimo kisses. Laugh. She helps him with another bite, congratulates him when he gets it right, then looks back at me. "How were your parents killed?"

She rarely asks personal questions off-the-wall, without any context, so I feel obliged to answer. "Plane crash, along with nine others, in a private jet on the way back from a benefit concert. Why?"

"I'm sorry." She stares into me, like she feels my sudden rush of sadness. "My parents are still alive, alive and vital and still living in the same house where I grew up in North Hollywood." She gives me a quirky grin. "I need the distance between us right now, but life without them seems unbearably lonely. Does it feel that way to you?"

"Yes. Sometimes...A lot, actually."

"You mentioned you have a 'real' father. I assume you meant a biological father?"

My breath catches in my throat. "Yes." She watches me. I look away.

"Family is a big part of my foundation. Always thought when my parents died, I'd still have Jack. But now, when my parents and in-laws are gone, Cam and me will have no one. And where do orphans go for Thanksgiving?"

I catch the laugh in my throat and it comes out more like a cough. Can't tell if she's serious. Her expression seems genuinely sad. "I'll make you and Cam Thanksgiving dinner, 'Lizbeth. Don't worry about it."

A surprised smile sweeps across her face, eyes more green than brown this morning sparkling with delight. "So... what are you making for this Thanksgiving feast?"

"Whatever you desire, my lady."

"You think you're that good?"

"I was taught by a master, and I learn quickly with things I want to know."

Her smile takes on a Cheshire grin, mimicking mine perhaps. "And will the guest list include your father to this holiday dinner?"

I stop breathing, force myself to start again when I realize I'm not. "I have no relationship with my father, and have no intention of having one in the future." I put my fork down, push my plate away. She studies me. I feel the wave coming. "And I don't want to talk about this."

"Okay."

"I don't."

"Okay."

I stand, push the chair to the table and hold on to the back of it. "My father was the one who had me set up for dealing." Everything starts to spin, and I grip the chair and close my eyes and words fall out of my mouth. "And I hate him. I really hate him. I want him dead, gone, off the face of the earth for the hell he put me through." I try to control my trembling, open my eyes to stop the spinning. She's staring at me. Cameron is, too. I try to laugh off my anger but it clings—chokes. "You don't understand. The controlling fuck *set me up,* ripped my life apart. He had no right, and I'm justified in hating him." I feel warm tears spill down my face and look down, wipe them away with my shirtsleeve.

I feel Elisabeth fixed on me. "James, I'm not your judge," she says softly. "Only you are."

"'Ames sad. *Ah.* Make awl beta, Mama," Cameron instructs.

I laugh off my tears, comb my hand through my hair and smile at Cam. "No worries, little man. Your mama's already helping me get better." I finally look at her.

She studies me, trying to get inside my head.

"Up. Up. Up, 'Ames." Cameron lifts his tiny arms to me to lift him from the high chair. I do, thinking he wants to get down, but then he hugs me, throws his arms around my neck and pulls himself into me, wrapping his legs around my side, pushing his face into my neck. There are no words to describe the feeling that overwhelms me with his tender action. I wrap my arms around him, holding him to my chest, my hand on the back of his head; soft, fine wisps of his hair caressing my fingertips. It takes every bit of my will not to break down again.

Cameron pulls back, put his tiny hands to my jaw and holds my face. "Awl beta, 'Ames?"

I smile from the inside out. "All better, Cam. Thanks."

Ear-to-ear grin across his angelic face, then he looks at his mama.

Misty eyed, but no tears, she gives us her beautiful, soft white smile, but it fades when she focuses on me. "I'm sorry for what you've been through, James, for whatever you're going through now. But I believe things happen for a reason, even if we can't see it at the time. Maybe the road you've traveled was the only way to enlighten you." She says it gently, simply assessing the possible, but it still irritates. "And, as harsh as it sounds, whatever led you here, well, for that I'm grateful."

I glare at her. "You shouldn't be." She stays fixed on me, waiting, and I want to hate her right then, but I can't. I give her Cameron, start clearing the dishes from the table. Feel them watching me, finally I turn on her. "Whatever you see when you look at me is an illusion. I killed a man 'Lisbeth. What you said last night is right. I'm not nothing without music. I'm a killer. Look at me. *See me*." Her clear hazel eyes become clouded with my confession, and I feel her withdraw. And it feels like she's knifed me.

"It was self-defense." She whispers. "Tell me it was self-defense and I'll believe you."

I hesitate. "It's complicated."

"No. It's not." Her eyes are liquid amber. "I see you, James. And I know it was self-defense." She stares at me with certainty.

I'm instantly humbled, sated. Sigh. "Thank you." I want to kiss her right then, imagine reaching for her, drawing her in, but I don't. I wait for her to probe further, but she just stands there with Cameron on her hip fixed on me. His little legs wrap around her waist; he holds onto her neck, their soft faces right next to each other, and I'm momentarily awestruck by their radiant beauty.

"I don't need to know what happened," she says, her eyes still fixed on mine. "But you're going to need to talk about it—put it out in front of you to move past it. You know that, don't you?"

I hesitate to proclaim my ignorance, then shrug.

"Well, just to let you know, I'm here, and available." She flashes a shy smile.

I smile. Nod.

Cameron yanks at her sparkling diamond stud, and she yelps and grabs his hand from her ear. "Ouch! Stop that! Let go." Elisabeth holds his hand. Cameron pouts but she sticks his knuckles in her mouth and sucks on his small hand with a big, wet kiss. His ear-to-ear grin is infectious. "I'm going to change him. Be right back."

I finish putting the dishes in the sink and wash them. I'd confessed. She knows now. Beyond her initial confusion, there was no fear in her eyes or change in her demeanor when I told her what I'd done. She exonerated me. Absolved me. Saved me.

Elisabeth comes back in the kitchen without Cameron, her cottony dress flowing with her graceful movement revealing her soft, sensual curves. She stands next to me, picks up the dishtowel and starts drying the dishes. "Cam decided he'd rather play with Thomas than be with us." She falls silent, but I feel her curiosity—her unspoken questions between us.

Regardless of what she said, I know she wants details of what happened. I would. Trust is a thin line, and borders belief without the knowledge to make your own assessment. I'm gonna have to cop to, I know. But the twisted ugliness of it is in such sharp contrast to the present, that for right now, I'll dare to rely on her faith in me.

The sun streams through the kitchen windows. The turquoise to twilight Ionian sparkles lazily beyond the shoreline and out to horizon, promising a spectacular day, which beckons.

"Thanks for breakfast. Delicious as always." It's my usual cue I'm leaving. Done it every morning for months now. But I don't want to leave today. I feel safe here, privileged to be with them. Alone in my house reading, or blowing one more morning playing Tavli will not do. "Ever been up to Sidari?"

"No. Why?" Her shy smile reappears.

"Want to go? It's only about an hour away, and I hear the tide pools up there are spectacular."

Her smile broadens and she nods, and the room fills with her lightness, displacing the darkness within.

-

-

Chapter Twenty-One

-

First really hot day since I've been here hints at the coming heat of summer. I take the top off the Jeep, go into Agios Gordios, get a baby seat for Cameron and secure it in the center of the backseat while Elisabeth gets him, and his many accouterments ready for the short trip.

Cameron laughs for the first fifteen minutes straight with the wind blowing all around him. He raises his little arms up in the air and lets the wind sway them about. His unadulterated joy is infectious and spreads to me and Elisabeth, and we laugh along with him, and then together at the duration of his amusement.

The roads are narrow and winding. I take them slowly and with care. We get to Sidari in the early afternoon, stop in town for some bread, cheese and fruit, and bring it out to the sandstone cliffs overlooking the crystal sea where we lunch. After eating, we scurry down to explore the sandy cove inlets created from the eroding hills. The water is shallow and warm, perfect for Cameron to wade in and be amazed by the small fish swimming around his feet.

The three of us play for an hour or so, then find an isolated cove and set the blanket on the warm sand near the base of the hills so Cameron can take his afternoon nap. He's asleep within moments of breastfeeding, his little head falling back away from Elisabeth's breast, his mouth still in the motion of suckling even in sleep. She covers herself quickly, then lays Cam between us in the baby carrier and loops her arm through one of the straps. Finally, she lays beside her son and snuggles her body next to his, spooning him.

"I love the way he feels, how his warm little body fits perfectly along mine. I love the way he smells." She presses her nose into the base of Cameron's neck and inhales his scent. "I feel so unbelievably lucky to have him."

I lay on my side, lean on my elbow and look at them. Cam's curled into her, his pouty lips slightly parted, his fine hair just over the top of his brow, his full face peaceful in blissful sleep. His tiny hand grips his mama's finger. Elisabeth's cheek rests on the top of his head. Soft wisps of his hair brush her naturally ruby lips. She's exquisite. Her sheer cottony dress and the maroon leotard she wears under it reveals her curvaceous form. Her hair is loose, cascades around her shoulders in soft waves. Her hazel eyes more green than brown against her suntanned skin.

"Don't stare at me like that. You're embarrassing me."

"Sorry. It's just…you're stunning. A Rubens masterpiece—'Mother with Child.'"

"First, Rubens is not a compliment. Rubin, and his fat women."

"Voluptuous. Not fat." My eyes keep drifting to her ample cleavage.

"Whatever. Besides, look who's talking. It's ninety degrees out here and you're wearing a long sleeve shirt. I'm not the only one with body image issues."

"I'll stop if you will."

"What?"

"Hiding. Take off your dress."

Her eyes narrow but there's humor in them. She sits up and very slowly begins unbuttoning the tiny row of beads down the middle of her dress. With each button the smile on her face broadens. "Come on, James. It's your challenge. Are you going to pick up the gauntlet?"

I sit up and start unbuttoning my shirt. No one around. She's already seen my wrists and had her say about them, but my heart beats hard, reverberates in my throat. I want to stop the game, but I keep unbuttoning. Because she is. I can tell she's feeling the same way I am. Her eyes dart to the edges of our inlet checking for intruders.

When our clothing is unbuttoned all the way we both freeze, and then smile. Her eyes are fixed on mine—we're connected, inside each other's heads. Feel her trepidation, know she feels mine.

"All the way." She leans over Cameron and unbuttons my shirtsleeves. When they're loose, I let her pull my sleeves off me. The shirt falls off of my shoulders. I cross my arms over my chest and tuck my hand against my sides, hiding my scars.

"No. Let me see."

"No. Not until you finish. Dress off."

She slides her dress off of her shoulders and lets it fall to her waist, the skin tight, spaghetti-strapped leotard essentially exposing her form. She doesn't look away. She holds my stare, her eyes pleading with me to stay with hers and not scan her body. So I don't. We keep our eyes locked on each other even while she reaches for my wrists, pulls my hands from my sides and turns them upward. I look down at the jagged red lines extending down the middle of my forearms. *There was so much blood.* Lunch rises in my throat.

"Talk to me. Don't let it swallow you up. *Tell me.*" She whispers.

"I couldn't feel it," I hear myself say. "I couldn't feel anything by that point. Used a broken shower tile—took six months to scratch it out with my fingernail. Blood was everywhere, instantly, the water splattered it. I didn't make a sound. Stood there and let the water run down my arms and watched my blood go down the drain. It turned the water red, the tiles red, gathered in the grout as it ran down the walls. But it was like watching it on TV because I couldn't feel it. There was no pain. Don't even remember thinking anything, except that I didn't want the orderly to wake before the blood loss killed me. I have no clue how long I stood there blanked out like that before I passed out."

She runs her fingers lightly over my forearm. "Feel this?"

The scar's numb, but around it tingles, touches pain as she strokes. "Yeah."

"Good." She smiles, and then releases my hands. Elisabeth lies back down, flat on her back and closes her eyes. After a moment I do, too, and we both fall asleep until Cameron wakes us, crying to be fed an hour or so later.

I put back on my shirt, button only my shirtsleeves, leaving my torso exposed, then lay on the blanket and watch her son suckle her. First thing she does after breastfeeding is put on her dress. I smile, shake my head knowingly as she buttons up.

She catches it. "Stop mocking me."

"I'm not. I'm empathizing."

She glances at me with her soft smile. "Then stop staring."

"Sorry. You're really quite alluring under your rather loose wardrobe."

I can tell she's taken aback. She looks away, out to the sea, but she's smiling. Cameron starts toddling towards the water's edge. She follows him down, and I do, too, and we play in the tide pools for another hour or so, and then head for home.

We stop in Ermones for supper. The small tourist town is virtually empty. Still off-season, though in just weeks from now it's sure to be packed here. The sun is setting over the spectacular beach of golden sand. We sit on the patio of Café Odysseus, and watch the sunset after finishing the best grilled snapper I've ever tasted. We linger over our Espresso, mostly quiet, occasionally laughing at Cameron's antics chasing and roaring at the seagulls until he's finally worn out. He crawls onto me and grips my shirt firmly, sticks his thumb in his mouth and sucks contentedly.

Feels fantastic—warm, connected, valued the way Cameron nestles his sun-drenched body into me; his soft, fine mass of hair a pillow under my chin. Elisabeth *is* unbelievably lucky. I nuzzle my nose into Cameron's hair and breathe him in as she had done. Clean. Fresh. New. I feel her watching and look at her. I smile. So does she. And the three of us are one. Connected. And I am complete.

I have to have more...

-

-

Chapter Twenty-Two

-

I insist on the terms of the original agreement when Elisabeth extends her lease through the summer. She insists on continuing to pay rent, though it seems gratuitous since I'm practically living with them. I stay later and later every day. After dinner, and a book before bedtime for Cameron, Elisabeth and I settle on the patio and talk into the night. We talk about nothing—abstractions of belief, politics, morality, reality, world affairs, books, art. We talk about everything—her childhood in the Valley, the only kid of 'two middle-class liberal intellectuals'; her years with Jack, her fears without him.

We swap L.A. stories: cycling from Santa Monica to Huntington Beach on the Stand, eating strawberry pie slathered with fresh cream at the Apple Pan. She knows The Wedge off Newport from her short-lived surfer days. I tell her about road trips with rock bands, how, even with the smell of the bus after a few days of eating and sleeping in it, the creative space from the confinement was worth it. I try and explain why I haven't performed live since my late teens, how I prefer to be in-studio than on display, but she doesn't really get my shyness—a la being 'graced' with my 'talent and looks.' I share with her what it feels like creating music—how the notes resonate through my fingers right into the pleasure centers of my brain, even confess my misconception about what mattered that first night I learned to play with Mike. I share tales of growing up with my parents in Boston. I leave Edward out, don't refer to him, or Ian, ever. Sometimes, we just sit and watch the stars, and don't talk at all. Every morning upon waking, I look forward to seeing them. Every night after climbing the hill to my house, I miss them.

I start playing the guitar at night, often well into the early morning hours. Music helps kill the aloneness that looms without Elisabeth or Cameron. Get past the initial wave of pain with practice and become more fluid with scales. By the end of summer I'm actually starting to improvise. Still don't feel ready for an audience, and refuse to play for, or even practice in front of them, and by her grace, Liz doesn't push it. She does nudge every so often, though.

Cool evening in late summer. We're walking back from supper at an open café where a bouzouki player squared off with an acoustic guitarist in an impromptu jam session. I'm holding Cameron, asleep in a blanket we've devised as a makeshift carrier. Elisabeth walks beside me. Her expression is placid; her face awash with moonlight. Her backdrop is the velvet sky scattered with a billion sparkling diamonds that reflected in the glassy sea.

"Musicians were great tonight, don't ya think? That last bit, they were strumming so fast their hands were one big blur. Amazing they could hold that rhythm for so long, almost as long as you do sometimes when you're practicing at night." She doesn't look at me, but I catch a glimpse of her smile.

Sudden, absurd trepidation of lascivious invasion. "How do you know I practice at night?"

She hesitates. "I can hear you playing when your back door is open. And you've had it open all summer, except the last week or so, since it's been getting cool in the evenings. I sit on the porch and listen until around midnight. How late do you play?"

"I usually quit about an hour or two after that. I had no idea you can hear me." I fiddle with Cameron, adjust my body so his face isn't smothered in the cloth, then stroke his fine hair back, let it run through my fingers, then do it again.

"You play beautifully, James." She looks at me. "Even with just scales you play melodically, rhythmically. Every time I hear you play, you're faster, smoother, sharper. It is quite obvious that you are still a gifted musician."

"Thank you."

She shakes her head and looks away. "I didn't really mean it as a compliment. Honestly, I'm more afraid than thrilled by your recent awakening."

"Afraid of what?"

"Losing you."

I stop walking. "You won't." She stops and turns back to face me. She stares at me, into me, and I touch her fear. "I love our days—the three of us together. I love our nights—just you and me. But silence is death to me when I'm alone, Liz. I've been playing at night to kill the void that comes without you."

A wide smile of pure delight spreads across her face, and lights up her eyes that are fixed on mine. I pull her in then, gather her face in my hands and kiss her. Passionately, sexually. She surrenders to my kiss and returns it. Her lips are soft, warm; her mouth open, inviting. She sucks me in slowly, her tongue gently caressing mine. I slide my hand through her silky hair and around the back of her neck. Then her hand's on my face, and her touch ignites me, excites. I want her to swallow me up. Want to be inside her. Connected. Her breasts brush against my chest as she pulls back slightly for breath, tantalizing. She lets her lips linger on mine, until Cameron squirms between us.

We separate and both look down at him, smack foreheads, laugh. Elisabeth strokes her son's head, then strokes my cheek. I take her hand, kiss her palm. A moment's pause and she pulls her hand away from my lips but keeps her fingers laced in mine and gently guides me forward as she resumes walking again.

We're hand-in-hand until we get back to her house. I put Cameron in his crib. Elisabeth makes some sweet Tunisian tea, and we go out to the patio, under the blanket of stars enjoying the last of the mild summer nights. I sit on the bench that runs along the back of the house under the kitchen window per usual. But instead of the lounge chair, Elisabeth sits next to me, brings her feet onto the bench and leans back against me, cradling her sippy cup mug in both hands.

She stares up at the stars.

"Look there. Wow." She says it with childlike amazement. Like Cameron. Same delivery. "You can see the Milky Way perfectly. That is so beautiful."

"It is." The stars of the Milky Way are so dense it looks like a white dust cloud arcing across the night sky. The moon's setting, allowing individual stars to twinkle and dance so brightly their single images are mirrored in the flat sea, making the water sparkle. We sit and watch the light show, her body warming mine, silently absorbing the scene and committing it to sweet memory.

"You know, I've been angry at Jack for the longest time—years before he died." She pauses to sip her tea. "Thought about leaving him a thousand times. We talked about breaking up a good amount, too. I was always wanting more of him than he was willing to give me. At least, that's how I saw it." She's going round about to what she really wants to say, and I feel her hesitation. "But lately, it's been dawning on me that my anger may have been...well, misplaced."

I wait for her to continue, but she just sips her tea, stares out at the sea. "You're going to have to take it further if you want me to understand." Her soft profile is dimly lit from the ambient light from the kitchen, and I catch a glimpse of her smile.

She pulls away from me, brings her feet to the deck, straightens and sips her tea again, then scooches next to me, so our legs and hips are touching, but she doesn't look at me. "Jack was a brilliant journalist, not only because he objectified everything, but he strove for excellence, pursued it with passion. It was one of the very things I loved about him. His commitment, regardless of the risks or hardships, inspired *me* to be equally dedicated. So I followed him around the world, providing the visuals for his stories. Got my first NPPA when I was twenty-five." She flashes a tentative smile. "And I'd like to tell you it was the pinnacle of my dreams, but truth is, it felt rather hollow. Even then I was tired of the *reality* of it all, and ready to go home, *make* a home, start a family and settle in."

"I'm getting Jack wasn't on that page."

"Good guess. We fought about it constantly. I'd spent all those years acquiescing to *his* way. He *owed* me the turn around. Closing in on thirty, and my biological clock became a time bomb. Yet, even when Jack agreed to work at having a kid, it wasn't enough for me. I'd assumed I'd have more of him, but, of course, that wasn't the case. His pursuit of excellence still dominated his time." She sighs with the weight of the memories. "Thing is, I'm beginning to see my expectations were out of line. It was absurd for us to marry. I should never have agreed to a life with a man whose priorities I couldn't accept, nor fault, since I knew of, even admired him for his dedication to his craft from the start." She drinks her tea, still does not look at me. "I didn't realize it then, that obsession is the price of excellence." She sighs. "I just don't want to go there with you." She practically whispers.

"I'm sorry?"

"I don't ever want to put you in the position of having to choose."

"Between what and what?"

"Between music, Cameron and me."

I sit up and face her. "You win. You don't know that by now, or is it that you don't trust it?"

She looks at me. "James, you're clearly a purveyor of excellence, and must have devoted a huge amount of your time and energy passionately pursuing, at least the guitar, to get as good as you are. Singularity of focus is how one becomes great at anything. I didn't get that with Jack. I just got hurt that I was so rarely the focus of his passion. He denied me what I felt I was due. But I get it with you."

"Lisbeth, I. Am. Not. Jack."

"No. You're more insular than Jack ever was. Our first twenty years

I thought were connected at the hip, but it's more likely I was his missing rib from the start. It wasn't until half way through college that his career took off, and took over. Music isn't just your career choice, James. Anyone who plays like you do, well, it's obviously more of a lifestyle, one you've pursued since you were a child, and probably deeply ingrained in your self-perception."

I smile at her phrasing. "Thank you, Sigmund."

Her clear amber eyes flicker with humor, but suddenly darken with her expression. "And while I've come to realize, sacrificing for excellence on occasion is essential to periodically achieve it, I beseech you, don't ever make me ask you to choose, James." Her eyes hold me captive, pleading. She's deadly serious.

I'm fixed on her, inside her head, feel her fear, and underlying anger. "I won't." I reach out to her then, hold her face in both my hands and kiss her again. Her warm lips part and I draw her in, get lost in contact, her taste, smell sweet sex on her skin. We part slightly, but stay lips to lips. She runs her tongue over mine, kisses me again, and again. I feel her smile, then mine, kiss her again and we finally pull back. "I promise you, you and Cameron will remain my priority." I let my hands fall from her face but keep my eyes on hers.

She smiles, nods humbly, then reaches up with both hands and cups my jaw, kisses me quickly, drawing my face up in her hands before separating them, and releasing me as she stands.

"Be with me tonight." Elisabeth's tone is tender, and teasing. In the dim light I can barely make out that she's extending her hand to me, the night sky behind her silhouetting her form.

Their forms descend on the bed like a pack of wolves. Laughter is loud. A woman yelling "No! Don't!" is in the background, like on TV. And there are faces in front of me. Men, boys really, Cheshire grins plastered on their faces, like the animated cat from the Disney movie. And the white snakes are rushing up my arms and I watch them coil round my wrists. Then a woman is on top of me, smiling down at me with the same Cheshire grin the boys wear, and what must be her hair but looks like glowing blond feathers of a Mardi Gras mask. The feathers surround her face and cup her ample breasts which she's sticking in my face. And the snakes keep me pinned though I'm trying to get her off me, writhing and cussing, and they're *laughing*, especially when I scream in terror as snakes wrap around my cock. But I fight and kick until I get one someone's head between my calves and I lock them around his neck, clamp down as hard as I can, lifting him off me, crushing his larynx by the sound of his gurgling, and breaking his neck. I hear it crack, like snapping a large twig, feel his body go slack between my legs, the weighted silence that follows, then someone whispers, "Holy fuckin Christ. I think he's just killed Billy."

I sit on the bench paralyzed, except for the trembling. My heart's coming through my chest. Feel Elisabeth looking down at me, feel her shame, her confusion when I don't reach for her hand. I can't move to save my life.

Take her hand. You want to be with her, be *with her.*

"I can't." I shake my head. *It'll hurt.* "I could hurt you." I can barely breathe. Want to crawl under the bench.

Run.

She drops her hand to her side. I look up at her, her face suddenly illuminated with the kitchen's dim light. I feel her uncertainty, her eyes searching to see into me. Then her expression slowly morphs with understanding into her casual smile. "Move over."

"I'm sorry?"

"Scooch." She sits next to me and bumps up against me until I'm two-thirds down the bench, then brings her legs up, stretches them out and rests her head in my lap.

Her hair cascades over my legs like a warm blanket. She stares up at the stars, dark lashes framing her glistening eyes scanning the twinkling sky. Hard to make out the color of her wide-set eyes, or see the strong features of her long, oval face in the dim light, but her dark, thick lips are closed, set in a placid expression. In fact, her entire demeanor is calm, relaxed, and I sense no confusion, nor ire. I manage to stop trembling. She laces my left hand in her right, brings my hand across her to rest on her stomach. I stroke her hair with my free hand, try slowing my heart rate.

Can she feel my heart pounding? Does she sense my shame, my moral dissonance—fearing my own essence now, more than anything outside of me. She closes her eyes, surrenders to my touch, the way I've seen Cameron mesmerized by hers. I lean back against the house, let my head drop back and close my eyes, but continue stroking her hair—bringing its silky smoothness between my fingers again and again.

Fifteen minutes pass in silence and I'm thinking she's fallen asleep, but then I hear her inhale to speak.

"You know, the first time Jack and I had sex it was very awkward." She pauses. "We were seventeen, on a road trip up at my cousin's house in the Berkeley hills. We stayed in his unfinished upstairs master bedroom of their second floor addition. Only three of the four walls were up. The west wall was just framing, which gave us a fantastic view of the bay, and even San Francisco beyond, but it was freezing in there. We had separate sleeping bags, but decided to share one and snuggled really close to keep warm."

She holds my hand on her stomach, connecting us, spinning a parable for what she's afraid to say straight out. I don't open my eyes. I want to stay in her story, watch the scene unravel with the offhanded manner of her telling.

"Well, of course, Jack got a hard-on almost instantly. We were both virgins, and although I wasn't committed to keeping it that way, I was afraid if we had sex it would wreck our friendship. Like death and taxes, adding sex to the mix certainly changes things, like it or not."

I smile down at her. Her eyes are still closed, her expression still placid.

"Anyway, to make a long story short, we did it. I let him, in other words. He'd been wanting to for so long, and I'd always stopped him. But that night I figured there was no turning back once we were in the same sleeping bag. I've always abhorred the idea of being a prick tease. And it was painful and clumsy and over in about a minute once he was inside me, which honestly, I was glad for because it hurt like hell with him in there."

Surely, she's not randomly sharing this slice of intimate history. There's something she feels a need to communicate, but fears her usual direct approach. And though I feel trepidation rising, curiosity overrides it so I spur her on. "And you're telling me this story because..."

"No reason in particular."

"Right." I catch her whisper of a smile, shake my head, but with humor, before dropping it back against the wall and closing my eyes again.

"The thing is, it got better. Sex, I mean," she continues softly. "Our first few times it was awkward, or it hurt, or it just didn't feel the way everyone always raved about. But eventually we found our rhythm, and somewhere after that I had my first orgasm and realized what all the hype was about." She pauses. "And even though I haven't had sex in almost a year now, desire has not abandoned me." She pauses again. "Just thought I'd let you know." She yawns, let's go of my hand and rolls onto her side, curls up and buries her hands under my leg, using my lap as a pillow. Within moments her breathing becomes even and I realize she's fallen asleep.

I let myself free fall into her warmth; her softness; her sweet, rich, seductive scent. I know she's just come on to me. I'm just not quite sure what to do with it. Yet. I smile, which persists as I drift off. The sleep is restless. The bench is hard. It gets cold out there at some point. There are dreams—exploring the tide pools with Cameron;

laughing while gorging on mangos with Elisabeth, the fruit juice dropping on her chest and dripping slowly down her cleavage. In one dream, I'm on her porch, guitar in my lap strumming a fast, rhythmic progression—Em-Am-E-F#-G#-F#-Em...a new one that sticks when I wake late in the night. But the nightmares do not come.

-

-

Chapter Twenty-Three

-

ELISABETH

James removes her head from his lap and stands. She tucks her hands under her cheek to lift her face off on the weathered pine bench and opens her eyes as the screen door shuts. It's dark, even the stars seem dimmer. She sits up, still groggy, looks around for James but doesn't see him, then hears the screen door again, feels the weight of her quilt over her shoulders and looks up at him.

"Sorry I woke you." He takes her hand and brings her to her feet, then guides her to sit on the lounge chair, then kneels in front of her. He smiles his adorable, single-dimpled grin. "Go back to sleep. I'll see ya later." His full, soft lips cover hers with warmth, and then he's gone. She falls onto the lounge chair, curls her feet up under her blanket and listens to him crunch the earth as he climbs the hill.

And Elisabeth is alone.

Except she isn't. Cameron sleeps just the other side of the wall. Five minutes later, James starts playing and they're connected again.

She gets up, checks on Cam while heating water for tea, then pours herself a cup and comes back out to listen. Connect. She craves him now. She wants to be with him, or hear him all the time, know he's close. Safe. Alive. Even if Jack were, he wouldn't be enough anymore. Not now. Knowing what is possible.

Elisabeth sits on the bench cradling her tea, listening to him strum the guitar—fast and fluid, then switch to picking, keeping the same tight rhythm without missing a beat. The music resonates off the hillside and echoes down from his house. He knows she can hear him now. He means for her to. She smiles, wonders if he is, hopes he is...and is suddenly chilled with the notion. *Will the very thing connecting them now eventually tear them apart?*

She would never ask him to choose between her and music. But she didn't have to stay with him if she doesn't like his choice. *I won't. Not again.* James *is* with her now. More often than not he's present, pays attention, listens, questions. This is nothing like with Jack. She had no idea this was even possible. She's the best part of herself when she was with James. He engages her. Challenges her. Empowers her. He sees her as beautiful. She feels beautiful.

Elisabeth has listened to him play all summer, night after night, getting better and better. But since he's crossed the line to great, her fear of losing him to his muse has become pervasive, constantly looming. Like losing Cameron. And that's how she knows she's in love with him.

She felt compelled to bring up her concerns on their way back from the café earlier tonight. And James said exactly what she wanted to hear, and she melted, even though she knows it was bullshit. She doesn't think *he* knows. He probably genuinely wants to stay connected. And then he kissed her. Totally out of the blue. *Wow!* It was electric. Set her body tingling…

She sips her tea. Warm and sweet. He stops playing. She's sure she feels him smile. She smiles. It's close to midnight, way too early for him to quit for the night. He'll pick it back up at some point. Ten minutes or half an hour. No telling really. She hasn't caught a pattern yet, except that he plays longer and longer each night. Lately, she hears him in the mornings sometimes, too, after going back up to shower following breakfast. His muse's talons are digging in. *'I play to kill the void that comes without you,'* he'd said. She laughs, shakes her head. It's impossible to believe him, even though she wants to.

Weeks pass, and most feel like a dream. James takes them to Mortaitika and Messogi on the east side of the island, where they spend hours exploring the shallows of the Messonghi river that flows from the pine covered hills. They go to Corfu City, shop but don't buy anything, then on a whim go up to see the crystalline bay of Gouvia. They go para-sailing. Elisabeth loves it. Spectacular view from above—lush rolling hills blanketed by groves of olive and citrus; rocky coves bordering the turquoise Ionian; a funky adobe church built on a jetty in the middle of the bay.

A week of adventures is followed by a quiet one at home. Then they're off again, back north past Sidari, out to the glassy lagoons of Acharavi. Then to the long sandy beaches of Kavos on the southernmost tip of the island before rounding out the week in the emerald pine forest in the hills of Skipero.

They laze three days in a row on *their* beach, reading, napping, talking, playing. They spend hours shopping, chopping, preparing meals. They trade off cooking. With minor resistance, Elisabeth agrees to trade off reading to Cameron at night, since they both love it, and Cam doesn't seem to care as long as it's *One Fish, Two Fish* or *Go Dog Go.*

"How come you won't play for me?" They're on the deck, enjoying the last of the evening sunset.

"I do." James says softly, as if he doesn't want to disturb the crickets' song.

"In *front* of me, for me and Cam." She lays on the bench, her head's in his lap. He sits leaning up against the house. He's running his nails lightly against her scalp, pulling his long fingers loosely through her hair over and over. It feels fantastic, tingling, yet soothing.

"Why do you need to see me play? You can hear me. I'm your lullaby."

"You are at that." She falls asleep every night to his playing, comes right through her bedroom window. She blushes, a twinge of lewd invasion. "But you're turning this around. I don't want to talk about me. I want you to answer my question."

He laughs. "Okay. Let's see. Hmm...The guitar, of late, is kind of like playing Tavli—to pass the time of day, or night as the case may be. I've always been more player than performer. I don't like being watched. I get that enough without the guitar." He stares out at the sea, then drop his head back against the house again. "But what *you* want to know is what I'm afraid of. And that would be you seeing me as a musician, and a mediocre one at that."

"So, you won't play for me, in front of me, because you're afraid I'll see you as less than brilliant?" Liz says as she sits up to face him. "I already see you as deeply flawed, honey. No worries." She grins at him.

"I'm afraid you won't see *me*." He looks at her, pleading, or scared, or both. His chestnut hair frames his sculpted face in wild waves. Soft strands hang in his eyes and mingles with his long lashes. "I don't want you to confuse the man with the music I make. Most everyone sees the later. I have a hard enough time separating them myself. You're my lighthouse." His deep green eyes are fixed on her, imploring her to be his ballast.

She smiles, humbled. "My father used to tell me, *'Fall in love with the art, not the artist.'* I didn't listen, of course. I've always been enamored with creative excellence. Like I said, it's a big part of what attracted me to Jack."

"Your father is right. Truth is, most woman I've been with were more enamored with the musician than me. But to be fair, I wasn't much to be with. It scares me who'll you'll see, how you'll see me forward if I introduce you to my muse."

She looks at him, manages a soft smile to hide her trepidation. She is grateful, at least, he's admitted his muse has returned. "No worries, then. I was in love with the man before the music, so we should be okay." Her breath catches in her throat. It's the first time she's confessed to being in love with him.

He stares at her, then puts his huge hand around the back of her neck, pulls her to him, meeting her halfway, and kisses her. His lips are warm, thick, wet. He's inside her mouth with his tongue, swallows her in for an instant, then withdraws, holds his lips to hers for a split second, then parts. Her entire body flushes, tingles. She smells sex oozing from her pores, but resists her powerful desire to pull him back to her or reach out to him, knowing she must wait for him to accept her invitation.

James straightens, lays his head back against the house and closes his eyes. "There were times when I would be creating music with someone, or a group of musicians, and we'd achieve what felt like this perfect harmony, the sound we were generating transcending the boundaries of the physical, venturing into the surreal. It was wild. Like we were one, all of us one being, intertwined, blended." He pauses. "Kind of like what I feel with you now."

She smiles, watching him. He doesn't open his eyes, but she catches just a hint of a smile whisper across his gorgeous face. It isn't 'I love you.' But it'll do. She lays back in his lap, closes her eyes and snuggles in.

-

-

Chapter Twenty-Four

-

Syrup drips from his fork like the sweat that trickles down his neck. He sits at the table, his usual place, eating pancakes. She's across from him, Cam's empty high chair between them, her son current entrenched in his morning Clifford videos. Elisabeth is sipping her coffee. This is her first cup of many today. Since she's recently weened her almost two year old son, her body is back to her own. James is in his running attire—his white linen shirt hangs open, unbuttoned all the way, his dark gray sweatpants almost black at the sweat-soaked waistband. He takes a large bite of his stack, looks up at her and smiles.

"What?"

"I see you."

"I'm sorry?"

"I see the child in you, when you're with Cameron, and the two of you are creating, building, or pretending to be pioneers colonizing Mars. And there's the angry, insolent teen when you're shutdown and inaccessible, and the orphan, the lost boy—self-involved to self-protect."

"OK...?" He narrows his eyes at her, justifiably coaxing her to get to her point. To be fair, her delivery is more dramatic than she'd anticipated this morning when she was constructing her narrative while making pancakes for Cameron earlier.

"OK. Here's the deal. The truth is, whether you play for me or not, I can't help but see the musician in front me. The way you hold your hands, the *size* of them, your bizarrely elongated fingers." She smiles. He does too, sort of, then he sighs, picks up his empty plate and puts it in the sink. "I hear you at night and in my head now, even when you're not playing. You're driven. I want to share your passion, befriend your muse so she doesn't get between us."

James turns to face her. "*She?*" He arches an eyebrow.

"You know what I mean. Please play for me."

He stares at her. "You are relentless, woman." His smile morphs into a mischievous grin. He leans back against the counter and folds his arms across his chest. "You want to see the other side of me 'Lisbeth? Then show me the other side of you. Haven't seen a portfolio, a photo album, not one photograph you've shot, not even those first ones of Cameron and me from way back."

She looks at him quizzically. "*'The other side' of me?*"

"You know what I mean."

"No. I don't." She gets up, goes to the end of the counter a few feet from where he stands. "Sounds rather bipolar to me. I have a thousand *sides*," Elisabeth grins at him, then pours herself another cup, the last in the glass carafe on the coffee maker. "You want to see my *work*, James?" She smiles with the idea that just popped in her head, like a light bulb switched on, or a lighter's flame sparked in the dark. "I will, if you will." Her smile broadens. "I sent my portfolios to my folks, but you can see my online book, though we have to go into town to get a connection, which I'll be happy to do later this afternoon, right after I see you play."

She can't help smiling. He doesn't. He cocks his head to the side again but stays fixed on her. "I'd love to see your book, but for this exercise, I'm not sure car bombings, riots, war scenes are...*appropriate*—which is what I assume you've got."

"Yeah. Most of what I have online is pretty much standard AP stuff."

"I'll agree to your challenge if you agree to mine." He's grinning at her, and she knows he thinks he's got her cornered. "Show me what captivates you, turns your head, catches your eye, turns you on. Show me your passion, besides Cameron. Then it's a deal. You show me your other side, I'll show you mine." He smiles teasingly.

"My fine photos were among the portfolios I sent to my folks before I left Israel."

"Create another portfolio. Show me the world through your lens. Shoot anything you want, because it inspires you, not because it sells."

Love to! And she's back on top of their banter of wits. "Okay. I'll pick up the gauntlet." *Game.* "I need a subject." *Set.* "I choose you." *Match.*

He laughs. "Why does it have to be me?"

"Don't be coy, Sweetie. You know why. You challenge me to be beautiful. Let yourself be."

He flashes a conciliatory smile. "Who sees the pics?"

"Me and you, if that's what you want."

"Okay," he says unexpectedly. "But I have some rules. You have *today*, and today only. After dark we're done. This is a one-time thing. I don't want the camera in my face, minimal intrusion, just like any other day when you happen to have it with you. I say when it's okay. I say when it's not. And it stops if I say so." He stares at her, searching. "And I expect to be dazzled."

"No pressure there." She barely refrains from sticking her tongue out. "Well, I have some rules, too. When you come back down after your shower you bring the guitar with you. You play for me when I say so, and where I say so. And throughout the day I want to hear more *your* music than covers of other artists."

"No way."

"Why not? I'll be as reasonable as you. It's for today only, right? A one-time thing..."

"Damn it, 'Lisbeth—"

"Oh, and since you've already dazzled me, I expect greatness."

He flashes this 'fuck you' grin. She laughs. So does he. She turns away, gets the digital Canon tucked against the wall at the end of the counter and takes the lens cap off as she turns back to James. Focuses on him. He watches at her. Doesn't flinch. *Click.* She catches his insolent grin. "Get ready to be dazzled." *Click.*

He smiles, raises an eyebrow. "I'm going up to take a shower." He's looking at her, but is somewhere else in his head. "I'll be back down later." And instead of doing the dishes per usual, he pushes away from the counter and walks out.

"Don't forget the guitar."

James waves goodbye without looking back, and just as he clears the kitchen doorjamb she notices he's dropped all but his middle finger and is now flipping her off.

She's about to take Cameron on a hike up the hill after changing his new pull-ups, when James shows up almost an *hour* later. He has Jack's guitar. Even still, she's on him the moment he walks through the door. "I thought we were going to be reasonable. I can't put together a series in one day without my subject."

"Sorry." He gives her a sheepish grin, stands the guitar case up and rested his hands on the narrow end. "This is hard for me. Harder than I thought."

"Which part?"

288

"All of it. Look, I told you, I'm not a performer. The few times I've been on stage have always been as back up and I've lurked in the curtains. So, in the shower I'm trying to figure out what the hell you're looking to see. And it occurs to me that you're not looking to be serenaded. You want to meet *'her.'* You want to see if I go away when I play, confirm your suspicion my muse consumes me, and ultimately I'll choose to be with her exclusively." He renders his analysis as a statement of fact.

"Thank you, Wilhelm Wundt," her witty retort, mocking his earlier Freud comment. He flashes a grin. "Though fear is not my motivator here. Taking the male approach, instead of wishing and whining, I'm proposing *solutions* to potential problems. I want to meet one of your *many* sides, hear what you hear in your head, witness your process of creation when your muse beckons so she never gets between us. I'm looking to share as much as I can get of you, James," Elisabeth boldly confesses.

He nods, thank God. "I know. It's just, well, not a space I'm terrifically familiar with, or comfortable in. Never really have been." He runs his fingers through his hair, but it falls back in his eyes instantly.

"I know—"

"'Ames!" Cameron comes bounding into the living room and goes after Jack's guitar. "Ooh, mine." He grabs the case around the narrow neck and pulls it away from James.

"Hold on a minute, Cam." James catches the guitar before it falls on her son, then lays the case on the floor and shows Cameron how to open the locks. "Here. Like this." His face is right up against Cameron's, both in profile, both exquisite.

Elisabeth goes to the kitchen, gets her camera and comes back to the living room. James kneels in front of the open case. Cameron is up against him plucking and stroking the guitar strings.

Get the two of them, and just a suggestion of the guitar. Stop it down to 2.4, blur out the background. Focus on Cameron's eye. Sharpen. Right there. Click.

"Play for me." She watches James through the lens, hoping to capture any change in his expression, focuses on his tiger-eyes.

He doesn't move. He stares down at the guitar.

Click.

"Cameron's playing right now." He glares at her.

Click. Shit. Missed it.

"Cameron. Come here, baby." She lowers the camera, smiles at James. Cameron gets up and comes to her.

"Not fair," James says laughingly.

"Hey, sweetie pea." She kneels, opened her arms to her son and gathers him in. "Look at James." He does. "Would you like to hear him play daddy's guitar?" Then she whispers in his ear loud enough for James to hear. *"He can play it very well!"*

"Pay daddy's tar, 'Ames!"

James glares at her, shakes his head, but he's smiling.

"Peeezzze!"

"Woman, you have no shame." He lifts the guitar from the case, so Elisabeth holds back another witty retort, though none actually comes to mind. He leans back further, sits on his heels and positions the guitar in his lap, strums it, tightens a few strings, strums it again, nods and looks up at them. One of his huge hands is spread over the strings silencing them. The fingers of the other are poised like a spider frozen on the neck.

She doesn't lift the camera. She can't move. Liz sits on her knees, Cameron stands wrapped in her arms. They both stare at James. There is little separation between him and the instrument. His arms wrap around the guitar like a lover, melding the two into one. "Play anything." She has to hear the sound of the image before her.

He cocks his head, narrows his eyes on her, then he looks down and starts picking the guitar. Fast. Smooth. Measured. Like rain. The rich melody bounces off the wood floors and bare walls and vibrates right through her. He mixes in strumming, like the building of a storm, until he's only strumming. Totally fluid. Holds a perfect rhythm as he builds tension intertwining minor and major chords, like heavy wind and lashing rain, his long fingers sliding the length of the guitar neck with only an instants pause as he lands the chord, then he brings back in picking, until he's only picking again, like droplets hitting tin in a summer shower, then freezes as he plays the last note, letting it resonate, then holds his huge hand over the strings deadening the sound, looks at her.

"Don't stop. Keep playing."

"Pay, Ames. More!"

"No."

"*Ahh!*" Cam pouts.

"Let's go to the beach. Come on, Cam, let's go build a masterpiece." He puts the guitar back in the case, shuts it and stands. Cameron pushes off his mama, goes to James and lifts his arms.

"Soder's 'Ames."

"You've got it, little man." He lifts Cameron onto his shoulders and they look down at her expectantly.

She dismisses them with mock demands of castle craftsmanship worthy of photographing, and comes out to the deck fifteen minutes later with a lunch basket full of sliced turkey, hard cheese, a box of crackers, three apples, and bottled water, of course. She brings the Canon. She acquiesces to digital to view the shots on demand. She can always Photoshop for color correction and effects later.

James refused to take the guitar, claimed sand could ruin it. Grains under the frets or something. She'd felt like screaming, but really, there was no point in arguing. Be back in the house for the rest of the evening in just a few hours. She'll get him to play later.

The boys build an elaborate sandcastle a few feet above waterline while Elisabeth sits on the lounge chair on the patio reading *Crime and Punishment*. When she calls them for lunch half hour later, they're both covered in wet sand—hands, arms, knees to toes.

James rinses them both with the hose next to the back gate. Cameron giggles and splashes, James right along with him. Elisabeth gets her camera, and focuses on them as James lifts her son onto his hip and cleans his toes with the hose while Cameron kicks at the streaming water. Droplets fly around them like fireflies, lit from the afternoon sun.

Click. And again. And again.

-

-

Chapter Twenty-Five

-

After their meal, when the remains of lunch are cleared, Elisabeth attempts to put Cameron down for his nap, but he refuses. It's becoming his new thing—not wanting to sleep during siesta anymore. James and Cam are looking at the Dr. Seuss book, *Oh, The Places You'll Go,* balanced on James outstretched legs when she comes into the room. Cameron sits happily among the pillows on the floor, curled into the cove under James' arm, his little body pressed against James' torso, practically in his lap. Her son touches the illustrations, tracing his pudgy fingers over his favorite images as James reads. Both look up at her standing with the guitar a few feet from them.

James shakes his head. Cameron pushes himself up, goes to the guitar, grabs the neck and tries to pull it from his mama. "Pay, 'Ames. *Peezze!*

Elisabeth realizes her son is trying to give the guitar to James. She helps Cam carry the instrument over to where he now sits cross-legged on the pillows, then lets Cameron hand it to him.

James takes the guitar before Cam drops it, but holds the neck, balancing it upright on the floor and doesn't bring it in his lap.

"Make tar sing, 'Ames." Cameron stands in front of him waiting expectantly. "Peezze..." he adds softly, as if he's forgotten his manners.

"Here's the deal, sweetie pea," Elisabeth negotiates. "James will play for you only if you're in your crib, lying down, and settling down for a nap."

"*Ahh.*" He pouts, looks at James beseechingly.

"You heard your mama. Take siesta for an hour and we'll finish our castle after quiet time."

"*No* quiet time. 'Ames pay tar." Cameron actually folds his little arms across his chest.

Elisabeth and James crack up laughing.

"Only if you're in bed, munchkin." She sweeps her son off his feet and places him in his crib. He stands up, his small hands holding the wood railing looking down at James, waiting.

James smiles, shakes his head, then brings the guitar to his lap and positions it. Again, the two meld into one as he hunches over the instrument and focuses his attention on playing.

He starts picking, then mixes plucking the strings in a rise and fall of major and minor notes that are instantly familiar, but she can't place it. High, then low, in a smooth ebb and flow that wraps back into itself and begins again. He plays a known lullaby, and then it strikes her— it's the most famous lullaby of all, the classical piece by Brahms.

He glances up at her. A smile spreads across his face with her awareness. They both watch Cameron as he plops down on his mattress and curls onto his side, never taking his eyes off James. He grabs the edge of his blanket, brings it to his face, sticks his thumb in his mouth and sucks while he watches James play. Elisabeth sinks to the floor, sits near the crib and watches him, too.

Plucking chords changes to precise picking of notes, in an ever increasing complex rhythm. Somehow, James makes the instrument sound like a piano as the lullaby merges into another familiar tune, or part of the same piece, maybe, she isn't sure.

"What is that? I mean, I know it, but not exactly like you're playing it."

He smiles. "Sort of a mash-up of Chopin's *Berceuse* and *Brahms's Lullaby.*"

"Oh. Of course." She meant to sound sarcastic, but it came out with authority.

His smile broadens. She catches his grin just as he looks down again, his long hair like a hood hanging around his face, hiding his expression from view. The intricate, melodic tune he's playing creates a barely perceptible, fluid vibration that resonates through her—warming, calming. It's quite mesmerizing watching him play, picking so fast his hand is a blur; elegant fingers of his other hand crawling up and down the neck of the guitar like a massive brown spider.

The guitar swells with a series of high notes, then falls back to mid-range, then high again, but not as high. He slows the tempo to half time, and stays in mid-range, infusing bass notes as he slows to quarter time, picks a few low notes and lets them resonate before he silences the guitar. She catches a glimpse of his enamored expression, a whisper of a smile filled with child-like wonder, seemingly with the closing harmonics he's just created.

James looks up at Cameron. Elisabeth would have, but she can't take her eyes off James. His hair falls over his forehead and tangles in his eyelashes. He blinks several times then runs his hand through his hair sweeping it out of his striking green eyes, for about a second.

"He's asleep," James whispers, gives her a soft smile.

Elisabeth looks at her son, curled on his side, finally napping. Fine hair hangs just over his brow. His wide-set eyes look large under his closed lids, enhanced by his long, dark lashes. His pouty red lips are slightly parted. One arm lay over his small chest, his tiny hand outstretched on the mattress in front of him.

She glances back at James as he gets up off the floor, still holding the guitar. He moves to her, puts his free hand out to help her off the floor. She takes it, the contact more than just tactile—warmth resonates with his touch, up her arm, through her body, right to the pleasure centers of her brain. She feels the tingling of desire, and can't stop it building, vibrating in her belly, her jeans against her, overwhelmingly stimulating, rubbing her genitalia as she rises.

They stand face-to-face, eye-to-eye, hand-in-hand for a second. Every part of her wants to kiss him, but if she does, she knows she won't be able to stop herself from mauling him. About the last thing she wants to do is scare him, like when he recoiled with her last attempted seduction. So instead, Elisabeth releases his hand, turns away, and walks out of the bedroom.

She spends siesta reading on the lounge chair on the deck. James reads the New York Times on the other lounge, but within minutes is dozing under the late summer sun. No point in shooting at mid-day. No shadows to give a 2D photograph dimension with the sun directly above. The warm afternoon, the cool sea breeze, Cameron and James are safe, and Elisabeth is sated...She wakes to Cameron beckoning an hour and a half later.

After a cereal bar, the boys go back out to the beach to finish their sandcastle. Elisabeth continues reading for another half an hour. When the sun finally arcs far enough for chiaroscuro, she puts the book down and wanders over to their latest masterpiece with the Canon.

Approaching quietly, she comes up behind them, along the waterline and stops a good thirty feet away, hoping they don't notice her. Cameron's putting long reeds into each of the castle's turrets. James kneels next to him, putting small seaweed leaves into the hollow tops of each reed. They're making flags. She lays in the sand to get on their level. *Focus on Cameron through the sand turrets. Pull back. Pick up James in profile absorbed in his task. Click.*

A lazy wave settles on the shore, pushes its way up the beach and fills the moat they've dug around the castle. Cameron is thrilled, but James looks dubiously at the rising tide. *Pull both in clear...sharpen—pick up the contrast in their expressions. Click.* Cam splashes the water around with both hands. *Click.* He splashes James, who splashes him back, both of them laughing with child's delight. *Focus...Click.*

Cameron sees her. A big, happy smile. *Click.*

"Mama!"

James looks over at her. The sun is behind him, haloing his chestnut hair in fine gold highlights. *Click.*

Cam gets up to come to her, trips over the moat bringing down part of a wall before she reaches him and picks him up. He wraps his arms around her and squeezes. She squeezes him right back. She loves the way he feels.

"Look! Maserpez for you, Mama. You and 'Ames and me. 'Ames says so." He squirms to get down and she sets him on the sand.

"*OK*..." She can't wipe the smile off her face to save her life.

She looks at James as her son rejoins him. He fixes the crumbled wall with Cameron, then brushes off as he gets up and stands next to her, letting Cam finish the job.

"Yeah. Well, so much for our masterpiece."

Regardless of the crumbing wall, their sandcastle is exquisite, with six main turrets, four on the corners and two at the entrance, complete with stairs and windows. Inside the wall is a multilevel castle right out of Disney. "Good job, gentlemen." And she means it, floored by the excellence James models and is instilling in her son. "You boys ready for dinner?"

"You bet." James kneels to Cameron. "High five on our latest," and the boys slap hands, then slam their knuckles together. "Good job, little man. Ready to go?"

"Soders!" Cam lifts his arms to James.

They meander along the shoreline towards the house. "What are we making for supper?"

"Let's keep it simple tonight."

"Zucchini quiche?"

"Sounds good."

She sets the camera on the end of the kitchen counter, puts Cameron in his highchair then cuts up some banana onto his tray. James opens the fridge and stares at the contents, then retrieves the eggs. He's getting a bowl from the lower cabinet when she stops him.

"I'll make it. Why don't you get the guitar?" She takes the bowl from him, opens the carton of eggs he put on the counter, takes one out and cracks it against the lip of the bowl, then splits it all the way and lets the contents fall. He stands watching her. "James, I'm being very reasonable." And she gives him her warmest smile.

He stares at her a moment longer then walks out of the kitchen. There's about a fifty-fifty chance he'll leave for the rest of the day. Surprisingly, thirty seconds later he reappears in the kitchen doorway holding Jack's guitar by the neck. He crosses between Cameron and her with his head down as he sits in his usual seat and nestles the guitar in his lap. He doesn't look up.

-

-

Chapter Twenty-Six

-

"Play, 'Ames." Cameron articulates the 'L' clearly, a rarity, and noticed by both. Elisabeth smiles but watches James.

James smiles, picks the guitar quickly from high to low, like water falling. The opening is familiar, but again, she can't place it. The cascade of notes moves into an easy melody of an old blues tune, and Elisabeth recalls it had originally been done with a piano, she's sure. Just the singer and the piano. *Who was the singer?* Scratchy, smoky voice...

"This is a little known tune by an eclectic musician named Leon Russell, that I'm not sure I got until now." He still doesn't look up. He picks the guitar note for note, exactly as she remembers Leon's piano. "It's called 'A Song for You.' And it goes something like this."

He picks the guitar like falling water again, from high to low. Stops, silences the strings, then clears his throat and begins picking the ballad's melody, finally looking at her.

"'I've been so many places in my life and time. I've sung a lot of songs, I've made some bad rhymes.'" His voice is smooth, a rich tenor, deep resonance though he sings softly. He keeps his eyes fixed on hers as he sings Russell's song about life as a musician, how he's acted out his love on stages in front of thousands, but this song he sings now to 'her,' is *for* her and her alone.

James smiles shyly, glances at the guitar as he repeats the melody, then at Cam, then looks back at her and continues singing.

"'I know your image of me is what I hope to be. I've treated you unkindly, but darlin can't ya see..."

He sings Leon's words as if they are his own. *"'...There's no one more important to me,'"* James fixes his gaze directly on her, like plugging into her brain, and she suddenly feels his urgency. Then the lyrics implore her: *"'Darlin can't ya please see through me?,'"* essentially *to* him, past the fiction we pretend to be, and the facades we all wear.

Cameron stares at him mesmerized. James smiles with quiet amusement, his fingers slide casually up the neck of the guitar as he goes into the bridge, his focus back on her.

"'You taught me precious secrets of the truth, withholding nothing. You came out in front and I've been hiding. And now I'm so much better, so if my words don't come together, just listen to the melody, for my love's in there hiding...'"

James picks the guitar like cascading water again, high to low. Silences it. He looks back down at the guitar. Returns to picking the melody then looks at her again.

"'I love you in a place where there's no space and time. I love you for my life you are a friend of mine.'" He looks at her with an intensity she's not felt from him before as he sings the last of Russell's song: *"'And when my life is over, remember when we were together. We were alone and I was singin' this song for you.'"*

Elisabeth shutters as James picks the closing melody, lets the last note resonate almost to silence then holds his hand flat against the strings. Cocks his head. Winks, then a whisper of a smile.

She stands there, staring at him. Awestruck. Humbled.

"'Gen 'Ames. Play 'gen."

"Ah, from the mouths of babes," she whispers.

"Maybe later, Cam. Your mama needs help making supper right now." He gets up, sets the guitar against the wall and he takes the bowl out of her hand before it registers she still holds it. He picks up an egg, cracks it on the rim with a grin and lets the contents slide from the shell into the bowl. "Why don't you cut some zucchini?" He flashes a grin. She narrows her eyes at him with a low growl. He laughs. "Just a suggestion."

She goes to the fridge and gets several vegetables, then retrieves the cutting board and knife. They make supper without much talking. The quiet is comfortable. The song he sang keeps playing in her head. James' version. She can no longer recall Leon Russell's. Elisabeth smiles, knows that James sees, catches a glimpse of his smile.

James gets to read to Cam before bed tonight. She gets the dishes. If they don't keep a spotless house, the ants come marching in. And Elisabeth hates bugs. James comes into the kitchen after Cameron is tucked in and finishes up the dishes while she bids her son goodnight.

She meets him outside three minutes later. Long shadows from the short pines stretch across the deck. James sits on the bench, slouched against the house, crossed-legs stretched out in front of him. His arms are folded loosely across his stomach, hands lay against his sides. He squints against the blinding light of the setting sun. She lifts the camera and aims it at him. *Click.*

He looks up at her. The insolent glare is back. *Click.*

She doesn't think she got it. *Don't check now. Keep the camera on him.*

"Knock it off, Liz. Enough already." He squints back at the sunset.

Click. "It's not. I need to burn through a lot of shots to pull a few great ones. If I can't dazzle with a subject like you honey, I shouldn't pursue the arts."

He laughs, to himself, shakes his head. "So, how will you know?"

Focus on his iris. Sharpen the forest green. More. There. Click. "Know what?"

"If you're any good." His question cuts, though she doesn't think he means it to.

She stops shooting, holds the camera to her side. "I have no idea."

"Exactly. It's subjective. You'll never really know." He looks at her. "That plagued me for the longest time. It's part of what drove my obsession. Do yourself a favor Liz. Don't ask yourself if you're good. And don't expect to find out through other people. Ask yourself if you enjoy the process. If you do, if it engages you, excites you, then keep doing it."

Once again she's humbled by his insight. He's right, of course. She smiles. "Thank you for today."

He grins, nods. "Did you challenge yourself?"

"Yes."

"Did it engage you?"

"Yes."

"Did it excite your creative process, ignite your muse?" His smile broadens.

"Yes." Her smile fades with her gnawing sense of trepidation.

"Do you crave her even now?"

"Yes." She can't help smiling, blushes, and looks away. He's right again. She does. She's framing his face through the lens, softly blurring the wood planks behind him in her mind as they speak.

He studies her. Smiles, then laughs. So does she. He squints at the remains of the orange ball as it sinks into the sea. His tiger-eyes twinkle behind his long, dark lashes. *Click.*

And the sun is gone. She sets the camera on the bench, goes to the rail and watches the blue absorb the last of the yellow light. A bright shooting star blazes across the darkening southeast sky and disappears into the ambient sunlight as it blazes west towards horizon. "Wow!" She turns back to him. "You see that?"

"Yeah." He stares up into the twilight with his wide-eyed kid look.

Elisabeth looks back up at the sky, searching for more fireworks. She hears him get up, thinking he's going to join her at the rail, but when she doesn't hear his footsteps she turns back to him. James stands by the screen door, the camera in his hand. He's still smiling, but the kid is gone.

"Ready to look?" He holds her camera up.

Suddenly she's paralyzed, anticipation choking, and she can't move.

It's one thing to view them alone. It's a whole other thing to see them, raw, with *him*.

"I'm gonna make some tea." He stretches, still holding the camera. "Why don't you come inside, plug this in and see what you've got?"

She just stares at him. She still can't move.

He smiles this disarming grin. "Think of it like a game of Tavli, Liz—to pass the time while waiting for the water to boil." He turns away and goes in with the camera. The screen door slams and she loses sight of him inside.

-

-

Chapter Twenty-Seven

-

Follow him. Don't let him plug it in.

He's at the sink when she gets into the kitchen, filling the teapot. He glances over his shoulder at her, then turns off the tap, sets the kettle on the burner and ignites it. He's set the Canon on top of the laptop.

She glares at him, growls low in mock anger. He ignores her, busies himself preparing their tea. When the mug and sippy cup have teabags and milk in them, James turns to her, leans back against the counter, crosses his legs and wraps his long fingers around the edge of the counter top behind him. "We have a deal." He flashes his punk grin. "I'm being very reasonable."

Elisabeth goes to the laptop, opens it and turns it on. The day has been unbelievable, damn near perfect. Whatever the pictures look like, they can't take away the day, sure to be etched in her mind for as long as she's sentient. She plugs the camera into the USB on the side of the laptop and pulls up the file of pictures, then double clicks on the first and holds her breath.

Onscreen, James sits in the kitchen, almost glowing. It's earlier this morning. Light pours in from the window over the sink, bouncing off the wood floor, the chrome rimmed table, the whitewashed cabinets, his white linen shirt. He's standing slouched against the kitchen counter near the sink—white, long sleeve shirt buttoned at the sleeves but open in the front expose his six-pack abs. The delicate lines of his hipbones move below the waistband of his gray sweats. He's staring straight into camera, so the picture gives the illusion that his eyes follow the viewer. She's captured the insolent child.

She glances back at him, standing behind her looking over her shoulder at the laptop screen, his expression impassive, unreadable.

Next. James and Cameron. In profile. In the living room. The clarity of their images and the bronze of their skin is in sharp contrast against the gray stone fireplace in soft focus behind them. They're exquisite. She'd captured the moment.

The kettle whistle blows, and blows, and blows, until James finally goes and turns it off.

Next. James stares down at the guitar in soft focus on the ground in front of him. He's sharp, in profile, his eye somewhat shrouded by his hair, but she's caught his trepidation. *Got ya.* Elisabeth smiles, remembers thinking she'd missed it. She hears him pouring the water into the cups and clicks to the next shot. It almost doesn't matter what he thinks. *Almost.* She can tell they're good, or, at the very least, what she was aiming for.

On the monitor, James cleans Cam's feet with the hose. Focus is only on James' huge hands and Cam's tiny toes partially covered in sand. Grains falls away with the water stream, exposing the virgin skin of her son's toes, and most of James' exquisite fingers, like they're sandmen turning human.

He sets her mug on the counter within her reach and resumes his position behind her again, holding his cup. She hears him blow on his tea, then take a sip. *It doesn't matter what he sees.* Good, bad, or indifferent, capturing dynamic moments—stopping time and directing perspective onto beauty instead of strife is beyond fulfilling. It's intoxicating.

Next.

Cameron full-faced, through the turrets of their sandcastle. James in profile just in front of him, focused on his task. They look remarkably alike, could easily be father and son with their mass of fine hair to their shoulders, and falling over their brows; their wide eyes and long lashes, full lips set in a whisper of a pout.

Next. Cameron splashing, sunlight faceting the water like diamonds falling all around him.

Next. He and James in a water fight. Beads of water flying off James' long fingers are frozen in motion, the stream only two inches from hitting Cam's face. Cameron's eyes are hugely wide, as is the smile on his laughing face an instant before the water hits him.

Next. James stares into camera, head shot, his hair haloed with the sunlight behind him. He looks cast in bronze.

One shot after the other resonates. The images vibrate on the screen as if they are breathing. Breathing life into her. She holds her breath every time she clicks. When the next image appears and tells its story, she exhales. The camera is a portal to the past; her aim with every shot—to create a time machine back to the scene to relive it, or to view for those who missed it. And it occurs to her right then that James is right again. She loves engaging with the camera. *It doesn't matter what he thinks.*

Last shot. James is just to right of center, staring straight ahead. His soft mess of dark chestnut hair frames his young face. His green eyes are striking against the whitewash exterior of the house, and the complementary colors of orange to violet to deep indigo of the sunset reflected in kitchen window above him. The balance, chiaroscuro and juxtaposition are as exquisitely aligned as he is beautiful.

She looks at it another moment then picks up her tea, sips it and turns to face James. He stares at his image on the screen. He does not look at her. And she stops breathing again.

"Don't quit. Ever. No matter what." He takes at drink of his tea then looks at her casually. "And don't give me shit about not being an artist. You're as intimate with your muse as I am with mine." He turns away, picks up the guitar against the wall as he walks out of the kitchen, leaving her with his image on the screen.

She hears the screen door shut, and a moment later he starts playing. She stares at his image one more second, a warm glow of contentment, even achievement enveloping her. Liz closes his picture, closes the file, shuts down the computer and clicks the laptop closed, then disconnects the camera and sets it back in the corner against the back-splash. Then she goes to join James on the deck again.

Elisabeth shuts the screen gently. No indication he's heard her. He's picking a fast riff she's never heard before. His fingers crawl up and down the frets quickly and precisely. He gets a sharp, tonal resonance from each string he plucks, his fingers a blur of fluid motion. His eyes are closed, and remain so as she stands watching him. She sips her tea. Tastes rich from the milk. The night is warm. Cameron is safe in his bed. James plays on, lost to his muse. It will never be her. And suddenly she recognizes loneliness, or at least that feeling she used to get so much with Jack. And she freezes up inside.

He looks at her, holds his hand over the strings silencing the guitar. "What?"

"I am so screwed." She glares at the guitar. She can't help it.

"You're not." He sets the guitar down, leans it against the bench. "I won't touch it again tonight."

"Don't say that. I'm sorry. Continue. Please."

"No. I don't want to. I was just hanging out, waiting on you." He stands, moves to the railing. "It's a nervous habit. I can't help picking it up if one's around." He turns back around, leans against the rail, shoves his hands deep in his jeans pockets and glares at the guitar. It reflects the moonlight and the ambient light from the kitchen windows. He gives a quick laugh. "I'll knock it off. I promise you, I won't go back to obsession. I can't get there anymore anyway, even if I wanted to."

"Do you want to?" She holds her breath even though she knows the answer.

"In moments, yeah."

She sighs. Any other answer would have been a lie. "This moment?"

"No." He flashes his single-dimpled grin. "I'm right here, 'Lisbeth. I want to be with you."

Her ire dissolves. She so wants to believe him...

He comes to her then, takes her face in his hands and kisses her, hard but soft, gentle but with power. Deep, intertwining, connected. He sucks her in, almost swallowing her up, pulling her to him, his hand now on the back of her head, the other at the nape of her neck, his body pressed firmly against hers. Her nipples graze his chest as he pulls back. He lets his lips linger just barely touching hers, and whispers, "Will you be with me?"

Elisabeth is literally swooning, dizzy with desire, lust. "Yes," she whispers, not to frighten him. Then he slides his hand into hers and leads her inside. She can hardly breathe, let alone walk as he guides her down the hall to her bedroom.

He stops next to her bed, stands facing her and begins undressing her. He kisses her again as he unbuttons her shirt, then softly kisses her neck down to the top of her breasts, and every part of her tingles. He gently pushes her now open shirt off her shoulders then moves his huge hands over her breasts, his slender fingers lightly grazing her nipples.

Elisabeth gasps with pleasure. James smiles, bends his head to put her breast in his mouth, massages her nipple with his tongue. She groans, her nipples harden to rocks, and she runs her hand through his hair and gently holds the back of his head to her a moment. Then he moves back to her mouth and kisses her again, and again. She doesn't touch his sex, fearing any approach by her may startle him and spark evil memories.

James slides his hand down her belly, unbuttons her khaki's, slides his hand inside, combing the tips of his long fingers through her pubic hair and cupping her crotch. Another gasp escapes her lips and he smiles again. She does, too, then kisses him gently, passionately. He unbuttons his shirt while they kiss, unzips his jeans and dribbles them off his narrow hips, then sits on the bed, puts his hands on her hips and gently pulls her pants down. She steps out of them as he pulls her to him and she joins him on the bed.

He's very gentle, almost cautious, but tantalizing to the extreme, with a slow hand focused on pleasing her. He separates only to get a condom from his wallet, shyly explaining it was gifted from one of the locals he plays tavli with, on the day they'd fought—the old man's solution to all problems with women. Elisabeth quivers with his touch, welcomes him exploring her body, directing the scene. James strokes her inner thigh, her body arching with desire, then moves his long fingers through her pubic hair again, up her belly, then runs his hand ever so lightly over her nipples again. Her body shudders and she draws a quick audible breath, which solicits another smile from both of them. She's breathing in quick gasps now, her heart coming through her chest, lust consuming her.

"Please..." she begs. "Be inside me."

Then he's on top of her. Then inside her, filling her up. He's kissing her neck, up to her lips, finds them with his, but Elisabeth feels his shift as he pulls back and stares down at her, but not at her, more like through her, clearly seeing something else in his head. His eyes are wide with terror. She grabs his face with both her hands and kisses him. He resists at first, for an instant pulls back, glares down at her, but then his eyes narrow and he draws her into focus, seeing her, and returns her kiss, but hard. Aggressive. It almost hurts, skates the pleasure/pain line.

"Don't stop. Don't pull away. Stay with me." Elisabeth whispers in his ear. She slides her hands to his back, presses gently at the base of his spine to get him deep inside her. She groans, breathing fast and hard, then striking pleasure climaxes in her groin, the pit of her belly, her toes curling with the intensity. Her body shudders and quivers with lingering delight. She grins up at him. "Thank you," she whispers.

He smiles down at her, kisses her lightly then rolls on to his back, pulling her on top of him in a swift, smooth motion as if she were virtually weightless. Elisabeth laughs, puts her hands on his chest to adjust him still inside her, then feels his stomach go rock hard and his expression morphs from pleasure to rage. His hands go rigid on her waist and she's locked in his grip. He's back in his hell again, eyes filled with fear and anger, she feels him trembling beneath her. His jaw is tightened, squared, lips set in a hard line. He looks like he wants to kill her.

She draws another quick, audible breath. Then she slowly brings her hands to his face, and gently holds his jaw line. "James."

He grabs her wrists, hard. It pinches but she doesn't resist as he pushes her back but doesn't let go, then flips her on her back and moves on top of her again, keeping their bodies pressed together and himself inside of her. He looks down at her now, studies her, his anger gone. He grins, releases a nervous laugh. Elisabeth slowly puts her hands on his face again, pulls him in and kisses him, gently at first, then passionately, and lingering. His hips begin moving, in an ever increasing rhythm. His breath quickens, his muscles tense, his jaw tightens again, but he keeps his eyes fixed on hers. She moves with him, totally wet again with his balls gently tapping her ass, the base of his cock slamming against her clitoris again and again. *Don't come. Don't come. It's not about me this time.* She stares back at his gorgeous face, his hair hanging in his eyes, now distancing with mounting sexual tension. She follows his motion, syncs with his rhythm, arches her body to maximize his pleasure and James groans, closes his eyes, throws his head back and opens his mouth as if screaming, though no sound comes out. Elisabeth isn't sure if he's experiencing pain or pleasure as he climaxes, his expression masked, unreadable as he empties himself. His body convulses into hers and she spontaneously comes again, pushing herself against him, relieving her tension. James looks down at her. There's a hint of a grin on his face. "Thank you," he whispers, and she feels no need for further clarification.

He relaxes on top of her a few moment, keeping them connected, then rolls off slowly, takes off the condom and tosses it in the small bin under her nightstand. They laid side by side for quite some time in silence. They hold hands.

"There was always this moment of realization that there was no way out." He whispers. "It happened every time they tortured me, that moment I knew the restraints would hold me, that I was absolutely helpless. There was this weird dual to it. Unmitigated terror. Complete surrender." He pauses. "It's what I feel for you now, only in reverse."

"What?"

"I love you, 'Lisbeth. And that scares the hell out of me."

She can't help smiling, even though she knows he isn't. She tries to stay focused on his declaration of love, and ignore the twisted reality behind his analogy. She knows he'd been institutionalize, but *tortured*? Why? How? What the hell happened to this beautiful man? She feels her smile fade. She hopes he doesn't look at her and see that she suddenly feels ill. Beyond her natural guilt of making it with a man other than her husband, she's scared out of her mind that whatever happened to James will haunt him, *them*, forever, if they stay together.

-

-

Chapter Twenty-Eight

-

Fall blows in cold and hard with an early storm. Rain and wind pound against the thin plate glass windows and doesn't let up for three days. Outside has been cold, and damp for upwards of a week now, keeping them inside. The trick is amusing Cameron. He colors, he paints, he builds, he makes messes. James holds down the notes and chords and teaches him to strum the guitar. Elisabeth spends hours with him in front of the laptop playing learning games. She and James read to him book after book until their own exchanges take on Dr. Seuss speak. And one more time around the track with Thomas and she's going to throw that little blue train right out the window.

James stays. He shares her bed every night. The last two mornings she's woken before him, lay on her side and watched him sleep. This morning he watches her. She opens her eyes and he's leaning up on his elbow with his head in hand, watching her. His hair hangs in his eyes, framing his sculpted face like a soft, hooded shroud. The pine-filtered sun pours in through the bedroom window haloing him a moment, but it's short lived. The sky darkens again and shadows the room, and James, momentarily distancing him. A chill passes through her, from the outside in.

"Morning," he says casually.

"Hi." She smiles up at him, then Cameron starts crying. "Bye," she frowns, then kisses him as she gets out of bed and she goes to her son. James stays in bed. As she lifts Cam up out of his crib, she hears the guitar through the wall. James keeps it in the bedroom at night, in the corner next to the closet, practically in arms reach of the bed. She changes Cameron's diaper and listens to James play, smiles at his choice with the opening pick of the old rock tune, *When September Ends* by Green Day. He switches to strumming and the wall between them buzzes with the guitar's resonance and his rich tenor as he sings softly. She holds Cam's hand against the wall to feel the vibration and they both giggle with the shared experience. Remarkably, sometimes James makes the instrument sound as if a full band is backing him.

As she finishes up with Cameron, James stops playing. He has the timing down. She has to give him that. She hears him get off the bed and put the guitar down, then rustling, then a zipper. A few minutes later, she and Cam meet him in the kitchen. He's already started breakfast. Blueberry pancakes today. And they're good.

He picks the guitar up throughout the day and fiddles with it, but it's yet to feel like it's between them. Quite the opposite. Surprisingly, Elisabeth finds she enjoys being the recipient of his passion. It's Cameron's daily lullaby; a soundtrack while reading, or a melodic background behind casual conversation.

They play countless games of Tavli, fondle and tease while Cameron naps, and make love several times during the evenings until she surrenders to exhaustion. Only then does he leave the bedroom, go to the living room and practice, often late into the night.

By the time the stormy weather finally passes, the three of them are climbing the walls to get out of the house. A few days pass with a breath of summer past, warm and splendidly languid. Then the beach turns windy and cold again, with only intermittent sun through most of October. Their excursions to the beach are shorter each day. Today, Elisabeth gets only a few good shots of James and Cameron running with the kite before losing the sunlight to the darkening sky. They're back inside within a couple of hours, and Cameron is bored. And so is she.

"Let's go somewhere."

"Where?" James sits on the couch, the guitar in his lap. He's picking at it softly, almost unconsciously, a smooth blues riff.

"Let's get off this island. Go to the mainland. Down to Athens. It'll be warmer there."

"Athens is five hundred miles away."

"I know. So?"

He gives her a vague smile, shakes his head and then his forest eyes veil, and he gets sucked inside. Lost to her.

Shit. "James!"

He startles, his eyes flash awareness as they fix back on her. "What?" He's back in the living room with her, sort of.

"Where did you just go?"

"Down to Athens, with all those people."

Cameron's on the floor ripping apart a Lego castle James built.

"Let's leave in the morning."

It takes some convincing, but they do. Elisabeth takes the Canon. James flat out refuses to bring Jack's guitar.

They take the auto ferry across and spend two glorious days driving down the coast of the Greek mainland. She thoroughly enjoys watching James drive, his body an extension of the vehicle, casual but in control, his hair blowing wildly around his stunning face, talking about everything and anything. Driving keeps Cameron entertained, especially when the top is off—he lets his arms fly in the wind, or just stares at the passing scenery taking it all in, or naps.

They stop often, exploring the rich history of the regions they pass through. Up the hill to Nekyomanteion, where they're awed by the massive stone ruins of the Oracle of the Dead; then down to the Acheron River, where James laughingly mocks her when she refuses to let Cameron wade in the water that ostensibly carries souls to the realm of Hades. They lunch in the beach town of Riza, then roam the ruins of Roman Villas there, then move on to the city of Nikopolis, where they stop for the night. Thick Byzantine walls of stone and brick are crumbling throughout the city, enhancing the essence of its ancient history.

After supper, they stroll along the shore of the quiet Mediterranean. The evening is warm. The sky is violet fading to indigo. Cameron sets a slow pace, stopping every other second to explore a shell or sand crab. She and James meander along the water's edge. The sea reflects the last of the light and looks like wet stone.

"What does your father do?"

She's taken aback by his question. He's never asked about her family before. She'd been careful to avoid the subject of family since their one encounter going down that road. "My dad is a retired English professor. Why?"

"What about your mom?"

"Middle-school English teacher. A brief stint as an aspiring writer, but she never followed through. Why do you ask?"

"You're clearly well versed in the history of the places we've seen along the way. It's impressive. I'm wondering how you come by your breadth of obscure knowledge."

She smiles at his backhanded compliment. "It has nothing to do with my parents, I assure you. I studied art history in school. And with my job I traveled a lot of the world in the last ten years, gathering snippets along the way. My mother prefers her house and her garden. My father reads about places, studies their cultures through their literature, but he never goes anywhere. The man is sixty-eight years old and he's never been out of the United States."

"Well, at least they were home at night for dinner."

She laughs, looks at him, feels him withdraw. He hadn't meant it to be funny. "I'm sorry. I know you didn't grow up in a typical suburban home."

He smiles, sort of. "For the first thirteen years I did. I've told you tales of growing up in Wellesley—snow days; fireworks over the Charles river." He picks up a flat stone and rotates it between his elegant fingers.

"What were your parents like? What did they do?" She's trying to keep it light, not be too intrusive, just volley his question to her back at him.

"My step-dad was a jazz musician. My mom was a teacher, in Cambridge, at Berklee School of Music. I went to Paul Revere Middle School." He's in the Way Back Machine, describing some other time, but miraculously isn't lost there. Elisabeth feels him with her, present. James throws the stone in the sea with a flick of his huge hand. It skates a dozen times or more then sinks. Cameron's very excited by this and begins picking up stones and tossing them into the water, but is quickly disappointed his don't skip. He throws his fistful of stones at the sea in frustration. James kneels beside him.

"Go easy, little man. Takes a lot of practice to skip stones." He picks up a flat stone, places the stone in Cameron's hand and together they throw it. It skips a few times then disappears into the sea. "Practice is how you get good at anything, ya know. You do it again and again."

"Do it 'gen! Pactice 'gen, 'Ames." Cameron goes running around gathering stones, then comes back to James and shoves the rocks at him. Elisabeth laughs when James looks at her with a twisted grin and shrugs. Both of them know Cam can keep this up for a very long time.

"OK. Let's see what you've got. The stones need to be flat like this one, and this one, and this one. This is no good. Let's get rid of these. We'll throw these three, and when they're all gone, we'll head back. Okay?"

"OK, 'Ames.'" Together they throw in three more stones, with James counting them down through the last toss.

"Good job. Let's go." He swings Cameron onto his shoulders and they head back to the hotel. Her 'little man' is all worn out and lay his head down atop on James' head. Cameron stares down at her and gives her a sleepy smile, then closed his eyes. Again, it strikes her how madly in love she is with her son.

"I never anticipated what I feel for him." She walks close to James but they don't touch. "I was expecting him to demand my time and attention, my affection, consume me with concern for his welfare. And I was okay with all that. But what I never expected is how much I need him." She strokes his soft round cheek. "I got *so* lucky."

James holds Cameron's wrists to steady him while he sleeps. "He did, too."

It's dark when they get back to the hotel. James gently puts Cameron into the portable crib they set up in the sitting area of their suite, and tucks the blanket around him with care, making sure it covers his shoulders but not his face. He stands, watching Cameron sleep. "You know," he says after what seems like quite a while. "Who you love may have have elements of chance, but *how* you love clearly doesn't. Your attention to his care, response to his needs, your constant concern for his safety and well-being—your *actions* show him he's loved, which will give him a solid foundation for life. Cameron's very lucky, indeed."

James just gifted her, perhaps the greatest compliment she's ever received. She pulls his face to her and kisses him, trying to transfer all the respect, all the love she feels for him right then. He responds in kind. They navigate to the bed while kissing, and made love quietly, with Cam just the other side of the french doors, until they both finally collapsed into a comatose sleep.

-

-

Chapter Twenty-Nine

-

They trudge across white sand surrounded by orange hills lit by the late day sun on their way back to the Jeep. Cameron's on James' shoulders, his preferred perch. Elisabeth keeps pace with James, a weighted silence between them.

They'd been exploring the sandstone inlets of Tourlida beach a few hours north of Athens. James stopped on a whim, but Elisabeth gets the feeling there's more to it than that. He's been engaging less and less the closer they get to the city. She was sure she'd lost him to himself completely until he suggested stopping at the orange cove, but then they didn't exchange five lines during the entire hour they were out there under the turquoise sky.

They finally get back to the car. James buckles Cameron into the baby seat and gets behind the wheel. Elisabeth puts the day pack in the back of the Jeep, gets in the passenger seat, and they're on their way again. She thinks he's consumed, deep inside his head, and it startles her when he speaks.

"I want to talk to you about something." He stares straight ahead, his eyes on the road. "I'm telling you this now because if my past comes back to bite me in Athens, you'll want to know why. You deserve to know why."

Elisabeth feels the ground slip away, as if the car is gliding, sliding out of control. He glances at her then looks back at the road and releases a quivering sigh.

"After my parents were killed, I was sent to live with my real father on a Gothic estate in England. At least, that's what I thought was going on. As it turned out, I ended up living with my whacked-out half-brother and Castlewood's staff. My father was the invisible man." Quick frown, then it's gone.

"I was sent away to school, to the Royal Academy of Music. And I became invisible, too. Tried to anyway. You know, like when Cameron closes his eyes he thinks we can't see him. Well, I did the same, with music. If I let it absorb me, then I couldn't feel anything around me, anything at all, like it wasn't there, because I wasn't. I was inside the music. The real world was harsh, scary, lonely, lonely, lonely. I was the youngest kid at school, and American nonetheless, yet privileged class—a British royal. I could play better than most there, including the teachers. I'd been practicing obsessively since I was five, and all summer long at Castlewood with maestros. No one knew what to do with me. I was an outsider from the start." He sighs heavily. "Music sheltered me. So I let it consume me." He shrugs. "And I did whatever it took to feed my addiction." His expression softens to remorse, then flat lines as he crawls inside his head.

She draws a breath but holds it. *Don't scream. Just don't let him get lost.* "Was music all you were addicted to?" She recalls him telling her he was arrested for drugs.

"Yes." He keeps his eyes on the road. "But to maintain my obsession, I did a bit of speed. Quite a bit, at times, actually. Which, in a round about way is what got me into this mess..."

There are times during his telling that Elisabeth wonders if he's sane, if the bizarre series of events over the past two years had actually happened to him. There are moments when her belief in the truth he speaks leaves her afraid of him, scared of the part of this man that can kill. And there are times of raging anger at the people who brutalized him, traumatized him, and left this talented, beautiful man so lost.

"I couldn't get out of there, 'Lisbeth. I couldn't get them to stop."

"Why?" she hears herself whisper. "Why were they doing this to you?"

He glances at her then, his expression masked again. "Ostensibly, for my ejaculate." Then he half-laughs, in a disgusted sort of way, as he focuses back on the road.

The lamb from lunch rises in her throat, burning hot and greasy, and her entire body flushes as she swallows it back. How better to mess with a man's sanity than through his sex?

"I'm not sure why," he continues. "I don't know what they did with it, but they took it from me every month or so. They put me in a padded cell, for a week, sometimes longer, pin me down and get me off, one way or another, over and over, regardless of my resistance. Parker, a nurse in common confinement, told me they were selling it, that five hundred years of royal lineage was valuable to the right sort, but she could have just been messing with me."

Tell him to stop. Shut up!

No. Don't. He needs to say it. She needs to hear it to begin to understand.

"It got pretty far out there, more and more warped. They kept me restrained for days at a time, completely incapacitating me, leaving me open to repeated rape, by staff at first, then others I didn't recognize. And filmed it all." He shudders, shakes his head. "Towards the end, a couple months before I sliced my wrists, a seemingly endless parade of women started mounting me, torturing me until I ejaculated into them. Could have been for some internet porn site, or some sort of twisted power trip, or they were looking to get pregnant. Maybe they just wanted to screw with my head. I don't know. But on the beach that day, when you asked me if I had any kids, well, I can't exactly be sure, now can I?" He stares straight ahead, blinks, and tears slide down his face.

Look away. If she looks at him, she'll cry. And then they'd both be crying. *And what the hell good would that do?* So she stares out the passenger window at the picture postcard coastline, swallowing repeatedly. "I'm sorry, James." She can't look at him. *Don't cry. Don't let him see you cry.* Anxious to the extreme doesn't touch what she's feeling.

"I'm sorry, too, Liz, for not telling you sooner—giving you the knowledge to make a wiser choice than getting involved with me."

She looks at him then. He stares at the road, his long lashes made even longer, darker with his tears. "I made the right choice, James." *Don't look away. Help him.* "The problem is you're still out on a limb. If you don't deal with this you'll be running from it the rest of your life."

"What would you propose I do at this point?" He grips the wheel with both hands and she sees his jaw tighten, his cheeks hollow.

"I don't know. Maybe you should confront your father. Find out why he did what he did, if he knew what was happening to you after he had you set up?"

"What difference would that make?"

"Well, if he got you into this mess, maybe if he knew what happened, he could get you out of it. I absolutely refuse to believe that any father would knowingly condone the torture of his son."

"I'm not going back to England, 'Liz. Even if I managed to get to Edward before they arrested me, my father may not believe me, or care, get me thrown in jail, or even worse, sent back to Langside."

"What about the States? You can go back to the States, ask for sanctuary, get a lawyer and a good private detective to prove you were set up, and fight him on legal grounds."

"How am I supposed to do that exactly? It's my word against his. The investigation showed that I'd been using when I was arrested. A case can easily be made that I had speed on me. And dealing isn't a huge leap from possession for most people. Anyway, none of this is relevant. I'd never make it to court. They'd send me back to England the moment I set foot in the States as James Whren."

"They can't just extradite you. You're an American citizen. You have rights."

"Yeah, that's what I used to think." He sighs. "Look, I can't handle going back to that hospital, or even prison for that matter. I'd prefer dead."

"Don't say that."

"I won't go back there, 'Lisbeth. I can't let them do that to me again."

"Shut up! I don't want to hear anymore. How important could Cameron and I possibly be to you if you're so keen on killing yourself when faced with a little adversity?"

"*A little adversity?*" He flashes her a look like hate, then looks back at the road.

"You know what I mean. I need you to listen to me very carefully now." She hopes he can hear her through his anger, and her outrage. "I promise you I will never let it happen to you again. You are not alone this time. You will not disappear off the face of the Earth with no one searching for you. There is not a court in any land that can convince me you belong in a mental institution, or even in jail for that matter. I'd go to the press, to my contacts with the state department, to Amnesty International if that's what it took. I promise you, I will not let them lock you up and throw away the key. It will not happen again. Do you hear me?"

He doesn't say anything. He stares straight ahead and drives.

"I need you to give me your solemn oath that you will never try and take your life again. I need that commitment from you, James, *no matter what.*"

He grips the wheel so tight his knuckles are white. "Don't ask me that, Liz." He doesn't look at her.

"Promise me. There is no space for compromise on this." She glares at him. "I'll keep at you until we have an agreement. And the only acceptable resolution is your word that you'll never attempt suicide again."

"You really are relentless."

She smiles. "You don't know the half of it."

He seems to soften, but still does not look at her. "You have my word."

She lets the silence ride for quite some time. Cameron naps on as the sun sets and lights up the golden hills of swaying grass before dropping into the sterling sea. She thinks about what James told her, what it must have felt like to be raped and tortured. She pictures him tied down, helpless, struggling, crying, trying to scream. No wonder he's so afraid. And so full of rage.

"My mother is convinced that family is the most important thing there is in life." She isn't sure she has his attention but talks anyway. "You wouldn't believe the tantrum she threw when I told her that Jack and I were moving to Israel for a few years. She raised me under the guise that friends come and go, but family is for life, the only people that you can count on to be there for you always. And to a large degree, she's turned out to be right."

"Not all families are like yours, Liz."

"I know that. Quite frankly, even my mom wasn't there for me a lot of the time. But overall, I know she and my father love me, as I love Cameron, that unconditional love that parents feel for their children that supersedes all others. And I think that's what she meant about family always being there, that their *love* would always be there."

"Cut to the chase, 'Liz." He gives her a weary smile. Both hands are still on the wheel but he isn't gripping it so tightly, and his jaw isn't clinched anymore.

"Do you really think that your biological father doesn't love you?"

He sighs heavily. "If he does, he sure has a fucked up way of showing it."

"Isn't it possible that he had you arrested to save you from what he perceived as the same fate as your half-brother?"

"I don't know."

"And isn't it possible that he has named you the sole heir to your family's estate because you are his son, his blood, but also because he believes in you, trusts you, loves you?"

"I don't know. I don't know. Damn it, 'Lisbeth. What are you getting at?"

"If you knew your father's intention came from love, would that temper some of your anger, at least towards him?"

He pulls the Jeep over suddenly, turns off the engine leaving the keys in the ignition, gets out and walks a few yards in front of the car without looking back. He stands facing the setting sun, clasps his hands on top of his head as if to hold himself to the ground. Still, he does not look at her. She checks Cameron quickly to make sure he's still sleeping, pulls the keys and pockets them and goes to join James.

Tears slide down his face and drip onto the soft dirt at his feet. "I don't know how to answer you. I don't. I hate him. It's true. I do. Don't ask me not to."

"I'm not." She's afraid to speak, afraid of hurting him anymore. "I'm trying to broaden your view, give you some space for forgiveness."

"Fuck forgiveness." He glares at her, then shakes his head and looks away, out across the golden hills to the azure sea beyond.

"I love you, James. More than I ever really knew was possible. But the love I give I want back in equal measure, and I expect no less extended to my son. And how can you possible achieve this when so much of you is consumed by *justifiable* rage from your current point of view?"

James rubs his eyes dry on his shirtsleeve, blinks her into focus and connects. Softens. Smiles. "I love you, 'Lisbeth. And Cameron too, unlike any other love known to me—without reservations, withholding nothing. Hope that'll be enough for you, because I don't know if I will ever achieve a resolution with my father."

"I'm not asking for a resolution, James. I'm asking you to consider, just consider, forgiveness."

"I'll consider it, if that's what you need."

"Thank you." *It's what* you *need, honey.* She doesn't say it, of course, but she can't help shaking her head as she hands him the keys and walks back to the car, completely spent.

He walks back to the Jeep a few minutes later and glances at her as he gets in, his expression back to masked, unreadable. Then he starts the car and they're on the road again. He focuses straight ahead, doesn't look at her, doesn't speak unless spoken to, and then only with monosyllabic responses even after they get into Athens, check into their hotel and settle for the night.

-

-

Chapter Thirty

-

They stay in a small bed and breakfast near Kolonaki Square, across the street from where she spent her summer there all those years ago. The whitewashed flat has only four tiny bedrooms for travelers, but the charm is in the trellised courtyard in back of the building, rare for the middle of the city, and shrouded with bougainvilleas blooming bright pink flowers everywhere. The old stone wall surrounding the courtyard keeps Cameron in check, so Elisabeth and James linger over their coffee and scones in the morning. They hang out that first day, passing the time at a local park, exploring the expensive shops, galleries and boutiques of the neighborhood, then relax during the afternoon hours of siesta while Cameron naps, play Tavli and soak up the sun. In the evening they go to the Achilleion Café in the square, feast on roasted lamb with peppers and olives, and listen to the bouzouki players.

It's close to ten, and the café's still crowded with diners. James lifts a sleeping Cameron from Elisabeth's lap to leave when one of the band members calls out, "James Logan! Is that you, man?"

James looks up at the stage, holding Cameron to him. He stands frozen, looking at the thirty-something, lanky, long-haired, rough bronze-skinned man on the stage, but doesn't say anything.

"That *is* you! *Dude!* Where ya been, man? Ladies and gentleman, let's try and convince one of the best guitar players around to come up and join us on stage." The man starts clapping, then the audience follows his lead, and James looks at Elisabeth, his eyes wide. He clutches Cameron. "James, get your ass up here, man."

"Not now, Curtis. Don't want to wake my son. Take care, man. Good to hear you playing again." He moves towards the door, making his way carefully around the packed tables. Everyone watches him, stares actually, especially the women. Elisabeth feels their eyes on her, too, sizing her up as she follows him out.

"Who was that?" She finally asks when they're a block away, feeling somewhat annoyed he isn't more forthcoming.

"Curtis Weston. He was a friend of my half-brother's. Good player. Lost his way for a while. Glad to see he's at it again."

"Did you recognize him when we sat down?"

"No. Until he noticed me, I didn't make the connection. Space…the final frontier." He flashes a quick grin and shakes his head slightly. "This is why I didn't want to come to the city. I shouldn't stay here now. Maybe it's best if we go back to the island tomorrow."

Each step becomes more weighted with his words. "James, do you plan on spending the rest of your life running every time someone recognizes you."

"'Lisbeth, you know my situation—"

"I do. And it scares me to my core, almost as much as it does you. I love you. I don't ever want anyone to hurt you. And I don't want to lose you. But I can't, I *won't* condemn Cameron to growing up on an antiquated, forty mile long island. Eventually, we'll have to integrate back into the real world. We can't hide on Corfu forever."

"Is the end of forever now? Is that what this trip is all about?"

She blushes, smiles. "Maybe. I hadn't thought of it, but maybe. Cameron is almost two. He's going to start to get it. And I want him to get there's more to life than that tiny island."

Cameron's head rests on James' shoulder, his full face angelic in sleep. James holds him close, supporting him in the crux of his arm, his huge hand on Cam's tiny back. "I don't want to leave yet, Liz. I'm not ready."

He'd said, 'don't want to.' Not 'can't,' or 'won't.' "How long then?" she whispers. "A month? A year? Two? Ten?"

"Honestly, I haven't given it a whole hell of a lot of thought." He doesn't look at her, his delivery sharp, angry.

She stops. He stops, turns back to face her.

He studies at her, and his expression softens. "I'll follow you to the ends of the Earth, 'Lisbeth. Just give me a little time."

She feels his tension and, for once, backs off. "Okay." She goes to him then, puts her hand on his face and pulls him in for a tender but quick kiss as Cameron stirs between them. She takes her son from James, careful not to wake him, holds him close as James did and they resume walking. James is lost inside his head, again, and she damns herself for chasing him there. "Do you want to go back to Corfu in the morning?"

He doesn't respond, walks beside her, hands deep in the pockets of his worn leather jacket.

"We can leave straight-away if you want."

He looks at her then, studies her again. Smiles. "Let's hang in Athens a few days, do the tourist thing, then head back to the island. Give me a month or two, Liz, and hopefully I'll come up with someplace workable for all of us by then." He runs his hand through his hair, sweeping it off his forehead momentarily. "I'm scared out of my fucking mind, 'Lisbeth. For me. For you. Without you." He practically whispers the last line.

"I'm right here, James." She glances at him, smiles. He looks at her, but his expression remains stolid. "We'll stay on the island for right now if that's what you need." They walk beside each other without touching, the distance between them palatable. "We'll merge seamlessly into the real world, together, when you're ready."

He smiles. Nods. They walk the half block to their hotel without further exchange. After settling Cameron in the portable crib, they shower together, massaging, then kissing, then teasing, tantalizing, finally ending up on the bed making love.

There's a desperate quality to his passion that night. James holds her close, his arms and legs still wrapped with hers after they've both climaxed, and he stays intertwined up against her even as they are drifting off to sleep.

-

-

BOOK THREE
Balance
Chapter One

-

JAMES

Cameron runs around the corner of a narrow cobbled street. I go after him but can't find him. And then Elisabeth is standing with Cameron at the end of the same narrow street. It's packed with people blocking my way, pushing me back, preventing me from getting to them, and the closer I get the further away they appear. And then they're gone.

Wake frequently from frightening dreams with disjointed images throughout the night. I finally get out of bed at dawn, put on some jeans and my fleece shirt, sneak out of the room quietly and go down to the courtyard for a coffee. The lobby, which is the living room of the B&B, is deserted when I pour myself a cup of fresh brewed from the coffee maker. Go outside to the courtyard to watch the sunrise.

Elisabeth is right, of course. She has to leave. She has to take Cameron from the cobbled streets, back to his family, to today's world of technology, instant access to knowledge and communication. He should be presented with every opportunity to challenge his mind and ignite his imagination. Elisabeth and I alone cannot provide even a slice of the spectrum, nor can that small, ancient island.

Stop bouncing your leg. Hold my hand to my knee to still it. *How did I get into this? What am I doing here?* Who the hell am I kidding pretending I can be a part of this scene? I can't be in the real world. I don't blend. It doesn't matter on the island, with the transient population, and the few locals who don't care where I'm from. I can't risk leaving Corfu right now, maybe for a long time to come. I have to let her go—tell her to take her son and go.

No! The notion physically hurts, like getting slugged in the gut.

'You choose.' I see her tear-streaked face. She's on her couch, holding the pillow and staring into me, certain of the truth in her words.

I choose to be with her. I want to be with them. Wherever we end up will be better than anyplace without them. Unless they catch me, lock me up again. Then it's all academic.

I'm scared out of my fucking mind.

Breathe. Just breathe. I inhale the bitter, rich smell of steaming coffee, pick up my cup and take a sip. It's good. Warm. Wet. Quenching.

Think. I have identification that gives me license to move fairly freely. I am James Matthew Pierce, a U.S. citizen with a residence abroad who hasn't done anything wrong. Technically, I should be able go almost anywhere. Just have to stay out of major cities. Wouldn't mind going back to the States, the Golden State in particular, though that's probably not the greatest idea. Stay away from L.A., and the Bay Area, even out of Manhattan, for that matter, where I could be recognized.

Who am I kidding? I've worked everywhere. I'm screwed out there.

I look around, drink my coffee and watch the yellow dawn through the trestled magenta flowers. Courtyard is quiet, and empty. Scan the five and six story buildings of whitewashed flats that surround the patio. Their windows are dark, no movement. No one is watching me.

Stop being so paranoid.

Where can we go? Think further out, but plugged in. College town maybe...Princeton, or Boston. What about Boston, just outside, like around Concord, or even near Wellesley where I grew up? Easy to stay anonymous in those swampy hills if we got a place with enough property around us.

Images of bright red, orange, and yellow hills, dense with birch and maple bending with the fierce wind, flash in my head. And I recall the brook in back of my neighbor, Tony Roselli's, house. I'm nine. Tony's eleven. We're standing in the rushing water building a dam. It's pouring rain. There's a hurricane coming, the wind tearing up the trees around us. We finally run for cover inside my house, blow the rest of the day with me playing, and him singing along with YouTube videos of our favorite songs. Our little dam held so well it flooded Tony's basement and several more houses along the waterway. Somehow, we managed to keep our adventures in flow control a secret, and no one ever found out it was us.

I remember watching my stepfather play the violin with the Pops on the half-domed stage every fourth of July. Mom and I sat on the Boston Esplanade, so absorbed in the music that the steamy, bug filled air is lost to me, until the music stops. Mom sits next to me in the first row swatting at the thousands of tiny gnats thickening the evening sky. Her short, thick hair flows around her alabaster face as she bobs and weaves while batting the bugs. She's clearly freaked out, but laughing, probably to lighten the mood so not to freak me out.

Then I'm in her car, and it's spinning, spinning, spinning across the highway on the ice that stormy afternoon on our way to my recital at Berklee. The car slides into a snow bank, hits it with a puff. Snow dust sparkles in the headlights. "You OK?" I nod. "We're good. We're fine." She looks at me with her wide, white smile, her emerald eyes twinkling with relief as she starts the car and we're off again. But I can't shake my trepidation with her and Mike leaving for Haiti in the morning.

And I'm back in the empty courtyard and my mother is dead.

I sigh, try to let go of my longing. *Play it as it lays, James...* Sip my coffee. Concord area, or Lexington may be doable. Produced a few singles at The Bridge, but that was ages ago. Don't know anyone in

Boston now, except Michelle Devlin, and she probably doesn't live there anymore. When I left her in Harry's Porsche to drive cross-country, she'd told me she wasn't planning on staying in their Cambridge flat. Lots of good things about settling in the Boston area. Liz could showcase in a major city, even in New York since it's so close. Great place for Cameron, from fireflies and lightning storms to snow days and fall colors. And Massachusetts is a progressive state with good public education—

"What are you thinking about?"

Nearly have a heart attack, jump up, knocking the small iron table, almost spilling my coffee. Didn't hear her approach.

"Sorry. Didn't mean to startle you. May I join you, or would you prefer to be alone?" She gives me a gentle smile. She's wearing her loose white summer dress that falls just past her knees, and makes her look very tan. Her hair is tied back, but long strands of soft auburn waves are coming out, cascading past her shoulders. Her hazel eyes are deep brown this morning, and fixed on me, like she's trying to get inside my head.

"Please, join me." I pull out the metal chair next to me. "Cameron still sleeping?"

"Yeah. Don't worry. We'll be able to hear him when he wakes up. So, what were you thinking about?" She sits and takes a sip of my coffee.

"Boston."

"Didn't you grow up there?"

"I did. Which is why I'm thinking about it. Wellesley was a great place to grow up. Ever been there?"

"Boston, Cambridge, around the city, a few times. Concord, Lexington area once, but not Wellesley in particular. Why?" She smiles. *She knows.*

"What do you think?" I smile back at her.

Her smile broadens. So does mine. Can't help it. Her delight is infectious. "When?"

My breath suddenly catches in my throat. Choking panic. *Breathe. Take some coffee.* "Soon, if you want."

"For how long?"

"For as long you'll have me." I stay fixed on her. I do not look away. Neither does she.

"If we leave next month we'll get there for the tail end of the fall colors. Early November is beautiful in New England." Her demeanor radiates her excitement. She sits perched on the edge of her chair, bouncing her feet on the tips of her toes. "I don't know about you, but I much prefer living rural, with trees and space to breathe. Where's Wellesley?"

"Fifteen minutes east of Boston. Maybe a bit too close, actually. The further out the better. Concord maybe? I'd like to stay away from major cities, Liz."

"Okay." She practically whispers, and I catch her disappointment. "I'll start packing up when we get back to Corfu. We can leave at the end of the month. What do you think?"

I hate the idea. *I'm scared out of my fucking mind.* "Okay. That's less than two weeks. We should book tickets straightaway. Unscheduled international flights can raise eyebrows. There's no sense in arousing suspicion."

Her eyes drift and it's clear she's not listening. *Where is she?* I stare at her and she focuses back on me, smiles.

"What do you think of taking a cruise back to the States instead of flying? Take our time returning to the real world, enjoy the ride. It may make the transition easier." She raises an eyebrow at me as she steals another sip of my coffee. We both hear Cameron crying through our room window facing the courtyard. "And the best part of a cruise is they have childcare on board." She gives me a big, happy grin as she rises to attend to her son.

-

-

Chapter Two

-

We do the tourist thing through Athens after booking a cruise to New York on the Windstar, because it's the only cruise line that boards in Igoumenitsu, the mainland port-of-call for Corfu. We hike up to the Acropolis one day, check out the almost three thousand year old temples of Athena and Poseidon; go out to Delphi the next, roam the sun-dried hills and sample the flavors of local vineyards. Over breakfast this morning, we decide to explore Athens and tour some of the famous museums for the day.

Start south of the Monastiraki Flea Market, at the Museum of Popular Instruments. We're on the third floor, perusing. Cameron's free to roam, since the entire collection of over twelve hundred musical instruments is protected in glass cases. Elisabeth is grilling me.

"Do you play that?"

It's a fretless Zither, rosewood with ivory. "Yes."

"How about that?"

A hammered dulcimer, seventeenth century. "Something like it.

Yeah."

"Have you ever played one of those?"

"What's with the third degree, 'Lisbeth?" Cameron takes off down the stairs and we go after him. I catch up with him close to the second floor and pick him up. He wraps his legs around me and sits perched on my hip. I look up at her a few steps above us. "Are we done here?"

"We can go if you want."

I do. Continue down the stairs with Cam grinning ear to ear from the bouncy ride. When we reached the ground floor, Cameron spies something in a case, wriggles down and runs over, presses his face up against the glass.

"What dat, 'Ames?"

"It's called a Daoulia. It's a drum."

"Did you ever play one?" Elisabeth's behind me. Her face over my shoulder reflects in the glass case and overlaps mine. And we are one. I smile. So does she.

"What difference does it make what instruments I used to play?"

"Just curious." She gives me a pleasant smile and turns away to join Cameron at the entrance, who's using all his might to push open the heavy glass door.

"Right." I follow her. "With you, there's always an agenda."

"And with you, there's always a reason for one." She puts on her sunglasses as she reaches over Cameron, pushes open the glass door and steps outside.

Cameron bolts and I go after him, down the steps and across the sidewalk, pick him up before he gets near the street and swing him on to my shoulders. Cameron starts bouncing, so do I, jump up and down and he laughs with delight, and so do I. Elisabeth's deadpan. "Okay, Liz. Just ask me what you want to know."

"I *am* curious, that's the truth."

"Yeah. About what?"

"About what you're going to do back in the States. About how you're planning on spending your days when we get back there."

"I don't know. Maybe I'll become a glider pilot. I'll take Cameron up with me and turn him on to soaring."

"Over my dead body." She glares at me. "I'm serious, James."

Can't help laughing. "I don't know. What do you want to do? I mean, how many days can you take Cameron to the park? I can't imagine you're going to be satisfied just doing the full time mom thing."

"*Stop that*. We're not talking about me. I asked *you*."

"I don't know. I haven't gotten that far yet. I'm still trying to come to terms with moving back to Boston, to the States, to humanity." The warm Athenian sun bakes through my shirt, deep into my skin. Cameron sits on my shoulders and holds my head. I hold his ankles as we meander through the congested city. "What do you think about us moving to Boston, Cam?"

"'ostn. What dat?"

"It's a place on the other side of the globe, but a world away from here." *A crowded, potentially dangerous world where I'm recognizable.* I cringe, and feel her watching me. *Relax. Talk. Say something.* "I'm thinking about growing a beard. What do you think?"

She gives me a knowing smile. "When we get back to the real world, I'm going to create fine photography, and try and get an agent to represent my work. And other than the full-time dad thing, which will last about another year before Cam goes to preschool, what will you be doing?"

"Finding us a place to live, especially if you're busy producing art." I grin at her. She sticks her tongue out at me. I'm too far away to suck it. I waggle my tongue back at her, teasing. She laughs. So do I. "Seriously, Concord is about a half an hour outside of Cambridge. Some great old Colonials out there. Land, too. Interested?"

Her eyes light up and go dreamy. I like the look very much, her features soft, her eyes wide, her toughness abandoned. "I *love* Colonials, especially the original ones with the tall windows and those huge central fireplaces—" She cuts herself off, and glares at me in exasperation. "You're doing it again! God, just answer the question."

I stop, turn back to face her, laugh. *Shit.* "What was the question again?"

She rolls her eyes, but I see the hint of a smile. "When are you going back to music?"

I stare at her. She's serious. "Maybe never." I don't want to talk about this. "We don't need the money. I've got enough for all of us, for this lifetime and Cam's too with the right investments. What difference does it make if I ever go back to making music?"

She stays fixed on me. "I just want to be ready when you do."

I feel her uncertainty, her doubt, and it hurts—literally, physically, like she's sucker punched me. I need her to believe in me, that I'll be there when she needs me, and even when she doesn't. *Tell her anything to quell her fear.* But I know mere words will not satisfy her.

"Wow!" Cameron wriggles off of me and runs down a path leading to a large open area with several partially destroyed Greek temples, and a labyrinth of old stone walls and building foundations. It's past noon, the beginning of siesta, and no one's around.

"What is this place?" Elisabeth follows Cam down the path. I follow after them.

"I don't know. Kind of creepy, though." Setting is park-like, takes at least five square blocks and surrounded by three and four story residential buildings. Dried grass and dirt paths meander through the ruins against the backdrop of the crowded, whitewashed city.

"Hey, he looks like you." She points to a decapitated statue of a Greek god-type figure mounted on a massive marble pedestal. "'Cept your head, and that brilliant brain inside it, is one of your best bits."

"Thanks." We follow Cameron and keep close while he climbs on the ruined structures. It's hot. Sweat trickles down my neck, my ribs. Liz isn't sweating. She doesn't even look hot. She walks beside me, close but not touching, her white dress moving like waves on the shore of the Med.

We pause at what's left of the entrance to a building. Only columns and part of the back wall still stand. Most of the marble floor remains, though it's pockmarked, eroding.

"Doric columns, early twelfth century. Can tell by the minimal fluting." Elisabeth points to the design on the top of the column, and smiles with her delivery.

Cameron runs around the cavernous space, then the perimeter, in and out and around the columns and disappears behind the back wall. I take off after him. So does Liz. I go right. She goes left.

Prickling panic sweeps through me the second Cam's out of sight. Then I round the wall and see him running towards Elisabeth at the other end of the crumbling remains of a columned corridor. She picks up her son, settles him on her hip and they both look at me. I stare back at them, breathless.

She's with him at the end of the narrow cobbled street. I can't get to them. Then they're gone. I convulsively shiver. *Forget it.* It was just a dream.

Elisabeth is wide-eyed as I join them. She, too, seems breathless as they resume walking.

"Remember I told you I'm scared of everything all the time," she says almost cautiously.

"I do."

"Well, now I'm afraid of losing you, too. I think about it all the time, just like with Cam. The love I feel for you, well, I can't imagine my life forward, or Cam's, without you now." She keeps her eyes on mine. "I'm sorry for the third degree earlier. I know you'll find your way back to making music eventually, and it scares the hell of of me. I want all of you, James. Forever, as selfish as I know that is."

Cameron wiggles down from her hip and is off again. He climbs into a dry fountain and walks inside the long, shallow leaf-filled pool, stomping and crunching. She slips her hand in mine and we pace Cameron slowly along the pool's edge.

She wants something from me. Needs something. *What is it? Does she even know?* "Elisabeth, music for me now, and forever forward, is my pleasure. You and Cameron are my passion. I would not be leaving my sanctuary, and risking my freedom, if I were not merely a slave to my passion."

She stops, stands in front of me, then releases my hand and holds my face with both of hers. "I love you." She kisses me and I return it, passionate, deep, lingering, but it does not quell her doubt. I see it in her eyes when we separate. She turns away, goes back to tracking Cameron. She still seems breathless, edgy, though her cadence is graceful. Her dress flows with her motion.

"We're going to need a fairly large house, with a guestroom for family." Her tone is certain, but she speaks softly. "And I just want to give you a heads up that my mom won't be too pleased we'll be living across the country, which to her might as well be the Middle East. And you can bet she's not going to be all that thrilled that I'm raising her grandson with a man I'm not married to, either."

OK....So that's what she's been getting at. I have to laugh. She turns around and scowls at me. *Wow. She's really mad.* A simple solution presents itself. "So, do you think if we got married that would please your parents, and galvanize my commitment to you?"

Cameron does a head long chasing a lizard, but gets up undaunted and continues the chase. I watch him over her shoulder, feel her staring at me. Look at her and spread my arms as if to say "Well?" I can't help smiling at the look on her face. Classic stunned.

She moves to me, locks her arms around my neck and whisper in my ear. "Yes!"

I wrap my arms around her. Pick her up, hold her to me, body to body, twirl her around and suck in her sweet, carnal scent. "Yes! Yes! Yes!" Louder and louder until she's practically yelling.

She grips my face and her lips on mine, our tongues intertwine and I get lost in her taste, her smell. I never want to let go. Then Cam's between us, trying to squish in between our legs. I pick him up, grab her face and snatch a quick kiss, then sling Cameron onto my shoulders. She smiles at me, winks. I laugh, then slide my hand back in hers and we walk out of the ruins, back into the bustling, noisy city—a stark contrast to my quiet contentment. The sun penetrates into my muscles. Cameron's weight massages my shoulders as we walk. Her hand is soft, our finger's laced. Feel her excitement pulse into me and fuel mine.

"If we get a Colonial, let's find one built in the mid-eighteen hundreds, before they got so ornate, one that isn't perfect, so we can fix it up and make it our own. And, you know, it's only right that we give Cam some siblings." She slips it in but with conviction.

I smile. "How many?"

"Just one, or two." She smiles. "I want to reproduce your genetics."

'I want to reproduce your genetics,' Parker says to me while I'm spread and bound naked on the padded floor. I'm vaguely astonished she even knows words like 'reproduce' and 'genetics.' "Royal-blooded baby be worth a pretty penny." She smiles her crooked brown-toothed grin as she mounts me. "You been givin it up and I been givin yours away. My turn now."

Holy Christ, *no!* But I can't stop her. She'll torture me until I give it up, let her take me.

My inner thighs burn with the memory of the electrodes repeatedly shocking me into a rhythm. My stomach cramps, goes hard. Everything spins. Think I may be sick. Stop walking, let go of Elisabeth's hand, take Cameron off my shoulders and hand him to her. He instantly starts whining.

"No. Soders, 'Ames. Soders."

"What is it?" She takes Cam to her hip and they stare at me, concerned.

I shake my head but can't say anything, swallow hard and turn away. I don't want to frighten Cameron. I comb my hands through my hair, pull it from my eyes and try to focus on the warmth of the sun, the sounds of the city, anything to force the images from my head and the bile back down my throat.

"Talk to me. Please!"

Turn back to them. Her expression is horrified.

"God, James. Whatever I said, I'm sorry."

"Don't be. It's not you." Look away again, swallow back my rage. "I'm okay. Just give me a second." Take several deep breaths in a row then turn back to her and Cameron. "I'm sorry, Liz." I take another breath and exhale slowly. "Look, what happened to me isn't just going to go away. It gnaws at me constantly, what they did to me...my response. You ought to think about that before you agree to spend your life with me, 'Lisbeth."

"Whatever was done to you was beyond your control. You didn't do anything wrong, James."

"I committed *murder*. That doesn't bother you?" I stay fixed on her, looking for any change in her demeanor. She stares at me, casually, shakes her head and turns away, resumes walking again.

"It was self-defense. It wasn't murder. Imminent danger falls under self-defense." She pauses to let Cameron down. He runs back into the park we still pace to explore an ancient temple where the front façade and the columns still stand, but all else has crumbled to dust. I look at her. She stares after her son.

"When I look at him I see his potential," she says, staying fixed on Cameron. "When I look at us, I see ours. I wouldn't if I didn't see you, James." She finally looks at me. "And I don't see a murderer. I don't see a man with a wanton disregard for others."

Her belief in me is unwavering, and untenable. "Look closer. I've been a coward, afraid to let anyone in. Careless. Cruel." Have to tell her. She has to know. Her decision to be with me should be made with knowledge. "You're right to be afraid of me, of losing me. I'm afraid of me—of losing me to who I used to be."

She stares at me. "You mean a solipsistic, self-serving son of a bitch?"

I crack up laughing. She doesn't. "Yeah, I guess you could say that."

No smile. No humor. She meant it. And it suddenly cuts.

She turns away and walks back into the park after Cameron who's examining chipped pieces of marble, and colorful leaves as he encounters them. She stops at the crumbling marble steps of the temple and watches him. I stand beside her.

"I love you, James." She whispers, slides her hand in mine. "Promise me, Cameron and I will always be your *first* priority, and everything else we can deal with together." She squeezes my hand till it hurts, then lifts it to her lips and kisses my fingers laced in hers.

I look at her, fix on her, hoping she'll hear me, feel me. "I promise." Not sure she believes me, but I'm damn sure she doesn't have a clue how out there things may get if my past comes back to haunt me.

-

-

Chapter Three

-

I first notice them on Iftseou Street, a narrow cobbled alley packed with vendors and shoppers at the expensive end of the flea market. There are four of them, men in their late thirties, early forties maybe, properly dressed in Dockers with Izod type shirts. Though a lot of other people are similarly dressed, most are older tourists traveling in groups, young students, or parents with kids.

Elisabeth goes into a ceramic gallery to look at some Raku-fired bowls. I take Cam a few doors down to a bakery to get a sweet treat, an easy distraction from the ceramic shop with all the delicate pieces on display. I catch all four of them looking at me in the reflection of the bakery windows as we enter. Take Cam off my shoulders and turn back to look at them but they're gone. It takes him several minutes to choose a moon-shaped shortbread cookie. Get one, too, we go back outside, and Cam sits in my lap at the small wooden table. We share the bottle of fresh milk, cream still floating on top.

"Did you get me anything?" Elisabeth stands behind the only vacant chair.

"I'll get you whatever you desire, my lady." I arch my eyebrows, give her a teasing grin.

"How about if we just share." She sits down next to us.

"No! Mine!" Cameron hordes his cookie and grabs the milk too, spilling it everywhere, all over himself and his mama. I stand, pulling Cameron up with me. Elisabeth gets up too, brushing the milk from her dress.

"Wrong, Cameron. In this family we share our stuff," she says as she helps me clean up the mess. We toss the wet napkins and the milk-soaked cookies, and we're on our way again.

I notice the four men again at the end of Normanou Street. They're gathered in front of a small corner furniture shop, seemingly talking among themselves, but I get the impression they're watching us.

"Here." I take Cameron off my shoulders. "Take Cam for a while, would you?"

"Sure." She takes her son, who isn't pleased to be off of his perch again.

"No! NO! NO! Soders. I want soders." Louder and louder. Over and over.

"Stop it, Cameron." Elisabeth gives me her exasperated mother look.

"Here. Give him back to me."

"James Michael Whren?" Someone says over Cam's screaming.

I see the alligator on his shirt then look at the face of the man in front of me. Tight-lipped, pinched chin, blank, gray eyes. The other three have surrounded us.

Fuck. Run. *Slam him and run.*

Elisabeth stares at me, wide-eyed. Cameron still wriggles, but has quieted, distracted by the men. One of them stands behind her and Cameron, at arm's length. I'm not going anywhere.

"Are you James Michael Whren?"

"Nope." *Be calm. Stop shaking.* "I'm Jim, but my last name is Pierce." My heart's coming through my chest. I take my passport out and hold it open for the alligator man to see. "Sorry. You must have me mistaken for someone else." Look him straight in the eye as I speak. The man's glare is unwavering. He doesn't even glance at my passport.

"No. I don't think so. I'm agent Robert Townes with ICPO, and I have a warrant for your arrest, Mr. Whren." He flashes a silver star badge, with a small crown atop it. Silver letters against deep blue resin read Notthinghamshire Constabulary around the large ER cut into the center of the star. "Please put your hands on top of your head." He pockets his badge in his pants.

I hear the guy behind him take out cuffs, and hold my breath to control my trembling.

"Wait a minute—" Elisabeth starts.

"Ms. Whitestone, if you open your mouth again, I'll arrest you for obstruction of justice. And even if the charges don't stick, we'll take your son away from you in the interim. Am I perfectly clear?" Agent

Townes speaks in a low, menacing tone with a cultivated British accent.

"Don't say another word, 'Lisbeth." I pocket my passport. "Walk away. Turn around and walk away." I implore her, then speak to them, but look only at her. "Let her go. She has no idea who I am and you can't prove otherwise." I clasp my hands on top of my head.

"No." Elisabeth stays fixed on me as the man behind me grabs my wrist and yanks my arm down shoving my hand against my back. Shooting pain through my arm and shoulder and I grimace.

"Wait." She glares at agent Townes. "I want to see your I.D again. Show us the warrant."

"Don't take me to task, Ms. Whitestone." Agent Townes says.

I clench my fist as cold metal tightens around my wrist. "Leave her alone. I'm doing what you want." Can hardly breathe as I feel metal tighten around my other wrist. "You fucking piece of shit you better leave her alone."

Townes nods to his men and the two on my sides grab my arms and start to lead me away. Try to stay fixed on her. "Go home, Liz!" I yell as they escort me to the end of the street. "Go back to the States. You'll be safe in the States."

"No! James. Wait." She grabs my shirtsleeve and Townes grabs her at the base of the neck and holds her shoulder, stopping her cold.

"NO!" I twist away from my captors and manage to kick one of them in the groin, then someone tackles me and I'm on the ground with my face slammed against the eroding cobbled stone street.

"Stop it!" I hear Elisabeth scream. "Get off of him! HELP! Someone help me! They're kidnapping my husband!"

"'Ames! 'Ames!" Cameron screams my name over and over in rising panic.

Then I hear gravel crunch under tires and a car pulls up only inches from my head, and men lift me up and shove me in.

"I'm going to the embassy, James." Elisabeth yells. "I'll get help! I promise you, I'll come after you!"

"Don't follow me, 'Lisbeth! Go to your folks and I'll come for you there!" I glimpse back. "Go home!" They stand where we'd stopped near the end of the narrow, cobbled street. She holds Cameron to her, their faces streaked with tears. She looks scared out of her mind.

Someone slams the car door and I struggle to get up but sudden acceleration throws me back down. Then a foot's on my back and holds me to the floor, and I lay still, flexing my hands against the stabbing pain shooting through them.

"Who are you guys?" I know damn well they're not Interpol. Went along to protect Liz and Cameron. "What do you want?"

No one responds. I twist my head to see agent Townes on his cell phone.

"We got him. We're on our way. Be there in ten." He touches the phone then pockets it.

"My hands are killing me. Could you take these off, or loosen 'em, or just let me sit up for Christ's sake." See Townes nod to someone across from him and the foot is removed from my back. I sit up, lean against the carpeted wall of the limo. I'm on the floor between two facing seats where the four men sit. They all looked at me with blank stares, then go back to looking at their cellphones or out the windows. I rub my wrists, try to move the cuffs around them so they're not biting into me so much.

It's hard to see out the tinted windows from my angle. I can tell we're passing through Athens, the top floors of whitewashed buildings flash by, but I don't know what direction we were traveling, or what part of the city we're driving through.

Elisabeth is holding Cameron in the cobbled street. They're getting further away.

Shut my eyes and focus on the pain in my hands and arms to make the image go away. But it doesn't. Look of terror on her face remains. Pull against the cuffs so they dig into my wrists, feel the metal edge pierce my skin and fight the urge to scream out. I flush, am drenched in sweat in seconds but I keep pulling anyway.

"Stop it." Agent Townes yanks me forward by my shirt collar so he can see my hands. "For Christ's sake. Carter get me a cloth or something. He's bleeding all over the place."

Carter hands him a handkerchief and Townes tucks it under one cuff, then the other. I try to pull it out, but Townes pushes me to the ground so I'm lying face down again, sits back down and sets his foot between my hands, immobilizing them. Sharp, stabbing pain is so excruciating I almost pass out. I lay still and relax my body as best I can. The pain subsides because I can't feel my hands anymore. They're numb. I wish to hell I was.

"Where are you taking me? What do you want?"

Still no response. This time no one even acknowledges me. Think to kick, to fight, possibly do them some damage, but really, what's the point. They know about Liz, may hurt her and Cameron if I resist, or get away. I'm at their mercy, helpless again. My eyes fill, and I look down. I refuse to let them see me cry.

It's unbearable torture being taken from Elisabeth and Cameron. Am I damned to the will of captors the rest of my life? I can't go back to Langside. I won't let them take me back there. *Feeling nothing is better than that. Nothing forever is better than another second of that.*

'Give me your solemn oath that you will never try and take your life again. No matter what.' I see her face, her determined hazel eyes waiting for my confirmation. And I'd given it to her. Gave her my word. Suicide is no longer an option. *No way out.*

She'd promised me she wouldn't let me rot in a cell somewhere, and I touch hope. And then feel conflicted, guilty wanting her to save me, afraid for her and Cameron if she becomes tangled in my twisted mess.

The car stops and they pull me out. Pain shoots through my wrists, into my hands, my arms, and a scream escapes my lips. We're at a rural airfield, just one runway and a hanger-type warehouse next to a squat, two-story control tower. But by the angle of the setting sun, I guess we're somewhere northeast of the city. I'm escorted to a small jet a few yards from the limo. My hands and wrists throb, the pain making me light-headed as I climb the step ladder of the plane. Takes my eyes a moment to adjust to the dark interior. There's a wet bar, an entertainment center with an enormous T.V. mounted to a wall, and an office area complete with an extensive computer set-up with several large monitors.

I'm ushered into a tall leather seat. A steward shuts and locks the door to the aircraft and I hear the engines winding up. Agent Townes disappears and a few seconds later comes back with a small black case, sits down next to me and opens it. Inside is a needle and a small clear bottle.

"Please don't." I almost get up but the steward throws me back into the seat and straps me in. Taste salt from my tears as I sit there and watch agent Townes insert the needle into the bottle and draw out the clear liquid. "There is no reason for this. I'm not resisting. Please don't do this."

Townes unbuttons my shirt and pulls it off my shoulder exposing my upper arm and inserts the needle. The liquid burns as it goes into me. I close my eyes, feel warm tears fall.

I hate this. I fucking hate this. Muffled voices. I open my eyes.

349

Everything's blurry. Can't focus. Squint at someone coming from the cockpit towards me. Medium height, slight build, short, receding hair graying at the temples, dark wool suit. *Harvard?* "Howard? Is that you?" *It is.* Fuck. These people work for my father...

-

-

Chapter Four

-

I'm afraid to open my eyes. Bittersweet taste in my mouth. Feel sick from the drugs. I'm in a soft bed, under a plush, heavy quilt. Hear fire crackle, rain hitting glass.

Elisabeth, Cameron where are you? If they hurt you in any way, I swear, I'll make it my life's pursuit to hurt them.

There's something around my wrists. Bolt upright and open my eyes as I push the quilt back. My wrists are wrapped, and they ache, but I'm not restrained.

Blink the room into focus, surprised, even relieved to see I'm in my old bedroom at Castlewood. There's a fire blazing in the marbled fireplace, but the cold rain that pelts the thin leaded windows creeps moisture in, and the high ceiling keeps the cavernous room damp. Instruments still lay in their cases about the room as they did two years ago, and ten on that—my old Powell flute, the 'Swan' Strad fiddle my father gave to me that his father had given to him, the Fender electric, and an Ibanez bass he'd gifted me. Took only two acoustic guitars when I left, a dozen years ago now—the Gibson SJ200 my step-father gave me when I was five, and my thirteenth birthday present, the Takamine 12-String my mother had given me a month before she was killed.

Halogen lights illuminate half the coffered ceiling squares, making the others look dark by comparison, which is why I notice the tiny red light on a small box directly in the center of an unlit square near the bedroom door. Looks sort of like a fire alarm, but it's barely the size of a cigarette lighter with a small glass-covered hole in the center. It's a camera. I glare at it, feeling exposed and disgusted, then angry.

I get out of bed, relieved to be dressed in my jeans and fleece shirt still, though my wallet and passport are gone, and I'm shoeless and don't see them anywhere. Move towards the door, stare up at the camera.

"Where's 'Lisbeth and Cameron? I'll do anything you want if you promise me you'll keep them out of this." Not sure I'm actually talking to anyone. For all I know, the thing's not even on, but I'm desperate. "Do you hear me, Edward? I surrender." I hold my hands in front of me, my wrists together like a prisoner. "I'm not even checking the goddamn door. I'll do whatever you want me to do." My voice cracks. My eyes fill. "Fuck." Wipe tears away but they come anyway. Sink to my knees. "Please, Edward. I'm begging you, leave them alone."

There's a light tap on the door, then it opens. Howard moves into the bedroom only a few feet from the threshold.

"Your father is expecting you in the study in ten minutes," he says in his crisp, cultivated accent.

I stand, glare at him, wipe my eyes and nose on my shirtsleeve again. He's dressed almost as he was on the plane, in a dark wool suit, perfectly coiffed. "Where are they, Howard? Where's Cameron and 'Lisbeth?" He stares at me with contempt, but remains silent. Then he turns on his heels and is about to walk away but I go after him before he makes the doorway and block his path. I'm five inches taller, considerably more muscular, and at least thirty years younger, but, like my father, Howard still intimidates me. "Where's is she, Howard? I know you know, you fucking prig, and you're gonna tell me."

"Remove yourself from my path." His gray eyes are fixed on me.

Heat rush of raw fury. *Slam his head into the threshold*, but instead I unclench my fists so I don't move on him. "Talk to me old man, or I swear I'll make you." Know I sound absurd, straight out of the movies, and cannot fault Harvard his disdain. Tears of frustration blur my vision. "Damn it, Harvard. *Please*. I need to know they're okay."

"Ms. Whitestone and her son were not detained." Howard stays fixed on me but remains expressionless. "To my knowledge, they are well."

My anger dissolves, my knees give way a little and I lean against the doorjamb for support, still blocking Howard's path. His expression softens with my surrender, but otherwise he stands statue still with that stick up his ass. "Harvard, *please,* help me get out of here. Don't let him lock me up again. For Christ's Sake, do you have any idea what they did to me? Does he?"

No response. No change in expression. Still stone cold.

"I can't handle going back there, Howard. I won't."

"I'm aware what was done to you, and I'm sorry for your suffering, James. It was never intended, and it will serve you well to remember that. Now move aside."

I don't, though I know he won't say any more. I want to put my hands around his throat and crush his larynx in. But what's the point. Howard's already beaten me.

"You now have five minutes." He keeps his eyes fixed on mine.

I step back, gave him ample room to move, watch him walk down the wainscoted hall, past Dutch masterworks of Vermeer and Rembrandt, marble busts of dead relatives on pedestals, the gold-leaf table with a huge floral bouquet, then he disappears down the stairs.

If Howard is 'aware' what was done to me, then my father surely knows. My body tightens, my blood starts to boil and I tremble with rage as the idea takes hold. Can't swallow. Can hardly breathe. Edward *knew*, and he did *nothing*.

Five minutes, my ass. I'm gonna kill the motherfucker. *Right now.* It's father or son, cuz there's no way in hell I'm letting that sonofabitch lock me up again.

Make my way down the hall, the split staircase with the massive portraits of my ancestry lining the walls of the Great Gallery. *It'll be self-defense.* 'Imminent danger' Liz called it. My heart races, pounds hard in my chest, reverberates in my throat. *He let them* torture *me. He did nothing.* And I hate him. I want him to bleed.

-

-

Chapter Five

-

Cold marble is under my bare feet as I move across the gallery to the arched threshold of the plush carpeted hall, and finally down the south wing hallway into his dim study. My father stands at the bar, holding a glass of what looks like brandy, staring at the collection of bottles along the terraced wall. He's slightly hunched, his body considerably thinner. His face, reflecting in the mirror over the bar, looks aged and tired. Though his hair is still thick, it's no longer salt and pepper but stark white. He runs his fingers through it, pulling it off his brow as he turns to me.

"Would you care for a brandy, James?" He asks like he's offering the topper to a satisfying meal.

"No." And I don't give a shit about the harshness in my tone.

Hit him. Go slug him. Pound his fucking face in.

He looks so old.

"Perhaps a smooth gin, then?" He gets a shot glass from the metal rack at the end of the bar, retrieves a black, gold-labeled bottle of Nolet's Dry, and slowly pours me a shot.

Rage crests. Can't stop shaking. Can't unclench my fists even though my nails are digging into my palms. *Kill him and run. Get the cops to kill me instead of catch me, and it won't be suicide.* I look around the room for a weapon. Mounted to one of the walnut walls is an elaborately sculpted family crest, with crossed swords. *Take one down and run him through.*

Edward puts the filled shot glass in the center of the bar then takes a long, slow sip of his brandy. He finally moves to his desk, and studies me as he stands behind it. "You look well. I'm pleased."

In two years, the man has aged twenty. His green eyes are set deeper now, surrounded by darkness, the tone of his skin a pasty white. Craggy lines cut across his forehead. Perhaps he's got some fatal disease and is in the process of dying. *Good.* He deserves some hideous form of cancer that will ravage his body until his last wheezing breath.

"You look like shit. And I'm pleased." I glare at him, move closer to his desk to get in his face. My father doesn't flinch. "What do you want? What am I doing here, Edward?"

He sits heavily in his leather chair and sets his glass down carefully. "Please sit down, James."

"Go fuck yourself, old man."

"Well, it seems we've been down this road before." He takes

another sip of his brandy, then smiles at me as if he has a secret.

"What do you want from me, Edward? Haven't you fucked with me enough?"

His smile fades. "You'll be please to know Elisabeth and her son are well. She seems like a fine woman, and Cameron sounds like a charming boy."

Feels like the hairs on the back of my neck rise. "You mess with them, old man, and I'll kill you." Place both my hands on his desk and swallow hard to still my quivered breathing. "*What. Do. You. Want.*"

Edward doesn't answer. Want to grab my father's shirt collar and bash his head into the desktop. Instead I reach out and sweep everything off the desk. Edward jumps up as the crystal snifter, the desk lamp, his laptop—everything flies off his desk and hits the ground with a clattering thud. A few papers flutter in the air as they float down gracefully.

"Do you know what they did to me!?" I scream at him standing three feet in front of me, only his desk between us. "How could you let them *torture* me!? How could you leave me locked up there *knowing* what they were doing to me? I HATE YOU! You are a monster and I HATE YOU, and I will *never* forgive you!" I turn away to control my impulse to strike him. Howard and several other men have come into the room. "GET OUT!" I yell at them. "*Get the fuck out!*" And my father must have indicated for them to do so because they leave. Howard turns back only to shut the doors after him, and as he does, glances at me with his thin-lipped, scornful frown.

"I am not seeking, nor do I require your forgiveness, James." Edward is calm, collected. He stands behind his desk in that hunched position. "I thought it important we meet again, not as father and son, but man to man." He looks so old, and frail. "This meeting is not for me, son."

"My father died in a plane crash when I was thirteen. And I'll never be your son. *Your* son is dead. You killed him, and his mother. They couldn't tolerate your pompous, self-righteous arrogance without drugs."

"This meeting is for you, James," he speaks softly, seemingly unruffled by my aggression. "I hope to enlighten you to the...*conditions* that led to my decision to have you incarcerated. This knowledge should help you to move beyond the unfortunate events in your recent past, and on with your life."

"*What life, Edward!?* You stole it away from me. I'm wanted for murder, for trafficking a controlled substance, for escaping from a secured facility for the *criminally insane*. And you *set it all up!* How the hell am I supposed to *move on* with my life when you've destroyed it?"

"The charges against you have been repealed."

"What?"

"You have been exonerated. You are a free man." Edward stares at me from behind his massive desk.

Vertigo. He gets distant. Everything spins. "What are you talking about?" I put my hands on the desk to steady myself and look outside, through the tall, narrow leaded windows behind him to find ground. It's gray, looks cold. It's always cold here.

"The Crown Court has rescinded all charges with recent evidence that has come to the fore. Additionally, you were denied your civil rights, never made privy to council or court, unlawfully detained and illegally incarcerated. You've been acquitted of all drug charges, the unfortunate incident regarding Mr. William Ferrell, and granted release from Langside Priory Hospital. The Crown will not agree to any reparations attendant to the circumstances surrounding your arrest, however, if you choose to do so, you may pursue a civil action against them, or myself, and our estate if you wish, and in all likelihood, receive a substantial settlement."

I'm still stuck on, 'You're a free man.' My knees feel weak. If I don't sit I'm gonna fall. My entire body goes limp as I slump into one of the padded armchairs across the desk from my father. Exhaustion takes me. It's hard to think, gather my racing thoughts. "I don't understand. Are you saying they found out you set me up? So what? I *murdered* a man. And I *escaped* from Langside. I wasn't released. What the fuck are you talking about, Edward?"

He sits down heavily, laces his huge hands in his lap casually. "Your case was appealed to the magistrate, then re-examined by the House of Lords. Your role in William Ferrell's death was determined to be self-defense. Your departure from Langside Priory Hospital was initiated by a medical emergency—your attempted suicide. Your release was granted retroactively. The ICAS and the PHS have each launched independent investigations of the facility. You've been given absolute immunity, James. Your records have been ex-sponged and cannot be legally obtained by anyone. This unfortunate series of events is now past, and will no longer directly impact your life forward."

"Directly impact my life?" I practically grow at him. "Are you *mad*, Edward? You let them take a piece of me. And now I have to live everyday with what they did to me." I feel myself energizing, my rage mounting again. "And regardless if I'm free, I'm still a killer. Is this who you wanted me to be, old man? Because I don't know *who this is!* You took my life and ripped it apart, and I can't go back now. I'm angry and scared out of my fucking mind most all the time. And I hope to hell what you did to me impacts *you* till the day you die, you *fuck!*"

"Exhilarating isn't it?"

"What?"

Edward stares at me. "Living."

I glare at him. My father twists everything. Arguing with the man makes me crazy.

"Tell me, son, do you wish to go back to when nothing touched you but music?" Edward shakes his head.

I just stare at him. Would have spit in his face, but I'm too tired.

"You are who you have always been, James. Your experiences over the past two years simply brought to the fore aspects of your character yet utilized. I will offer no judgment on who you are, nor on what you wish to become. That is for you alone to determine. All I can offer you are some answers, and perhaps a broader perspective on your current interpretation of the circumstances that lead to my actions."

Edward has me by the balls again. We both know it. I have to know. Need to know why this man, my *father,* had me locked up and then abandoned me in hell. Edward alone can provide these answers, and he sits before me now, offering them. "Is this your attempt at penance, Edward?"

"Perhaps." He smiles, but it fades quickly. "Indulge me this one last time, and you may just learn some things about yourself, James."

I can't move. Weight greater than gravity holds me in the chair. Stare at the man before me. He looks so tired. Old and tired. I feel like Edward looks. I nod for him to continue.

Edward nods back with another weary smile. "At the time I met your mother, I was married to Kathryn, Ian's mother, though we were estranged, and in fact, we'd been living apart for several years."

"Are you trying to justify fucking my mother while you were married to someone else?"

His eyes narrow slightly but he does not look away. "I have no need to justify loving your mother. She was a consenting adult, and was privy to my situation from the beginning. When she found out she was pregnant with you, it was her choice to move back to the States and terminate our relationship. She refused to be a catalyst for breaking up my family. Your mother married Michael Logan two years after your birth, and I agreed to the adoption upon their request, their union offering you what I could not."

"You want a fucking medal for doing the right thing?"

"James, will you give no quarter?"

"Why should I?"

Edward shakes his head, takes a deep breath and releases it slowly. "Ian was not as fortunate as you have been."

"*Fortunate*? You are insane, Edward."

He continues as if I'd not spoken. "My marriage to Kathryn Croft, then Countess of Brookshire, was a business union to merge our family's holdings. She was a socialite, an alcoholic, and addicted to pain killers. In fact, she was only twenty-nine when she died of an overdose, only seven years after your brother was born."

"Half-brother. And I already know all this Edward. Ian told me about growing up with, or, actually, I should say, *without* a mother, or father."

"Of course." He nods slightly. "As my first born, it was Ian's birthright to take over the Trust upon my retirement or passing. It was all he had, and it was all I had to give him. It wasn't until his teen years that I began to see this may not be feasible. Ian was already addicted to drugs, just like his mother had been." His eyes drift from mine for a moment, and slowly scan his office like he doesn't know where he is. Seems more like he's addled than thinking. I'm not sure if I'd be glad or mad if it's Altzhimers. He didn't have the right to forget what he did to me, but watching him watch himself go insane may be worth him getting it.

"Your mother granted me visitation rights before she and Mike

Logan married, though, unfortunately, I only availed myself of the opportunity twice when you were an infant. You were still quite young when I came with Ian, to relinquished my parental rights to your mother and step-father. Part of the adoption agreement stated that you were to retain the Whren name on all legal documentation. Anna understood the significance of our lineage, the enormity of the Whren Family holdings, and the importance of family." His eyes flash with...affection maybe, picturing my mother. "It is likely my notoriety was the mitigating factor in her refusing to marry me. She was unwilling to risk the scandal that would surely come from our affair, and your illegitimate birth, afraid the media coverage might hurt the both of us."

Picture my mom, her wide, white smile after we hit the snow bank. Imagine her stunning young face kissing my old man, and feel sick. "Why are you telling me this, Edward? What difference does any of this make now? Thrilling though it is traveling memory lane with you, I don't want to hear about your affair with my mother."

Another portentous sigh escapes his lips. "When you were born, your mother agreed you'd be added to the House of Windsor registry as my direct descendant—a cautionary measure to discourage legal challenges to the disbursement of the Whren Family assets due to you, as my heir, upon my death—"

"All I want from you, Edward, is to leave me the fuck alone. In fact, I'd like my name stripped from every association with yours. Barring that's not possible, I don't want to be named in your will, or on any documentation involving the family Trust. We're done. You get that, right?"

Hint of a frown and he shakes his head again. "James, you are my son, my only remaining direct descendant, and now the 22nd Earl of Carham. With that title comes responsibilities—"

I rise abruptly, put my hands on his desk again, glare at him. "I don't want the goddamn title. Why are you not hearing me? Why is it we're still here, right back where we left off two years ago? Damn it!" I turn away, sweep my hair out of my eyes and pace a few steps, then turn back on him. "I told you then, I'll tell you again. I *don't care*, Edward. I fucking don't a shit about any of this. Why do you insist on fucking up my life? Haven't you done enough damage?"

"James, I do not have the authority, nor the desire to leave almost two billion in assets, garnered and preserved through countless generations before us, to anyone but family. It will be passed to you, as a matter of course, as it has been for over five centuries. Your net worth will substantially increase with the transition. And there will be serious tax implications, of course. However, at least initially, your involvement may remain as minimal as you choose, modeling our current structure of operations, only with Howard at the helm."

"Go ahead, wanker. Screw with my taxes. Try and get me locked up again. But you won't force me to sacrifice my life to serve your needs. I don't care what they are, now more than ever."

Edward inhales deeply, exhales slowly. "When we sat here discussing this two years ago, I did not infer you abandon your music career. In fact, I thought I made it quite clear that overseeing the Trust would take only an initial investment of your time to familiarize yourself with our holdings, and get acquainted with the people managing them. As I recall, however, you were not listening, could not hear me, as you were on drugs at the time."

"I wasn't on drugs, Edward." *I was crashing from them.* Sudden pulsing in my temples emerging into a massive migraine that feels like my head's splitting open. I glare at my father. "And even if I was, you had no right to *set me up*, to rob me of my freedom to control my life. There is *no justification* for what you did to me."

"I am not here to justify myself to you, or to defend my position. I had you arrested because I believed you were abusing drugs and in need of professional intervention. You are an adult, an American citizen, James. I had no authority to help you once you were back in the States. I was forced to act quickly. Priory Manor is a world-renowned, private treatment facility. You were slated to complete their highly touted twenty-eight day program and then be released, your records sealed, case closed. I could not foresee the events that took place after you were incarcerated. Nor could I prevent what followed after you killed Judge Ferrell's son."

"Gross miscalculation on your part, father?"

"Yes, I believe it was."

I can't believe the words actually come out of his mouth. Never before has the man admitted culpability, to me, or anyone else I can recall. I'd anticipated this moment my entire life. But no lightning bolts come shooting through the window. No brass band begins playing. The only thing in the room is a defeated old man, and there is no victory here. I turn away from his debasement, move to the bar to put distance between us. "Are you finished playing God, Edward? If I'm truly a free man, will you let me walk out of here and control my own life?"

"It was never my intention to control your life, James. If I had taken any course of action to help your brother when I first became aware of his addiction, it is quite possible he would be alive today. Had I taken no action with you, it is equally possible that you would not be."

"You're wrong, Edward. I was never that strung out."

"You were addicted to your own mastery, chose to let it consume your life, denying those in it their due. Drugs were a dangerous means to a distorted end, son. Somehow, I failed to impress upon you the importance of a balanced life." He sighs, shakes his head. "While much of your experience over the course of the last two years has been unfortunate, and without condoning nor minimizing your suffering, you are fortunate to have broken the bonds of your obsession. You've achieved a greater understanding of your place in the world around you, and your effect on the lives you touch, forging the foundation to extend yourself in love." He pauses, lets his words resonate. They do. Tingling in my head, racing over my scalp overrides my headache. "I assume you and Elisabeth are to marry, and you'll adopt her son, Cameron, move back to the States?"

My shoulders tighten. My fists clench and I look away, at the full shot of gin on the bar. *Pick it up and throw it at his head.* I need him to bleed. "Don't speak their names again. It doesn't matter how you know. You can watch me, but I'll never let you in."

Edward nods. "I understand."

Again, I'm dumbfounded. His stance has always been domination, never conciliation. Where's the lightning? I can't get a fix on my father's expression in the reflection of the smoked mirror behind the bar. He just looks old. Turn back to face him. "You expect me to stand here and have a civil conversation, a casual dialog between father and son?"

I have to get out of here.

"Well I'm just not ready to do that, Edward." I shake my head, turn away. My eyes fall back on the shot glass. I go to the bar, pick up the glass, down the gin in one gulp and swallowed back the burn, then set the glass back on the bar and walk out of the room.

-

-

Chapter Six

-

The sonofabitch knows everything about my life. He's been tracking me, who knows how long, and I've been blissfully unaware. I stand in the hall. No one's in sight. Can walk out the front door, except I have no I.D., no money, no shoes, no jacket. It's pouring rain and maybe forty-five degrees out there. I'll probably freeze to death before I ever make it off the property.

Oddly, I feel very calm, the gin having encased my brain in a fuzzy haze. To leave, I'll have to get my wallet back, or at least ask for help, and I'm not about to ask *him* for anything. The limousine kid, Steven, I think it was, something like that, might help me with the right numerical incentive, and a good alibi to deny any culpability in my departure.

I manage to find his bedroom with the aid of one of the household staff, but he's not there, nor the suggested library or media room. Find two housemaids in the kitchen, but they only speak German, which I know about five lines of, though they make it clear 'Stefan' has been summoned to drive Edward and Howard somewhere. The blond, blue-eyed matronly woman and her younger version don't seem to know when they're coming back.

Fuck.

Neither has seen my wallet or passport, but tell me to check my bedroom again for my shoes. I request a phone. The older woman indicates my father's study, and I go back to where I left Edward, but he's gone. I enter slowly, fighting the anxiety that's overwhelming me as the gin wears off.

I want out of here.

There's a sleek black portable phone on a small antique table near my father's desk and I pick it up and pace with it, considering how to reach Elisabeth. I need to talk to her, hear her tell me she and Cam are fine. I'll tell her what's happened, what's going on. Check if she still wants to be with me, even with my twisted history shackling me to this fucked up family. But I don't know her cell, or their land line number on the island. I'd never had to call her. We were always together. Regardless, it isn't likely she's gotten back there yet. A day, maybe two have passed since I was taken. I wonder if she's still in Athens, at the U.S. Conciliate, and I'm not sure how I feel about that.

Spend twenty minutes on the phone trying to find someone at Villa Vacation Rentals in Corfu City, and leave two message for my property manager to call me back as soon as possible with Elisabeth's contact information. Could try her at her parents, if I can get their number, but it's six in the morning there, and probably not the best introduction to possible future in-laws.

Can't call a cab without money. Can't get a plane ticket without I.D. Can't leave this fucking house without shoes. I fight the urge to throw the phone across the room, but set it down on my father's desk instead. Someone has picked the lamp and the laptop up off the floor and put them back on the desk. The brandy and crystal snifter are gone. The papers I'd scattered now sit in a neat pile next to the laptop.

I'm about to turn away, but the top paper catches my attention. A metallic British Crown Court identity is at the top of the page. There's a raised government seal at the bottom. It's a court order, issued to my father to appear before a grand jury inquiry in regards to my arrest two years ago. It's dated from December of last year and is scheduled for—*tomorrow*. The warrant gives few details. It simply states the date and time Edward is required to appear. One of the few things it does specify is that my father must submit his "signed statement" on or before the inquiry date.

I search the small stack of papers for any other pertinent information but don't find anything. Desk drawers are all locked. The laptop, well, it doesn't work anymore. Why were the drug charges rescinded? Was the 'recent evidence' to which Edward referred supplied by my father? Edward had me locked up, but is he the one to set me free as well? He knew about my suicide attempt, knew I was sent to an outside hospital. The idea burrows into my brain and my head starts pounding again. Press my palms into my eyes, holding them closed, blacking out all light. Edward's aged face and diminished stature come to the fore.

What has my incarceration cost my father?

What has it really cost me? Hear myself screaming in my head from searing, tearing pain, feel the restraints around my wrists and ankles, pinning me spread, ripping my limbs apart. *Stop it. Don't go there.* Drop my hands and open my eyes and I'm alone in the silent study.

Elisabeth, save me. I need you. And I see her laughing, her lightness brighter than the fire we had blazing that rainy afternoon. We're on the floor, I'm fingering the chords to Itsy Bitsy Spider, Cameron's in my lap learning to strum, my hand guiding his. We're on the fiftieth rendition, though he's finally getting it, and doesn't want to quit until he can make the 'tar' sound like me. Liz is laughing with me, at me, my beleaguered expression of fatigue, but we don't want to discourage his enthusiasm. We're both awestruck by his unwavering tenacity. It was then, I believe, the moment I fully understood love without reservation.

What has my incarceration cost me? My freedom, most of my fortune, my dignity, my seed. *My obsession with music.* What has it given me? Elisabeth and Cameron. *Maybe she's right. Things happen for a reason.* Round about though it may have been, my father has actually presented me an opportunity.

No! That's bullshit. I could have died. Nearly did. Wanted to countless times.

But I didn't. I'm still here. And life is richer, more intense than ever. *Play it as it lays, James.* And move on.

My head still pounds. Inhale deeply and release it slowly, but it doesn't stop the pulsing behind my eyes. *To hell with this.* I grab the bottle of Nolet's off the bar and go looking for someone, anyone, who knows where my wallet and passport are, but the invariable rejoinder from the staff is to wait and speak with my father when he returns to the estate, whenever that is. No one seems to know, or willing to tell me. Go back up to my old room, stop in the doorway. My head spins, buzzing from swigs of gin while on my quest. I stand in the threshold not sure what I'm looking for then spy the guitar. Retrieve the Fender and pull the strap over my shoulder, then plug it into the custom Hiwatt 100watt amp and turn it up, blast the old stone walls with its resonance and proceed to finish the bottle of gin.

A loud noise wakes me during the silent night, then I hear a dog barking. I'm cold. My head hurts. Feels like I'm laying on stone.

Open my eyes to see I'm on the oak floor where I passed out, the guitar still in my hand. Suddenly feel the gin rising up from my stomach. Leave the Fender on the ground, get up, and after using the toilet, I crawl into bed and fall back asleep.

My tongue is glued to the roof of my mouth when I wake in the morning, and I have a fantastic headache, the kind that reminds me why not to drink anymore. Venture downstairs to find my father or Howard, and encounter a lot of people I don't recognize rushing about with purpose. Everyone looks at me, stares really, except not in the usual way. When I look back, most look away and avoid eye contact. Creep factor becomes gnawing. At the bottom of the stairs someone grips my arm. I recoil, almost lay Howard out.

Howard jerks back and releases me. "Come with me, James."

I follow him into the library. "What's going on, Howard?"

He doesn't answer. He turns and shuts the double doors then turns back to face me, fixing his gray eyes on me. "Your father is dead."

"What?"

"Your father shot himself last night. He's dead." He stares up at me with contempt—like I'm the one who shot him. He waits for my response, but I can't think. *'Your father is dead,'* keeps repeating in my head.

Nausea overwhelms me and I run to the bathroom and throw up into the toilet. *Don't think. Wipe your mouth. Get up.* Fill the sink with cold water, dunk my face in. *Don't think. Hold your breath for as long as you can.* 'Your father is dead. Your father is—*dead*.' Pressure builds in my chest until it feels as if my lungs are bursting. I stand, gasp in the cool air, water dripping off my hair, onto my fleece shirt and all over the marble floor. Pull a plush towel from the bar and hold it against my face, pressed it deep into my eye sockets until I see sparkles, then go back into the library. Howard is gone.

-

-

Chapter Seven

-

HOWARD

Howard Engel met Edward Whren in his first year at Harvard. Howard had been pursuing a graduate degree in philosophy, of all things, with the intention of becoming a professor. Edward's diplomacy saved him from a beating by some neo-Nazis one night, back when Jew hating in the U.S. was all the rage. They walked to evening classes together a few times a week after that, and enjoyed animated discussions debating Nietzsche, to the Internet.

Completing his graduate degree in Business, Edward was brilliant, well read, versed in history, and had a great sense of social conscience. 'Prince Edward' was his nickname on campus, and though he knew many people, he had few, if any friends. He kept his distance with everyone. Even Howard. Their conversations always focused on philosophical or moral abstractions. They were never personal.

He'd read the celebrity rags most of his life. His mum was obsessed with them. But Edward was the first Royal that Howard had ever actually met. His new friend's family lineage could be traced back over *five hundred years*. Howard Engel was nobody, from generations of poor Manchester steelworkers who died young of lung cancer, and left wives obsessed with their children's potential while drowning their own with gin.

Edward offered him the position as his Secretary Director, with an extremely generous compensation package, while sharing a celebratory drink for their graduations at the Queen's Head pub. The upcoming 21st Earl of Carham cited Howard's moral character, his reliability, the demonstration of his stamina in completing his degree in just three years. They'd toasted each of his fine characteristics with a fresh shot of Beefeater's, then Edward reminded him, that, but of course, what clinched his choice for Howard as his SD was his British antecedence. His interests were larger than his own. He had a country to represent. And Howard knew even then that Edward Whren was a man of honor, and he'd be privileged to work for him, along side him.

They returned to Britain that summer. Together. And he'd managed Edward's affairs ever since. Through the years Howard learned the finer points of business. Edward sought his opinion often, respected his choices, and walked his bride down the aisle at his wedding. Edward was Amelia's other love, second only to Howard, and Edward mourned her loss almost as deeply as Howard did. He'd seen Edward through his marriage, the birth of his sons, the lost of his love, the death of his wife, the rise and a few falls of many companies, his father's death, and the death of his first born. And the last two years he'd watched Edward wither under the weight of his mistake having James incarcerated. He'd aged ten years in one, when he was made privy to what was happening to his son, and Jame's subsequent suicide attempt.

Howard sits in Edward's chair at the massive Partners desk, remembering, and silently weeping, only noticing the wetness on his cheeks when James bursts into the study. He doesn't bother to rise. The boy doesn't deserve that level of respect.

"What is going on, Howard? Why would Edward kill himself? What the hell happened here last night?"

"Your father put a bullet in his head in the chapel at four-thirty this morning, while you were passed out upstairs. Of course, I cannot speak for Edward, but my best assessment as to why he did this would be related to you."

James stands in a halo of halogen light glaring at him. "What is your problem, Howard? What did I do to you? You knew what was going on. You could have stopped him in the beginning. But you didn't.

Why?"

His ire rises and it takes great effort to stay seated and calm. "I was not Edward's keeper. His decision was made without my knowledge and did not require my consent. Your father is dead, yet you still mourn your own loss." He sighs deeply. "What is it you want here, James?"

"My passport and wallet. And I want to know what the hell happened. Did he leave a note, an email, a voicemail? You got anything, maybe a text, and I wanta see it."

"You are in no position to make any demands. And I am in no mood to give into one of your tantrums."

"What's my crime, Howard? How do you justify my father framing me? What do you accuse me of that warranted him fucking with my life like he did?

"Indifference." The impertinent child still glares at him. How is he to get through to this man? "Edward took you into his home, his life, after making the painful decision to agree to your adoption by Mr Logan, and hoped you'd come to know him and your linage on your own one day. He provided you with a stable environment after your parents were killed. He supported and funded your musical gifts without limits. And you walked away, disavowed his name, and severed all connections, lacking even a modicum of consideration for anyone but yourself. You shame me as a man and a mentor. I thought you knew better than that."

"That's right, Howard. You thought you knew me. You, and the endless parade of tutors and teachers. A valiant effort. Really. More than my father ever bothered."

"From the day you came to Castlewood, you had your music, James. Perhaps it was *you* who never bothered. Regardless, that Edward was not able to coddle you because of his job requirements, should have long since been resolved by the son who has spent the majority of his adulthood emulating his father quite exactly."

His eyes narrow with indignation. "You fault me my obsession, yet sit there asking me to have reverence for a man who devoted himself to his career and nothing else."

Howard tries to temper his anger, soften his galled expression to avoid aggravating their fragile interaction further. Edward would have hoped for this to be a teachable moment for his only remaining son. "Charles Dickens', *A Christmas Carol*, tells the tale of a man going back to his past to see the truth of what happened. The first ghost shows him scenes of his history from an observers perspective, and Ebeneezer is forced to view his real life, not the falsehood's he'd wrongly committed to memory." He paused. "It is criminal that you will never have the opportunity to thank your father for his contributions, and to forgive him for his error in judgment, with the understanding that the actions he took were motivated by concern for your welfare."

"And for his. Let's not forget that his precious Trust is without a willing heir to adopt it. My father is, was, a master manipulator. You're not going to sit there and convince me that he was a Saint, and that his sole intention was for my own good."

"I will not engage in any dialog to the finer points of your father's intentions, as he is not present to define them. Nor will I sit here and listen to you assassinate his character. Your father loved you, James, and whether you want to believe it or not, he bitterly regretted the outcome of his decision to have you incarcerated, and devoted almost every waking hour, and quite likely millions trying to correct his mistake."

James laughs, and Howard wants to backhand him. "My father loved me so much he left me rotting in an *insane asylum* for over a year *knowing* what they were doing to me."

"Your father was unaware of your experience at Langside until after the fact. From the beginning of your incarceration there, he used every resource available to him to get you released. Judge Ferrell blocked his efforts, compelled by retribution for killing his son. When you tried to take your life, Edward took the radical course of paying off key personnel and coordinating the team that facilitated your...early release."

"Edward got me out?" James presses his palms to his temples as if he has a blinding headache.

"Yes, he did. The torture you and others endured came to light only after Edward received your admitting records to Southern General following your suicide attempt. The mutilation of your wrists and ankles from restraints, the toxic levels of haloperidol and phenobarbital found in your bloodstream were enough to warrant a federal investigation of the institution. Your father felt compelled to testify about his involvement in your arrest to secure your legal release from the facility, in the process destroying his name, and quite possibly risking his own freedom had he remained alive to play the hand."

James moves to the armchair and sits across from Howard, but doesn't look at him. He runs his hand through his hair, his long, elegant fingers combing it out of his face momentarily. He slumps in the chair, folds his hands in his lap and stares down at them. "The snowball from Hell..."

Howard's ire spikes again with the man still acting the insolent child. "A snowball that you set in motion when you walked back into this house still absorbed in yourself and strung out from drugs, directly after burying your brother, your father's first born—from an *overdose*. Regardless of your perceived autonomy, you did not, and do not function in a vacuum, James. You, too, are culpable."

"I've done my penance, Howard."

"Your penance will never be over. You killed a man not yet twenty five. Your action, warranted or not, does not invalidate this outcome. You've spent a lifetime fundamentally indifferent to many who've deeply cared for you. And it's not hate, but indifference at the root of all evil. For these things, and others to be sure, you are culpable. You will bear the weight of them for the rest of your days."

James stares at him, eyes narrow, hands still folded in his lap. Though he's clearly angry, at least Howard has his attention.

"Everything is connected, James. Your actions play a key role in the actions and reactions of the people in your life—like a note of music, your resonance is felt by everyone you touch." Howard stays fixed on the insolent child, sees his jaw tighten, his eyes well, his demeanor soften.

James looks away but Howard sees tears stream down the man's sculpted face. He stands after another minute, runs his fingers through his hair again, wipes his eyes and nose on his shirtsleeve, and looks at him. "I'm sorry, Howard. I'm sorry for your loss." James does not mock him. The boy means it. Howard feels his surrender. Then he turns away and walks quietly out of the room, shutting the doors quietly behind him. Perhaps he's learned something after all.

Howard sits back in Edward's huge leather chair and recalls more of their time together, sometimes weeping, sometimes laughing, the entire time wishing that the outcome had been different.

I will miss you, Sir Edward Whren. I am honored to have known you, and privileged to have called you my friend.

-

-

Chapter Eight

-

JAMES

I stand over the open hole and watch them lower my father's casket into the ground. Elisabeth stands next to me. Cameron is back at the estate. Liza, one of housekeepers at Castlewood, watches after him.

Elisabeth and I agreed it isn't appropriate for him to be attending a funeral at his tender age, fearful of instilling a premature fear of death, or invoke nightmares of being buried alive. Wish I could've used either excuse.

Biting fall wind whips my father's full length wool overcoat around me. Fallen leaves crackle and snap as they skate across the brittle lawns and gather at the base of the stone markers in the High Halden graveyard. This will be the last time I'll stand here. My name will never appear on the giant marble monolith listing my family members buried here over the past two hundred years. Hold Elisabeth's hand, only realizing I'm squeezing too tightly when she flexes her fingers laced in mine, loosening my grip, and gives me her soft, indulgent smile.

The priest hands me a shovel, but I refuse it. Avoid looking at the crowd around me as I kneel down, grab a handful of dirt, and release it slowly onto the casket. A coating of moist soil clings to my hand, and for a moment that remaining soil connects me to my father until I brush my hand clean, the filth of the past to be buried with him, along with my anger. No tears come. Don't feel much of anything, only a vague sense of a similar disconnect I'd experienced two years ago, when I stood here watching them lower Ian into the ground.

What am I doing here? Again.

People start coming up to me with hangdog faces extending apologies. I don't know how to respond to them. Don't know if I'm sorry my father is dead. They grab my arm and shake my hand. I pull back but they hold tight and pump, showering me with accolades for Edward.

I want to take Elisabeth's hand again, but can't. And suddenly I'm falling. Spinning. Vertigo. *I have to get out of here.* I look at her. She stares at me—nods. She takes the hand of the next person who extends one to me, introduces herself as a friend of the family, graciously thanking them for their condolences. I walk away from the crowd to the limo and get into the first in the row. Stefan shuts the door and I lean my head back and close my eyes.

Edward had sent for her. She'd arrived yesterday morning, and was waiting for me in the library after I left Howard in the study. She presented me with the note Townes had given her as I was taken from the marketplace.

-

Ms. Whitestone,

It is necessary at this juncture I meet with my son. I have taken him at this time, and in this rather abrupt manner, to address an urgent family matter. I implore you, as a parent, to understand my son's welfare supersedes all else to me, and I'm acting in Jame's best interests, regardless of appearances. As I'm sure you know, my son must achieve some measure of closure, which I can provide, to help him marginalize his anger. However, my timeline is extremely limited.

Love should know no bounds, so I put none between you. You are welcome at Castlewood. If you choose to join James here, a driver will be at your hotel in Kolonaki at six o'clock tomorrow morning for you and your son. A private jet will be waiting at AIA for your comfort and convenience. A driver will be at Heathrow airport to receive you. I request twenty-four hours alone with my son. Thank you for your indulgence.

My profound apology for any undue stress my actions may have caused you and Cameron.

Humbly,

Edward Whren

-

I look out the tinted windows at the sun setting over the rolling hills of Kent on our way back to Castlewood. Hold Elisabeth's hand, and try not to squeeze too tight. Just have to get through tomorrow and then we're gone. Away from here. We have a 4:00p.m. flight to Logan out of Heathrow. *Just get through tomorrow morning and everything will be fine.*

"What are you thinking about?"

"The reading in the morning."

"You have any idea what you want to do?"

I want to burn it. Want to bury it with him. I want my name struck from wherever it appears. I go back to staring out the window. "Let's see what the Will says. Maybe he found enlightenment and left me out of it."

"And if he didn't?"

"I don't know. Play it as it lays, I guess."

"What does that mean exactly?"

"I don't know, 'Lisbeth. I don't want any of it. They can run the estate into the fucking ground for all I care." Regret saying it instantly, but she's all over me anyway.

"I thought you said the Whren Family Trust has interests in over fifty companies, employing something like seventy thousand people worldwide. Are you telling me that you don't give a damn what happens to all those people, and the families those businesses support?"

"I didn't mean it that way. You know it. It's just...you seem to have some misguided belief that I can ever become competent at overseeing something of this proportion, even if I wanted to, which I don't."

"My belief in you is not misguided, nor is it limited to your business savvy I know you are an honorable man, and I believe your father knew it, too. As set as you say he was on the blood that bound you, do you really think your father was a fool, James? I'm sure he saw in you what I do."

She stares at me with tender conviction. I have to look away. Want to be the man she sees, but I'm scared out of my mind of disappointing her.

"And I don't think you should take on the Trust. I think you should look into it, not dismiss it out of hand."

"All I know is music. It's the only thing I've ever been any good at."

Her expression softens and her full, ruby lips spread into a casual smile. "How did you get so good at music, honey?"

I smile back. "Practice."

"That, and this." She taps my chest lightly where my heart is and lets her hand linger there a moment. Her smile broadens into a teasing grin, though I know she's serious.

I grip her face, bring her to me, meet her halfway and kiss her. She returns my kiss with sensual sweetness, transferring all her compassion, her passion, her desire. She fills me up and quiets my fear, having her here—knowing she wants to be, is choosing to be with me.

Look back out the window and let myself free fall into the rhythm of the trees as they flash by, the white noise of the tires on the road, the melody of the wind; the sweet, fresh scent of Elisabeth next to me, the feel of her hand in mine. The tantalizing anticipation of Boston, starting a new life together, energizes me. And for that moment, I let myself embrace the ride.

I hear the tires crunch on the gravel drive of Castlewood. Open my eyes. It's quite dim outside. Thickening clouds block the late day sun. The estate is lit up and looks like a golden castle at the end of the long, tree-lined drive. Lots of people in the Grand Gallery. A few I recognize from the funeral, know them vaguely as distant relatives. I accept their condolences again, then introduce them to Elisabeth, as my fiancé. Others are household and contracted staff, busy with preparations for the memorial that will take place in the rose garden tomorrow after the reading of the Will. We'll be gone by then. Castlewood will become a memory, and I can bury it with my old man if I chose to do so. Or can I? It isn't so easy to shut it all out anymore.

Elisabeth, Cameron and I attempt to sleep together in my old double bed. Cameron is the only one who actually sleeps. An hour or so before dawn I finally get up, and after assuring Liz I'm fine several times, I quietly slip on my jeans, pull on my shirt and leave the room.

Moonlight bathes everything in blue, lights up the marble staircases, the massive Grand Gallery, the arched thresholds leading to each wing of the estate. I pause at the base of the stairs, consider getting a cup of coffee. Too much of a hassle in that enormous kitchen, and I don't feel like talking to anyone who's probably already in there working. The library's too closed in, with only that small ring of windows in the dome. The darkness would likely accentuate my darkness within. So I just stand there, alone at the bottom of the stairs, remembering my time here, aching for my mom, and Mike, wishing I'd never known this place.

A ghosted image of my father crosses the checkered marble floor with an open book in his hand. He reads as he walks, and disappears down the hall and into his study. I follow the memory.

Study is empty, quiet, dim. Only the recessed bar lights are on. Edward's huge desk has been cleared, his leather chair empty. Flash on him sitting there the evening of Ian's funeral, then again yesterday afternoon, having aged ten plus years in two, then shake my head with a quick jerk to dislodge the starkly contrasting images.

Wander among the shelves of alphabetized books lining most of the walls, everything from Bettelheim, to Machiavelli, to Shakespeare. Had Edward actually read even a small percentage of his collection? What were his favorites? Whose words resonated with him? Why? I really knew so very little about him. I, too, had never invested the time. And I see Howard's thin-lipped expression of disdain, then sweep the hair from my eyes, and sigh with weighted awareness.

Small torn piece of paper sticks out of a worn copy of Kipling's *Rewards and Fairies,* and I pull the book from the shelf. On the marked page is the poem *'If,'* one of my personal favorites, though for the life of me I can't recall who turned me on to it. Read it through, rereading lines that resonate again.

-

If you can dream—and not make dreams your master;

If you can think—and not make thoughts your aim;

-

If you can meet with triumph and disaster

and treat those two impostors just the same...

-

Close the book after I finish the prose, almost put it back on the shelf, but the last four lines of the poem linger, almost irritate, so I open the book and read it again, and again, and again.

-

'If you can fill that unforgiving minute,

With sixty seconds worth of distance run,

Then yours is the earth and everything that is in it,

And which is more, you'll be a man, my son.'

-

I don't know how long I read it over and over, but suddenly I get it, like a brick to my head, opening up my skull and releasing all residual anger.

"You completely and utterly fucked up, Edward! And fucked me in the process." No one to hear me, and I know it. Don't care. I need to get it out of my head. "And I hate you for what you did to me. And I love you, too." Cover my mouth to stop more words from coming out. Tears blur my vision, fall on my fingers, feel warm. I wipe my eyes on my shirtsleeve and will myself to stop crying.

"If you knew your father's intention came from love, would that temper some of your anger?" I see Liz, in the passenger seat of the Jeep on our way to Athens, her long auburn waves blowing around her shoulders and across her exquisite face. Her hazel eyes, deep brown right then, penetrate me, imploring me to find forgiveness.

Yes. I'd been unable to answer her then, but now, the voice in my head is definitive.

Exhaustion consumes me, and I lean back against the bookshelves to stay standing. "I'm sorry, Edward. I never let you in. I couldn't. I couldn't risk another loss. And I'm so sorry." My voice absorbs into the walls of the study and the rejoinder of silence is resoundingly painful, like pin pricks from the flu. I've blown the opportunity for a merited truce with my father.

I can't stop trembling. Close my eyes to control my quivered breathing and slow my heart rate, but have to open them and focus on the misted lawns emerging with the sunrise through the leaded windows to calm of my body.

Don't know when I slid to the floor, no longer able to bear my weight. Don't know when the tears came again, but suddenly I'm aware of them, and the unbearable, intolerable ache of longing that I've not experienced since the death of my parents. I sit on the hardwood floor hugging Kipling's book, rocking, crying, missing my mom, yearning for her and for Mike to hold me, touch me, to *feel* them. And finally for Edward, suddenly missing him too, craving a second chance, a do over. And a floodgate of memories I'd locked away since I left here light up my brain like flashbulbs, bringing images to the fore...

We're hiking in the Highlands of Scotland. It's just a month after I'd come to the estate and he's requested I join him on a business trip. We're standing on a windswept hilltop. Edward is showing me 'our' land, an endless three hundred and sixty degree view of grassy hills and forest groves of oak and birch along meandering rivers, punctuated by ponds of rich blue reflecting the morning sky. I don't care. I don't want to be there. It's cold. I hate the UK. It's always wet, cold most everywhere, and not just in the winter like Boston. I want to be back in the States, with my mom, and Mike, and ache for them, standing on that hillside, freezing my ass off. My father is just behind me, close but distant, lurking but not touching, as he points out features and regales me with history of the landscape. All I can think about is getting out of there, away from him, at the very least, get back in my room at Castlewood, with my guitars.

We're in London, at the Palladium. Edward's introducing me to the famed choreographer Miguel Joseph. He's gotten me a gig to co-write the score to his latest. I'm fourteen. I don't want to. I don't even like musical theater. I like rock. Electronic, electric, acoustic, raw rock. The only music I wanta hear or create. Anything else won't, 'broaden my foundation' as he claims. And I don't care he's merely adopted my mother's position supporting my talent. She's dead. And everything else but rock is a mere distraction.

He's talking at me, insisting I stay home and continue my lessons during school break instead of touring Europe with Mayhem. We're in the music room, with the renowned pianist Paul Michelson, my latest tutor. I hate practicing piano, but don't say so, with maestro

Michelson there. I only want to play guitar. I'm fifteen. Don't want to stay at the estate all summer, be near him. I want to get away from him. Forever.

Edward must have known, must have felt my distance. There were surely many times he tried to reach me, but I wasn't receptive, or outright rejected him, his mere presence a glaring reminder I was with him because my parents were dead.

Sun stretches across the study and lights up the face of the grandfather clock against the far wall near the walnut doors. I see my father standing in front of it, setting the shiny brass hands to the proper time. He turns to me as he shuts the glass door. 'Time is all we will ever really possess, James. Use it wisely.' I'm sixteen, and don't care what Edward says. I was shut down, and he retreated. Howard nailed me. My father and I were one and the same.

"I'm so very sorry, Edward." And my voice catches in my throat. *I've missed the opportunity to love you.* And I sit on the floor and weep, grieving his loss.

Don't know how much time passes before I get it together and stop crying, wipe my face with my shirtsleeve and stand, slide *Rewards and Fairies* back on the shelf. It's well into the morning when I finally leave the study to shower and shave. Find Liz coming down the Gallery stairs, looking for me, she says breathlessly. I meet her on the landing, her expression goes soft when she sees my eyes, blasted from crying. I gather her face in my hands, assure her I'm fine, kiss her passionately, but quickly, then take her hand and head back to our room. Cam is downstairs in the kitchen with Liza, so I fill her in on my enlightenment over the past few hours while we're in the shower. We just make the 9:00a.m. convening time in the Library. Elisabeth and I, Howard, Miles Bartlett, and one of my father's solicitors, along with a small team of others I don't know, are gathered for the reading of Edward's Will.

-

-

Chapter Nine

-

We all sit around the enormous maple table, Miles at the head doing the reading. The language is contractual legalese directing distribution and management of the family assets—companies, properties and holdings that are all part of the Whren Trust collection. I only understand about ten percent of it.

Elisabeth sits next to me, and I hold her hand on the armrest of my chair. I'm made acutely aware I'm squeezing too tight when she unlaces her fingers from mine, puts my hand on the armrest to squeeze, leaving her hand over mine.

Miles drones on, ultimately confirming what my father had told me—the Whren Trust has been left to me, but is to be overseen by Howard. The individual companies are to retain their current boards, and to continue to function in their present incarnations. Upon Howard's retirement or death, the management of the conglomerate will become my responsibility, or that of a suitable replacement for Howard, but only with my authorization, as the sole direct heir.

Only one stipulation was directed solely at me. Upon my death, the Trust transfers to my blood heirs, or it will be dissolved as a distinct entity, its assets dispersed. The Castlewood estate, and a few other real estate and art holdings of the Whren family for many generations are secured in registry trusts. With the dissolution of the Trust, they'd be awarded to the Crown and deemed national historical treasures.

Miles Bartlett stands after the reading. Everyone rises, and they cue up to shakes his hand, and mine. One by one, the entourage I do not know, all wearing hangdog faces, introduce themselves with their condolences. They are lawyers, CEO's and the like, who have worked with my father for years. They extend their sympathies, then drift away, gather in groups and talk discreetly among themselves.

Miles gives me a warm smile and hands me a bound copy of the will. "Questions? Comments? Concerns? Email or call. I'm at your service."

"I will. Thank you, Miles." I tuck the inch thick document under my arm.

"You're welcome to join us." He sweeps his hand towards a small group of men. Only men, most rather older men. I have no place among them. I meet Howard's disdainful glare.

"Can't stay. Sorry. We've got a flight to catch." I look at Elisabeth. She meets my eyes and slips her hand in mine.

"We'd like to know your plans, James." Howard addresses me from across the room.

"My immediate involvement isn't required here, so for now we're going back to the States. I'm going to marry 'Lisbeth, if she'll still have me." Glance at her. She smiles and squeezes my hand. "And adopt her brilliant son, if she agrees." She squeezes my hand again. "Then work at establishing a relationship with Cameron that eluded me with my father." I look at Howard. His expression is stoic, unreadable.

"Congratulations!" Miles smiles at me, then Elisabeth.

"Yes, congratulations," one of the men I don't know says, followed by a few other well-wishers.

"Thank you," Elisabeth and I say in unison then look at each other and smile. Howard stares at us, nods, but remains silent.

"Well, let us know where you settle and how to contact you," Miles says. "I look forward to working together in the future. Good luck to you both."

"And to all of you as well." Elisabeth speaks when I do not. "It was a pleasure meeting you."

I watch Howard. "Good afternoon, gentlemen." I bow slightly as I grip her hand tighter, then escort her from the library.

"You okay?" She asks for the tenth time this morning as I lead her down the dark hallway.

I nod. "Yeah." It's about all I can manage to say and she must get that because she does not question me further. We walk the maze through the drawing room, then the music room, then the solarium to the leaded French doors of the rose garden where we find Cameron at the lily pond.

"Is that the real one by Rodin?" Elisabeth marvels at the Madonna, mounted on a three foot marble pedestal in the center of the pool.

"Yes."

"Oh, your son is just precious," Liza says to us in her thick Cockney accent as we approach. "And such a curious child. He's been runnin round non-stop explorin just 'bout everything, but I think this may be his favorite spot."

Cam lay on his stomach, on one of the large slate stones surrounding the twelve foot pond, his face hanging over the edge of the slate to look into the water.

"Look, look." Cameron points to a Koi swimming in the pond.

Your son really is an angel, Mr Whren."

"Thank you." Feel no need to correct her about Cameron's parentage. "We've got him from here. Thanks for all your help, Liza."

"My pleasure, sir." She stares up at me a bit too long, then finally looks at Elisabeth. "Mum," she says softly as she crosses in front of us to leave the garden.

"Look 'Ames. *Fis.* Wow!"

I hand Liz the bound Will and lay next to her son on another of the large slabs surrounding the pond. Cameron scooches his tiny body next to mine, nestles into me, and joyfully points out every fish he sees. So do I.

"Look at that one. Wow. Check out the rainbow on it's back."

"Red one! Red one!" Cam points out excitedly.

We watch the fish quietly for a moment, and I revel in his warmth, his scent, his wonder.

"Our flight's in two hours." Elisabeth speaks softly. "We have to leave here soon if we're going to make it. You ready?"

"Yeah. I am." I look at Cam. "You ready to go on an airplane?"

"Fy, 'Ames. For real?"

"You bet, little man. Let's go."

"Let's go!" And he pops up, suddenly standing, with agility only a child possesses.

Takes me a bit longer. I rise to my knees, then Cam's hand is in my face, extended to help me up. I smile down at him in front of me, and clasp his waiting hand. Love the feel of his warm grip on my fingers. He pulls hard with both hands, and I rise as if he's helping me. I thank him and we fist bump when I'm standing. Then we follow Liz, hand in hand, out of the garden. The air is sweet, but rustic, like good brandy. Reminds me of Edward.

Elisabeth stops and turns to us just after we clear the arched, double French doors that cap the side of the Grand Room. She stands in the middle of the parquet floor, wearing a simple knee length black dress that shows her curves against her backdrop—the gold leaf paneled walls, carved in complex Victorian floral patterns. "Is there anything you want from here?" She looks around the opulent room, virtually vacant of furniture beyond a small iron table and three small maroon silk padded iron chairs.

Is there anything from the estate that I want to take back to the States? There is only one thing I can think of at the moment. "You ready to go?"

She nods.

"Give me a minute. I'll meet you and Cam in the Gallery, OK?"

"OK." She kisses me softly,

I kneel to talk to Cam. "I'll meet you at the front door in a few minutes. Then we take a car ride to the airport, and then *fly*. OK, little man?"

"OK, 'Ames."

I give his hand to his mama, and she takes Cameron from me.

I go back up to my old room and scan it, breathless after running up the stairs and down the long hallway to get there. I spy the Strat my father gave me when I was fifteen, that his father gave him, and go to get it on the bench along the window. I have no idea why he'd leave a valuable instrument lying about like he had, for over a decade, but I've got no time to ponder it. I open the case, and of course the violin is in there, shiny, as if it had just been polished and placed back in the case yesterday, which is also dust free, and ding free. I clip the case closed, take the ancient instrument, and go. On my way back down the stairs it hits me—the violin, and the case are too clean to have been sitting there for years. It's likely someone had been placed it there before I got in the room, as I was expected, both times.

Continue down the South hall to the South Tower and back to my father's study. I look at his huge desk, see him sitting there, old and tired, as I go to the bookshelf and pull Kipling's *Rewards and Fairies* from the shelf. I make sure to keep the bookmark on the poem 'If," when I tuck the book under my arm and leave my father's *space* for the last time.

Then I go meet Liz and Cam in the Grand Gallery.

We pile into the limousine. Cameron is instantly amused with all the electronic gadgetry. We let him explore, though Elisabeth's tracks his every move making sure he stays safe. I hold her hand and stare out the window as we drive around the green square of perfectly manicured lawn in the massive central courtyard of Castlewood, then down the gravel, tree-lined drive, finally turning onto Covet Ln, leaving the estate behind.

I do not look back.

-

-

*****

EPILOGUE

-

JAMES

Don't know why I chose this particular afternoon to stop. Must have passed by the house twenty times on my way into Hollywood, or Santa Monica for a studio gig since moving back to Southern California. I turn onto Heathercliff off Pacific Coast Highway when I get out to Zuma on an impulse, really.

Sun is setting over the coastal hills. Sagebrush is tall and tan from the long summer, the small pines dark green against the azure sky. Turn onto Cliffside and pull to the side of the road across from my old house. Someone has fenced the place. Seven foot tall, inch thick poles with twisted spikes at the tops surround the property. Two tall brick pillars guard the entrance to the gravel drive. What an asinine thing to do.

I know Mitchell Tesch, the producer, bought the house from the feds. Never met him, though I've heard the stories, and for the moment I pretend they're all true since I want to hate him. I mean, what kind of jerk puts a wrought iron fence around an acre and a half of chaparral overlooking the Pacific. And what the hell does a film producer need with a homespun digital recording studio anyway?

Sit in the Jeep, staring at the house through the iron bars, fighting my mounting outrage. They obliterated my life. All of them. Each took a part of me. Mr. Mitchell Tesch, the DEA, the UK, Langside, Parker and her cronies, my father. They put me through hell, and stole my house. And even though five years have passed, a part of me still hates them all. *This house is mine.*

Other than the fence, the only change to the front of the place is the row of small lights that border the drive to the base of the stairs.

Flashbulb images begin popping in my head, so many, *so fast*. I see myself going up the slate steps—running in the pouring rain, lugging equipment in summer heat, holding Julia's hand as we cut a path through thick fog. Fragmented images, snapshots of moments whiz by. It becomes surreal, like watching a movie at a drive-in.

Don't know how long I sit in the Jeep, staring at the stained glass doors, recalling time after time coming home and retreating inside, but it's almost dark when I get out of the car to catch my breath, and come back to the moment at hand. I lean against the front fender and stare across the street at my beautiful, custom-built, five-bedroom Craftsman Ranch. *Mine.*

It's mine.

Not anymore. *Focus, James,* on what I came for.

Cameras mounted on top of the brick pillars follow as I cross the street, blinking red eyes at me. When I get within three yards of the gate, a motion sensor floods the area with light. There's a small monitor inset into the side of the left pillar. On the screen blinks an access code that dials the house. Press the appropriate sequence. The screen prompts, 'One moment, please.' Then a man, maybe in his mid-fifties, almost bald, with a stubbled, athletic face appears on the monitor.

"What can I do you for?"

"I'm looking for Mitchell Tesch. My name is James Whren. He may know me by James Logan."

"James Micheal Logan…" He rubs his stubbled face. "Why does that name sound so familiar?"

"Because I used to own this house." *Too harsh.* Back off. "Sir."

"No. That's not why." He says it with a wave of his hand. "That's interesting, but I'm thinking of the musician. That you?" He squints into the monitor, ostensibly at my image on his end.

"Yes, sir." Guess he's heard stories of me as well. "Are you Mitchell Tesch, sir?"

"Drop the sir. I'm barely old enough to be your father. Come in."

Hear a click. Iron gate rolls apart and I walk through, along the gravel drive. Front door opens, and the warm light from inside silhouettes a man coming out. Gate behind me starts to shut. I fight the impulse to run from here, jump the fence, forget about this whole thing. It's suddenly hard to breathe, like a weight on my chest.

The silhouetted man on the porch looks husky, or fat, it's hard to tell against the light from the house. But what I can see is something in his hand, that glows blue at the tip. A vape pipe maybe. The iron gate clicks shut behind me and suddenly I'm caged. *I have to get out here. I have to get out.* I stop, look around for an escape route if he moves on me...and they do. Two burly morons knock me off my feet in the common area at Langside, hold me down and shoot me up with something that knocks me out. I wake, my wrists restrained above my head with thick leather straps to the sides of the padded examine table, my knees pinned back to the metal sides of the table. I see a small blue light but can't see who's holding it. They're in silhouette against the dilapidated walls sagging from age and moisture. Then searing pain rips through my groin with the memory of the electronic shocks burning my balls, my anus. And I writhe in agony spread fixed to the table unable to move, or stop them from torturing me.

Stop it! Don't panic. Nothing bad is happening here. Relax. Focus on the sound of the waves echoing against the cliff behind the house.

Swallow back the nausea and resume my pace. Suck in the dense ocean air, feel it on my skin, the weight of it in my lungs, taste the salt on my lips. *It's okay. I'm fine.* See the man from the house cross the slate deck to the redwood railing, welcoming my approach.

This guy's not going to hurt me. No one here wants to hurt me.

Breathe. Just Breathe.

Navigate the paving stones without tripping, I get to the base of the stairs and stop. He looks five months pregnant standing on the landing, leaning against the railing, holding a beer and smoking a cigar. "Hey, how ya doing," he says cheerfully.

I hate cigars.

"So you're James Micheal Logan."

"Yeah," I say, looking up at him from the base of the stairs.

"Come up. Come up." He waves me up as he talks. "Good to finally meet the legend." He's trying to be nice, but I don't know how to respond, so I don't. "So, you used to own this house? Explains the recording studio. I've wondered about that." He takes a deep draw off the cigar. Red embers flare and he flicks them on the deck.

It's odd he doesn't know I was the previous owner, with all the paperwork that changes hands when purchasing property. "Are you Mitchell Tesch?"

"Nope. He's on his way home from Burbank where they're editing his new star search series. He should be here within the hour, depending on traffic. I'm his brother, Elliott. Come in. I'd be honored." He moves aside revealing the open door with this big, happy smile on his face. He's cultivating California casual— barefoot, in ripped jeans, his ponderous belly forcing the pants to fall at his hips, a ripped white t-shirt covering the love handles on his sides.

My heart's still pounding hard. Nauseating smell of cigar smoke hangs in the crisp fall air. Walk up the gray steps slowly, recalling every crack, noticing some new ones. Feels so familiar, yet bizarrely distant, like crossing over a dimensional time warp, but not all the way.

This is my house. No. It's not.

"I heard you were back around. Aren't you working with the Damsels over at Capital?" Elliott snubs out the cigar on the railing that borders the landing and leaves it there.

"I'm sorry." I look at him carefully when we get close. "Do I know you?"

"We never met formally, but I saw you at Dylan's house around the corner a few times. I played with his band years ago. And your reputation precedes you. Elliott Tesch." He extends his hand.

"James Logan. Good to meet you." I shake his hand and meet his eyes for an instant, but am drawn to the open front door.

"Come in." Elliott sweeps his hand towards the door. "Want a beer or something?"

"No, thanks." Step across the threshold and stop breathing. The sonofabitch has barely changed anything. The long, low agate table I bought at that Asian gallery with Julia in Laguna is still up against the glass bricks that separate the entry from the dining room. In the living room, *my* leather couches still sat in the L shape Julia's younger sister, Rachael, had insisted was best for the fireplace, the view, and the feng shui of the room.

How can someone just adopt another's life like this? *What is wrong with this guy? What a twisted fuck.* I imagine him coming through the door and punching him, lay the guy out for taking my home, my property. But what's the point? It won't get me my house back.

"Look familiar?" Elliott stands next to me, takes a swig of his beer. "Mitch hasn't changed much since he bought the place, including the recording studio that he practically hasn't opened the door to since he moved in. The sonofabitch won't let me use it either." He gives me a lopsided grin. "Want to see it?"

I nod, and with a wave of his hand he lets me lead him down the hall to the control room. Again a tidal wave of memories flood my senses, and I hear Dave, alone in the studio, wailing on his D-35 Martin; the smell of Sheryl's perfume lingers, like her melodic voice drifting down the hallway back in the day; Kurt's wicked bass vibrates the walls and reverberates inside me. And I'm massively humbled by the spectacular talent that has graced this place.

The solid oak door with the long thin window opens with a suctioned-swish ushering us in, and suddenly I'm back in the rubber room, restrained naked and spread on the quilted floor. I shiver, then compulsively shake my head to dislodge the image, then comb my hand through my hair as I flip several light switches on the wall.

Recessed lighting along the top of the walls cast the silent room in muted tones of creams, browns and metallics. Thick layer of dust covers the SSL console. Two of the five flat screen monitors have been removed. Dust is so thick in the black Yamaha speakers mounted in the front, side and back walls that they look gray. The studio is dark and hard to see into through the window with only the ambient light from the control room.

"Told ya. Exactly like you left it, right? Mitchell hasn't been back here in four years."

I assume Elliott's question is rhetorical so I don't say anything. Then the three remaining monitors light up in my head and digital wave forms streams across their screens. And the guys from the Zone are in the studio. Max's electric is pulsing through the speakers, vibrating the wide window and carpeted control room walls, resonating in my chest, my lungs, sucking me into their sound. And then I see Julia, sitting on the couch that last night, and my indifference grounds me with shame.

Elisabeth comes to the fore, waiting for me at home with the kids, safe, and there's a moments peace. Red numbers on the electronic clock I'd mounted above the window between the speakers years ago changes to 6:40. At this rate, I won't make it back to Montecito until after eight tonight.

"What the fuck are you doing in here, Elliott?" A smoker's throaty voice shouts from the doorway, startling me. "I told you to stay the fuck out of here, and you're *bringing people in here*? Who the hell is that?" Then he turns on me. "Who the fuck are you?"

Late-fifties, maybe even L.A.-sixties, buff, with a buzz cut, and a tanned, chiseled face, he stands with hands on his hips, filling the studio doorway. Think he may be drunk, though I'm not sure. The smell of alcohol permeates the control room, but it may be Elliott's beer.

"James Logan." I extend my hand. Heart's coming through my chest again. Never got on with drunks, and I really don't want to mess with this guy. Though he may be double my age, we're the same height, he's easily thirty pounds heavier, and it looks like muscle to me.

"Well, I don't really care who you are." He doesn't take my hand. "I don't want you in here. Get the hell out before I call the cops." He glares at me from the doorway.

I feel my fingers fold into my palms as I clench my fists. *Relax. I was invited in. Let him call the cops. No one is after me. He can't hurt me.* I fight the rising panic and focus on why I've come. "Mr. Tesch? Mitchell Tesch?"

His eyes narrow, and he scowls at me but he doesn't answer. He turns away abruptly and walks back down the hall.

Elliott gives me an apologetic grin.

"GET THE FUCK OUTTA THERE, Elliott!" He yells from the hallway. "NOW!"

Hear a lot of slamming around in the kitchen as I follow Elliott there. The man I assume is Mitchell Tesch stands by the kitchen sink, glaring at his younger brother. Only thing changed in the kitchen is that the granite top on the center island is now butcher block.

"I told you I didn't want any drug dealers in this house." Mitchell scowls at Elliott.

Feels like he's delivered a blow to my jaw. And I have the impulse to slug him back, set him straight. *Forget it, James. What the hell does he know. We all believe what we want to.*

"I thought we had an agreement, Elliott." He shakes his head and turns away, looks out the picture window behind him that frames the Santa Monica bay, all the way out to the lights on the Huntington Hills. "What do you want here?" He speaks to me.

"He's not a drug dealer, Mitch."

"I know who he is, Elliott. And I know what he did. How do you think I got his house?" He spins around and glares at me. "You're not getting this house back." He gives me an opening for a comeback, but I'm not about to go there. "Or I'll be dead, and you'll be old by the time you do."

Years ago I would have told him to fuck off. "I'm not here to lay claim to this house, Mr. Tesch." *Asshole.* Relax. *Deep Breath.* "I'm hoping you'll be interested in a business proposition— with a lot of tax free cash."

He laughs. "Why on earth would I ever get in bed with you?"

"I'm not suggesting a union, sir. This is a one-time thing. A quick exchange, and you'll never see me again."

He crosses his arms over his chest, leans against the counter top and waits for me to continue.

"Two acoustic guitars that are very important to me were mistakenly included in the sale of this house. And I would pay quite a bit to get them back." To hell with tactical negotiations. *I want out of here.*

"Are they your guitars?"

His question throws me. "Yes."

"Prove it."

"Excuse me?"

"Do you know where they are?"

"Yeah. I think so. If no one moved them, they're still in the studio room."

"Let's go check." He walks past me. Elliott and I follow him back to the studio. He flips on the light upon entering, illuminating the menagerie of drums, giant speakers, full-scale keyboards, mini soundboards, mics on stands, stools, amps, all cluttering the space. I spy both guitars still sitting in their stands against the cork wall, covered in dust so thick I can write my name on them. Instinct is to grab them, clean them, cradle them, but I just stare at them from across the room, much the same way I watch the twins sometimes.

"That them?" He goes and picks up the Gibson Mike gave me when I was five.

"Yeah." *Don't hurt it. Don't bang it. Be careful.*

"Here." Mitchell hands me the guitar. "Play something."

He has to be kidding. I take the guitar, smile at him, sure he's joking. "What?"

"Play something that proves you've been intimate with that guitar. Do that and you can take 'em. Both of 'em. I don't want your money. I have enough of that."

I look at Elliott and he shrugs, but the big, happy grin is back on his face. Mitchell stares at me. *Okay...*Whatever. As long as it'll get me my guitars back. Sit on one of the many wooden stools, position the Gibson in my lap and wipe it clean with my shirtsleeve, then tune it, its unique, rich resonance bringing me home. *What to play...* Start with an even pick, Dm, Am, Em, Gm, and faster; repeat, then slide down in D on 5/3, 5/7, 7/9, 9/12, *keep it smooth,* and stop; beat; and pick it back up, C, G, Am, Em—fast, faster; repeat, *fluid.* Stop. Look up at Mitchell.

"They're yours. Take your guitars and get out." And he walks out of the studio.

Still holding the Gibson, I hesitate only a second then go get the Takamine 12-string my mom gave me.

I have them. They're mine. They're safe.

Clean them both entirely with my shirtsleeves, making sure they're dust free, then put them in their cases. The click of the lock is surprisingly loud as I snap the last case shut. Practically echoes in the dead quiet of the abandoned room.

One last look around, and again I'm swept up in memory and rushing with the rhythm Bob Greene and I are creating strumming acoustic guitars. I'm trying to block out the cramping in my hand as we battle it out to see who's faster. His face breaks into this huge smile, and then I burst into laughter and surrender. We must have raced at least ten more times on that stormy afternoon all those years ago, and I seem to recall in the end we came out fairly even. My smile lingers with his punk image as I pick up the guitars, and leave the studio for the last time.

Elliott walks me back out to my car and waits to shake my hand while I put the guitars in the back of the Jeep. "It's great meeting ya." He grabs my hand in both of his and pumps. "An honor really, especially to hear you play." He has that happy smile on his face.

It's hard to take Elliott seriously. I smile back at him. "Good to meet you too, Elliott." I retrieve my hand and get in the Jeep. One last look back, and the distance is complete. It's a house I used to own.

There's no more music here, just the sound of the surf echoing against the cliff. I've jumped the dimensional warp all the way to present day. Can't wait to get back to Liz and the kids, on my way home again, out on the highway, away from this place.

Take Hwy 1 all the way out to the 101 to stay by the ocean. Living by it again, back to surfing in it almost daily, and I still can't get enough of the Pacific. The water shimmers in the full moon as I drive up the coast. Coming over the hill at Leo Carrillo it looks like phosphorescent sea the way the moonlight reflects in the crashing waves. Wish Liz was with me to share the view.

"Call home," I tell the car without adding a please, or a moniker. Unlike my wife, I don't feel compelled to name the UI's disembodied voice. But, of course, I can't get a connection around Point Mugu. 'No Service' is printed in the center of the glowing monitor mounted in the dash. Strong onshore winds bringing in the fog and buffet the Jeep with whistling gusts. The highway is virtually empty this far out on a Thursday night past the evening commute. I'm out of contact, and fight the familiar panic with reason. I'm a free man, no wants or warrants under any of my names. No one is out to hurt me, except maybe Tesch. He could've reported the guitars stolen the moment I walked out the door with 'em to fuck me up—a hedge against me going after the house.

Scan the sides of the road for cops. *Stupid, James,* taking the guitars without some sort of contractual agreement. Really idiotic. My throat constricts, my heart pounds again. Force myself to focus on driving, tighten my grip on the wheel. Check the monitor every second or so to see if I have service, fear collecting and taking form, panic rising, until I finally get a connection to Elisabeth coming into Oxnard.

"Hi, honey." Smooth, rich tone of her voice calms me. I'm not alone in the middle of nowhere. "Where are you?"

"Coming into Ventura. I'll be home in half hour, tops. Are the kids in bed?"

"Sara and Kyle are. Cam's doing his homework, or on the net playing video, but he doesn't think I know. A pox on you for getting our son into that." She's mad, but there's humor in there, too.

"You've got it wrong. He got *me* into it with—"

"Who got him online, James?"

"Just the online part, for school research, access to knowledge. He found Zero-G all on his own. And it isn't so bad, really. He's building all kinds of structures with respect to physics, designing complex cities on alien worlds—"

"To have *guerrilla warfare in*, honey!" She growls in frustration, this rather cute mid-range roar. I laugh, which she does not find amusing. "I can't believe I'm having the exact same conversation with my thirty-three year old husband that I did this afternoon wi- my fiv- y--r old s-n." Her voice starts breaking up and I think we've dropped the connection and tension creeps in again, but then I hear Elisabeth say, "Kyle? What are you doing up?"

"Can I have some water?" I hear Kyle's high pitch in the background. "Is that daddy? Can I talk to daddy? Can I talk to daddy, *pleezze*?"

"Tell him I'll be home soon and come kiss him goodnight." Hear rustling and water running above the constant din of road noise. The hybrid Jeep was Elisabeth's idea of a 4x4 SUV. Except she likes the concept more than the noisy, drafty, bumpy reality, so I'm stuck with it most of time.

"Your three year old son is playing the 'let's find ways to stay up' game." There's more rustling. "I'll take that. Now, get in bed, munchkin." She speaks to Kyle, and I picture her long auburn hair bouncing softly against the small of her back as she followed him down the hall.

"Tell him sweet dreams from me. And kiss him for me."

More rustling. "OK. You warm enough? Kiss from daddy. Goodnight, sweetie pea."

"Tell him sweet dreams."

"And daddy says sweet dreams."

"Sweet dreams, daddy," I hear Kyle yell.

"Night, baby," Liz says softly. Then more rustling, and then I hear the door click shut. "Hi," and she's back on the phone with me.

"Hi."

"You okay? You seem kind of...weird."

"Yeah. I had an interesting experience tonight. I'll tell you about it when I get home."

"Good or bad?"

"Well, hopefully good, ultimately." Oncoming headlights sweep across the guitar cases crammed in the back of the Jeep. Looks like people sitting back there.

"Then why are you feeling sad?"

I smile. She's right, of course. I've just failed to acknowledge it. "It reminded me of what I had, and how I got here."

"Let's get off of Mars and come down to Earth, shall we? Less abstracted, please."

"Okay." I laugh. "I love you." I pause, then add, "I love my wife, my kids, my life."

She laughs. "Cool." I swear I feel her smiling.

Lose our connection at the 101 connector, our signal now competing with countless other cells for transmission towers. And I'm alone again, though the freeway is packed. Heart beats hard, loud, hear it in my ears above the road noise. I want to be home, in my sanctuary. But maybe it's not safe there now, or won't be if Tesch called or calls the cops. It's hard to breathe again. My entire body flushes and I break out in a sweat, pull my sleeves up to cool down and expose the light red scars up my forearms. I can't help but flash on slicing them with that broken shower tile. *I had to get out of there.* It was the only way out.

Grip the wheel and try to focus on driving. But the highway becomes background, the oncoming headlights turn to ceiling fluorescence that flash by as they drag me almost unconscious into the ancient treatment room.

And then I'm back in hell, naked, my wrists and ankles strapped with three inches of padded leather around them, pinning my body spread on the examine table. Parker is standing beside me, sticking small patches on my upper thighs next to my balls and the thick plastic edges cut into me as she presses them on my skin. I'm screaming at her to stop but only muffled grunting comes out with my tongue pinned and mouth gaping from the gag holding my head to the padding.

"You got a special visitor today, sweetie. A real fine lady, all the way from Cambridge, some poor rich lady lookin for a baby." She holds an iPad and it washes her face in electronic blue light. She looks like the bad witch out of Harry Potter—long, black, stringy, damaged hair frames her ashen face, sunken cheeks and eyes. "A royal baby." Her eyes are black marbles from speed and reflect the blue light of the screen as she touches the tablet. And white hot shocks constrict every muscle in my body, burning my balls, my limbs, my legs, constricting my stomach into a tearing cramp as I pull against the restraints. Parker lifts her finger off the pad and the shocking stop. She stares down at me like a child after stepping on an ant hill, then giggles with delight. "Just testing. Feels grand though, don't it." Parker puts the tablet on my torso and turns away. "Come on. Step up," she says to someone out of my view.

A woman, mid 30s maybe, rail thin and pinched, like so many elite Brits tend to look, comes along side the table I'm strapped to. She looks down at me with a tentative expression, like she's uncertain, but still curious, and, like Parker, without empathy.

"Go on, then. Don't be shy," Parker says as she grabs my cock. I groan, beg, but it's nonsense, garbled grunting. I can barely move my head, try and shake it NO, but the woman takes hold of my cock from Parker, and I lay moaning, gasping, helpless. "Ready?" and she grins perfect white teeth at me. Her breath stinks of alcohol. She strokes my hair from my eyes and then picks up the tablet still on my chest.

"NO! NO!," I try and scream, but she presses the screen with her long, polished red nail anyway, and stinging, white hot burning shocks come over and over, along with my muffled screams.

"God, you're fantastic. A work of fucking art," she slurs. "They promised me you'll give it up for me, gorgeous, sire me a royal child today. I am paying a tidy sum, so we'll be here until you make it happen."

I writhe and pull against the restraints but can only lay there, my muscles contorting in agony as my body rises and falls with the shocks while she holds my cock, jacking me off. I hate her. Want to kill her, strap *her* on the table. I try to fight the stimulation, but my balls and penis surge with blood and I feel my cock stiffen, and tears well, then slide down the sides of my face.

Then she climbs on the table and mounts me. And I'm inside her, and she leans over and buries her breasts in my face, and laughs as she sits back up and rides me. And I can't stop her. Cramping in my loins and stomach is excruciating and the pain becomes intolerable, and I'm with her in hell as she forces me to ejaculate into her.

A loud horn brings me back to driving. Drifted to the right so I crank the wheel left and get the Jeep back into my lane, miss hitting the guy next to me by about half a second. He guns his BMW and passes me, then sticks his hand out his sunroof and flips me off.

Monitor rings. Liz's beautiful face appears on the screen. Press the green button while trying to shake off my fury, my fear. I take a deep breath, clear my throat and hope I sound normal. "Hi."

"Hi." Again Elisabeth's warm, sultry voice fills me up and I am not alone. "I missed you this week."

"Me too." I did, more than I ever dreamed possible—her face, her touch, her taste, her smell, lying together, safe inside her.

"I'm really glad you're coming home."

"So am I." Decide not to mention my irrational fear of Tesch calling the cops on me with no real reason, and Elliott as a witness to what really happened. Anxious to get home. Bad memories rarely came to the fore with the distractions of family. And I flash on Elisabeth's casual smile; Cameron slapping me a high five; Kyle and Sara's toddling gait when they run to me. I'm not alone anymore.

"I have the Vanity Fair shoot in the morning out at Sea Ranch, so I'll feed the twins and get them over to Beverly's so you can sleep in—give you a chance to recover from just cat naps all week," she scolds. "But you'll have to get Cam to school."

"No problem.

"Have to swing by the gallery after the shoot, but I'll get the cake and pick up the kids on the way home."

"Is Larry still rearranging?"

"It's always a floating point with him. He'll probably keep changing the layout right up until the opening. He's decided to go with the pictures of you playing guitar as the window teaser."

"Lizbeth, I told you I don't want my body displayed in a gallery storefront, no matter how great the shots are."

"You can't even tell it's you. Besides, you should be honored."

"And I am. Just a little shy."

She laughs. "I love you. We can argue about this later. See ya when you get here." And she hangs up without any salutations, which I find somewhat irksome. Hear her laughing even after she's disconnected, which saves me from getting sucked back into the black hole of the past.

Get off the freeway at San Ysidro Road and release a deep breath. It's dark, shrouded by the canopy of old knurled cypress that block the streetlamps. Road is tight, and parking for Cameron's birthday on Sunday is going to be a bitch. Invited way too many people—somehow it's exploded into this extravaganza, but Liz tries to convince me that social gatherings are, if nothing else, excellent creative stimulus. Truth be told, I looked forward to spending time with Aaron and Mimi, and the kids love having grandma and grandpa around. And it's always a kick seeing Martin, and even John now, since Martin deemed them the kid's official Godparents, whatever that means.

Turn onto Edgecliff, pull into the drive and up to the house. Cameron's light is still on. After five long days away I can hardly wait for that first hug—him slamming up against me, body to body, his head nuzzling into my neck. Lately I've been thinking about giving him something for his birthday just from me, turning five being a milestone and all. As I pull the guitars from the back of the Jeep, I decide on the Gibson, the one my stepfather gave to me when I was five.

The night is damp and cool, and fragrant with foggy sea salt and pine. Trudge up to the house with guitars in hand, anticipating the warmth within. I'm home. Safe.

But the past is never past. And somewhere deep inside me I hear derisive laughter.

****

About the Author

"Writing fiction is intoxicating," author J. Cafesin said in a recent interview. *"Fully engaging. Hot. Sexual. Physical. Mental. Spatial. Virtually touching real as I enter the scene. And I'm a million miles from Lonely."*

J. Cafesin is a novelist of taut, edgy, modern fiction, filled with complex, compelling characters so real they'll linger long after the read. The original REVERB was her debut novel, and was a Kindle #1 Bestseller. Her works include her speculative fantasy short story series, **Fractured Fairy Tales of the Twilight Zone:** *"5 Stars! Great read for young adults, and even some not-so-young adults."* Her second novel, **Disconnected**, called *"unabashedly unafraid, completely honest writing,"* released 2014.

The Power Trip (the first in this upcoming speculative fantasy three-book series) unveils the misanthropic adventures of the four Stanford students, who implement an online game in which players manipulate each other using predictive modesling. Due to release 2020.

Her essays and articles are featured regularly in national publications. Many have been translated into multiple languages and distributed globally. Read them on her blog: jcafesin.com/cafe-42/

J. Cafesin lives in the S.F Bay Area, with her husband/BFF, two gorgeous, talented, spectacular kids, and a bratty, but cute Shepherd pound hound.

J. loves to hear from readers! Reach out via email: connect@jcafesin.com.

♦ ♦ ♦ ♦ ♦

Post-Traumatic Stress Disorder (PTSD) is a psychological disability often developed by a person who has experienced one or more traumatic events, such as sexual assault, warfare, serious injury, or threats of imminent death.

For information, resources for treatment and support for those suffering from PTSD, and/or affiliated family and friends, please contact The National Center for PTSD: http://www.ptsd.va.gov/

♦ ♦ ♦ ♦ ♦

www.ingramcontent.com/pod-product-compliance
Lightning Source LLC
Chambersburg PA
CBHW071112290626
47170CB00018B/210